ROGUE'S
MARCH

ROGUE'S MARCH

a novel

by W. T. Tyler

HARPER & ROW, PUBLISHERS, New York
Cambridge, Philadelphia, San Francisco, London
Mexico City, São Paulo, Sydney

1817

FIRST EDITION

Designed by Ruth Bornschlegel

Library of Congress Cataloging in Publication Data

Tyler, W. T.
    Rogue's march.

    I. Title.
PS3570.Y53R6 1982   813'.54   82-47544
ISBN 0-06-015048-3   AACR2

82 83 84 85 86 10 9 8 7 6 5 4 3 2 1

To my youngest son, Hugh

I tell you, worthy little people, life's riff-raff, forever beaten, fleeced and sweating, I warn you that when the great people of this world start loving you, it means that they are going to make sausage meat of you.

—LOUIS-FERDINAND CÉLINE

Empire is over,
Bedlam's in charge—
Bushmen in tatters,
Consuls, and clerks;

Copy-book Bolshies,
Bagmen and narks:
Two-penny soldiers,
Playing at farce.

Muster the trumpets,
Let the drums start
Jeer in the bagpipes—
Play a rogue's march.

—ANONYMOUS

book one

chapter 1

✧ A warm wind blew over the Mediterranean from the Algerian littoral, where the saffron light of late afternoon hung like dust above Mers-al-Kabir. The near waters of the port were as lifeless as brine, but beyond the breakwater the sea raced in the sunlight, drawing the eye out across its broken silver surfaces toward the horizon, where distances were suddenly lost and no ships were, only the immense empty mirror of sea and sky. At quayside a gray Soviet freighter inbound from Odessa creaked in partial shadow between two rusty coastal steamers, unloading its deck cargo of trucks, jeeps, and shop vans. The Cyrillic letters on the stern read *Kirman Vishnevskiy*. Four days earlier, it had sailed the Bosphorus declared for India. Now, under new orders, it was at Mers-al-Kabir. Anchored in the roads a hundred meters offshore was the East German freighter *Potsdam*, bound for West Africa.

On the quay stood a small olive-skinned Algerian, a clipboard under his arm, silently studying the Russian ship whose name he couldn't pronounce. His name was Hamoud. On his shoulders were the chevrons of an Algerian customs official. His lips moved as he re-counted the vehicles but stopped again as his eyes came to rest amidships, where a series of long wooden crates were tied down, their shapes unfamiliar to him. A group of Russian seamen stood on the fantail, some with their shirts removed to catch the last rays of the sun. Their faces were shrimp-pink, but their shoulders and bellies were as colorless as plankton. One was eating an orange, gouging out great mouthfuls of fruit like a dog. Hamoud studied them disapprovingly and looked back at the strange crates, searching their flanks for letters, numbers, or symbols; but he saw nothing. As he watched, a small dusty Fiat with official license plates led a canvas-covered army truck onto the quay, lifting ribbons of dust from the worn footpaths along the tarmac. Hamoud turned as the caravan

1

stopped near a set of stone steps that led to the sea below where a lighter waited for cargo for the East German freighter *Potsdam*, its clattering diesel engine pumping thick black smoke out to sea.

Three men left the Fiat, two Algerian and the third an African, a head shorter, wearing an olive twill uniform and green fabric boots with rubber soles. The uniform was new, like the cheap metal suitcase and the portable radio he lifted from the back seat. In his small size and his wrinkled new apparel, he looked to Hamoud like a child being sent off to school for the first time, pencilbox in hand. Six Algerian soldiers dropped to the roadbed, unshackled the tailgate, and began removing the wooden boxes.

"You're late," Hamoud said as he joined the tall Algerian near the Fiat.

"It's that way with these Africans." The Algerian officer wore neither rank nor insignia, but his cotton uniform was camouflaged in the brown and sand of the Algerian commandos. He was a captain, hawk-faced, with short wiry hair and a weeping black mustache. His soft brown eyes had a curious shine, as if he were just recovering from a fever. A long scar curved like a sickle up the cord of his neck and ended in a small fishtail under his left ear. He handed Hamoud the shipping manifests as he turned to look toward the East German freighter bound for West Africa. The African was also watching the ship from the top of the stone steps, his small figure dwarfed by the flooding light from the sea.

"Just him?" Hamoud asked.

"The others have influenza."

Hamoud looked back at the African, who made no move to help the Algerian soldiers struggling with the heavy ordnance boxes.

"I fought too," he said, "but I carried my own guns." From the offices and warehouses other customs clerks, inspectors, and laborers were leaving for the day, moving toward the gate where the buses would carry them back to Oran. Hamoud watched them resentfully as he unfolded the invoices. His own motor scooter was broken, and he would have to return home by late bus, arriving after dark. He glanced at the African again before he studied the manifest. "Agricultural implements," the document read. He knew it was a lie. "Machetes, hoes, mattocks, shovels, and barrows, disassembled." All lies. The heaviest would be mortars, he guessed— mortars and base plates. All destined for "Bernard Delbeques, Frères, Pointe-Noire, Congo." The deceit annoyed him as much as the crates' late arrival, and he blamed the African. He looked at him again as he stood at the top of the steps, a small frightened figure looking out to sea.

Congo? Hamoud wondered, memory releasing the image of a rain forest deep in the equatorial jungle. Where had he seen it? At the cinema? In the coffeehouse magazines? Rivers and swamps, fever, rain and more rain shrouding the sky. In the warm Mediterranean sunlight his imagination faltered and he remembered only the chilling winter rains of Algiers, relieved suddenly that duty no longer obliged him to go where the guns were going, like the little African, and that there was nothing left to his life that might force him to go.

Life had sucked him dry, his wife had accused two days earlier. He had his freedom now, yes—he had earned it himself with his fellow Algerians, but now there was oppression of another kind. His useless motor scooter lay in the rubble of the rear courtyard in Oran, a piston broken. Chickens squatted on it by night, fouling the leather seat; his three daughters banged on it by day when his mother-in-law turned them out into the yard. She had broken her tooth on an almond and howled for three nights. "Can't you take pity on her!" his wife had cried after he'd threatened to push the old woman's bed out into the courtyard. "Has misery robbed you of all feeling? Has life sucked you dry!"

Attached to the documents on his clipboard were the secret manifests prepared by the ordnance officer at the Skida Commando School and countersigned by the ministry of interior. They wouldn't accompany the shipping manifest. The guns were listed in a single column: ten boxes of 7.62 assault rifles, Kalashnikov, folded and fixed stock; five crates of Degtyarey light machine guns; two crates of 7.65 machine pistols; two crates of 9-mm Makarov pistols. He removed the copies and returned all but one to the Algerian captain. "Who is he?" he asked, nodding toward the African.

"A friend from the south," the captain muttered, moving away from the stone steps. A secretive man, like most of the Algerian military who fought in the *maquis* and still bore the scars of French brutality, he disapproved of Hamoud's indolent curiosity.

The African was the last to board the lighter. He passed his tin suitcase to one of the deckhands and stepped aboard uneasily, the radio cradled in his arms. The Algerian soldiers and dockworkers watched him silently. None of them could have afforded such a radio, and they looked on resentfully, as if he were a child bearing away the gifts paid for by their misery. The lines were cast off; the lighter drifted away from the stone steps and settled in the slough of the sea.

Hamoud watched from the quay as the lighter retreated in the distance toward the East German freighter. He had never been south of Djelfa, never beyond the Atlas mountains, and had never had the desire to go; but the thought of the African's long journey had a peculiar, repellent fascination for him. He thought of the rain forest again—the leaden skies, the insect-filled hovels, and the sheets of devouring rain: lichen would multiply; ammunition would turn green, like moldy bread; flesh would rot from the bone.

He knew no more, imagination failed, remembering instead the brutal winter cold of the Italian mountains where he and other Algerian recruits had fought with a Moroccan infantry regiment. As homesick as a street orphan, he didn't know who the Germans were; they meant less to him than the French troops, whose officers he despised. In his right knee he still carried the fragments of a French grenade from his days with the FLN fighting the French in the streets of Algiers. He had helped liberate Algeria, but he felt no kinship with the black man in the lighter. They had fought the French with primitive *mousquetons* purchased in Europe and brought in by night over the beaches of the Rif coast. No one had given them shortwave radios, wrinkled green uniforms, and Russian-made automatic weapons. He didn't know the enemy the African would fight—French, British, Portuguese, or American—but it didn't matter. They were all colonialists.

"Congo," he muttered as the Algerian captain turned away toward the Fiat.

"Congo, then Angola," the captain said over his shoulder.

"Angola?" Hamoud muttered dumbly as he watched the lighter draw alongside the East German freighter. He knew nothing about Congo or Angola, lying somewhere within that vast darkness to the south. But standing in the warm Mediterranean sunlight, he knew that there was nothing left to his own existence that would again make these foreign wars his own.

Four days later, on a Saturday, Hamoud was in the quiet back streets of Robertsau in Algiers. He entered an old apartment house in a cul-de-sac, climbed the narrow staircase, and waited silently for a few minutes on the third floor, looking down the stairwell to see if he had been followed. He rang the bell, and a dog growled fiercely from beyond the glass door. He rang a second time, the dog barked, and he moved away. The chain was drawn and Fachon's ugly face

4

appeared, damp with perspiration. He was a short, powerfully built Frenchman, as bald as a stone, with thick lips and pale blue eyes, a UN technician who worked at the port. He'd been sleeping, and the imprint of the pillow lay like a fern leaf on his cheek. He wore a pair of shorts and leather sandals; his white cotton shirt hung open across his chest, covered by a cuirass of gray hairs. He'd been up at dawn for his daily exercise—a walk along the deserted beach with his brindled German shepherd, followed by his morning swim in the chill gray Mediterranean. The dog now lay inside on the cool tiles of the areaway, the leash knotted to the handle of the inner glass door. Gouts of beach sand lay over the terrazzo floor; the brindled coat stood out in stiff spikes from the sea brine. The dog growled again, ears pricked, as Hamoud, frightened, followed Fachon across the entryway. The hallway smelled like a kennel to Hamoud, the flat beyond so tepid with its alien unknown Continental aromas that it smelled to him like sickness.

They sat on the rear balcony off the kitchen, out of the sunlight. Fachon brought a pitcher of lemonade from the refrigerator, his bald head now covered with a handkerchief knotted at the corners. The lemonade was watery and sour, but Hamoud drank it as he described the Russian ship he'd seen at Mers-al-Kabir. Fachon's face was impassive as he told him of the deck cargo. He smoked a cigarette and then another, irritated at Hamoud's imperfect memory, for which he was prepared to pay nothing at all. The streets were silent; the sun beat down on the roofs and balconies.

Where was the Russian ship going? Did he have a manifest? How many crates were unloaded?

Hamoud didn't know. Fachon gave up in disgust, taking back the lemonade glasses and preparing to stand up. Only then did Hamoud take the damp papers from his waistband and hand them to Fachon, waiting hopefully as the Frenchman studied the secret gun manifest destined for Bernard Delbeques, Frères, Congo. He saw the interest stir in Fachon's face.

"For the Congo and afterward Angola," Hamoud added, trying to provoke additional interest from this Frenchman who had once lived in black Africa.

Fachon lifted his vulgar eyes toward Hamoud: "Guns for what?" he asked, taking the cigarette from his mouth. Hamoud's clumsiness made his voice even harsher. "For what? The revolution? Independence? For what?"

Hamoud didn't answer, studying the Frenchman's eyes. He remembered then where he had seen the equatorial forests. There was a large brightly colored painting of the African jungle in Fachon's salon. He had once lived in Cameroon. He had lived in a well-screened cottage shaded by jacaranda and flowering hibiscus at the edge of the coastal savannahs. His shadowy porch looked down laterite lanes winding between the trees toward the wide silk of parrot-green river which the afternoon sun turned to bronze when the women and young girls came to bathe. Now he kept a dog and walked the beach at dawn before the Algerian urchins and beggars came to claim it.

"*Que voulez-vous?*" Fachon asked, provoked to cruelty by Hamoud's awkward silence. "*Avec de la merde, on ne fait pas de la menthe.* You don't make these fine things with shit, do you?"

Hamoud nodded blankly, his olive face suddenly warm with shame. Fachon would keep the manifest and pay him for it, even if the guns were intended for African insurgents, not Russian-equipped armies; but he had intruded too far into this curious Frenchman's personal life, that little space of privacy, like their little gardens and private clubs in whose sanctuary Hamoud would be regarded as a savage and infidel too, like that little African whom Hamoud now described for him.

He had even managed to learn his name from an Algerian officer who'd come the following day—he was Lieutenant Bernardo dos Santos of the Movimento Popular de Libertação de Angola—but Fachon thought the name unimportant. Hamoud left the flat with the slip on which he'd written the name still in his pocket.

chapter 2

❖ Andy Reddish was alone in his villa that Saturday evening and had just finished dressing for a diplomatic reception when the telephone interrupted him in the downstairs hall. Within the walled courtyard outside the night guard was preparing his evening *mwamba* on the charcoal stove under the avocado tree shading the study window. The lamps had been lit in the downstairs rooms by the houseboy before he'd pedaled his bicycle out the gate through the warm African dusk toward the sprawling native commune of Malunga on the fringes of the capital, the family laundry freshly washed and bundled on the rear seat.

He hadn't known the houseboy had used the washing machine that afternoon. The roof reservoir had emptied before he'd finished his shower, like the hot-water tank; now he couldn't find the key to the liquor cabinet. He could overlook the half-finished shower but he wanted a drink.

He took the call in the downstairs study, still pulling on his seersucker jacket. An American diplomat had been kidnapped in Khartoum two days earlier, and the crisis had dominated the incoming cable traffic for two days as Washington brought sleepy embassies to life across the continent with instructions for action and support. He thought the call might be from the communications watch officer at the embassy. As acting station chief in Haversham's absence, he'd twice been summoned earlier that day.

But the call wasn't from the embassy. The voice belonged to a frightened African who sounded vaguely familiar but who refused to identify himself.

"That's right, this is Reddish. Who's this?" In a sprawling African nation devastated three times by rebellion during the first years of independence, anonymous voices usually brought warnings of impending coups or foreign plots; and after four years Reddish had heard them all. Now he listened morosely as his caller told him the army had guns brought in from Congo-Brazzaville and was preparing to stir up trouble. Did he understand what that meant—for the President, for him, for the Americans?

"Yeah, I get the message, friend," he drawled in a vulgar voice calculated to discourage whispered intimacies, whether from bored embassy wives or Third World diplomats looking for the American bagman. "Loud and clear, like the last time or whenever it was, but it's not my problem. You've got the wrong number. Try the police." He turned, pushing his arm through his jacket, looking out through the window at the night watchman's fire under the avocado tree.

"*Mais non, non,*" the whispered voice came back, very shocked. "*C'est M'sieur Reddish?*"

"That's right, Reddish. Like last time. So what? Who the hell's this?"

His caller renewed his warning: the army was preparing to overthrow the President. Reddish still couldn't place the voice. There were few in positions of power whose voice he wouldn't have recognized. For nearly four years their history had been his history, their lives grown over his own like a kind of scrofula, a canker, separating him from his own past.

"*C'est votre ami,* your old friend," the voice continued in an agonized whisper. "*Vous me connaissez très bien—très, très bien.*"

For an instant, the voice was fleetingly familiar, but Reddish was impatient: "You've got the wrong man, friend. Sorry. Why don't you try the internal security directorate. Maybe they can help you." He looked across the room. Atop the locked liquor cabinet, the houseboy had set out the ice bucket, soda siphon, and a single glass on the silver tray, but no bottle.

"*Mais non, non,*" the voice pleaded. "*C'est à vous, mon ami!* It's up to you, the Americans! The paratroopers have guns, Russian guns, brought in from across the river! I tell you it's true. The paras and their mercenaries too! The first trucks have gone out. Tomorrow they'll send more. It's up to you, you the Americans! *Vous êtes notre espérance, notre conscience! Vous, mon ami! Il faut donner toute votre puissance au président!* We want no more rebellions, no more anarchy!"

The emotion of the appeal was suddenly as familiar as the voice, and for the first time a face swam into focus—the gold-rimmed spectacles, the dark face, the damp, embarrassed toffee-colored eyes.

"Look," Reddish said, "if you've got something to say to me, maybe we'd better meet someplace."

"There's no time. They're watching me. They know, you see. *C'est à vous, mon ami.*"

Somewhere off in the background a goat cried out, two women were shouting in Lingala, but then a truck engine revved up, drowning out everything else. The connection was broken.

Reddish stood with the dead phone in his hand, remembering too late his caller's name. He was Mr. Banda, an obscure little civil servant who worked in a dusty little office in customs clearing incoming shipments. Reddish had once done him a favor, a small thing, of little consequence at the time, but one the older man had never forgotten.

During the Simba rebellions, Banda had been assigned to a provincial town in the north, where he'd been captured, imprisoned, and sentenced to death by the rebels. The death sentence hadn't been carried out by the time the town had been liberated by government troops. The prison had been blown to rubble by army mortars, but Banda had escaped, bloody yet alive. The army was systematically killing the wounded in the small rural hospital, and Banda had taken refuge in the deserted UN compound, where he was discovered by the team of UN doctors and nurses who reoccupied the clinic. By then his name had appeared on the army death list as a rebel collaborator.

When Reddish visited the town following the Simba retreat, a dossier had been assembled on Banda's behalf by the sympathetic UN staff—attestations and affidavits gathered among the townspeople, all duly signed or thumbprinted, swearing to Banda's imprisonment by the rebels. The senior UN doctor, a nervous Austrian, had tried to present the dossier to the army commander, who refused to meet with him. The doctor asked Reddish to discuss Banda's case with the colonel. It was filthy hot that day and Reddish's C-130 was waiting at the airfield. He looked at the dossier, all tricked up with red ribbons, green ink, and official cachets, the way the UN would do it, guessed that it wouldn't solve Banda's problem with a drunken, brutal army colonel who'd twice been humiliated by the rebels in battle, and he had done the simpler thing, smuggling Banda through the military roadblocks in his borrowed Landrover and flying him back to Kinshasa in the C-130 for hospitalization.

Banda was reinstated at the ministry of interior after his convalescence. Reddish saw him from time to time on the streets and had been invited to meet his family. He'd attended his daughter's wedding. Banda, like many other minor officials, had become effusively pro-American, part of a small frightened middle class who found in American military and economic support their only escape from the bloody legacy left them by the Belgians. Maimed by the past and frightened by the future, they were patriots of the status quo, even a corrupt or oppressive one, which protected them against the mindless anarchy of the truly dispossessed and the waiting sedition of the Russians and Cubans across the river. Their fears, like those of the pro-Western regime, were those American success hadn't solved.

Night had fallen beyond the windows. The watchman's fire blazed brightly in the side garden. Reddish left the villa and walked out into the darkness, light with wood smoke, to stand near the iron gate listening. Trucks were being sent out now, Banda had said, but sent where? To do what? That made as little sense as the infiltration of foreign guns from across the river. What kept the paratroopers and the army loyal wasn't lack of guns, but tribal antagonisms and fear of Western reaction if they smashed parliamentary rule and toppled a pro-Western regime.

The mercenary threat made even less sense. Less than two dozen were left in the country and all of them in prison, a handful of killers and psychopaths rotting in their felons' rags in the maximum security dungeon at the para camp on the hilltop behind the city. He knew a few of them, foul-mouthed liars and braggarts, most of them; others pathetic in their weaknesses, like Cobby Molloy and Rudy Templer, the two Brits who once hung around the airstrip at Stanleyville before the mercenary rebellions, cadging cigarettes and whiskey from the incoming C-130 crews hauling in ammo, offering free favors from their fifteen-year-old bush bunnies in return. From time to time he still received appeals for his help, smuggled out of prison and posted to the embassy in dirty envelopes, his name misspelled.

Standing at the gate, he heard only the sound of traffic on the boulevard a few blocks away. He returned to the study and telephoned Yvon Kadima, the minister of interior, his controlled asset. There was no answer on his private line at the ministry. He called his villa, and the houseboy who answered told him Kadima was still at his office. Kadima kept a suite at the old Portuguese hotel where he entertained his métisse concubines and mistresses, but if he was there, he was probably drinking.

"Tell him Robert called," Reddish said irritably. "Tell him he can reach me at home after ten."

He called Bintu, the President's *chef du cabinet* and another controlled asset. The switchboard operator said Bintu had gone to the coast for the weekend. He searched the drawers of the desk for the local phone directory. Banda's name wasn't listed. He looked instead for the spare key to the liquor cabinet, but couldn't find that either. A man without memory is like a lizard without legs, he recalled, taking out the screwdriver. The President had told him that, at their first meeting nearly four years earlier, but it wasn't until later that he'd finally understood what he meant. A man without memory wouldn't survive his enemies.

He knew what Banda's memory was. The poor little bastard was scared to death of the army.

The liquor cabinet lock was single-toothed and tightly mortised. He tried to jimmy it with the screwdriver, but the teak doors were stouter than the old metal and the tooth snapped off. Only after he brought out the whiskey bottle from the cabinet, opened it, and picked up the glass did he see the missing key, lying there on the napkin in front of the soda siphon where the houseboy had left it, concealed from the discovery of the cook. From separate Kwilu tribes, they mistrusted each other, each complaining of the other's peculations. Tired of their accusations but unwilling to fire either, he'd taken possession of both pantry and liquor cabinet keys, but frequently misplaced them. When he did, they were always returned to him on the sly, like the key on the napkin, the truce kept alive.

But he'd broken the lock. "God damn it," he swore softly. The cabinet had been made in Saigon, the only piece he'd brought back with him.

◆ ◆ Reddish was of medium height, with sandy hair receding from a high sunburned forehead and a crooked nose that looked as if it had been broken a few times over the years and never reset properly. The eyes were neutral. He was in his mid-forties, a bit thick in the waist, his hair thinning on top. His suits were usually rumpled and nondescript. They were bought off the rack from a Baltimore wholesaler every three or four years during home leave and never settled into comfortably until they were out of fashion. He looked like a man already reconciled to whatever face or destiny the age of fifty would settle upon him, a man who probably drank

11

and smoked too much, whose ambition might have slipped some since his divorce, like his hairline and tennis game; but he was an intelligence officer, not a career diplomat, and for him appearances didn't count for much. He'd joined the overseas ranks as a case officer after five years as a weapons expert in the Agency's technical services division, where appearances hadn't counted for much either. To his foreign colleagues, he was simply another diplomat. He stood with three of them now near the rear wall of the Belgian Ambassador's residence, come to say farewell to the departing Belgian counselor.

"Terrible about your chap in Khartoum," the Pakistani Ambassador said.

"Very bad news," agreed Abdul-Aziz, the Egyptian chargé.

"Have you any information?" inquired Federov, the Soviet Ambassador.

"No," Reddish said, his mind elsewhere. "Nothing at all."

"A pity," Federov murmured.

"The PLO office in Damascus denies any knowledge," Abdul-Aziz offered consolingly.

"It's impossible to know which terrorists are doing what," the Pakistani complained. "Who blew up the Portuguese oil tanks at Luanda? The MPLA claimed credit. So did GRAE."

"Freedom fighters, not terrorists," Abdul-Aziz disagreed.

"Terrorists," the Pakistani insisted, smiling slyly at Federov, who said nothing. The Russian was short and paunchy, with stiff gray hair and a scholarly squint that sometimes stirred mysteriously in the gray eyes lurking behind the steel-rimmed spectacles. His peers sometimes found the squint an annoyance, a cipher they couldn't read. Did it signal myopia, contempt, or secret amusement at possession of the facts they didn't know? Vanity sometimes provoked the more aggressive to thrust and parry, as the Pakistani was doing now. "When they're our chaps, they're freedom fighters," he said to Federov. "When they're yours, they're terrorists. You don't agree it wasn't terrorism that blew up those oil tanks?"

"I don't know that I disagree," Federov replied politely.

"Oh, but you must disagree," the Pakistani chided, "otherwise what would Moscow say?" His brown eyes darted toward Reddish, inviting his complicity. "Isn't it Moscow that supplies those MPLA chaps across the river with rockets?" Reddish said nothing, looking away. A provoked Soviet diplomat was one who'd stopped thinking, retreating clumsily into the trenches, dug in behind the official line, but it wasn't the thunder of cold war artillery Reddish wanted to hear. Federov was only interesting when he thought quietly aloud, as he sometimes did when he and Reddish talked together, but the Pakistani's vanity made that impossible.

Federov asked the Pakistani when his home leave commenced.

"Oh you can't slip out of it that easily, old chap." The Pakistani laughed.

"How is the weather now in Karachi?" Abdul-Aziz asked.

"Islamabad," the Pakistani corrected immediately.

Federov's reticence was characteristic. He had nothing to gain from cocktail party debates, unlike the Pakistani, who thrived on them. The latter's principal task was to sell used and obsolete textile machinery to the Africans while keeping open the local market to cheap Pakistani textiles made on more modern Swiss machines. Apart from that, his diplomatic triumphs were merely personal, like the silver-plated cups and cigarette cases he won playing bridge at the Belgian Club, where he could be found four nights a week.

Federov's situation was more delicate, the tactics more complex, the stakes higher. The government was hostile, the Soviet mission small, his staff curtailed, his front gates monitored, like his telephone and his small talk. If he erred, the Soviet mission would grow smaller. So in his silence Federov belonged much less to the gossip of the moment than the other diplomats; in his presence Reddish sometimes sensed a figure of more remote but no less certain future expectations, like a priest practicing among lepers.

"It will be splendid in the hills," the Pakistani was saying, "a relief from this terrible heat, but then I'd fancy anyplace else on earth these days, wouldn't you?"

Federov offered no comment. Reddish looked with Abdul-Aziz across the terrace toward the french doors where more guests were emerging. More than a hundred were already assembled, but Reddish saw no local military officers. Federov, his glass empty, gestured to a white-coated Congolese waiter carrying a tray of drinks, but couldn't catch his eye. From ten feet away, Richter, the East German chargé, saw the motion, plunged after the waiter, and fetched him back.

"Please," Federov insisted, embarrassed by Richter's deference, offering the lowered tray to his companions, "after you."

Richter remained with them, tall and dour, saying nothing. A minute later the Spanish Ambassador joined them too, but by mistake. He'd seen the Pakistani but not the others, whose backs were turned; now he was trapped with Federov and Richter, two men he scrupulously avoided. He'd served in an Eastern European capital, and the experience had been a humiliating one. He made the most of his current ambush, however, shaking hands all around, slavishly following protocol. He was small and dark-haired, nattily dressed in a blue blazer and ascot, as if he'd just come from his boat on the river, where he entertained the Scandinavian secretaries and the nurses from the Swedish hospital. His energies were much more muscular than inquisitive, probably the source of his embarrassment in Bucharest, Reddish sometimes thought. A hunter and horseman, he kept an Arabian stallion stabled near the coast on a Belgian-owned beef ranch. In Karachi, he'd played polo and learned to shoot from a pony. The protocol dispensed with, he disappeared immediately, pulling the Pakistani after him. Richter's reproachful eyes, unlike Federov's, moved with them.

"What was it we were talking about?" the Russian now asked, turning to Abdul-Aziz.

The Egyptian couldn't remember. "The American in Khartoum?"

"Before that."

Federov looked at Reddish.

"Tribes," Reddish said, naming a small rebellious tribe living high in the hills near Lake Tanganyika on the remote eastern frontier. An article in the daily Le Matin a few days earlier had claimed Peking was smuggling them guns from across the lake. The story had been planted by the Republic of China's embassy press officer, but Reddish doubted that Federov knew that. The President feared Peking as much as Moscow, and the Taiwanese Embassy did what it could to keep those fears lively.

"You've been there?" Federov asked.

"No, no one's been there for years."

"Bandits then?"

Reddish said, "The Belgians were never able to pacify them. They just left them alone, like this government."

"And the story in Le Matin?"

"Very doubtful."

Federov nodded, satisfied, the fact tucked away. Ethnology interested him; so did geography; he never asked the same question twice, an uncommon talent in a capital where the memory of small talk seldom survived from one cocktail party to the next. After a year in the country, he understood far more of its tribal divisions than the other diplomats Reddish knew. He'd once told Reddish that he'd taught geography and natural sciences in a small town in the Urals before joining the diplomatic cadres. His interest wasn't

14

merely scholarly: internal politics made little sense without some sense of the more complex tribal declensions. He'd also admitted that he read a great deal to keep himself occupied, as genuine a concession of professional failure as Federov had ever made to anyone—the hostility of the government, separation from his wife in Moscow, and the small prison his local world had become, no larger than his tiny office, the small flat in the chancellery a few steps away, and the dusty compound yard outside, where he'd planted a small garden, trying to grow tomatoes and cucumbers. At receptions such as this one, where the Eastern European diplomats greeted him like curates receiving an archbishop, his power seemed more real; but the impression was illusory, surrendered as quickly as the trailing car from the internal security directorate picked up his limousine outside the front gate and returned with him to the Soviet mission.

"Would the Tanzanians allow them to send guns?" Abdul-Aziz asked. Federov had served in Dar es Salaam before his current posting.

The eyebrows lifted. "The Chinese? No. Never." His voice was brusque. Reddish never talked to Federov about Peking. Soviet and Chinese troops had clashed along the Ussuri River earlier in the year and along the Sinkiang frontier a month later. Moscow's diplomatic offensive to further isolate China in Europe and the Third World was then under way, the principal priority of Soviet foreign policy.

Reddish said, "The problem is that Dar can't control its frontiers any better than this government can."

"True, but they can control the Chinese."

"But you're no longer in Dar to remind them."

"But this government doesn't recognize Peking either," Federov replied with a smile. The moon broke from behind the clouds, lighting up the sloping hillside behind the terrace. "Would you say that was my doing?" he added wryly.

"Maybe it was you that planted that story in Le Matin," Reddish suggested.

Federov laughed, his eyes lifted toward the tropical moon. He'd fared as poorly at the hands of Le Matin's editors as Peking had. Richter said something in Russian, but Federov only shook his head. "Mr. Reddish was making a joke," he explained in English.

"Georgy! Oh, Georgy!" Cecil, the British Ambassador, raised a gangling arm from a circle of diplomats nearby and came to fetch Federov. "Sorry, but we've a bit of a problem with the Bulgarian. I wonder if I might borrow your good offices." The diplomatic corps was meeting at Monday noon, a *vin d'honneur* for a departing envoy, but the Bulgarian chargé, newly arrived, was reluctant to cooperate, since Sofia didn't maintain diplomatic relations with the envoy's nation. "I wonder if you might talk to him. I suspect he may be a bit confused."

Left alone, Reddish moved away from the rear wall, drink in hand, searching for a familiar African face. He saw no army officers. Most of the Africans present were the young technocrats the departing Belgian had cultivated, the ex-socialists from the university who were now part of the detribalized intelligentsia, men vaguely anti-Western in everything but style and taste.

Bena Mercedes, his friend Nyembo called them—the Mercedes clan.

He made his way around the edge of the terrace, moving toward the side entrance from which he could slip away into the darkness without being noticed.

"Not leaving already, are you, Reddish," a sly voice called to him from the dark corner near the terrace steps. "How lucky you are. That late already?" Guy Armand, the French counselor, leaned indolently against the stone wall, ankles crossed, drink against his chest. A dark-haired woman stood with him, her face partially in shadow. Reddish joined them in passing, and Armand introduced them with a casual wave of his hand. "Madame Bonnard has just arrived from Paris, visiting the Houlets. I was pointing out the celebrities while we waited for the ambassador to leave. Were you at the Houlets' for drinks the other evening?"

"No, sorry."

"Then you and Madame Bonnard haven't met. I was trying to identify a few cabinet ministers for her, but none seems to have come." Armand was tall, his pale skin as dry as parchment, the color now gone from thinning hair that had once been blond. In the lapel of his jacket was a French military rosette, like the souvenir of some lost childhood. He was a faithful disciple of de Gaulle's *stratégie tous azimuts*, the enemies everywhere policy which allowed him to treat American diplomats with as much suspicion as the Russians; in his case, the practice not only promoted French grandeur but gave full rein to his talent for duplicity and conceit. "I've known such men," the American Ambassador, Walter Bondurant, had once scrawled across a memo of conversation with Armand sent him by Simon Lowenthal, the embassy political counselor, "an exhausted, malicious mind, drinking its own hemlock. Please send me no more of these Cartesian epigrams."

"We came early, God knows why," Armand continued, looking sleepily at the Frenchwoman as if she might remember.

"The Houlets brought us," she reminded him.

"Oh yes, so they did. In the absence of the cabinet, I suppose Mr. Reddish might pass for a celebrity. I should have mentioned that."

"Oh? Is he?"

"Oh yes. He's been here longer than any of us," Armand said dryly. "The senior American diplomat north of the Zambezi, a virtual walking encyclopedia of all that's happened here. Only he never shares it with us, you see. Quite selfish in his seniority."

"And how long has it been," asked Madame Bonnard. Her hair was dark and cut short. Reddish was uncomfortably aware of her perfume.

"Almost four years."

"Four years." Armand gave a brittle laugh, and Reddish saw her mouth stiffen, her eyes still lifted toward him. "And I believe Lowenthal told me you were leaving soon. Is that true? Lucky fellow. Where will they send you next—Africa again? You've earned your pardon, God knows. All of us have."

"Is it so bad as that?" she asked, turning to confront Armand.

"Oh I'm absolutely the wrong person to ask. Reddish is leaving. Ask him. Going to an embassy of your own now, are you?" He put down his drink carelessly and opened his cigarette case. "An African embassy, no doubt. That's the recognition we get, isn't it? Twenty years in a brothel and they promote you by making you its mistress." He laughed and turned away to light his cigarette. "But we must have a long talk before you go," he resumed, suddenly serious, "just the two of us. Or maybe you'd prefer a small dinner."

He turned to the Frenchwoman. "Diplomats tend to be much more frank with one another on the eve of their departure, much more honest. In places like this, we all tend to become very much the same, very old, very dull, very cynical. But I wouldn't say Reddish has become the oldest of us all. No—quite the contrary. He's managed to keep quite young, but then most bachelors do, don't they?"

"And honest too, I suppose," she said calmly, "or is he like you?"

"Oh no, not like me." Armand laughed, surprised but pleased. "Not at all like me—"

"Only because you're not a bachelor?" she said coolly, looking away across the terrace, her interest in the conversation ended.

"Armand speaks for himself," Reddish told her. "I hope you enjoy your visit."

"Thank you. That's very kind."

Reddish moved down the steps and across the lawn. On the dark road outside the gate, he heard a rumble from the east and stopped to listen. It came a second time, but he ignored it, walking on toward his car. It was the sound of a thunderstorm moving out across the savannahs.

chapter 3

◆ Reddish didn't sleep well. It was a little after five o'clock on Sunday morning when his bedside phone woke him. He groped for the receiver on the bedside table and rolled to his side without turning on the light. The communications watch officer was calling from the embassy. "Sorry to get you up like this but I thought I'd better call. I've got something."

Reddish sat up. "Local?"

"No, sir. Khartoum. I've got an instruction for you."

"That's all?"

"Yes, sir. That's it."

"Thanks. I'll be in about eight."

He dressed in the darkness and went downstairs to put the coffeepot on while he shaved. Nothing during the night at the embassy, he thought, standing at the bathroom mirror. Banda hadn't telephoned again; neither Kadima nor Bintu had returned his calls. Even the villa seemed unnaturally silent. If there were those within the army plotting to bring down the government, the Americans would be the last to know, as much a target as a corrupt president or a paralyzed parliament. Isolation was the price most often paid for political success, and the embassy had been successful. In their success, they'd come to know everything about the country but the secret despairing faces of the opposition, those who mistrusted the Americans as much as Banda and others mistrusted the Russians and Cubans across the river.

He waited in the kitchen for the dawn to come. As the first gray light came into the back garden along the thorn-grown wall, he carried his coffee cup out to the rear patio. The dew was heavy in the grass and the first finches were moving in the shrubbery. He'd once been a late riser, but in recent years, living alone, he was usually up and about at this hour. Solitude didn't explain it.

Growing up in a small town in Wisconsin, he had heard his father moving about in the morning darkness in the downstairs kitchen in the same way, before his mother was awake, and solitude hadn't explained that either. He'd worried about his father then, afraid his parents were getting a divorce, that his father was losing his job or the house, or had cancer like the dying machinist next door. Lying in his upstairs bedroom, half awake as he speculated about what might be making his father old before his time, he would hear him lighting the wood stove, filling the coffeepot, fetching the paper in, and in the winter filling the bird feeders in the crabapple tree outside the kitchen door. On those mornings when they'd gone duck or grouse hunting together, he'd shared the chilly kitchen with him, but those mornings were different. The stars were still out, the icy air took your breath away, and even the frying bacon and the coffee bubbling on the stove had a special aroma, not to be found on any ordinary morning.

The summer before Reddish went off to college, he took a job operating a stamping machine at the same corrugated box factory where his father worked as an accountant. The noise was deafening, the work brutal. After the first hour, his mind went blank, numb with boredom as he watched the time clock, not the clock just inside the employee entrance on the loading dock, but the office clock on the rear wall of the glass-windowed enclosure where his father and two other accountants sat, summer and winter alike, bent over their desks, the light always the same. It was the sight of that silent gray figure hunched over his ledgers that finally explained for Reddish his father's early-morning restlessness. He told himself then that he would escape the world that had trapped his father; yet now, twenty-five years later, his restlessness was the same.

He left his coffee cup in the sink and drove out the front gate. The tree-shaded villas nearby, occupied by government ministers and diplomats, were still silent at this hour. A few arriving cooks and houseboys stirred along the roadbed under the trees. He turned away from the embassy and drove out the empty boulevard toward the sprawling police camp at Bakole. He saw no signs of activity and drove into the hills past army headquarters, deserted at this hour except for a single Mercedes parked near the front steps. He followed the tarmac higher and circled the paramilitary cantonment on the adjacent hilltop where the mercenaries were imprisoned. They were still an embarrassment to the regime, a political problem for which no one had found a solution. The President, like the army, was too frightened of European reaction to hang them and too terrified of their bloody talent for retribution to pardon them; so they rotted in prison, a sure sign of everything else that was wrong with the regime.

The gates to the para camp were open, the barriers lifted, the motor pool filled with idle and disabled vehicles. The gate guards were gossiping with old women and young girls from the nearby village who brought fruit and vegetables to sell at the gate.

He drove back down the hill to the presidential compound. The ornamental gates were drawn closed, the white ducal villa beyond the slope of green lawn somnolent in the morning light. The royal peacocks hadn't yet been released from the aviary to parade under the trees and along the walks. On the side terrace, a solitary gardener was stooping to turn on the underground sprinkler system, a gift from the same Belgian *société* that built the small lake and the Swiss-chalet boathouse tucked away in the corner of the grounds, invisible from the gate. The same firm had been awarded the contract for improving the municipal water system, but progress had been slow. The *cités* where the Africans lived still had their communal faucets, Reddish his roof tank.

A handful of ragged Africans were already gathered on the bare earth under a tulip tree, some holding ten-franc copybooks, others folded newspapers concealing their petitions. Most wanted jobs, medical treatment, or the release of imprisoned relatives. A few simply wanted money, relief from the evil eye, or to pay homage to their president. They'd spent the night there sleeping on scraps of cardboard. By eleven o'clock, when the gates opened and the President's motorcade swept by, speeding him to mass at the old Belgian-built cathedral, they would have been dispersed, their petitions received to be burned in the incinerator at the guard barracks, the supplicants sent back down the hillside, the President spared the humiliation of their rags and tatters, the contagion of their nameless diseases. But even as the speeding Mercedes roared by them far down the hill or along the boulevard, they would turn to greet him, their spirits lifted from the roadside dust for a moment to flap their rags at the splendor such men make across the Africans' miserable planet in whose ancient, abiding helplessness there seemed to be no such thing as moral outrage.

Reddish circled the stone kiosk near the gatehouse, ignored by the presidential guards, who wore chrome-plated helmets and carried newly arrived American M-16 rifles. He drove back toward the city. He'd once made the same reconnaissance each night, accompanying the chief of the internal security directorate on his rounds as he locked up the city each night for an uneasy President, making certain that the capital was quiet, the police on duty or safely dispersed, the mud and tin hovels of the native communes asleep with their misery, the army secure in its barracks. The midnight patrol had ended in the study of the presidential villa, where they reported to the old man and his *chef du cabinet*, but that was before his power had been consolidated and his own security apparatus in place.

He turned off the main boulevard to idle past the Soviet and East German embassies. They were as peaceful as the surrounding streets, their gates locked. The gray shutters were drawn; the courtyards empty. Two policemen sat on the curb opposite each gate watching the compounds. They didn't turn as Reddish drove past.

At the *grand marché* the morning sun had broken through the overcast, the quick yellow light flooding the open square. African women were unloading their produce in the stalls; trucks from the interior were discharging cargo in the narrow lanes. Five sleepy soldiers in jungle-green twill, on furlough from the interior, climbed from beneath the canvas of an old Mercedes truck and straggled off stiffly, still cramped from their long journey, still carrying their weapons. A few street orphans who made the *marché* their home chased after Reddish's Fiat, mistaking him for an early shopper. At an intersection he watched a policeman in gray khakis flag down a Portuguese merchant who'd run a stop sign. The Portuguese gave him a package of cigarettes and drove on.

Business as usual, Reddish thought. *What guns?*

He left the commercial district and drove into the native commune of Malunga, the largest African *cité* in the capital. The sunshine was thick with the dust drummed from the dirt road and the adjacent footpaths by women in brightly colored *waxes* returning from the small native markets carrying baskets of fruit, palm oil, and dried fish. Jobless African youths stirred through the lanes or sat atop the concrete-block walls in front of open-air bars eyeing the young girls. It hadn't rained in ten days. The older women were lined up twenty deep at the communal pumps. The rising dust mixed with the smoke still drifting from the morning cooking fires that burned within the beehive of compound yards where goats had cropped the shrubbery and foliage bare.

He drove past the police station, searching for Banda's house. A policeman at the gate knew the name and pointed off down the laterite road. Behind him a few gray-clad figures lounged dissolutely on the porch facing the clay yard. The police post was half complete. Like rice, cooking oil, and flour, the price of cement had increased threefold since urban population pressures had forced the ministry of interior to begin new construction. A half-mile away he found a small concrete-block cottage that looked vaguely familiar, painted a pale blue, with yellow latticework along the porch. He saw no cars nearby, and he left his Fiat up the lane and walked back to the cottage.

The old woman who answered the door said that Banda and his wife had gone. *"Flamand?"* she asked curiously, moving her head from the shadows to study his face.

"Flamand te." He asked her where Banda had gone. Her French was poor; his Lingala made her smile. She wasn't sure where Banda had gone—West Kasai, she thought—and now she was embarrassed because Reddish's knowledge of Lingala made it impossible for her to conceal her ignorance. But she knew he'd left last night, taking his motorcar, taking his wife and daughter. Somewhere far away, where his brother lived.

Reddish went back to his car. A few hundred feet beyond the Banda cottage he was forced to the verge by fifty youths jogging in double time down the lane. They wore green twill uniforms and the red armbands of the Jeunesse Nationale de la Révolution, the youth wing of the teachers and professional workers party, whose headquarters compound was nearby. Most of the youths were orphans from the bush or homeless commune kids whom the workers party had tried to train with vocational skills, but resources were limited, its talent meager. A few foreign embassies exploited the vacuum, supplying the JNR reading room with a potpourri of Pan-African, Western, socialist, and Marxist material—the words of Ben Bella, Nkrumah, de Gaulle, Kennedy, Marx, Nasser, and Kim Il Sung. The party *jeunesse* had grown to over a thousand strong, and growth had brought suspicion and resentment, principally from the commune dwellers of Malunga. The cadre leaders were bullies and thugs, mixing socialist argot with fascist tactics, extorting money from the poor for the workers party membership cards, intimidating shopkeepers, and harassing Portuguese and Belgian merchants. The JNR had clashed with the army during the student and transit strikes of the previous spring, a few were killed, a dozen more arrested.

But the principal object of army and cabinet suspicion was Pierre Masakita, the rebel leader brought back from exile by the President to be named vice minister of interior in the new government of national reconciliation. He was secretary general of the workers party, reorganized with the President's sanction following his return from abroad.

"*Flamand te!*" a small urchin in the rear ranks shouted to Reddish as he marched by—"Belgians, no!" He was no more than eight or nine, barefooted, lifting his knees high with the other street orphans who were straggling along after the party *jeunesse*. But he couldn't resist turning his head to see the insult's effects, and when he did, he smiled suddenly, gap-toothed, too innocent to yet know who he or Reddish was.

Reddish drove back to the embassy. As he waited in front of the gate, a score or so of Congolese straggled along the street, moving away from the customs sheds a block away where the ferry from Brazzaville had just arrived. A few were traders carrying tin suitcases to set up shop in the Ivory Market. The Brazzaville Africa Cup winners were playing the national soccer team at the stadium that afternoon, and he wondered if the others were the first arrivals.

The embassy courtyard was deserted except for a Chevrolet station wagon drawn up near the front steps. It was the Sunday duty car, and the driver was asleep in the front seat.

"In kinda early, aren't you, sir?" said the young Marine as he unlocked the steel riot gate from within. He wore dress blues and a pistol case on his hip. The riot screen was newly installed and a nuisance; the Marine had to struggle to keep it on its track as he pushed it overhead. Taggert, the regional security officer newly arrived from South Africa, was responsible for the installation. His first official act was to install the screen, his second to ban all African employees from the second and third floors, an inconvenience which meant that the embassy staff now had to fetch their morning coffee from the first-floor snack bar. The Marines, with that vernacular quickness of the barracks room, called him "Shaky the house dick."

Reddish signed the registry and searched the night entries at the top of the page. No one had come in during the night—not Lowenthal, not Colonel Selvey, the defense attaché, and none of his own people.

"Quiet night then," he concluded.

"Yes, sir, all weekend, except for that Khartoum business. Maybe everybody's sleeping off the party for Mr. Harris. That was sure some bust-up."

Harris was the administrative counselor, departing for reassignment. The staff had given him a farewell party at the embassy recreation center in the suburbs, which would remain a quasi-official monument to his ingenuity in squeezing official funds for nonofficial purposes, like swimming pools, wet bars, and commissary runs to South Africa for fresh lobster.

"Was you there when they throwed Taggert into the pool?"

"I must have missed it," Reddish said without lifting his eyes from the log. According to the registry, Lowenthal, the political counselor, had been the last officer to leave the embassy the previous evening. At seven, twenty minutes after he left, the Marine had logged an incoming call from Armand. That was about the time Banda had called him. He wondered what Armand had wanted to talk about.

"They throwed him in clothes and all. Jesus, was he pissed. The whole bunch was smashed and maybe Taggert was too. Corporal Martinez was in on it, and Taggert said he was going to get him busted."

"That's too bad," Reddish said, returning the registry. "When the duty officer calls, tell him I want to see him. I'll be upstairs."

Behind the vault door of the third-floor commo room, the clerk showed him the incoming cable from Langley listing the names of five Palestinians who'd left Khartoum the afternoon prior to the kidnapping, traveling on stolen Jordanian passports. The Agency thought the second group was targeted against a second American diplomatic mission to the south. The station was instructed to pass the names and passport numbers to the local security service and request additional protection for the embassy and the ambassador.

In his office on the second floor, he unlocked his safe, turned on the coffee maker, and switched on the shortwave radio. He listened to the news bulletins on national radio and turned to the BBC from London. On the wall behind the desk was a framed diplomatic commission; a picture of his ex-wife and daughter standing in the rich golden light of the Roman ruins at Palmyra, Syria; and a black and white photograph of Reddish, the President, and Yvon Kadima standing with a group of black paras in the rubble of a tea plantation in the Kivu during the mercenary rebellions. After the newscast, he turned off the radio, disconnected his phone from the switchboard, and replugged the jack to a direct outside line. He called the director of internal security, but the operator said he was out. He called his residence and got no answer. He telephoned two other contacts at their private residences. Neither was at home. One was in the interior, a second had left for Brussels two days earlier.

What in God's name is going on? he wondered as he dialed Yvon Kadima's residence. The houseboy told him the minister had left for Matadi on the coast to visit his banana plantation.

"Did you give him my message last night?"

"Yes, I told him."

"Tell him again, will you. Tell him it's important."

He turned on the national radio again, puzzled. On any other Sunday he might have thought his sudden Coventry a coincidence. Now, remembering Banda's telephone call, he wasn't sure. It had happened once before—in Syria on the eve of a coup d'etat when his assets had suddenly dried up, vanished, been blown away—

"Looks like they traced those Palestinians, Mr. Reddish." The commo clerk stood in the door holding a teletyped sheet just torn from the code machine, sent from the CIA station in Nairobi. The five Arabs traveling south from Khartoum had left Nairobi the previous night, bound for Mogadiscio and Aden. Kenyan passport control had tracked them.

"Headed north again. Looks like they got scared off," the clerk said. "Do you want me to take that instruction back upstairs?"

"No, I'll keep it for a while. Thanks."

He telephoned Sarah Ogilvy, his secretary. "Do you realize what time it is," she complained. "You woke me up."

"That makes two of us. It's eight-fifteen. If you don't have anything better to do, why don't you come in. I may need a little help."

"I suppose you know I'm *not* the duty secretary this week."

"It's not duty I'm looking for, it's companionship. You'd better bring your lunch—for both of us."

"I haven't been shopping yet. I was going after church."

"No cucumber and lettuce. The same with the cream cheese. Corned beef's O.K. Smoked salmon's better."

She hung up.

In the old days improvisation had been his operational code, and old habits died hard. Swiveling in his chair, he typed out the five Palestinian names and their passport numbers on his old Underwood. From the bottom drawer of the desk he removed a dog-eared telephone book and found the paramilitary camp on the mountain. If his sources had all disappeared temporarily, others could be used. He knew Jean-Bernard de Vaux, the Belgian ex-mercenary who was now aide and equerry to Colonel N'Sika, the commander of the paratrooper brigade. He telephoned the para camp.

In the past he'd often been given credit for knowing far more than he knew or had the right to know. The Agency sometimes struggled with the same omniscient reputation. If it wasn't deserved, it was sometimes useful, particularly in coping with those lost in the conspiratorial murk of Third World politics. He thought the reputation might be useful now. If Banda was right, and the army, the paras, and others were planning something, they were amateurs, these ham-handed colonels and majors—and amateurs could be scared off.

He spoke to de Vaux, who, after some hesitation, agreed to see him at noon.

chapter 4

✧ Reddish had sat with Michaux that day two months earlier on the verandah of the old *cercle* at Kindu, seven hundred miles east of the capital deep in the African bush. Behind them, half in shadow, the whitewashed wall of the old sporting club was scaled by the African sun and pocked by the rifle fire of the rebellions two years past. Vultures and magpies flapped along the sagging fence behind the weed-grown courtyard where the tennis courts had once lain. Waiting in the sand drive under the laurel trees was the old Fiat Cinquecento that had brought him from the airstrip. Michaux's muddy Landrover stood near the concrete steps, the Mutatela driver squatting in its shadow eagerly turning the pages of the newspapers Reddish had brought from the capital. The trials of the leaders of the transit and student strikes had just ended; the photographs of the executed men, hands and feet bound, blindfolded, decorated the front pages.

"Still as suspicious as ever, is he?" Michaux asked, amused, talking of the President. "Terrified of strikes, foreign guns, Russians, Cubans, and God knows what else. Students now, eh? Is that why he brought back that scoundrel Jean-Bernard de Vaux? Someone told me he's the President's bodyguard. Doesn't trust the Americans now, just his old Belgian mercenaries."

Michaux knew Reddish as the President's shadow during the rebellions, accompanying him on the C-130 flights about the interior. Even during the most bitter days, when the nation seemed merely so much carrion for the UN and the cold war jackals, Reddish had never adopted the bush jackets or safari suits worn by other junketing diplomats or UN civil servants, but always the same drab rumpled seersucker or tropical suits, the coat settled damply about his shoulders like a barman's jacket.

"Not the President's bodyguard, Colonel N'Sika's, the new commander of the para brigade. Where did you know de Vaux?"

"Jean-Bernard de Vaux? Here," Michaux said. "I know him well. An ugly little guttersnipe, straight from the Antwerp slums—a mongrel, that's what. Clever though; everyone knows that. So now he's with the para brigade. Bodyguard, you say?"

"Aide and equerry to Colonel N'Sika, the commander."

"N'Sika?" Michaux frowned suddenly, memory gone. "Don't know him. Where's he from?"

"The north. Equateur."

Michaux brightened. "Then I wouldn't," he declared, relieved. He was no longer physically active, a crippled old crab on the beach; memory was the tide that lifted him away. He drank from the whiskey Reddish had brought him from the capital, smiling. "No, don't know him. Equateur, you say? No, too much jungle in the blood up there, like Maniema—too dark, too savage." He laughed.

He was almost seventy, his thatch of white hair crudely cut, the flesh of his face and neck scarred by the equatorial sun. He had lived in the bush for forty years, surviving fever, isolation, superstition, and disease, the murder and mayhem of the Simba and mercenary rebellions, and now the torpor of an exhausted countryside. The roads were worse now than forty years ago; he couldn't evacuate his palm nuts to the river or the railhead; the pressing plant, burned by the rebels, hadn't been reopened. After forty years, all he had for his labors were his crippling arthritis, a derelict palm oil plantation thirty kilometers to the south, and a middle-aged Batatela woman who kept house for him and whom he called his wife.

"They say the President is in poor health," Michaux continued, still eager for gossip from Kinshasa. "They say that's why he hides himself away in the capital—cancer of the throat, I heard. Paralyzed, they say—everything. Is that why he went to Brussels last month, because of this cancer?"

"Health isn't one of his problems," Reddish said, gazing out into the bright, windless African afternoon.

"But everything else is, eh? The army, the parliament, the cabinet, the Russians, now the students. Is that why he reorganized the paras, with his new colonel in charge? They say the regular army threatened to mutiny in the south."

"A little misunderstanding, that's all."

"The army and the students fought in the streets, but the national radio tells us nothing. Is that a misunderstanding too?"

"Probably. How well did you know de Vaux?" Reddish persisted, his curiosity stirred. He collected the odd anomalous fact as other men collect pocket pieces, pipes, or books. He knew de Vaux well enough to recognize that some of his information was false.

"Well enough. I knew him here. Why? Has he tried to hire himself out to the Americans? If he has, you've got a brass sovereign. Tried to hire himself out to me once. Wouldn't have him."

Their conversation had been interrupted by the arrival of the sedan from the internal security sub-office to take Reddish away to the army depot. There he examined a cache of weapons discovered at an army checkpoint aboard a trader's truck south of Uvira along the lake. They were concealed beneath bags of rice and tinned goods marked with Chinese characters, smuggled in from Tanzania. The major at Kindu had reported to his headquarters in the capital that he'd seized a shipment of Chinese-supplied weapons and rations intended for old rebels in the bush preparing to reopen the insurrections. The President had been alarmed at the report; so had Kadima, the interior minister, and Bintu, the President's *chef du cabinet*.

Reddish had been dubious. He'd told Kadima he would look at the weapons himself.

"*Chinois*," the army captain muttered, prodding a mud-caked carbine with his foot. He had a broad, stupid face; the whites of his eyes were muddy, the pupils dilated, like a hashish addict's.

The cache of weapons lay on a wooden pallet in an ordnance repair shop, half covered by a filthy tarpaulin. In the dim light of the shop, Reddish found what he'd expected to find—a potpourri of rusty old ordnance the rebellions had given back after a few years— old Belgian rifles, German 9-mm Schmeisser submachine guns, Italian 9-mm Berettas, and two Danish 9-mm Madsen submachine guns. The automatic pieces were once mercenary hardware, stolen, sold, stolen, and sold again, most recently to the trader who'd smuggled in the Chinese rice and tinned goods from across the lake. A few had a coating of fresh light oil, but the remainder had been heavily coated with fish oil and stank as oppressively as the tarpaulin. A few were missing firing pins; others had ruptured barrels. Pushed down the bore of a Belgian rifle was the shaft of a hunting arrow with a broad scalloped point of hand-forged iron.

"Masakita," the captain grumbled. He disappeared off into a dark corner and returned with an empty rice sack, pointing out the Chinese characters.

"He says the guns were for Masakita's followers," the security chief translated.

"How does he know that?" Reddish asked, cataloguing the guns in his notebook.

"He says Masakita was in China."

"Ask him which guns are Chinese."

The captain searched among the weapons Reddish had moved aside and dug out a Danish 9-mm Madsen. The hieroglyphics of the armorer's die might have looked like a Chinese character to a bush soldier, but the weapon was Danish, once a mercenary piece, now part of the gun traffic along the frontiers of this ramshackle empire. Poachers bought guns; so did brigands, provincial officials, and frightened tribesmen beyond the reach of an inept administration.

Reddish pulled the old arrow from the rifle bore and studied the arrowhead, intrigued. "I think it's a hippo arrow, isn't it? Used by the hunters on the lake?" He held the arrow out to the captain, who made no move to take it.

"He doesn't hunt hippos," explained the security chief.

"What does he hunt then?" Reddish asked, losing interest.

"He hunts what the soldiers always hunt," the chief said to him softly as they went back to the car—"rice, cigarettes, and beer from the trucks."

"Contraband, is that it? Everything they can get their hands on?"

The chief nodded. "When the army is hungry or bored, everything is contraband."

Michaux had guessed Reddish's purpose in coming. He greeted him at dusk as Reddish returned to the *cercle* for dinner, rising from his chair on the verandah, propped grotesquely on his heavy walking stick.

"Is that what brings you out here for a few hours, looking for new rebels *en brousse*? Look for yourself, *mon vieux!* What do you see except exhaustion?" His bright eyes swept the dimming desolation of the *cercle*—the fallen roof tin perforated by rifle fire, the litter of mortar rubble along the wall, the weed-grown fence where the magpies had quarreled.

◇ ◇ Michaux talked that evening of de Vaux.

"Oh yes—de Vaux. Yes, I remember. What can I say about him? He started off in Bunia up near the Sudan border after the war. That's where I first knew him. All he had was the cloth on his back. Hired himself to a Pakistani merchant as a mechanic and driver, smuggling tea and coffee into Uganda and Kenya. Brought back stolen lorries. Quick with a spanner or a knife, take your choice. Quick with other men's wives too, if you want to know. Tried to hire himself to me, like I said, but I wouldn't have him—a brass sovereign if I ever saw one! Twice he tried. So now he's with the para brigade, eh? Aide and equerry?"

"You say he was at Bunia in forty-six?" Reddish asked, drawing him on. "That's not what I remember."

They sat on the side gallery of the *cercle*, the table brought from inside, where a handful of UN technicians and local administrators were drinking and dining. Behind the latticework that divided the gallery from the kitchen area, the smell of couscous and roasting chicken drifted, mixed with the pungence of charcoal. Insects rattled against the hurricane lamp. Beyond the scapular crowns of the palms and palmetto, the sky was bright with stars.

"Oh yes, he was at Bunia then, maybe a little to the north," Michaux said. "You know him, do you? What'd he tell you about himself?"

Reddish had heard that de Vaux had served with the elite Belgian unit Chasseurs d'Ardennes but had resigned his commission after the war to serve in Indochina. Another source credited de Vaux with service in the crack Third French para regiment during the Battle of Algiers, after which he'd been decorated.

Michaux smiled as he noisily refilled his glass. "Chasseurs d'Ardennes? Never! Don't be fooled. A chaser of women was all he was in those days, women and money. A handsome lad, bright as a penny, but a thief. Stole the Pakistani bankrupt, they say, but no one minded. Good riddance, some said. After that a Belgian took him on. That would have been forty-eight or forty-nine. I think it was a Belgian, but he could have been a Greek. Took him on as overseer and mechanic. No—wait! He was Greek, that's right, an old Greek who married late, the way they do. From Rhodes I remember. He brought a Greek wife from there, a widow and her daughter, all in black. Pretty, both of them. Before the old man knew it, de Vaux had made a mistress of the wife. After he got tired of her, he had a go at the daughter.

"By God, there's a lad from Antwerp for you. His old man must have been a sailor, eh, off the ships. Anyway, de Vaux finally ran off with the girl and took over an abandoned tin mine up in the Kivu. Bought it for a song—but why not?—it was worthless, an old shaft filled with tailings and a smashed lift. Tried to sell shares in it, I remember, tried to create a world out there. That was the second time he came to see me. *Shares!* Had the Greek girl's baptism card with him, all gold and gilt, flowers on the margin, cupids blowing kisses through silver clouds, the way the Greek churches do it. Found his pot of gold at the end of the rainbow, he had. He was going over to Kampala to have it copied up, printing and artwork both. I had to laugh when I saw it—shares like a bloody baptism card.

"Anyway, all he got out of it was the three hundred thousand francs the Greek paid to get his stepdaughter back. De Vaux didn't care, not a man like that. He knew enough chiefs in the bush by then to pick his crop when the young lasses bloomed—jungle poppies, eh? What age would that be, twelve or thirteen? Next thing I heard he'd bought a tea plantation on the track to Goma, right at the edge of the lake. After that he bought another mine and lost everything again. It was as worthless as the first."

The waiter brought chicken and rice. Michaux began to eat hungrily, without waiting.

"So he was here in the bush all those years," Reddish said.

"He was here, no place else. Had a way with the blacks, no doubt about it. Hard worker too and clever as a snake. Went after what he wanted, but a swine too, for all the honest ambition he ever had. What good is his kind of ambition out here? Brings you closer to the grave, that's all. Take my word for it—leave your ambitions in the old world. Take this one as you find it. Don't try to make another. Battle of Algiers? Never. Did he graduate from Saint-Cyr too?

"He did disappear for a few years, that much I remember. Some thought he was dead, killed while poaching the King's elephants up in Parc Albert. Nothing was out of bounds for him in those days. Others told me he went up to Juba in the Sudan, as bold as brass, trying to corner the ivory trade. Tea prices had fallen. They say he had a fleet of lorries up there. Whatever it was, when I saw him again he'd learned a little English. Spoke it well too—talked like a limey though, dockside style. Maybe he picked it up in prison in Entebbe or Khartoum. Does that make him an Oxford man too?"

Michaux laughed, eyes lifted as he brought knife and fork together again on the plate in front of him.

"When did you last see him?"

Michaux raised his knife, waving it toward the dark courtyard behind Reddish. "Outside the gate there, during the rebellions. He was commanding a merc unit. Lost track of him after that." He frowned as he drank from his glass, memory fading again. "What happened to him after that?"

"He went up north," Reddish replied, "to Orientale." Michaux was curious, listening silently as Reddish explained. De Vaux had bought a coffee plantation in the north after the Simba rebellions were put down. When his old mercenary colleagues had rebelled against the central government, he'd refused their appeals to join them and had retreated with his African wife to a remote village on the Sudan frontier. Returning after the mercenaries were defeated, he'd found his house burned, his trees ravaged, his trucks stolen, and the bodies of his wife's two sisters rotting in the coffee-drying sheds, murdered by the retreating mercenaries and their Katangese soldiers. De Vaux had dropped from sight, reappearing a year later when he'd been named to the training staff of the old general who commanded the northern sector. A few months afterward, the old general had been killed in a plane accident, his small aircraft mysteriously blown apart as it descended through a rain squall to the Mbandaka airstrip. De Vaux had accompanied the general's deputy, N'Sika, to the capital as his aide. Among the Belgian commercial community in the north, a rumor had circulated claiming that sabotage was responsible, a bomb rigged to the aircraft's landing gear and wired to detonate as the wheels were lowered.

"Don't know anything about that," Michaux admitted. "A man's bound to make enemies, I suppose, but when Jean-Bernard is around, you have to be doubly careful. The last time I saw him he was outside the gate there"—he lifted the knife again, pointing off through the darkness—"standing on the front seat of a mercenary jeep with a captured Simba witch doctor in the back seat, a manioc sack pulled down over the poor bugger's head. There were flowers all over the bonnet, thrown there by the villagers as they'd driven in. He had twenty mercs with him, the worst of the bunch, I'd say. The Simbas were on the run, the last of them around here smashed just on the other side of the ferry by de Vaux and his unit. The blacks who'd stayed loyal wanted to put the torch to the poor old bastard de Vaux had in the back seat."

Michaux smiled with the recollection, gazing beyond Reddish toward the gate. "He wouldn't hear of it. Reading the riot act to them, Jean-Bernard was, giving them a piece of his mind. He was a merc captain by then. They say he'd been a real soldier too, all spit and polish, not one of those cutthroats or thieves masquerading as a Sandhurst field marshal amongst the bow-and-arrow savages of the bush, but a real soldier. Shot a Rhodesian corporal, they say, after he'd raped a young girl. So there he was, standing up for discipline again, standing up for that ignorant savage in the back seat with the manioc sack pulled down over his head. I called out to him from just inside the gate over there, wearing the same filthy rags I'd been wearing for three months dodging the rebels. They'd have had my tongue on a skewer if they'd caught me, same as they'd have had Jean-Bernard's. 'Jean-Bernard,' I called out to him. 'Hey there, Jean-Bernard! What's tin bring in the Kivu these days?'

"Everyone was a little out of his head that morning, and maybe I was too. I'd been burned out like everyone else, but that was all right too. I was alive, like them, and we were all delirious that morning. 'What are you cooking up now?' I shouted to him. 'What's next for you—a seat on the Brussels bourse?' I thought maybe the rebellions had changed things for him, everyone in town kneeling down to him and his men that way. Maybe he thought I was a ghost. Maybe he never saw me, I don't know, but he never said a word, not a bloody word. He just looked at me like I wasn't even there, still in the iron grip of whatever it was that brought him out here in the first place.

"So after a while the jeep went away with him in it, up the track like it was the road to Goma and Bunia again back in forty-six, the witch doctor on the back seat not moving a muscle, and that was the last time I set eyes on him. Now he's back in the capital, eh? Working for the paras?" Michaux laughed. "That's Jean-Bernard, all right, the same man. Make of him what you will, he'll never change."

chapter 5

❖ Reddish left his Fiat in the oyster-shell drive next to a para jeep. A black trooper sat slumped behind the wheel, dressed in the leopard-spot fatigues of the para battalion, sunglasses across his eyes, a red beret on his head. An American-made M-16 lay across his knees. A second para lounged against the front fender, ankles crossed, weapon in his arms, his eyes moving with Reddish as he passed in front of them. Reddish nodded, but the paras didn't acknowledge the greeting. Annoyed with himself, he crossed the drive to the gravel path under the palm trees. The paras were the pampered hoodlums of the presidency, insolent, brutal, and vain, eager to test their skills whenever GHQ turned them loose, as it had against the striking students and transit workers, but more often in the ugly ceremony of crowd control, clubbing a path for the President and his retinue through a mob of the urban poor already whipped to frenzy by the loudspeaker trucks and the paid political claques of the communes.

He followed the path toward a whitewashed cottage roofed in red tile, similar to the dozen or so other cottages scattered among the trees along the sand road. The hilltop had once been a Belgian police cantonment. A few of the cottages had fallen into disrepair, gutters gone, windows cracked, gardens unweeded, and the turf trampled to sand under the raffia palms; but de Vaux's cottage was bright and neat, freshly painted. Red blossoms bloomed in the flower beds along the foundation wall; a poinsettia tree stood near the front steps.

De Vaux waited for him on the porch, a slim figure in starched khaki drill shorts and shirt, knee-length tan hose, and high-topped boots. A red beret was stuck in his belt.

"Worried about terrorists, are you, Reddish? I wouldn't have thought it of an old bush sergeant like you." He didn't misplace the accent, like most French speakers.

"I lost my stripes, I suppose. Like you."

"I heard about your bloke in Khartoum. On the wireless. Too bad. Didn't know him, did you?" He was ivory-skinned, thin-faced, and slightly built, but tightly muscled, the sharp features under the blondish hair lit by eyes as cool as sea water. Size belied his strength. He had quick hands, as quick as his temper, which had once been unpredictable. At Goma, Reddish had once seen him drop an unruly mercenary corporal to the floor, jaw broken, so quickly he hadn't believed it had happened.

"No, I don't, but he's not dead yet, is he?"

"You're the expert, not me."

It was sweltering in the midday heat, and Reddish mopped his face and neck as he climbed the steps. At the gate he'd been kept waiting inside his boiling car for twenty minutes while the guard phoned ahead.

"Come inside. It's cooler on the side porch."

"Not on duty today, are you?"

"Always on duty. Why?"

"The uniform."

"My Sunday kit."

"I was thinking at the gate I should be playing more tennis," Reddish said, following de Vaux's trim figure, which reminded him of his own lack of conditioning. His blue tennis shirt clung to his wet back, sweat rolled from his cheeks and neck. He was annoyed at himself again. Small talk too was a surrender of strength, and de Vaux would surely recognize it.

"Tennis won't do. Not diplomats' tennis. Don't even chase their own balls at the Belgian Club do they? Not unless there's a thousand-franc whore at the end of it." De Vaux laughed, opening the screen door, and Reddish was conscious of the poor teeth, the result of his years in the bush. The trace of Cockney in the English was as strong as ever, but with an exaggerated nasality which bordered on parody, a navvy's version of how a sergeant-major talked.

"The ball boys go with the club. I don't think they'd chase them off, not with unemployment what it is."

"Frightened, are they? What do they think, those dips of yours, that ball boys will solve the bloody labor problem?" He laughed again.

"It's hard to tell what they think."

The sitting room was small and sparsely furnished. A few children's toys lay abandoned on the worn Wilton carpet. An expensive cabinet radio and phonograph sat against the wall below a dusty mirror and a reproduction of a painting of a Normandy cottage and hedgerow. On the footstool nearby someone had left a rag doll and a half-eaten croissant. There was no air conditioning. From the rear of the cottage drafted a babble of voices, children, women, and men, all gossiping together in an African dialect Reddish couldn't identify and which, for that very reason, sounded aggressively loud. It was likely that de Vaux's African wife, a cousin of Colonel N'Sika, the para commander, had brought a few of her family with her to the capital.

They moved to the side porch, separated from the living room by the dining area and a pair of louvered doors. "Something to drink?" de Vaux asked. "Or is it too early yet? Whiskey, beer?" The nasality again, the exaggerated manners.

"Beer would be fine, thanks."

He sat back as he waited, his shirt wet against his back. Beyond the white-enameled iron latticework the sunlight drifted through the trees, splintered in bright patches; but over the distant city, visible from the porch, it paled like smoke over rubble in the gaseous heat. A metal coffee table with a glass top sat in front of the rattan chair where Reddish waited. Nearby was a small bookcase, the lower shelves crammed with local and Belgian newspapers, together with the daily mimeographed bulletins circulated by the ministry of information, many yellow with age. Two books lay on the top shelf next to a candlestick, the only books Reddish saw. Behind the empty rattan chair at the far end of the coffee table was a reading light. Alongside was a table holding a telephone, yellow legal pads, and a clay pot filled with pencils.

He supposed de Vaux used the porch as a study, shut away from the distractions of domestic life. The two books drew his eyes. They were dog-eared, their bindings tattered, the cloth covers ringed with watermarks. He couldn't read their titles, but they interested him, clues to the man many had heard of but few knew. He'd been collecting the odd pieces for years, and now he leaned forward and was putting on his steel-rimmed reading glasses as de Vaux returned carrying glasses and beer bottles.

"The UN left them here," he explained, guessing Reddish's intentions. "A crate of them. That's all that's left, those two. Used this place as a reading room, game room. Even had an Indian librarian. That's the UN for you, wogs everywhere. This was the place where a soldier could write home, feel sorry for himself after the sun went down." He lifted one of the books from the shelf and pushed it across the glass-topped table. "You'll know this one. They say there's not an Englishman that doesn't."

Reddish adjusted his glasses and opened the tattered cover. It was a copy of *Robinson Crusoe*. "I know it," he muttered, studying the brittle flyleaf. Pasted inside the front cover was a faded gum sticker: "Property of Chapel Library, Birmingham."

"Chap I knew in the Fifty-fifth Merc Brigade used to carry a copy in his kit. A Yorkshireman. The way he talked, you'd think it was the only book he ever read. Maybe it was. Didn't save him though. Took a tracer in the throat, and his friends buried the book with him. He was clever with words. Maybe that's where he got them, out of that book." He took back the volume and opened it. "I read it to keep my English up, read it by myself to learn what a man can do, the way he did. It helps. Relaxation, see, but it's not a boy's book. Never was. There's a lot there if you've got the patience for it." He pushed the book aside. "So what's this about the PLO. On their way south, you say?"

Reddish gave him the typewritten list of Jordanian passport numbers and the names of the Palestinians. De Vaux studied it silently. On the wall behind him was a military map of the nation, the location of army groups and their zone of responsibility marked in heavily with a grease pencil. Before the President had moved Colonel N'Sika to the para brigade following the student clashes, N'Sika had been the chief of intelligence at GHQ and de Vaux his aide in charge of the foreign intelligence collection effort. Reddish guessed that the map probably dated from those days at G-2.

"I was wondering if anyone over at G-2 would be interested in the list," Reddish began as de Vaux lifted his eyes. "I don't have any contacts over there, not since you left."

"There's a major who follows it now. He might be interested. But the internal security directorate would have responsibility. They're the chaps that would take charge."

"I can't get hold of anyone at internal security. A little odd, I thought."

De Vaux shrugged. "It's the way they are. You can't find them until they need you. I can get this to them."

"We have another report that interests us more. It could have something to do with this Palestinian group. Maybe not."

"You brought it with you?"

"No. It's not that kind of report. We think guns might have been brought in from Brazza, smuggled in." He watched de Vaux's eyes. "You still follow that, do you? Guns brought in from across the river. It's something the para brigade watches."

"It interests us," de Vaux said diffidently.

"These would be Soviet guns, guns just shipped in."

De Vaux said nothing.

Reddish picked up his glass and drank from it, then took off his glasses, sitting back. "That worries us. More than the Palestinians. If this group isn't to use them, maybe someone else is. We wouldn't want that to happen."

"If these chaps are headed here, they'd be picked up at the frontier, at the airport. I'll talk to internal security myself."

"Then we'd still have the problems of the guns already here, wouldn't we? Someone else using them?"

"How many guns?"

"Quite a few."

"Where'd they come in?"

"That's not important, is it? They're here."

De Vaux smiled shrewdly. "What is it, your ambassador worried? His migraine comes on and all you chaps get a headache, just because some diplomat gets himself stuffed in Khartoum. Tell him no one is going to hijack him. I'll send a company down to your embassy myself if that's what he wants, another to his residence out on the river. Is that what he wants?"

"That still leaves the guns," Reddish replied. "Let's talk about the guns, what they're doing here, who's going to use them."

De Vaux turned in his chair, pulling a package of cigarettes from the table. He lit a cigarette quickly, fanned away the smoke, and picked up his beer glass, settling back in his chair. "I know bloody well what you're faced with, Reddish. We all know. Someone gives you a list like this and tells you you'd better bloody well do something about it. Go talk to x, y, and z. All right. I'll take care of it. Guns and terrorists, guns and someone about to blow your ambassador's head off. He's been in Europe all these years, hasn't he? What'd he learn there? Nothing that's any good here, I'll wager. So now someone's about to come through the embassy gates with rifles and grenades, someone with a grudge to settle, maybe because of the Middle East, maybe because of something else. A local problem, say. Well, you tell him this. It won't happen. We won't let it happen, see. I won't let it happen."

Reddish watched him, aware that de Vaux might have misunderstood.

"It's simple for you, you're dealing with a diplomat, a man who can understand these things if he wants to. But I know the corner he's backed you into. He wants you to *guarantee* his security, doesn't he? Well, you guarantee it for him. You tell him whatever you need to—"

"I'm not talking about his personal safety," Reddish interrupted, "the embassy's either. I'm talking about guns smuggled into the city, guns that might be used—"

"Guns? What guns? Tell him there aren't any guns. What's happened? Has someone gotten to him the way they have the President? Listen, why do you think Colonel N'Sika and I left GHQ? Because every morning there were guns somewhere in the city, every bloody morning! And we'd sit there, the way you're sitting there now, trying to write up the morning intelligence brief, knowing he wouldn't believe a bloody word. But you're not working for the President. You're working with a man who knows what a Chinaman or a Marxist looks like, a sensible man. N'Sika and I were dealing with something else—crazy superstitious wogs whose brains fear had eaten away, like gonorrhea. You know the President. You know him as well as anyone. He's made his pile now and he thinks everyone's trying to take it away from him. What happened, did the President talk to your ambassador recently?"

"He saw him last week."

De Vaux got up and closed the shade. "He wants to know everything these days. That's why N'Sika and I were ready to get out of GHQ. Who can keep up with all the rumors? You have to be half mad and a charlatan to keep up with them—Rasputin himself. Palestinians, you say?" He laughed bitterly and sat down again. "We were dealing with all of them—Palestinians, Russians, Chinese, Cubans, Belgian royalists, Maoists, anarchists, and God knows what else. Everywhere he looked, he saw a conspiracy. Everyone trying to get his knife in. Don't let your ambassador catch the same disease, all right?

"Let's put it all out on the table now, just the two of us. It was a Chinaman's nightmare up there at GHQ. Every morning. N'Sika got an ulcer. At six o'clock in the morning we'd meet to put together the daily foreign intelligence brief, N'Sika and I. Six o'clock in the bloody morning! At eight, the old man would be waiting for us at the *présidence*. It was our neck in the noose. We never knew when he'd spring the trap. 'What did the Russian Ambassador do last night?' he'd want to know. 'Who did the East German meet with at the finance ministry?' That wasn't our brief. Internal security had the

41

Soviet and East German watch, but he was checking on them. Sometimes we'd wing it, but that was risky. Half the time he was testing us. Then there were the rumors those little bastards in the *présidence* put into his head, and we'd have to chase those down too.

"We finally worked out a system. We watched his daily appointment schedule. If he'd met with the Belgians, we'd dig up all we could about what the French were doing and have it for him the next morning. If the Israeli Ambassador had been in, we'd cram the morning brief with what the Arabs were up to. For a time after the sixty-seven Israeli war all he cared about were UN and OAU questions. He could never make up his mind about the Sinai, whether it was in Africa or the Middle East. 'How many Bantus are there in the Sinai?' he asked N'Sika one day, and we knew the Israelis had gotten their teeth into him again. The sixty-seven war was a royal mess. Israelis in French Mirages and American Phantoms, Jordanians in American Pattons and British Centurians, Egyptians in MIG's, Jordanians in British Hawkers—who could make sense of it? Not him. Senility was getting to him, and that made it worse. He began to forget things, but that just made him slyer. Today is all he knows, and he's just hanging on."

He lifted his glass and drank, Reddish watching him silently from across the table.

"It was a regular Comédie Française," de Vaux resumed. " 'Worry about the Portuguese in Angola,' N'Sika muttered one day while the old man was lecturing us about the Chinese in Burundi, and the old man must have heard him. 'Your stomach growls,' he told N'Sika the following day. 'Get out.' It was the ulcer. He saw a MIG-17 over Brazzaville one afternoon as he was returning from the OAU meeting in Addis Ababa, and that worried him. It was after that that he began looking for someone to give him ground-to-air missiles. He asked the Israelis. He knew the Americans wouldn't supply them. N'Sika had told him that. After the coup attempt in Brazza last year, he asked for M-16 rifles for the para brigade and the palace guard, remember? You chaps came through in the end, and for a month or so he was his old self again."

The State Department had denied the M-16 request for policy reasons, a breach of the embargo on sophisticated weaponry for Africa. At Haversham's insistence, Reddish had contacted a former Agency colleague who worked for Euroarm, a Luxembourg-based arms broker, and the M-16s had come through commercial channels, bought in Hanoi.

"They say he's worse now than ever," de Vaux was saying. "He believes what he wants to believe. Fear poisons every cup you take him. God knows how the internal security people put up with it, but they do, every morning when they give him the internal security brief. Guns in every commune every day, old Simbas returning from the north every night with new Kalashnikovs on their backs, about to retake Kisangani."

Reddish watched de Vaux's face silently, knowing the falsity of much of his characterization but puzzled by something else. Sedition was in his words, but he spoke in the same level tone.

"What he wanted was what they all want, men like him—absolute security, someone to tell him he'll never die. And what does that mean for the poor sods around him? Absolute terror, every day. But your ambassador isn't like that. He's a sensible man. That makes it a simpler world. That's what N'Sika and I wanted too. What's a simpler world than one you make yourself, eh, like the para hilltop. Don't worry about guns. Tell your ambassador that—"

The phone rang and de Vaux picked it up, his eyes still on Reddish. "*Oui, oui*," he said easily. "*C'est ça. Non, non. Pas du tout. Rien. Je suis sur—oui—à cinq heures.*" He looked at his watch.

The voice hadn't changed, moving with the same fluency with which he'd dominated their conversation, and Reddish was struck by the ease of de Vaux's transition, moving from one interlocutor to the other, from English to French, with no change in tone or register.

"*Oui, Colonel. Oui. Bon . . .*"

The tone puzzled Reddish: the same casualness, the same familiarity, moving from Reddish, an outsider, to a fellow officer and colleague with the same ease. The caller was his confidant and Reddish wasn't; yet he might have been talking to either.

Or to no one, he thought suddenly, and he realized then that he'd been listening to a man wholly alone with his own ambition, as Michaux had said.

They crossed the porch and went out into the sunlit yard toward the car. Reddish had been right. De Vaux's caller was Colonel N'Sika, summoning him to para headquarters down the sand road in the center of the compound.

Reddish stopped at the edge of the oyster-shell drive, looking south along the road toward the dense growth of trees where the maximum security prison was located. De Vaux paused too, following his gaze.

"It's been a long time since I was up here," Reddish said. "Is the prison still being used back there, below the crown of the hill?"

"Still used."

"I wonder if Cobby Molloy is still there with the other mercenaries. He sent me a note a few months back asking for help."

"Crocodile tears, eh? Had to wring it out to read it, did you? Probably peed all over it."

"Still there?"

De Vaux shrugged, pulling on his beret, his gray eyes even blanker in the piercing sunlight. "Could be. I don't follow it. The ministry can tell you."

"I knew Cobby better than the others. Maybe I should try to see him. A little mixed up maybe, but not a killer."

"Our mates never are," de Vaux said dryly.

"I suppose they've learned their lesson, the rest of them—that they know the old days are over now, finished."

"It's not lessons we give them," de Vaux muttered indifferently, "just rag gravy and prison clogs."

Banda had said that the mercenaries would be involved too, but that made no sense either. Nothing did. He'd seen no emotion in de Vaux's face, but he remembered what Michaux had told him that day at Kindu months earlier, how de Vaux had looked through him as he stood in the jeep beyond the *cercle* gate with the blindfolded witch doctor in the back seat.

Michaux had been right. De Vaux wasn't a man of trifling ambition, whatever else he was, no more a man to find release in the hero's welcome given him by a grateful bush town than he would in the hot, empty silence of a hillside military camp that had rescued him from the President's paranoia.

"If not, we can teach them again," de Vaux added as he climbed into his own jeep, but Reddish only nodded as he went back to his car, still troubled.

chapter 6

❖ After Reddish disappeared down the sand road toward the front gate, de Vaux drove to Colonel N'Sika's headquarters in the center of the compound. Three jeeps, a gray Mercedes, and a weapons carrier were parked in the circular drive outlined with whitewashed rocks. The low whitewashed stucco building had once been a Belgian officers' club. An outdoor dance floor and open terrace lay to one side under the raffia palms. A few idle para officers sat behind the dusty shrubbery drinking beer. Two corporals stood on the wide porch, caps low over their eyes, watching the road. Inside the building, the NCO at the orderly table had been replaced by two para lieutenants with side arms. More officers waited in the rooms along the central corridor, four and five to an office, sitting on chairs and desks or leaning against the wall waiting, weapons in hand.

De Vaux entered Colonel N'Sika's conference room at the back of the hall. The iron shutters had been drawn and the room, airless and warm, was lit by the ceiling fixture overhead. Colonel N'Sika sat at the head of the table, a large man with powerful shoulders, neck, and arms, his glossy black face glistening in the heat, the color and texture of an eggplant. His short-sleeved khaki shirt was wet under the arms and along the V of the neck. On the table in front of him was a holstered side arm. At his side, drawn up on a chair, was a portable radio tuned to a security channel. Three other para officers, all majors, sat along the table in front of him, their holstered arms also on the table. They looked on suspiciously as de Vaux took his seat at the end of the table. On the wall behind him was the portrait of the President in morning coat and the blue and yellow sash of the republic, the colors muddy and indistinct, the face as lifeless as a rotogravure photo.

"He said nothing, you told me," N'Sika began curtly, his dark irisless eyes fixed on de Vaux. His voice was deep, carrying effortlessly across the room. "You said nothing has changed. What did he say?"

"He had a report Soviet guns were hidden in the capital, brought from across the river."

"He knows then."

"He suspects something."

"How does he suspect, why?"

"He wouldn't say."

"Finished then." Major Fumbe sighed. He was a short moon-faced officer, with bulbous eyes giving him the look of sleepy gluttony. "Finished."

"So what will he do?" N'Sika demanded, turning to him. "Send in C-130s, Belgian paras, Green Berets now, like you claim? Like Stanleyville? Crush you like the Simbas. Of course, when you talk like that." He turned back to de Vaux. "What did he say he would do, what did he threaten?"

"Nothing, no threats," de Vaux said. "We talked. He's worried about the embassy and his ambassador. His ambassador is worried. That's all he cares about."

The door opened and a major joined them, sweating and out of breath from his jog through the trees from the motor pool, where the trucks were assembled. Seeing the holstered side arms on the table, he unbelted his own and sat down heavily.

"Take off your hat," N'Sika ordered. Sheepishly, like a forgetful schoolboy, he pulled off his cap. "What else did he say?" N'Sika asked.

"Just that. He's worried about the safety of the embassy and the ambassador. That's why he came."

"*He?*" Major Lutete leaned forward. "He? He *is* the ambassador. *El Capo. Numero uno.*" He was thin, his skin pale and pockmarked, like a *métis*. "Of course."

"Who?" asked the newly arrived major.

"Reddish," Lutete replied. "CIA." He pronounced it as a single word, in two syllables. "Of course."

"So what will he do now?" N'Sika asked.

"He'll tell his ambassador not to be worried."

"What did he say about the President? What did he ask?"

"I told him the President was sick, senile, useless, an old man corrupted by fear and everything else. He understood."

"And what did he say?" N'Sika asked.

"Nothing."

"*Nothing?*"

The room was silent. The four majors gazed at de Vaux suspiciously. From beyond the door the para officers were talking softly among themselves, waiting.

N'Sika leaned forward, almost angrily: "And so what else did he tell you? 'Go do this thing, but do it silently, like a dead man's sleep, a virgin's dream, no blood spilled, no American blood, no President's blood!' "

The four majors were suddenly uncomfortable; de Vaux's face was as cool as ever. "No, not a word about that. How it's done isn't his business. It's the way it is with men like that."

N'Sika sat back slowly, his eyes still on de Vaux; but Major Lutete wasn't satisfied. "And after it is done, what will he do? He will tell his government, he will tell Washington. Then Brussels will know, Paris, everyone—"

"Afterwards doesn't matter," N'Sika said. "By then it will be too late." He looked at Lutete's pale face. "Besides, what will he tell them? The President moves three million dollars to Zurich—dollars, not francs. Everyone knows—the ministry, the Central Bank, even my chauffeur. Even your driver. But what does this man Reddish do? What do the Americans do? Nothing. Nothing except give him more dollars for the rural roads, ten million this time. Jean-Bernard is right. That's the way it is with men like that, your friend one minute, your assassin the next. Open the shades, open the windows."

Major Fumbe and de Vaux rose and pulled open the iron shutters as the others watched. Sunlight flooded the room, lighting up the presidential portrait and the map of the capital positioned on the tripod to the left of N'Sika's chair. Suddenly conscious of the President's glazed, dusty stare, one of the majors got to his feet and pulled the frame from the wall.

"If the Americans care nothing, as de Vaux says," Major Fumbe grumbled, returning to his chair, "why do we bother with Masakita and the *jeunesse?*" He sat down heavily, the bulbous eyes heavily lidded, gluttony gone, face glistening with water. "Why not go directly to the *présidence.*"

N'Sika turned in irritation. "And what would the army do then? Where would GHQ send its helicopters? To kill you, me, and the rest of the paras. If the President's generals and the rest of the army need a reason not to fight us, Masakita is the reason—"

"Lutete could go now, talk to the chief of staff—"

"It is too late!"

"It is not such a good plan," Fumbe muttered. "No. Masakita is trouble."

"It is the same plan we talked about last week, the week before.

Where were you then, sleeping! What is different now that it is going to happen?"

"The Americans know," Fumbe replied weakly.

"It was Reddish who went to Kindu to see the guns there," Lutete said. "Who can trust this man? He helped hire the mercenaries. He was with the President during the rebellions, always with the President . . ."

His voice died away. They waited in silence watching Colonel N'Sika, who sat with gaze lowered, toying with a cigarette package. He removed a cigarette without lighting it and continued to turn it in his hands like a child's puzzle.

The phone rang suddenly. Fumbe and Lutete sat up frightened. N'Sika didn't seem to hear it. As it rang a third time, he lifted his head and nodded to de Vaux, who swiveled in his chair to lift the receiver from the table behind him.

"It's Kadima."

N'Sika got to his feet to take the call at his desk in the corner. He listened frowning, turned toward his colleagues, who silently watched his face.

"Yes, all right," N'Sika said. "Yes, I understand. No, if you must go, you must go. Yes, he might be suspicious. But call me from the airport. I may have some news. All right. Yes."

He hung up and came back to the table. "Yvon Kadima said he must go to Brussels this afternoon for the President, a private mission. His plane leaves at four o'clock." His voice was tired.

"So it's over," Major Lutete muttered. "He's told them."

"He's planning something," Fumbe said. "He knows something."

"Of course he's planning something," N'Sika replied. "Of course. To save his own skin. He had no heart for it, not from the first. Kadima was a mistake. Your mistake." He looked at Major Lutete. "But our mistake now. Each of us." He lit the cigarette finally and crumpled the package. "He thinks we'll fail now, that the army won't join us, the army, the police, everyone. You see the weakness now, don't you?—the poison that's spread everywhere, even in this room. Every place you look, the same—"

"Kadima told Reddish," Lutete broke in. "Told him the way he's told him everything all these years, whispering in his ear."

"The police won't be with us," Fumbe said. "With Kadima against us, the police too—"

N'Sika said, "Who will go for Kadima?"

The four majors were silent, surprised.

"Who will go for Kadima?" N'Sika repeated, searching the black faces around the table.

"I'll go," de Vaux volunteered quietly from the end of the table.

"No!" Major Lutete objected, "not de Vaux! Keep him with Major Fumbe, where he can keep an eye on him. He spends an hour with Reddish and tells us nothing. Now Kadima! What else? Will he go to the prison and bring out his mercenaries? Go to the President next? Who can trust him? Send Captain Olinga."

"Olinga will have to go to the police camp at Bakole to keep the police in the barracks. I can't send Olinga." He turned to Fumbe. "Send your captain, the tall one from the north."

"So we go ahead?" Fumbe asked, surprised.

"At five o'clock."

"But what about Kadima, Reddish?" Lutete said. "What about the mercenaries? The President will send for them, like before. He'll give them guns."

"Kadima will be taken care of. Major de Vaux will handle the mercenaries. Reddish doesn't matter."

"If the President can't trust him, how can we?"

"Reddish? Because of what Jean-Bernard has told us. Because he came here to say he didn't care where our guns are pointed so long as his people are protected."

N'Sika stood up and buckled on his holster.

"He's not to be trusted! He'll arm the mercenaries!"

N'Sika hesitated, looking down at Lutete's thin face. "What are you saying—*trusted*? Who's to be trusted? You, me, Major Fumbe there, who's frightened still of Masakita after all these years, like the army! All of you, who're worried about these mercenaries? Are you like the President?" he shouted, angry now, his patience gone. "Are you weak and corrupt, like him? Because if you're weak and corrupt, you have no choice but to trust men who'll deceive you, deceive you because you're weak and corrupt! So sit there like a coward and talk about trust, or get to your feet and join us!"

They all stood, lifting their holstered arms. De Vaux remained behind with N'Sika, following him to the desk in the corner. Only after the door closed did Colonel N'Sika lift his head to glance scornfully toward the corridor and then at the Belgian.

"They are all women," he said, "each of them, each what the President has made him."

chapter 7

✧ At four-thirty that Sunday afternoon, the American Ambassador was alone at his residence on the river, an enormous stone villa with ivy-covered colonnades shaded by towering African hardwoods. A gently sloping lawn curved away from the rear of the house and down through the trees to the great pool of the river. In the front of the residence beyond the circling driveway was another lawn bordered by gardens and flowering trees within the high wall. At the rear beyond the frangipani and flame trees was a turquoise-green swimming pool.

It was a brilliant sunlit afternoon with a mild breeze blowing high in the trees, the distant drowsy rustle the only sound to be heard. Ambassador Bondurant was in the back garden when the Belgian Ambassador telephoned. He took the call at the poolside bar, dressed in sagging seersucker gardening shorts, leather sandals, and an old polo shirt. Under one arm was a pair of long-handled pruning shears, under the other two books cradled together, each held open in its middle pages by separate fingers of his right hand. One book was a copy of a British historian's essays, just received in the pouch, read that morning after breakfast, and the second a history of Soviet foreign policy 1929–39, drawn from his library. He'd been toiling in the garden that afternoon, pruning his absent wife's roses, when a passage from one had fused with a passage from another. It was this discovery he'd been pursuing when the telephone overtook him.

His caller was the Belgian Ambassador, who told him that fighting had broken out in the native commune of Malunga, where the socialist workers party was believed to be in armed revolt. Fighting had also erupted at the sprawling Bakole police camp on the outskirts. Two Belgian police advisers had been seized as hostages; a third had escaped and was in critical condition at the Swedish hospital. The Belgian military attaché believed Cuban infiltrators had come from Brazzaville during the night and had joined the socialists, reinforced that afternoon by a ragtag group of political exiles hidden among the crowds who'd come over on the ferry to see the soccer match at the stadium.

"I've asked to see the President," the Belgian shouted above the turmoil in his own suite. "I've just spoken to Bintu, the *chef du cabinet*. We've scheduled a meeting for six o'clock. Could you join us?"

"Yes, certainly," Bondurant agreed, perplexed. "How did the fighting start?"

"No one is sure, but it seems to be spreading. Can you hear me?"

"Yes, I hear you."

"The paras are trying to close off Malunga, but some of the insurgents have fled to other communes. *Hello!* Have you heard anything?"

"No, nothing at all. At six, you say? Yes, I'll join you at six. I'll call my people in the meantime. Yes, at six."

He put the phone down uneasily and turned back up the flagstone walk toward the house. In the center of the drive he paused, head lifted, listening; but he heard only the sound of the breeze from the river rustling high in the trees. The iron gates were pulled closed, and the African watchman sat dozing in his wicker chair, his transistor radio on his lap. He listened for another minute and continued on into the house, entering through the reception hall and following the black and white marble floor along the corridor to his right to his study, a deep high-ceilinged room with white woodwork and white bookshelves cluttered with the memorabilia of thirty years of diplomatic service. On the walls were prints from Berlin and Vienna, consular exequaturs from his early posts, and ambassadorial commissions from his recent ones. Two colorful modern abstractions on loan from a New York gallery hung behind the long couch. Behind the desk was a fragment from a Roman mosaic, retrieved from the southern coast of Turkey by his children during a holiday after the war.

The study that afternoon might have been in Newport or Palm Beach on a gentle summer day, with the blue sea bickering on the ceiling and the tanned guests changing upstairs, up from the tennis courts or the bay after an afternoon of sailing. On the malachite table next to the couch stood a silver-framed folio of color photographs taken in the White House Rose Garden, the ambassador and his wife smiling luminously, standing next to a now dead President.

The ambassador was a large man, well over six feet tall, his face broad, the jowls and lower lip drooping, pregnant with disapproval. He was sixty but looked younger, his gray hair as thick as it had been at thirty. Reserved, distant, and autocratic, he was as remote from most of the diplomatic staff as his study was from Africa. On Sundays he dismissed the servants, even the cook, making the most of his holiday privacy. But this Sunday his wife wasn't there, returned home a week earlier to prepare their house on Library Place in Princeton for their coming home leave; and the emptiness of the residence had driven him into the garden that afternoon with her pruning shears.

At his desk he telephoned the embassy, but the line was busy. He got no answer when he rang Becker, the deputy chief of mission, at his hillside house above the city. He was looking up the number of Haversham, the station chief, when he remembered that he was in Nairobi attending a CIA African Division conference.

Before he could find Andy Reddish's number, the phone rang and Lowenthal, the political counselor, was on the line. "I'm afraid I've got some dismal news," he began. "We've been trying to reach you—"

"I've just tried to call the embassy. I understand fighting has broken out in Malunga."

"I'm afraid so. Malunga's in open revolt, they say, and it appears to be spreading. I tried to send your car for you, but it was turned back by an army roadblock near the parliament building—"

"Open revolt? Who's seen the fighting?"

"No one yet. The paras have closed off Malunga, but you can hear the shooting from the boulevard. The French have had a few eyewitness accounts. So have the Belgians."

"How much have our people seen?" Bondurant asked. "I want to be sure we know what we're talking about." For Bondurant, Lowenthal was cleverer with words than with facts. Born in Germany, educated in France, and imprisoned with his parents in fascist Spain, he was a linguistic chameleon. Verbal agility had been his law of survival—German, French, and Spanish, all with equal fluency—but he'd paid a price, taught that all ambiguities could be resolved with a quick, facile tongue. After the President had thrown one of his political opponents in prison on a trumped-up charge, Lowenthal had reported to Washington that he had "temporarily quarantined political dissent among local elites in the service of national consensus and/or nation-building." Bondurant thought him an obscurantist, his quickness verbal, not conceptual, spawned in the stagnant ponds of the bureaucracy that overflowed every day in cables, instructions, and staff studies from the Potomac, polluting every well.

"I'd be skeptical of what the French told me. The Belgians too. What about Colonel Selvey and Reddish? Are they on the streets?"

"They're out now."

"Good. Are our people safe?"

"Yes, sir. So far as we know."

"All right. Send my car back. I'll call the President myself."

He was unable to reach the President. Standing at the front window, he waited for his car, searching the skies above the front gate for signs of smoke. Only a few clouds moved there. The sunlight was fading, the house silent, and he felt his isolation like a kind of fear. His wife gone, he had felt it earlier that afternoon as well, but in a different way: his age, his geographical isolation, the career that was now all but over. He'd attended, a month earlier, a NATO session in Brussels, invited out of courtesy by his old friends in the European Bureau to talk about Soviet strategy in Africa. The meeting had gone badly for him. He'd caught cold, the old friends he'd hoped to see were absent or retired, the remarks he'd prepared were no longer fashionable, heard too often in the past to stir younger imaginations now. Political fashions changed as much out of boredom as obsolescence. Kissinger was now in fashion, Kennan wasn't; but only the historically ignorant could be flattered into believing that the Kissinger NSC was now saying something new. The language was as old as Metternich's, attempting to impose a static order on a dynamic world, but no one he'd talked to at Brussels had seemed to count it important.

After his return, he'd summarized the NATO conference for a country team meeting, concluding that his remarks were old hat and out of tune, that he'd felt like a solitary flautist in a citadel of brass, listening to his young State Department colleagues talk so hawkishly about Vietnam and Cambodia. In a cable circulated from Washington a week later, State had told the field that an aging European diplomat, a man of Bondurant's generation, wasn't "hard-nosed" enough to carry out the Moscow negotiations entrusted to him by his government. Bondurant had underlined the locution, one he despised, and in the margin had commented in his own microscopic handwriting:

In Washington's parlance these days, I take it "hard-nosed" describes a disposition that will snarl after every bone atop the global table, like a Carolingian mastiff who would devour bone, gristle, and master alike to prove his ferocity.

*The Celts were ferocious; so were the Visigoths; Roman law is what we re-
member. Ferocity for its own sake, particularly among liberals, is suspect. It's
also primitive. Washington's failure to recognize this is a symptom of its present
distress, as the Cambodian bombings now make clear.*

The marked-up cable had been circulated among the senior officers and returned to him three days later. Rereading it, he saw
behind the words a man deeply wounded, isolated an ocean away
from policy councils which had once consulted him. As a younger
officer, he had been contemptuous of that weakness in ambassadors
he saw dawdling into old age with nothing left but their pedantic
self-conceit. Finding it in himself, he was ashamed.

The phone rang. It was the Belgian Ambassador, reporting that
his appointment with the President had been abruptly canceled by
an aide at the President's office. The Belgian military attaché had
tried to reach the minister of defense, but had been turned back by
roadblocks. "We've just learned that he was shot down near the
presidential compound, Walter. It's serious, very serious."

A coup, Bondurant thought for the first time. A coup d'etat. "It
certainly sounds that way," he muttered in confusion.

"Has your own staff learned anything?"

"Very little, I'm afraid." Had it come to that—the Belgians
keeping the American Embassy informed?

"You'll get back to me if you have any news?"

"Indeed I will, yes. Certainly."

He hung up and immediately dialed the embassy again. Where
was his car? Where were Becker, Selvey, Lowenthal? He got a busy
signal, hung up angrily, and climbed the stairs to his bedroom to
fetch the emergency radio from the bedside table.

He supposed he should have been more aggressive in using his
Agency resources, he thought, descending the stairs. Haversham, the
station chief, briefed him weekly on internal stability and had offered to give him more on Soviet and Eastern European activities,
but he'd declined. He had little interest in the peccadilloes of the
Russians and East Germans. Although the CIA station had once
played a certain reckless role in internal politics and with the President, its operations were now confined solely to Soviet bloc activities. Les Haversham understood that, but he had his doubts about
Reddish, his deputy, a holdover from the old days.

Turning on the radio at the desk in the study, he could hear
Lowenthal's voice over the emergency communications net. He
opened his microphone, but he had forgotten the call signals. He

was searching the instruction card on the rear panel when the phone rang again.

"Oh Walter, John here," the British Ambassador drawled from his residence down the road. "Bit of a mess, isn't it? That's what my chaps tell me. Malunga has guns—you heard, I suppose. Ugly business. The army is having a go at them, I'm told. I suppose we're in for rather a bloody bash, don't you think? Are you buttoned up? How's the staff faring—any casualties?"

"I don't think so. I'm trying to get more information."

"Aren't we all, yes. Look here, are they outside your gates too? I'm corked in—jeep in my drive. Can't get in or out. Don't know why. Can't imagine, as a matter of fact. Not personal, is it? Any suggestions?"

"I'm trying to get my car from the embassy, but it was turned back by a roadblock. Possibly the roadblock in front of your place."

"Could be, yes. They're turning back vehicles. Camped out all over the road, as a matter of fact, like a gypsy caravan. A little embarrassing too, I must say—"

"Sorry, John, but I've got a call on the emergency net. I'll call you back."

Lowenthal was at the microphone. He couldn't locate Becker or Reddish, but everyone else seemed to be accounted for. The embassy families living in apartments inside the military checkpoints had taken refuge in the embassy compound. Those in the suburbs had been told to stay in their residences and await word from their evacuation wardens over the commo net.

"What about Malunga?" Bondurant asked.

"It looks very bad. Some of the rebels have broken out through the paras' cordon and seem to be infiltrating guns into other communes. The French say a clandestine radio is operating from inside Malunga, proclaiming a peoples republic and appealing for foreign support. They think the radio is located in the workers party compound. Agence France Presse in Brazza picked up the report and put it on the wires. So did Reuters."

Bondurant was upset. "What about my car?"

"We tried again, but no luck. The soldiers wouldn't let your chauffeur through."

"All right, but try again. I'll speak to the President. Keep me informed. I'll leave my radio on."

Dusk was falling. He turned on the lamps in the study and carried the radio out into the drive, listening for gunfire. The evening wind from the river stirred high in the trees. Far in the distance he could hear for the first time the muffled detonations. On any other evening he would have identified them as thunder from an evening storm high on the savannahs. Troubled, he moved out to the gate, where the guard was standing uneasily, listening. The road beyond was empty.

He returned to the residence and unlocked the combination safe hidden away behind the card tables and folding chairs in the study closet. His confidential notebook and the embassy evacuation plan were inside. The notebook contained the President's confidential phone number at the private suite at the President's villa but Bondurant had never used it—a point of honor. The Agency had installed the line and had used it to deal with the President during times of crisis in the old days. He had never dealt with the President in that way—speaking to him over the phone while his sycophants, courtesans, and bodyguards listened from nearby.

Now he called the number, but it was busy and he waited, receiver in hand, phone button depressed, watching the sweep of the second hand across the face of the brass-mounted ship's chronometer on the desk. The clock had been a gift from a New York yacht club, aboard the winning vessel in the Newport to Bermuda race the year his son had died at the Inchon reservoir in Korea as a Marine second lieutenant. His son had once sailed under the same colors, aboard the same yacht. From beyond the window the reverberations came again, but he was still watching the clock, past and present mixed now—thunder, gunfire, dirty skies, high seas, and the cold, cruel heave of the Atlantic that last season they had sailed together in Maine. Nothing had ever made up for that loss. In his time, he'd seen Munich, the Anschluss, Yalta, the Truman Doctrine, and the creation of the Common Market. As a young vice consul, he'd learned Russian at Riga, and toured Manchuria before it fell to the Japanese. His wife thought he should have retired after Stockholm, others that he should have never accepted a non-European post, that his conceptual vision had died with the Treaty of Rome and lay buried at Bandung. They meant by that that the Third World meant little to him, that it lay outside his own historical memory.

They were wrong. After so many years of effort, he'd achieved a certain view of history, of events and men whatever their nationality. It had enabled him to value the past and understand the present, as he also hoped that it would give courage to the reflections of his final years. Implicit in that view was a certain order, certain values, and a certain tradition, all sustained by a certain continuity of change. Without such an order, neither the heroism of action nor of intellect was possible. He knew how delicate was the civilizing balance. Aberrations would occur, but fifty years later they would only appear as oddities of style, and the tradition would endure. He had never feared the future. Death didn't frighten him. What he feared most was that which had the awful power to wipe out that tradition and let him live on buried in the tomb his civilization had become. He didn't know Africa well enough to fear it, as some of his colleagues did, but he had seen enough to make him uneasy. He knew Africa had that awful power—its senseless suffering, its crushing poverty, the mortal helplessness of its people, and the awakening passion for retribution—cruelty groping toward consciousness—quick to be blown to flame by anarchy as mindless as this.

He waited, the receiver still lifted, still listening to the distant gunfire. Again he dialed the President's number. He didn't recognize the voice that answered. It was cool, distant, unhurried, its French not that of an African, but a native speaker's, a man in full control of himself, calmly mixing diplomatic proprieties with local colloquialisms in the nasal accent of the Antwerp slums.

"May I ask whom I'm speaking to?" Bondurant asked, troubled and uneasy.

The phone was still sticky with blood. The body of Bintu, the *chef du cabinet,* lay twisted in the white chair, his feet caught in the desk well, his black skull crushed, nose and mouth leaking blood to the carpet beneath.

The room was gray with cordite, as rank as ammonia. The President shrank against a damask sofa opposite, naked beneath his claret-colored dressing gown, spitting and gagging into the bloody towel the black para corporal had thrown to him. His lip was bleeding, his forehead gashed, and he was spitting out piece by piece the fragments of a shattered tooth crown.

A dead woman lay sprawled across the carpet, face down, her nakedness half covered by a satin sheet Major Fumbe had brought from the bedroom. The pair of gilt scissors with which she'd tried to protect her lover lay on the carpet just beyond her outstretched hand.

The man at the phone stood looking down at the scissors—gilt-handled, encrusted with stones, like her dark fingers. They stirred in his memory for a moment: a pair of cheap scissors lying on a wicker table in an alcove, a sewing basket and a few cards of cheap wool and thread nearby, the winter darkness of the Antwerp streets just beyond, through the small window.

"You said the President was with you," Bondurant's voice came again. "I'd like to speak with him. May I ask who this is?"

"*Son adjoint*," de Vaux said, moving his gaze from the scissors to the terrified President. "He'd like to talk to you, but in a few minutes—"

Entering the anteroom from the terrace were two paras from the presidential gate guard, prodding along a frightened technician and announcer from the national radio, carrying their portable gear for the President's appeal to the nation.

chapter 8

❖ "Oh, quite. A damned nuisance! Yes, still corked in! Bit of
bad luck. Chucked out? His own car! You don't say?" Cecil, the
British Ambassador, stood talking on the phone to his deputy, still
wearing his sailing togs from the river as he held the drape aside to
look out beyond his front garden toward the road, where a barricade of army trucks, lights on, was interdicting traffic. "No, I'll be
quite safe here, I assure you. It'll all blow over in a few hours. Not
our worry, old boy. Let the Americans bother it, eh. Yes, stay in
touch. Tell Gresham I shall need my car tomorrow, eleven sharp.
Vin d'honneur, yes. Cheerio."

A young American secretary, hair limp from the river, in shorts
and a halter, but her bare shoulders now decently covered by Mrs.
Cecil's gardening cardigan, watched Cecil tremulously, lip quivering. "What am I going to do?" she asked, close to tears.

"I haven't the foggiest," Cecil answered brightly, trying to put
the best face on it, "but I'm sure we'll manage something. The first
thing you should do is to ring up your embassy and tell them you're
safe."

"But I'd be so embarrassed." She seemed to have an exalted
notion of diplomatic rank and privilege, as if she had no right being
there. Even after she'd driven her moped over to Cecil's residence
that morning, invited by Cecil's secretary to accompany a small
group out on the river aboard Cecil's boat, she'd left her vehicle
outside the gate, waiting for them in the drive.

"Don't be silly. Of course you can."

He called the number himself but the line was busy.

"No answer?" She seemed relieved. Cecil found her little girl's
sense of propriety touching.

"Busy. We'll call back later."

"I really feel so terrible, such a terrible nuisance." She seemed on the verge of tears again. Cecil had only that day met her. She was a secretary in the American Embassy economic section, substituting for Bondurant's own secretary who'd left a week earlier for home leave in advance of Bondurant's own. The invitation that day had been tendered by Cecil's secretary as a kind of introduction to the senior members of the diplomatic corps who sometimes congregated aboard each other's boats on Sundays for picnics on the islands. She'd called the ambassadors she'd met there "sir" or "your excellency" in the case of the Swede. The Spanish Ambassador had suggested she water ski from his craft, but Cecil's secretary, a watchful matron, had waved him off. She was in her late twenties with a pretty face, full cheeks, and dark liquid eyes—rather like a lost rabbit, Cecil thought; a bit buxom too, he'd discovered, heavy in the hips as well; but his attention was avuncular, nothing more.

Cecil was in his late forties. He was tall and boyish-looking, his youthfulness in part the reflection of the age of his ambassadorial peers, most of whom were much older, in part his refusal to take his responsibilities too seriously. He often felt younger for both, still a spry young Oxford undergraduate, moving among creaking dons. His wife, now visiting the children in England, had no such advantage. She looked her age. Without her methodical gray-haired presence stalking the house, the servants, and the garden, Cecil felt even younger.

"I think I shall have a word with those chaps out there in the road," he now told Miss Browning. "Sometimes, you can solve these little misunderstandings with a bit of firmness. They're out of place, no question about that. Belong down at the boulevard, I dare say."

He crossed the dark lawn to the gate while Miss Browning watched from the window. "Look here, Lieutenant, Captain, you have my gate blocked off. Can't get in or out. That's not what you wanted, was it? Move, yes. There's a good fellow. Yes. Move. You speak French, don't you? *Motocar te! Te! Vous comprenez! Aye-bez?*"

The soldiers sitting in the jeep looked at him blankly. Beyond the jeep an army truck was pulled across the road with a second backing it up. A pair of flares burned brightly in the turf of a bank across the road where a few soldiers sat. They watched him silently and finally a lieutenant crossed the road, stuck his automatic rifle through the palings and pointed back toward the residence.

"Only one officer," Cecil explained in the front salon, looking out the window again. "I suppose that's the problem. Out of place and they won't admit it. When their officers come, they'll get a boot in the backside and get sent off again, I'd say. Terribly mixed up place, isn't it? I don't suppose you speak Lingala, do you?"

He heard a low moan from his side and turned. "But what's this? No crying now."

"It's awful."

"We mustn't have that, no, no. Chin up now. It's going to be all right. Certainly. We'll call your embassy, tell them you're here, and before you know it they'll have sent a car."

"But they won't understand."

"Won't understand? Won't understand what? Of course they'll understand. Who won't understand?"

"The girls in the embassy."

"No crying now. It's quite all right. Nothing is going to happen now. In a few hours, you won't even remember it. Oh look here now, you mustn't cry. We must do something to cheer you up. We'll have a drink first of all, how's that? We'll have a drink while we're waiting for the car and in a few minutes you'll have forgotten all about it. The trick is to put your mind on something else."

He led her down the dark hall to the huge kitchen, conscious of her suntan lotion, no longer aware of his own discomfort, of the wet bathing trunks under his shorts, the grit in his sandals, the river sand in his hair.

"We'll imagine it's not our worry for the time being. How about that, eh? Just the usual Sunday tedium outside. Sunday evenings tend to be dreadful here, don't you think? I mean you've had your Sunday on the river and quite suddenly it's all over, isn't it? Another Monday gathering itself out there in the darkness. What would you fancy? Gin, whiskey, a spot of vermouth? White wine? Gin then. Tonic? A slice of lemon?"

"I usually go to the USIS movies on Sunday night," Miss Browning said, drying her face.

"Do you? Takes your mind away, does it? I don't go much myself. Terrible films, really—I mean the British Council, not your own. Then the Baptists come too and you can't laugh at all. No, I prefer my Sunday evenings here, on the back terrace. Quite peaceful, actually. Then there's a Sunday evening program from Johannesburg, dance music by request. Curious names, though. After a time, you get to know them. It's quite pleasant. Soothing, I should say. Brings back younger days. Would you like to see the terrace?"

He turned on the outside terrace lights and led her out into the warm, fragrant African evening.

"It's lovely."

" 'Tis, isn't it?" Cecil was pleased. Her composure seemed to have returned.

"You even have a pool."

"Yes, didn't I mention that?" The swimming pool lay at the foot of the terrace steps, dark and cold in the shadows. A few erratic gunshots rattled in the distance, and Cecil lifted his voice to smother them: "Yes, I swim quite often. Keep fit that way. My wife enjoys it too. She's quite a gardener too, you know."

"It's awfully dark in the back."

"Yes, I suppose it is. Needn't be. We'll fix that." He came back to the terrace, opened the switch box, and turned on the pool lights. The pool and garden beyond softly came alive, shadows melted along the rear wall. The bright aquamarine swimming pool had the transparency of glass.

"If I had a pool like this, I'd never go anyplace else," Miss Browning murmured. "Never." Putting down her drink, she boldly shed his wife's cardigan and her sandals, stepped out of her shorts, and slipped down the steps to stand at the edge of the brightly lit pool, again clad, as she had been on the river, only in her bikini. "A pool like this really gives me courage. It really does."

"Does it?" Cecil murmured in turn, stirred by Miss Browning's transformation. He'd been glad to see the cardigan go, a sacklike garment in which his wife puttered around the side garden, pockets stuffed with crumbs for the finches, peanuts for the gray parrots, and a plastic-enclosed thermometer with which she took the daily temperature of her compost bed, a smelly treaclelike mound that lay behind the trellis near the back wall.

"You're not leaving me?" Miss Browning called in alarm as Cecil turned back to the house.

"No, no. I'd better fetch the radio." He brought the shortwave radio from the kitchen and put it on the table at the top of the terrace steps, next to the outside telephone. The national radio was broadcasting an old march tune. "A nuisance," Cecil said, "but there may be a communiqué." He called his office but the line was busy. He couldn't reach the American Embassy either. "Oh well, no use bothering about that, is there? Glass empty? What about another drink?"

"If you don't mind."

"I'll just be a minute. No cause for alarm now."

Like most women with a strong libido, Miss Browning had a clear eye for masculine guile but was perfectly innocent of her own. Ambassadors, especially English ones, were new game for her. Now she watched helplessly as Cecil returned to the pantry for more gin.

chapter 9

❖ "It's a fucking coup," said the Marine corporal, "that's what it is." He stood with Corporal Martinez atop the embassy roof, both wearing flak jackets and helmets, their figures clearly outlined in the light of the tropical moon that lit the sheltering trees and the wide pool of river. The warm African night smelled of decaying blossoms mixed with the mold of dead and decaying leaves. The dark streets below were silent except for the occasional rattle of army trucks filled with khaki-clad soldiers and a few jeeps carrying red-bereted paras in battle dress. From the distance came the intermittent crump of mortars and the crack of small-arms fire.

"Some bad shit out there," said Martinez. "Who's watching the back wall?"

"Tucker's doing it. Hey, Tucker, baby? What you see back there?"

A third Marine crouched behind the rear coping holding a tear gas gun. "Ain't shit back here. Ain't no mother fuckers trying to climb no wall neither. What's Gunny wanna go and send us up here for?"

"Cause that dude told him to."

"What dude, Shaky?"

"Squirrel Balls."

The side streets were empty, the street vendors gone, vanished with the mini-skirted prostitutes who habitually skulked under the trees along the avenue and the blond-faced *colons* who gathered at the nearby sidewalk café on muggy African nights. In front of iron-shuttered shops and garages, only the night sentinels remained, dark bags of bones crouching as silent as corpses on their pasteboard or raffia mats in front of guttering wood fires, clutching primitive spears or machetes.

In this neighborhood near the port, only the embassy was

ablaze with light, the windows lit to the top floor. On the roof, the dark masts of antennas, the microwave dish, and the transmission towers were visible against the stars and the frail glow of Magellanic cloud to the south. A red eye atop the tallest tower opened and shut. Security lamps flooded the inner embassy wall from the border of flower beds; in the front the iron gate was shut and shackled closed. A block to the north, a flood of dark river moved from the jungles and savannahs toward the rapids, by day an ocean of swift brown water laden with rafts of water hyacinth, by night a cold dark channel where no lights were. A Panhard armored car interdicted access to the quay, the customs houses, and the creaking ferries that stirred with the current against their hawsers.

"Hey, baby? *Habla español?* See any Cubans yet?" Martinez called to Tucker.

"Screw you." Tucker had wanted to bring a carbine aloft, but the Marine Gunny had given him a tear gas gun instead. "I got sumpin that'll wipe you out, baby."

"What's that?"

"What'll take care of all you wetback greasers—a shit-seeking asshole reamer that don't leave nothing but piss socks and pucker strings."

Martinez laughed. "This is the place for it, sucker. Din't they tell you that in Nam? The big A, the big asshole. It's all shit, ain't none of your jungle bunny cunt sacks told you that?"

"They ain't like your women. They don't wanna talk to my dick, baby. They just wanna listen to the music."

An embassy sedan spun into the drive and stopped at the gate; a dark face lifted into the headlights from the shadows of the bougainvillea inside. "*Fungola!*" the driver called. "*Fungola!*" The gateman dragged away the chain as the two Marines watched, and the sedan idled into the courtyard. The sedan belonged to Lowenthal, the political counselor, returning from the French Embassy a few blocks away.

"Who is it?" Tucker called from the rear coping. "Captain Cheese?"

"Shut up, God damn it. He'll hear. It's Squirrel Balls."

Lowenthal looked up toward the whispered voices as the two Marines stumbled backwards into the shadows. Martinez dropped his tear gas gun as he fell over an antenna guy wire and it clattered across the roof.

"What is it up there," Lowenthal called.

"God damn it, that mother was pointed at *me!*" Tucker whispered angrily, rising from the coping. "You coulda blowed my fucking head off, you goddamn Cuban—"

"Shhh." The two corporals crouched in the shadows out of Lowenthal's line of sight, laughing.

Lowenthal continued to look skyward, puzzled, but saw nothing. He was short and small-boned, wearing a dark turtleneck sweater under a bush jacket. A scalp disorder had compelled him to have his head shaved shortly after his arrival, and his hair had returned very slowly. "Just like his balls, I'll bet," the Marine Gunny had said morosely to himself one day as the small, fuzzy partially bald head disappeared down the corridor after the Marine sergeant had received one of Lowenthal's fatuous peremptory orders. Lowenthal's nickname was announced over a game of hearts at the Marine house bar the same night.

A siren wailed in the distance and Lowenthal turned away from the roof toward the street. The siren moved away from the embassy, but the headlights of a car came closer and turned into the gate. The sedan belonged to Colonel Selvey, the defense attaché, who parked behind Lowenthal's vehicle. As the engine died away, a voice from the car radio drifted into the courtyard: "*Citoyens! Citoyens! Déposez vos armes! Déposez vos armes!*"

It was the voice of the old President, urging the rebels to put down their guns. A volley of rifle fire echoed through the streets from the direction of the port; as the reverberations died away, a Panhard armored car lumbered slowly around the corner in low gear. A dozen soldiers trotted alongside.

"*Je répète! Déposez vos armes! C'est votre président qui parle!*"

Colonel Selvey reached through the window and turned off the radio. The rear window had been smashed.

"What happened?" Lowenthal asked.

"Someone clobbered it when I came through a roadblock." He was Lowenthal's size but trimmer. His square saturnine face under his military brush cut was the color of old saddle leather. He wore a white tennis shirt, red plaid golfing trousers, and white loafers with tassels.

"How are the paras doing in Malunga? Are they holding?"

"How the shit do I know," Selvey drawled. He wasn't unfriendly, just a Tennessee country boy with a soldier's disdain for nervous State Department diplomatists who wanted to fire off a cable to Washington every time a rifle shot rattled a window. He didn't know what was happening and he didn't think anyone else did either.

"You didn't get anything?"

"I couldn't get near GHQ. They got it bunged up tighter than an old maid's asshole—roadblocks all over the place. One thing I do know is an awful lot of folks out there are toting guns. Malunga looks like the worst. You can see the fires burning from the boulevard. I heard the President's gonna parlez-vous over the radio at nine, a special announcement. Maybe he's gonna tell us."

A crippled wind moved from the river, stirring through the trellised roses of the compound wall, dimming the distant sounds of gunfire and the baffled *crump-crump* of mortars from the besieged police camp at Bakole.

In the embassy reception hall, a dozen staff members were milling about in confusion. The Marine receptionist told Lowenthal the duty officer had been looking for him.

"Tell him I'll be upstairs. Any word from the ambassador?"

"Negative, sir. We sent the car back, like you asked, but the driver got turned back again."

"What about the DCM, Mr. Becker?"

"He's with the ambassador. He got stopped too, but he turned back and hot-footed it over to the ambassador's. That's where he is now. The duty officer says they got three roadblocks between here and the parliament building, closing off the downtown, real pissers too, with BAR's, shooting people."

"Any word from the foreign ministry?"

"Negative, but a whole bunch of people have been calling in about the evacuation. The phones have been tied up—"

"No one's said anything about an evacuation."

"Yes, sir, but everyone's been asking. We got almost a hunnert people back in the dispensary and motor pool, scared to go home."

"No decision's been made," Lowenthal said, "but tell them to stay calm. We'll keep them informed."

"Yes, sir, that's what I've been telling them. The Gunny wants to know can he take his guys off the roof?"

"What the hell are they doing on the roof?" Colonel Selvey broke in.

"I told them that's where they should be," Lowenthal said briskly, "commanding the optimum field of fire." In the absence of the ambassador and Becker, Lowenthal was in charge.

"What the goddamned hell for? The perimeter is back there, along the wall. Where's the Gunny?"

"In the security room, sir." From down the corridor they could hear the calls coming in through the emergency radio hookup in the security office. A second Marine standing at the desk behind the reception counter replaced one phone and lifted another.

"Yes, ma'am. A coup d'etat? I reckon so. Yes, ma'am. Stay inside and listen to the radio. Well, if you don't know no French, get someone else to listen. Wait for your warden to call you. No ma'am. No one's been evacuated yet."

Selvey dodged into the security office and told the Marine Gunny to pull his people off the roof. He rejoined Lowenthal in the stairwell. Standing at the cipher lock on the metal-clad door at the top of the steps, they could smell the forced air furnace from the floor above. The commo unit was already at work burning tapes and top secret files.

In the political section suite, two junior officers sat at glass-topped desks in the outer office, one taking queries from other embassies, the other monitoring the national radio and taping the communiqués as they were transmitted. The bearded officer at the phone put his hand over the mouthpiece, looking at Lowenthal. "The Brits don't have anything. They know less than we do. Cecil is holed up at his residence, just like the ambassador."

The commo chief from the floor above waited against the wall outside Lowenthal's office, ankles crossed, arms folded, holding a sealed manila envelope marked in red crayon: "Secret NODIS: Ambassador Only."

"He's immobilized at the residence," Lowenthal told him. "Becker's there too."

"So I heard." He gave Lowenthal the envelope. "You'd better get this to him pretty quick. Washington wants to know what the shit's going on." He went out quickly, before Lowenthal could detain him with an instruction. The political counselor wasn't popular among the commo clerks on the third floor, disliked most for the windy pedantry of his reporting cables, which invariably reached the clerks at close-down time, keeping them at their machines long after the diplomatic staff had gone home.

"What's the radio saying?" Lowenthal asked.

"Nothing right now." The young political officer turned up the volume. A military band was playing "Yes, We Have No Bananas" in three-quarter time. The recording was old, the clarinets and trombones blurred by surface noise, but Colonel Selvey recognized the melody and smiled.

"You got to get that in your next cable, son," he told the young political officer. "Back in Foggy Bottom, that'll tell them a ton."

A violent explosion rocked the silence somewhere up the street, rattling the windows. "Probably a stray," Lowenthal murmured as no sounds followed. He looked inquiringly at Selvey, who'd been in Vietnam and knew all the sounds.

"Maybe a gas tank too. How the shit do I know?"

Lowenthal turned to his secretary, a stout young woman from the Pennsylvania coal fields with rabbit-brown hair and a chain-smoker's cough. "Please get Andy Reddish for me. It's absolutely essential that I talk to him. Find out if he's come back."

She picked up the phone without enthusiasm, her eyes still registering the shock of the explosion. "They used to tell me it'd happen like this," she grumbled as she dialed Reddish's extension. "I wish I'd taken my R and R when I was supposed to. I'd be in Mombasa by now, soaking up sun and the Indian Ocean."

"Gin you mean, don't you, sugar," Selvey said with a sympathetic pat as he followed Lowenthal into his office.

"Yeah," she muttered irritably, waiting for the door to close. She spent most of her idle hours drinking bourbon at the Marine house bar and knew their secret nicknames for the embassy staff as well as if she'd helped invent them. The door closed. "Up yours too, Gomer Pyle."

Lowenthal pulled the drapes closed, turned on the desk lamp, and passed Selvey the three telegrams he'd sent to Washington. The first had been sent out a little before six o'clock when the fighting in Malunga had been confirmed. The second and third had been dispatched after the President had come on the national radio declaring martial law and asking the rebels to lay down their arms.

The Sunday had begun routinely for both men, neither warned of the possibility of trouble. Selvey had spent the morning playing golf at the Belgian Club with his Air Force attaché and the departing administrative counselor. Lowenthal had passed the afternoon on the rear terrace of his villa, reading old copies of the New York Times and Le Monde, which he'd been collecting for several weeks, while his wife Pam loafed in the nearby pool, sculling lazily from time to time to the pool's edge near his chair to remind him of some conversational or gastronomical triumph of the evening before. She was an Episcopalian from an old Philadelphia family, and Lowenthal was now an Episcopalian too. They'd met in Paris, where she was a staff writer for a New York fashion magazine, he, at the embassy, an American diplomat who spoke that flawless French she'd never expected to hear from a countryman. Diplomacy was for her the ultimate social pretext; perfection was what she'd always reached for; and she'd reached for Lowenthal. Now her ambitions excited his.

At their dinner the night before, the French Ambassador had remained until twelve-thirty, an unheard-of hour for a Frenchman who seldom accepted American hospitality, and departed promptly at ten-thirty when he did. The Belgian and Israeli counselors had stayed until one, the Italian until two. Not a word of English had been heard that evening; the cuisine had been French too, the gossip Continental, and the dinner not at all compromised by the failure of the French-educated minister of justice to appear.

After a nap, Lowenthal had retired to his study to reconstruct his talk with the French Ambassador for a Monday cable to Washington. The phone call from the embassy duty officer had interrupted his memo, the events that followed had demolished it. Nothing was salvageable. No hint of the afternoon's disasters had been implicit in the table talk of the previous night.

"I hope to hell you birds can do better than this," Selvey complained, returning the three cables. "There's not a goddamned thing there Washington couldn't get off the AP ticker."

The young political officer stuck his head in the door. "They've postponed the President's nine o'clock announcement again. Now they're calling for all off-duty doctors, nurses, and attendants to report to the hospitals. They've shoved back the ten o'clock curfew so they can bring the wounded in off the streets."

The bearded officer followed, carrying a report passed from the Belgians, advising that Radio Brazzaville across the river was claiming that the army was trying to destroy the local workers party. "They're saying that some army officers tried to pull off a coup this afternoon, but it didn't work, and now they're trying to blame the workers party. They say some workers party officials escaped across the river by pirogue." The young man with the beard was an ex–Peace Corps volunteer who spoke Swahili and had served in Uganda. "Sounds pretty logical to me."

"That's bullshit," Selvey growled. "The army's trying to put down a revolt, not start one." The army was his turf and the political section didn't belong there.

"I think that's most improbable," Lowenthal said.

"I said 'sounds logical,' I didn't say it was," the younger man retreated. "The Belgians don't believe it either."

"What do they think?"

"The same as us, that the workers party is behind it."

"You can't pay any attention to Radio Brazza anyway," Selvey said. "I wouldn't be surprised if Brazza isn't trying to infiltrate some of those Cuban-trained militia across the river to help out. What do they call it?"

"Défense Civile," Lowenthal said. Selvey's French wasn't very good; his Tennessee accent made it worse.

"With the Russians and Cubans over there, they've got more guns than burrs on a baboon's ass, and I wouldn't be surprised if some of them aren't in Malunga right now. I think that's why the paras have closed off Malunga, why you've got all these goddamned roadblocks—scared of the Cubans coming over."

Lowenthal's secretary came in. "Sorry, but it's Franz from USIS. He says it's urgent."

Lowenthal picked up the phone, listened for a minute, and turned to Selvey. "Dick Franz says there's a tank burning near the USIS cultural center. That's in the commercial district, outside Malunga, so the fighting has spread."

"That's bullshit too," Selvey drawled. "Everyone's an expert all of a sudden, even my wife. Tell him it's a sound truck from the national radio trying to scare them bimbos back into Malunga. I saw it myself. Some bird put a couple of rounds in the gas tank—shooting with his eyes closed, like you folks. You got any coffee out there, hon?"

"I'll see," Lowenthal's secretary answered. "Just instant, I think."

Lowenthal put the phone down. "How bad is it in Malunga? What's the Belgian military attaché saying?"

Selvey took out his notebook and pulled on his half-moon reading glasses. "He says the workers party has guns and is passing them out to anyone who can use them, automatic weapons, mostly. He saw a few crates of Molotov cocktails taken by the paras. He also saw a para ammo carrier loaded with captured weapons outside Malunga—Kalashnikovs, he said. The Israeli attaché saw a weapons carrier too, but it could have been the same one. That's another problem—everyone singing from the same sheet of music, so maybe it sounds worse than it is." He turned the page. "A few Simonov semi-automatic carbines too, some Makarov pistols—all Russian. The Israeli counted twenty-seven dead *jeunesse* at the government hospital, most dead of chest wounds, blown away at close range. Some had bandoliers of 7.65 ammo, he said, like Chinese bandits.

More dead bodies at the Swedish hospital, the British attaché told me, but the paras closed off the gate, and he couldn't get a body count."

"How much worse do you think it will get?" Lowenthal asked, troubled.

"I dunno. It's hard to say. But any time the communes have guns, you've got a peck of trouble, that's for goddamn sure, I don't care how many guns they've got. Then you turn the paras loose and the army too, you've got more, I don't care if all they're packing is beer bellies and barrel staves. If the native communes bust out, then we're in for it. This whole city will go up in smoke and there's not a goddamn thing GHQ or the para brigade or anyone else can do about it.

"You've got maybe a million nigras out there in the slums with nothing between them and us but a half-assed army that'll run sooner than it'll get shot at, and after ten minutes ain't an army any more. If the communes get mad enough, get the grit in their craw bad enough, and get moving quick enough, they'll take it all, the whole farm—the commercial district, the embassies, the port, all of it. Everything they can tote away they will, and if they can't tote it, eat it, or smash it, they'll burn it. They'll go through this town like salts through grandma, nothing but green gravy left where they've done their business—

"Thanks, sugar." He took the cup of instant coffee passed to him by Lowenthal's secretary, who stood listening in terror. "And after that the paras and the army will pull back to a hilltop perimeter around the President's compound and let it blow itself out. Then in a few days after everyone's dead drunk, sleeping it off back in shanty town, the army and paras will come on back in, shoot a few strays, and hose out the streets. But that's assuming the army holds together. You got this tribal mess to think about too—the President's generals on the one hand, the colonels on the other, the sergeants down below, the lieutenants and captains somewhere in the middle. So that could blow the army apart too, everyone fighting each other. So I wouldn't bet on anything right now. What worries me is the embassy, the dependents. My headquarters want to know what we're going to do about an evacuation. They've got a couple of C-141 MAC flights holding in Jo-burg, waiting for me to let them know."

Selvey drank from his coffee cup, grimacing painfully.

"The airport's closed," Lowenthal said, discouraged.

"Then we'll get them to open it. There's no fighting out there."
He looked at his coffee cup. "What the shit did she put in this—
saltpeter?"

"It's something we can talk to the ambassador about. I doubt
that he'd favor it. It would suggest he was not at all sanguine about
the regime's ability to keep order."

"What the hell does he want—a few dead bodies? I'm talking
about dependents, women and kids, not a few old grunts like us."

"We'll ask him, certainly. But what he'll want to know is how
the guns got into Malunga, where they came from." Lowenthal sat
back, picking up his yellow pad. "How do you think they managed
it?"

"Who managed it?"

"The workers party," Lowenthal said, surprised.

"I don't know," Selvey said. "I'm not sure of anything right
now. You'd have to say they came from across the river, I reckon—
from the Sovs and Cubans. Maybe they cut a deal with Masakita,
told him they'd support a peoples republic. You have to figure something like that, but I'd say it's goddamn stupid. Ask Andy when he
comes in. He's the one doing the bean count on the Sovs."

"It's clear it started in Malunga."

Selvey nodded. "I'd say so."

"At the workers party compound, where these radio appeals for
foreign help are coming from?"

"I don't know about that."

"We know they've been training a paramilitary brigade at their
agricultural camp at Mundi," Lowenthal continued, "just as we've
always known it was a Marxist party, masquerading as a professional workers union under the President's policy of national reconciliation. Why should we now be surprised to discover they have guns?
They've probably had guns for a long time."

The symmetry pleased Lowenthal. Nothing else he'd heard had.
But Colonel Selvey was silent, still undecided. He shared the army's
suspicions of Pierre Masakita. The return from exile had been a fait
accompli, arranged secretly by the President and kept from the
army, the cabinet, and the old politicians until the day of his return,
when the old cabinet was dismissed, new elections promised, and a
new government of national reconciliation formed. With the ban on
political parties lifted, Masakita worked to rebuild the old teachers
and professional workers party, but his activity only increased army
suspicions, convincing the general staff and GHQ, all loyal to the
President, that Masakita was quietly rebuilding his power base

while transforming the youth wing of the party, the *jeunesse*, into a paramilitary unit, similar to the old *jeunesse* who'd devastated the countryside during the rebellions.

"I'd say you're probably right, except for the police camp at Bakole," Selvey said finally. "Those grunts out there aren't socialists or Marxists. So how come they're getting clobbered by the paras?"

"There's always been bad blood between the police and army," Lowenthal replied, still searching for symmetry, "but it's primarily tribal. Therefore, it has no ideological base, while the other manifestly does."

"You mean it's still a little fucked up," Selvey drawled cheerfully, as bright as a street sparrow suddenly, bobbing after the junkman's horse.

chapter 10

✦ Between the mud walls, the laterite road in Malunga was blocked by abandoned carts, trucks, and cars. The commune was partially ablaze to the south. Africans were moving away from the fires and the tattoo of rifle shot, four and five abreast in the road and along the septic ditches. As Reddish watched, sixty meters down the road a wooden building took a phosphorus grenade through a window, flared like a gasoline-soaked rag, and began to burn. He stood in the door of his Fiat, his face wet, blue tennis shirt soaked, ashes from a burning hut nearby falling against his brow and shoulders. He heard quick bursts of rifle fire echo from the rear of a building beyond and watched a long flaming timber fall from the second-floor roof, pulling a tail of blazing embers after it to the road. A few minutes earlier, youths from the workers party *jeunesse* had been on the roof firing pistols at the paras.

"*Kende, patron,*" an old African voice urged him. "*Kende,* go now." But the dark wrinkled face passed beneath him in the shadows before he turned. Beyond the stalled vehicles further down the road, the headquarters compound of the workers party was under siege. A few weak muzzle tongues of flame licked from the darkness of the second-floor windows and along the roof under the trees. In the road a quartet of armored cars blocked the approaches from both directions. Firing popped from the rear of the two-acre compound where a dilapidated old building lay. Once a Protestant mission school, it had been converted by the party into barracks and classrooms for the youth wing. Behind the armored cars, crouched in the shelter of the compound wall, a score of red-bereted paras crouched or sat, their fire desultory. None wore helmets. In the light of a truck's headlights, a para captain with a swagger stick chased away the curious. A small boy who'd passed Reddish's Fiat a minute earlier pushed his way through the small crowd and dropped a wooden beer crate at the feet of the captain, who lifted a bottle for himself and pushed the crate with his foot toward his two subalterns squatting in the lee of the armored car. An old woman was selling groundnuts nearby.

Several vehicles were overturned inside the party compound. A cream-colored auto smoldered steadily, its upholstery ignited, its windows broken out.

Behind Reddish's Fiat, an army truck blocked the road in front of a small *petit marché*. The squad of soldiers who'd climbed from beneath the rear canvas were examining the identity papers of the Africans retreating down the road, searching for weapons and fleeing rebels. To the west, an orange glow hovered over the trees in the direction of the Bakole police camp.

The gunfire from the party compound was sporadic—small-bore handguns, he thought, crossing the road and moving through the crowd. He climbed the bank to the wall beyond, hoisting himself into the shadows of a barren avocado tree, looking toward the center of the compound to see if the paras inside had taken prisoners. He saw no one. A few dead bodies lay crumpled behind the burning vehicles, automatic rifles lying nearby. In the compound directly in front of him, hidden two walls away from the firefight, a plump woman was calmly sweeping the bare earth with a palm frond, indifferent to the gunfire. Two small boys were pounding a manioc pestle, brought back to their work by a sharp command from their mother when they let their attention escape to the nearby confusion. Government business, not hers, Reddish guessed, looking at a man in a blue fishnet undershirt who sat slumped against the wall of the house. An empty palm wine vessel was at his feet. He was massaging his woolly head drunkenly, muttering to himself, and lifting his swimming eyes from time to time to shout threats at the rifle fire beyond the two walls.

Reddish left the wall and went back down the road toward the *marché*. Old women still sat in the rush-covered stalls whose counters were stacked with piles of two and three cigarettes, silver flakes of dried fish, and bright red peppers of *pele-pele,* all husbanded in small frugal heaps purchasable for a few francs. Next door a small open-air bar still served customers, although most had fled. A pair of young prostitutes remained, drinking beer. The soldiers checking documents behind the truck sometimes called to them, but they only giggled to themselves, covering their mouths as they turned away.

A gasoline tank in one of the overturned vehicles exploded suddenly, and the crowd surged forward along the road, blown forward by the detonation. The Africans in their compounds were drawn to their gates to watch, even the prostitutes stood up to join the market women at the edge of the road. "Has the army finally finished with them?" called an old grandmother. "Sent them to the devil so we can walk in peace now?"

A burst of automatic weapons fire followed from the paras. Through the heat of the burning car, Reddish followed the curling images of a few paras dodging through the gate and into the compound. The army truck at the *marché* began to crawl forward, followed by the squad of soldiers examining identity cards. Reddish moved quickly back toward his Fiat before they accosted him.

"*Monsieur! Oh, monsieur!*" He heard a voice, as light and exhausted as the night wind, and stopped abruptly, searching the faces passing in the shadows. No one turned his way and he went back to the car. As he reached the door Alphonse Nyembo's face lifted through the open window on the far side where he'd been waiting. An embassy consular clerk, he worked as a librarian at the workers party headquarters on evenings and weekends. At four-thirty he'd called Reddish to warn him there would be shooting in Malunga.

"I've been looking all over for you. Get in."

"No, follow me. Quickly. Bring the car."

"Where? What for?"

"There's no time. Follow me. This way."

Nyembo dodged ahead and Reddish drove forward after him down the road toward the approaching truck, turned across a shallow ditch and into a narrow cart lane concealed behind the compound walls. The lane disappeared in a narrow footpath under the trees where a small white Volkswagen stood abandoned, engine hood up. Reddish left the car and followed Nyembo to a concrete-block wash house twenty meters beyond, hidden behind a screen of shrubbery. Reddish stopped outside warily, listening.

"Here," Nyembo called from inside. "Hurry, please."

The interior was dark. Reddish struck his lighter. Nyembo was kneeling next to a figure lying on the floor.

"Who is it?"

"They left him here, left him here for the soldiers."

"Left who here?" Reddish asked softly, kneeling. He supposed the wounded man was a tribal cousin. A bloody rag was tied across his forehead, partially masking his face. Blood soaked the front of his Mao tunic. His body was twisted awkwardly, as if he were protecting a shoulder wound.

"Masakita."

Reddish immediately stood up, extinguishing the lighter. He moved back to the door and looked out, listening, the blood pounding in his ears. He turned back inside but couldn't see Nyembo's face. "You've got to get out of here," he said harshly. "Get the hell out. There're soldiers all over the place."

"We must move him, take him—"

"Don't be an idiot! Come on! Move!"

"He's wounded."

"God damn it, it doesn't matter! Come on!" He moved forward, trying to find Nyembo's arm, his shoulders, anything to pull him out of there, but stumbled over the wounded man's ankles. "It's not your fight. Leave him and let's go!"

"Someone slashed him with a machete, one of the *jeunesse*."

"That's not your problem. Do you want them to find you too?"

"Lule and another brought him here," Nyembo said. "The car wouldn't start and they left him here."

"That's too bloody bad. Come on—"

"The *jeunesse* were taking guns from the crates and he tried to stop them."

Reddish turned. "*Crates?* What kind of crates? *Gun crates?*"

"Boxes with guns."

He kneeled down. "Are you sure?"

"I saw them from the library window."

Again he struck his lighter. "How bad is it? Is he unconscious? Can he talk?"

"He'll wake again. We must take him away."

"Use your head. We wouldn't get past the road out front."

"Your car has diplomatic plates."

"CD plates won't make any difference, not with this god-damned shooting going on. How much did you see?"

"Just when they were taking guns from the crates and he went to stop them. The soldiers will find him and shoot him. You could take him to the embassy, to your villa."

"And do what, for God's sake?"

The lighter flickered out and they crouched in silence next to the wounded man, Reddish's mind already racing ahead. He couldn't see Nyembo's small, bony face. His wife had been Reddish's Lingala teacher and he'd visited their village near Benongo on the lake. Like Banda, he had no faith in his own status, just in those of more exalted rank. Reddish got to his feet and went outside, listening. The gunfire had died away and he could hear the sound of the wind high in the trees.

"Can he talk yet?" he asked Nyembo as he returned. "Has he said anything?"

"No."

"We can't wait like this, there's no time." He crouched down. "Go outside and watch. Call me if you hear someone." Nyembo scrambled to his feet and Reddish leaned forward. "I'm going to lift you," he said. "Just take it easy." This is crazy, he thought, his face and shirt drenched. This is just goddamned crazy. He moved his position, got a grip under the knees and behind the shoulders, but Masakita cried out, and Reddish eased him back, still thinking about the gun crates. "It's going to hurt but I can't help that." Ignoring the cries of pain he lifted Masakita from the floor, got his balance, and reeled out the door. "Take out the back seat," he told Nyembo at the car. "Just jerk it out. How many crates were there?" Nyembo pulled out the rear seat and Reddish lowered the wounded man into the back. He took a raffia mat and two vegetable baskets from the Fiat's trunk, covered Masakita with the rear seat, and piled the mat and baskets on top. "How many crates did you see?" he asked, still breathing hard as he climbed behind the wheel.

Nyembo had moved away. "I'll go on foot," he said. "If they see me in the car, they'll stop you." His courage was leaving him. Reddish heard it ebbing away in his voice.

"We'll risk it. I need to talk to you. Come on, there's no time." He started the engine.

"I've told you all that I saw. I'll go another way."

"Come on, get in," Reddish called, but he knew it was no use arguing. His burden transferred, Nyembo was just another helpless African, like those out on the road. "Go the back way then," Reddish said, "but for God's sake stay out of sight. Not a word."

"Just my wife," Nyembo said.

Reddish drove back down the cart lane to the road. The army truck hadn't moved far enough to clear the road to the north. In the other direction, he was still blocked by the armored cars in front of the besieged compound. He left the car in front of the shallow ditch and walked along the road with the crowd, searching for another exit between the approaching truck and the burning compound.

"*Monsieur, oh monsieur, s'il vous plaît.*" The voice came again, stronger now. In the storm ditch at the far side of the road, a small Renault was mired to the axles where the driver had stupidly tried to cross. A woman leaned against the rear fender, her white face streaked with ash, her dark hair wet against her forehead. "Can you help me, please. I'm at my wit's end."

He saw the muck burying the wheels and splashed against her skirt and ankles. "Leave it," he called impatiently. "You can't get it out. Leave it." The vehicles in the compound behind him were still burning, lifting bolls of dense black smoke into the cordite-filled African night. She shook her head, as if unable to hear him, the brightness brimming in her eyes. He slid down the side of the storm ditch. "Leave it. You can't get it out. Come on. I've got a car up the road."

She seemed to recognize him then, looking up through her wet lashes, afraid she might be wrong. "Reddish?" He nodded, puzzled. "Last night," she reminded him, frightened that he might have forgotten. "At the Belgian reception."

He remembered then. She was the Frenchwoman who'd been standing with Armand in the corner of the terrace. "Not the same, is it? Let's go."

"I have these." She opened the rear door of the car. Two burlap bags lay on the rear seat. "Will they be too much trouble?"

Quickly he pulled the bags from the car, guessing by their weight and smell what they contained: African masks bought from a Senegalese trader who lived nearby. "Come on. This way."

"It's frightful," she said as they reached the road, "terrifying." The army truck had begun to move forward again.

"My car's this way, toward the truck."

She hurried after him, running to catch up as they were separated by the Africans moving past. "You came here alone?" he asked.

"It was terribly stupid of me."

"Whose car is it?"

"Houlet's secretary unfortunately. Do you know what's happening? Why they're fighting—" She was moved aside by a quartet of African women carrying baskets and then swept up in the throng in the center of the roadbed. When she joined him again, her face was as distraught as before, her breath dry and hot. "I'm afraid I'll get lost. I don't know the way. I'm completely turned around."

"Over there, toward the side road."

She saw the car. "Thank God. I didn't know what to do." He'd turned to look back, toward the burning compound. "Can you drive out? Are you so sure?"

Searching the road ahead for the paras examining identity documents, he seemed hardly conscious of her voice, her wet face, her muddy sandals. In a few days she'd be just another Frenchwoman at another diplomatic reception, like dozens of others, trading anecdotes about where they'd been shopping or sunning themselves when a few ugly Africans blew out the lights of the capital.

He put the burlap bags in the rear seat on top of the raffia mat.

They waited in the car, concealed in the shadows until the army truck finally passed, and then Reddish drove across the shallow ditch, and turned north through the thinning crowd. A few meters ahead, they were stopped by a group of men carrying a wounded woman across the road. As they waited for the litter to pass, a piercing glottal scream lifted from an old woman ahead of them, and the crowd scattered in terror for the safety of the ditches. Reddish immediately swung the Fiat over to the side of the road. "Get out," he told her. "*Now! Move!*" She stared at him in shock, unable to move, and he reached across her, opened the door, and pushed her out, scrambling after her to drag her down into the roadside ditch with him.

Twenty meters ahead of them three figures had leaped from the high wall enclosing an old Portuguese warehouse to the center of the road, each carrying an automatic rifle. One of the youths had lost control of his and it clattered to the clay of the roadbed, rupturing the magazine. One of the youths had a bloody handkerchief wrapped around his ankle and he half crouched, half squatted in the road, trying to reload his weapon. The third man also carried a pistol, and had difficulty managing both the pistol and the automatic rifle. He waved the pistol aloft with one hand while with the other he struggled unsuccessfully to steady the heavy muzzle in the direction of the paras far down the road behind Reddish, the Frenchwoman, and the Africans in the ditches. The three wore green twill uniforms and the red armbands of the Jeunesse Nationale de la Révolution.

Head down, Reddish watched from the shallow ditch, his arm forcing the woman down even lower. "You're hurting me," she cried weakly. He released the pressure.

"Shut up and keep your head down."

A young woman bolted suddenly from the deeper storm ditch across the road back toward the safety of the paras, a baby swaddled high on her shoulders. The taller rebel, his attention drawn from Reddish's Fiat with diplomatic plates, let the rifle muzzle drop and fired his pistol in the air. The woman collapsed in terror, the baby tumbling into the road ahead of her. A dozen black arms reached for mother and child, pulling them back into the safety of the storm ditch. The youth fired the pistol again, the muzzle flame a weak, dirty orange against the darkness of the trees, as if the cartridges hadn't been fully primed.

"*Lukulu*," whispered an old man from the ditch near Reddish. "*Lukulu*."

"Eh," Reddish grunted, the old man's explanation suddenly his own. *Lukulu* was a locally brewed intoxicant made from boiled hemp leaves and alcohol, drunk by the Simbas during the rebellions to get their courage up when sent against automatic rifles with bows and arrows in their hands. He studied the automatic rifle which had fallen to the road. It was a Kalashnikov, caked with dust, as if the stock and barrel were still thick with cosmoline, just removed from the shipping crate. The second rebel couldn't fit his magazine into the breech. It was a mismatch, he hadn't been trained properly, or he was too terrified to know what he was doing. The tall rebel was exhorting those in the nearby ditches to join him. "*Makasi!*" he cried, brandishing the pistol aloft. "*Makasi!* We have strength!"

Reddish thought the pistol was an old Belgian sidearm, not Soviet-made.

"*Lukulu,*" the old man's voice came again.

"*Makasi!*" The rebel lowered the pistol and aimed it down the road toward the paras hugging the shadows of the armored car that was now moving toward them. The gun jerked as he pulled the trigger, but no shot came, only the sharp *click-click* of the hammer. A single shot whined in response from a para sharpshooter lying atop the armored car. The rebel turned angrily, still urging the Africans out of the ditches. A few began to rise. The other rebels remained crouched in the road, fumbling with their AK-47 magazines.

A second shot came twanging up the road from the armored car and ripped through the impacted roadbed near the rebels. The Frenchwoman's shoulders jerked under Reddish's restraining hands, and a few Africans lifted themselves to wave back toward the paras, pleading to them to hold their fire. One of the rebels leaped for the ditch, but a dozen Africans rose to thrust him away, grappling with his flailing arms first, ripping his weapon away, and flinging him back into the roadbed. The two remaining rebels crouched on their haunches, their green uniforms dark with sweat, aware for the first time of the hostile circling faces. One rose suddenly, dragging his AK-47 as he tried to vault the storm ditch on the far side of the road to scale the concrete block wall, but four men seized him, twisted the rifle from his hands, tore the revolver from his belt, and sent him toppling backwards. He lay on his side, breathing heavily, his wet black face chalk-white across his cheek where he'd fallen in the dust. From the shadows of the trees, a few glottal screams came again from the older women. Looking over his shoulder, Reddish saw what they had seen, a dozen paras moving out ahead of the armored car, automatic rifles lowered.

The crowd moved ahead of them out of the ditches and culverts and over the walls, just a few at first, the younger men leading the way, the older following, joined by mothers, old women, and children, until the road was full of dark angry faces circling the three figures sprawled in the dust. The three rebels were hidden then, the night suddenly still. The violence came swiftly and savagely, the way it came to thieves trapped in the *grand marché*, but Reddish couldn't see from the shallow ditch—just the angry heaving shoulders and bobbing heads in the road, churning like the dark surface of a sea whose depths trawlers had chummed, voracious with hidden appetites blood had suddenly released. He lifted the woman from the ditch and pushed her into the Fiat. The mob surged behind them toward the advancing paras, encumbered by what they still dragged and were pounding mercilessly, with feet, fists, clubs, stones, and useless weapons; and as they moved away, Reddish saw from the car window only a single rubber tennis shoe left in the road where the three rebels had crouched.

"Don't turn, just look straight ahead," he told her. A single shot followed from behind them as the para captain stepped forward into the circle of faces. A second shot followed, then a third, and all seemed to reverberate together along the road and out over the rooftops.

She stared out through the windshield as the cry of the crowd reached her, head and shoulders unmoving, her lips slightly parted. They passed a few squads of soldiers advancing toward the party compound, some herding rebel prisoners forward, hands behind their heads. They were stopped twice, once by a pair of corporals without prisoners to whom Reddish gave five hundred francs, and a second time by a para captain standing behind an army truck. He probed their faces with his torch, looked at the CD plates, and returned to the window, demanding that Reddish get out. The Frenchwoman put her head back against the seat, her eyes closed, her hands clenched in agony on her lap.

Reddish refused. "She's sick," he told the captain. He examined her face in his flashlight beam, reconsidered, and waved them on angrily. Six dead *jeunesse* lay along the road beyond the truck, lying in a row, their green tunics pulled over their faces, revealing their naked rib cages. A kerosene lantern blazed at the foot of a compound wall behind them, where a small crowd of Africans had gathered, watching them silently. A few small boys darted along the ditches, some still wearing the paper hats passed out by a local beer company at the stadium during the soccer games. More lay scattered along the road.

He turned off into the back lanes to avoid those roadblocks where groups of *jeunesse* were under siege, but when he finally reached the debouchment into the commercial section he found that blocked off too. The paras were permitting Europeans to depart on foot, most of them Portuguese merchants and garage owners, but without their vehicles. The potholed road was filled with abandoned cars and trucks. He turned around and drove south, following the road toward Yvon Kadima's villa. The rear gate entered into Malunga, but the front entrance faced the arc-lit boulevard of the commercial section. He found the narrow lane and drove back to the screen of shrubbery. The night guard's fire burned in the cinder drive beyond the sagging gate shackled with a heavy chain.

"*Patron, azali awa?*" Reddish called, standing at the gate, asking if Kadima had returned. The old sentinel moved to the gate, peering suspiciously through the palings. He recognized him and unshackled the chain.

"*Ehhh. Kufi.*" Reddish heard him sigh grievously. "*Kufi.*"

"Dead?"

"*Kufi.*" The lips barely moved.

Many of Yvon Kadima's tribal kinsmen had taken refuge in his compound from Malunga, fearing the worst. They moved between the porch of the decaying old villa under the trees and the surrounding outbuildings; more gathered in the brightly lit rooms inside, where Kadima's body lay. Reddish found Kadima's chauffeur in the rear salon helping Mrs. Kadima's younger sister pack her bags. The room was in disarray. On the plush divan were two valises filled with clothes. A few European suits hung over a nearby chair, topped by a dusty tuxedo with satin lapels. A young African girl in a faded cotton dress brought freshly ironed dresses from the rear porch, where a shirtless African youth pushed an old charcoal iron over Mrs. Kadima's *waxes*. Two radios were playing simultaneously, one tuned to the national radio, the other to Congo-Brazzaville. On the table next to the divan were Kadima's blue-jacketed passport, his yellow shot card, a thick manila envelope, an airline ticket, and an opened bottle of Courvoisier.

The chauffeur, his eyes still red, told Reddish that a para jeep had arrived shortly after four, just as Kadima was about to leave for the airport. The para captain had insisted Kadima accompany him to the Bakole police camp to talk to the police. Kadima had argued with the captain in the drive, refusing to accompany him. The captain had shot him and sped off.

"Just shot him—without warning?"

The chauffeur nodded miserably, holding his hands to his face to describe the terrible wound.

"But why was he packing? Where was he going?"

"To Brussels—for a holiday."

The body lay in the rear bedroom, face covered. Reddish glanced in, saw the grieving relatives gathered there in the shadows around the bed, knew there was no time, and ran back the corridor. At the top of the steps, he collided with a small African just arriving. He was a gray-haired man wearing gold-rimmed spectacles.

"Banda!" he cried, his hands out to steady him. The eyes were hidden, but as they lifted, Reddish recognized his mistake. "Sorry!" He released the man and leaped down the outside steps.

chapter 11

❖ The Frenchwoman stirred as Reddish slammed forward through the gate and out into the boulevard.

"I must go to Bois du Fleuve," she muttered weakly, "to the Houlets'."

"I can't get you there. There's no time. The curfew's about to begin."

He circled the tall cenotaph in the square near the railroad station, tires shrieking. The massed flower beds were black in the moonlight. Two army trucks were unloading troopers in front of the stucco station. A block beyond, the boulevard was blocked by a third army truck, but he veered around it and sped past before the soldiers dropped to the ground.

"I'm sorry, but I've forgotten your name."

"Bonnard. Gabrielle Bonnard."

"Bonnard, that's right."

A caravan of troop carriers moved toward him, dropping off squads of soldiers at the deserted intersections. The lead jeep blinked its lights as he approached. He didn't stop and a second jeep swung out from behind the first and turned on its siren.

He spun into the next side street, smashing through the improvised barricade at the same instant he saw it, lifting aside the two-by-four and capsizing the two lanterns, spilling the kerosene in a sheet of fire along the gutter. He jolted the wheel to avoid the two leaping soldiers and immediately spun the wheel again, sending the sedan hurtling into the dark alleyway parallel to the boulevard.

"You know the route?" she said, her voice coming back.

"Yeah, but it changes after dark."

He kept to the alley for three blocks, lights out, entered an empty street and turned toward the river. The watchman came to the gate of the apartment compound, opened it, and Reddish drove down to the underground garage.

"This is your building?" she asked as she got out.

"A friend's flat. He's on leave." He swung back the seat, dumped the burlap bags in front, and pulled away the raffia mat.

She saw the wounded man, looked at Reddish in surprise, and then back at him, her lips pursed sympathetically. "He's wounded?"

"A little. Would you get the elevator?"

"My sacks?"

"I'll bring them later."

Stiff with his wounds and semi-conscious, Masakita was barely able to stand. Reddish carried him quickly to the elevator, held him upright inside, and unlocked the stainless steel control panel. He tripped the circuits closed, and sent the elevator creaking toward the fifth floor.

"So it is your building," she said coolly, lifting her eyes, almost like a stranger again.

"Not the building, just the elevator," he answered, closing the panel and locking it. She studied the wounded man silently, his face still hidden by the bloody scarf.

The apartment was airless, the air conditioners turned off. The flat was carried on the books as transit quarters, but was used sometimes as an accommodation flat, a kind of safe house. Reddish carried the wounded man into the small bedroom behind the kitchen, turned on the air conditioners, and led her to the bedroom down the hall at the rear.

"This is about as good as I can do. I'm sorry. I can take you to the embassy with me, but it's better not to be out on the streets. I can't get you to the Houlets'."

"I understand."

"We could make a run for the French Embassy. It's a couple of blocks away."

"I'd prefer not to go there," she replied, her voice as cool as the night before when she'd rebuked Armand.

"You're a guest of the Houlets'?"

"Yes."

"You're better off here—safer too, five floors up."

"With a wounded man in the flat?" She looked at him dubiously.

"He's an old friend." Reddish lied. "He used to be my driver. Now he has a taxi fleet. I'm leaving and he wanted to buy my car. When I got to his garage he was bleeding like that. Maybe a fight, I don't know."

She nodded, as if details didn't interest her. "I'm suddenly very tired," she murmured, her eyes closing for an instant. "I think I'd like to lie down."

"You feel sick?"

"No, I'll be all right. But I'd like to lie down."

She went into the bedroom, closing the door, and Reddish returned to the front bedroom, where he helped Masakita remove the bloody Mao jacket. The machete wound began at his shoulder and traveled down the outside of the upper arm, curving across the white bone of his elbow.

"It should be stitched up."

"It can be closed without stitches," Masakita said. "There's a trick to it. The Chinese taught us how."

Reddish lifted the table lamp to look at the scalp wound. The laceration was superficial, beginning at the hairline and ending in the brow above the right eye.

"You're Reddish, aren't you?" Masakita said. He was a small man with a thin face and wiry arms, his physical appearance usually a disappointment to those who knew him only because of the lore of the rebellions. His black face had a slightly Asiatic cast, the eyes hooded at the outer lid by a crease of skin. His enemies claimed his grandfather was Chinese, one of the laborers brought in by the Belgians at the turn of the century to help build the railroad up from the coast. The nose was small and flat. The mouth was full, the white teeth irregularly spaced.

"Reddish, that's right. Who told you?"

"Nyembo."

"When?"

"In the wash house. . . . He said he'd called you . . . that you were coming." He tried to lift his head but sank back, his black face leaking water to the pillow.

Reddish brought the first aid kit from the bathroom and cleaned the shoulder wound with alcohol as Masakita lay on the bed, eyes closed, his mouth twisted as the alcohol seared the raw wound. He dressed the shoulder and bandaged it crudely, as best he could.

"Nyembo has often told me of you," Masakita said with difficulty.

Reddish ignored him, raising the lamp again to look at the scalp wound.

"He's a simple man, Nyembo, an honest man," Masakita continued, watching Reddish's fingers the way a frightened patient watches the dentist's drill. He closed his eyes as Reddish cleaned the laceration, only opening them again as the bandage was pressed in place. "What does he make of men like us?"

"Save it."

"For what, for when the army comes here too?"

He closed his eyes. Reddish ripped the adhesive tape from the spool, looking down at the man who'd been the most feared of the rebel leaders in the interior during the uprisings against the central government. A peasants' war, the sympathetic Belgian scholars from L'Institut National d'Etudes Politiques now wrote, the revolt of the countryside against the new class of black bourgeois civil servants and administrators who'd replaced the departing Belgians with a colonization of their own, oppressing the countryside from the capital as the metropole had once done. Masakita had been the boldest of the rebel leaders as well as the most elusive. A hapless army command invariably reported him on all fronts simultaneously—in the Kwilu, where the first outbreaks began, in Maniema, West Kasai, or far to the east at Kindu.

The army feared him, originally because of his popularity in the bush but as the rebellions had spread because of the myths their clumsiness had created, making him the legend of local folklore wherever he appeared—the man they couldn't kill, who changed shape whenever capture seemed imminent, now a serpent, now a leopard, now a wisp of smoke or a toothless old man on a stick, melting away through the thick green twilight as the futile ambushes were sprung, leaving the terrified soldiers fleeing the smoke of their own batteries.

After the rebels had run amok and begun the systematic extermination of their government prisoners, Masakita had broken with the Simba leadership and again disappeared into exile. With the help of foreign mercenaries, the rebellions were put down, the leaders executed or driven abroad. Masakita was the most legendary of those who survived. The old superstitions persisted, fed now by faulty intelligence, local paranoia, diplomatic confusion, and cold war gossip. He was reported to be in Moscow one week, Peking the next, and Cairo the third, soliciting political and financial support to resume the guerrilla war in the more remote regions of that sprawling, ramshackle collection of tribes, tongues, and ancient animosities that independence had labeled a nation. But whatever his wanderings during those years, he was again working in obscurity on the staff of the Afro-Asian Secretariat in Cairo when the President had secretly offered him amnesty and a cabinet position in his newly formed government of national reconciliation, designed to bring to an end those old tribal and political rivalries that had devastated the countryside.

Reddish had never understood why Masakita had accepted the President's offer. He knew why the offer had been made. Despite the end of the rebellions, the interior was still in turmoil; pockets of resistance remained, ready to be exploited by outside powers. The radical leadership abroad was attempting to form a government in exile with political and financial support promised by a few African progressive nations, by a few Arab radicals, and possibly the Soviet bloc; but the radical leadership abroad was in disarray. Twice the leaders of the two opposing factions had met with Masakita in Cairo, offering to unite under his leadership, twice he refused.

After the President had learned that a third appeal would be made to Masakita, he made his own, sending word secretly to Masakita that he would form a new regime of national reconciliation if Masakita would return to take a cabinet post. To Reddish's astonishment, Masakita had accepted. The radicals in exile were outflanked, a few followed Masakita home, and the clandestine plans for a government-in-exile collapsed.

Reddish hadn't understood Masakita's acquiescence then and he didn't understand it now, a man as elusive to him as he'd once been to the army, which feared him as much as ever.

"I've heard of you," Masakita muttered, his eyes flickering open, "but not just from Nyembo."

"Bloody good," Reddish said. "That'll make it simple then, won't it?" He saw only confusion and pain in the dark face.

Masakita said nothing for a minute, staring at the ceiling. Then he closed his eyes. "I understand."

Reddish closed the first aid kit and moved toward the door, turning back in the doorway. "What about your family, your wife? Can I get word to her?"

Masakita said she'd gone to visit her mother, deep in the bush behind Funzi, in a village so remote that no one could reach her.

"You mean you got her out of the way," Reddish said. "You didn't have much faith in that little army of yours, did you?"

But Masakita didn't respond.

chapter 12

✧ In the embassy reception hall, a plump woman in tangerine slacks and a bloody white blouse lay on the leather sofa behind the reception desk, bleeding from her nose and mouth. A second woman in tight yellow slacks and sneakers was holding a towel to her forehead. "They just beat her up," Reddish heard her explain tearfully to Colonel Selvey, whose back was to him. "They just laid into her, all of them."

The two women were wives of NCO's from the US military assistance mission. In the brightly lit corridor a dozen or so American families were bedded down on blankets, the children sleeping with their faces to the wall.

"The doc's on the way now," explained a Marine guard. "The dispensary's so jammed up with people she couldn't get in."

"They like to tore her clothes off," said the woman holding the towel. Her hair was up in pink curlers. "It's all right, honey. It's all right, hon. Don't you fret none. They're sending planes. We're gonna bomb those baboons back to Alley Oop, that's what we're gonna do."

"What'd she do," Selvey asked, "run a roadblock?"

"Run her Mustang plumb into a ditch and they drug her out . . ."

Reddish met Lowenthal in the stairwell, descending from the second floor. "Did Miss Ogilvy tell you? The car's waiting outside. Where in God's name have you been?"

"Trying to find out what the hell's going on. Sarah told me the ambassador wants us at the residence, which is stupid. He should be here, where he has communications."

"He spoke to someone at the présidence, an adjoint—Bintu, I suppose—who promised laissez-passe for diplomatic cars in the parliament area, but no place else. He asked Bondurant to stay at the residence, since it's closer to the présidence. The President may want to see him, and they can get a helicopter in there. We'd better hurry, Andy."

"Go ahead. I'll be down in a minute."

Sarah Ogilvy was waiting for him in the station suite. He pulled her after him into his office and shut the door. "Kadima's dead. I've got to get word to the others."

"Bintu too."

"Bintu?"

"Walker got word from one of his sources before he vanished too. Everyone's disappeared."

He pulled open the door and crossed to young Walker's office. Todd, the newly arrived junior officer, was with him.

"Does either of you have anyone still operating out there?"

"Not me," said Walker. "Where have you been? This place is going ape."

"You, Todd?"

He shook his head. "All we know is that Malunga's got guns and the *jeunesse* is getting clobbered by the army, which suits just about everyone fine, as far as I can tell."

"What's the political section reporting?"

"Lowenthal thinks Masakita's party started the shooting with guns brought over from Brazza. That's what Selvey's beginning to think too. What about you?"

"Kadima's dead and so is Bintu. Everyone else has disappeared. I think we've been wiped out."

Reddish turned and went out.

"What if I hear something?" Sarah called after him as he crossed the suite.

"I'll be at the residence."

Selvey and Lowenthal were waiting in the courtyard below. "What the shit have you been doing out there?" Selvey asked as Reddish climbed into the back seat. "Putting your local pussy to bed? What'd they tell you?"

"If I knew, I'd be upstairs writing it."

Selvey laughed. "Don't tell me they caught you holding your dick too, like the rest of these birds."

Lowenthal joined them, carrying a portable radio tuned to the emergency net. A Congolese night guard had joined the Marine at the front gate, sent from the AID compound with his spear and bow and arrow.

Selvey turned as they drove out, watching him through the rear window. "Is that what the President's gonna protect us with?

Where's his tepee and squaw." He winked at Reddish and nudged Lowenthal in the front seat. "Is that bird one of yours, perfessor?" Lowenthal didn't turn.

Twice they were stopped by roadblocks. They talked their way through the first, but at the second the soldiers were more stubborn. Unlike the paras Reddish had seen in Malunga, they seemed less sure of what was going on and more frightened. They also wore steel helmets. Selvey had finally drawn the lieutenant away into the shadows and given him a thousand francs.

"How much?" Lowenthal asked as they drove forward again.

"A thousand," Selvey muttered, still angered by the trooper's insolence.

"That's a month's pay, isn't it?" Lowenthal asked. "One of their grievances, why extortion is so blatant?"

"For Christ's sake!" Selvey shouted.

"Just turn it off," Reddish muttered to Lowenthal. "For God's sake, not now."

The parliament building was dark. In the residential quarter along the river the air smelled of mown grass and flowering trees, all mixed with the musk of the great gland of water itself. The lights of Brazzaville glimmered from across the great pool. The streets would be quiet over there, the diplomatic missions closed—Cuban, East German, Russian, Chinese, and North Korean—but their staffs would be listening to the radio, wondering if this was the night the government across the river would die in the streets. For them its death was inevitable. Reddish watched the lights, troubled, wondering which jackals would drag off the bloody corpse.

After almost four years, he believed its end inevitable too.

The moon was high over the river, untouched by clouds as he watched it. Years ago, on a night very much like this one, he'd been declared persona non grata by the Syrians after he'd been compromised by a ministry of defense official with documents to sell— Soviet weapons agreements that supplied the sort of detail not available in those days: unit prices, terms, financing, barter clauses. Entrapment, they'd discovered later. He'd spent three days incommunicado in Al Mezze prison near Damascus. During the interrogation, a team of KGB advisers shuttled between the Soviet mission and sûreté headquarters. On the fourth night, he was driven to the border and released to Lebanese authorities. He'd been without sleep for two days. As they pulled him from the car to remove the handcuffs, a Syrian interrogator had broken the two small fingers of his right hand.

"The tools of ignorance again," his father had said when he'd learned Reddish had taken a job as a weapons specialist with the Agency's technical services division after his army stint. In the small Wisconsin college town where the townspeople still turned out for the spring baseball games, he was remembered as the catcher who'd hit .385 his senior year, but had failed his tryout with a Chicago Cubs farm club. He'd played Legion ball that summer. In the Agency, he was still remembered as the case officer who'd been PNG'd in Damascus, some blue-collar technician out of Legion ball.

Reddish climbed from the car in the ambassador's drive, the fatigue of the past six hours settled in his joints like rheumatism. He stopped for a minute to flex the stiffness from his back and legs, listening to the wind rustling in the treetops. He had no enthusiasm for the meeting with the ambassador. He knew he couldn't talk to him here and make sense. It was a different world.

❖ ❖ They gathered in the ambassador's study, Bondurant deep in his armchair next to the sofa, Becker next to him in a wing-backed chair. He was a Princetonian, like the ambassador. His short gray hair was carefully brushed to one side as it must have been during his undergraduate years, with the same mannered precision that marked his ambition, his conjugal habits, his drafting. The mouth was thin without being humorless, the blue eyes brisk without being unkind. He was clever, but with the intelligence of a banker or broker, an actuarial keenness which might have made him a success on Wall Street. Why he'd become a diplomat, Reddish never knew. Spontaneity meant for him a day on the tennis courts, where his enthusiasm was that of a small boy. Diplomacy meant for him neither vision nor art but administrative success, which solved problems as they were defined. He was, for Reddish, merely another careerist, a man who, after twenty years, could never be persuaded that bureaucratic truths weren't also moral and historical ones.

Lowenthal sat silently on the sofa with Reddish, watching Bondurant nervously as he read the cables they'd brought. Selvey puffed on a thin cigar, gaze lifted toward the modern abstractions hanging on the study wall. They'd never made sense to him but took meaning with his mood—circus balloons on bright afternoons, goiters or lymph glands when his prostate was acting up, empty anarchic shit on nights like these.

"Washington's confused," Bondurant began, handing the cables to Becker as he peered owlishly through his reading glasses at Lowenthal, Selvey, and Reddish in turn. "They say they're getting more from Reuters and Agence France Presse than from us. What's happening? I take it Malunga has guns. Where did they come from?" He looked at Selvey.

"According to the Belgians and Israelis, they're Russian guns."

"What does that mean, that it's a Soviet-backed coup?"

"No, sir, but right now, I'm not sure of anything."

"What else could it mean?"

The room was silent. Becker shifted in his chair, searching the faces, trying to find the consensus.

"I take it then we're not sure of anything."

"No, sir," Selvey volunteered, almost eagerly.

Bondurant asked, "Is Malunga under control?"

"It's under control," Reddish said.

"Can the army guarantee the safety of the embassy?"

"If Malunga goes up in smoke, so will the rest of the city," Selvey said. "The army will pull back to protect GHQ and the *présidence*—"

"That's a worse-case scenario," Lowenthal intruded, leaning forward, his notes on his knee. "The paras seem to be doing quite well at present. The hospitals are evidently full of *jeunesse* wounded, no military. And the commercial section appears to be free of disorders—"

Bondurant waited impatiently, listening to Lowenthal do what he did best, supply a clever rhetorical context in which unpleasant facts could be embedded and neutralized, like wasps in amber. He grew restless.

"—in addition we've heard that some rebels have escaped by pirogue to Brazza. That's a positive sign too. We've heard a few Cubans might be in Malunga. If so, they certainly must be in disarray by now."

"What Cubans?" Reddish asked.

"We've had reports. The Belgians for one."

There were three hundred Cubans in Brazzaville, some training the youth cadres, others the local militia, the Défense Civile. When the President had appealed to the ambassador for the M-16 rifles which State had denied, the Cuban threat was the one he'd cited. An ex–trade unionist with prewar ties to the Belgian socialists, he was convinced that his old colleagues would stop at nothing to destroy moderate Third World heretics like him. A few diplomats, like Lowenthal, shared his fears. Reddish had a different view.

A month later the station had handled the defection of a Cuban captain from the Défense Civile advisory staff who'd described Cuban problems across the river—the anarchy of local administration, local suspicions and hostility, but most importantly, the hostility of the Soviet mission which had insisted on restraint. Havana had supported the Russians and had ordered the Cuban support staff to confine its activities solely to cadre formation in Brazzaville.

Reddish had offered to brief the ambassador, but he'd received a peremptory note as acid as any Lowenthal had gotten back following receipt of one of his memos: "I'm sure this Cuban's motives were eminently ingenious," Bondurant had scrawled. "Men who betray their countries do so for a variety of reasons, all of them ingenious, but necessarily so, I'm sure, since all of them are despicable."

Bondurant felt the same disdain for Agency case officers like Reddish masquerading as diplomats, but it hadn't been motives or his success in managing the defection that Reddish had wanted to talk about, just Soviet and Cuban policy in the region.

"You've been in Malunga?" Bondurant now asked Lowenthal.

"No, but Houlet at the French Embassy had some firsthand reports from a few of his sources."

"I was in Malunga an hour ago," Reddish said. "The paras are mopping up. In another three or four hours, it will probably be all over."

"What about the other communes?" Becker asked.

"I don't know about the other communes, but my guess would be Malunga's the trouble spot."

"So you're encouraged?" Bondurant asked.

"The paras are mopping up," Reddish repeated. "What I don't know is what's happening at the presidential compound or GHQ."

"The radio station is still on the air," Bondurant said. "I take that as a good omen, or am I being overly optimistic, Colonel? Radio stations are the first targets of coup attempts, aren't they? Isn't that what your counterinsurgency texts say? The President's still on the air."

"He's still on the air, yes, sir."

"Telling the rebels to lay down their arms."

"Maybe with a gun at his head," Selvey suggested.

Lowenthal leaned forward. "We suspect it may be a taped transcription. We've recorded the broadcasts and replayed them. The same appeal is being made over and over—identical, even down to the surface irregularities."

"What does that mean?" Bondurant asked.

"They may have the voice, but it's not entirely clear they have the man."

Selvey turned to Lowenthal, annoyed. "When did you birds find this out?"

"Are you saying the President may be a prisoner?" Becker put in.

"I'm saying that the voice is transcribed," Lowenthal replied. "Drawing no conclusions, not yet. It may be simple prudence on his part. The presidential palace is some distance from the radio transmitter. With guns in the streets—"

"I thought he had a private hookup at his office," Becker remembered.

"Whether someone has the voice, the body, or the man, it's a plea for civil order," Bondurant interrupted, his patience wearing thin. "Let's return to our problem. Reddish says Malunga is under control, but he doesn't know about the rest of the city. Neither do the rest of you. A breakdown in order is still very much a possibility. What if the rebels grow in strength and the President asks us for additional military aid, as the rebels seem to be doing over this clandestine radio? What do we say if he asks for military help, immediate help—helicopters, armored cars, even tanks?"

"He's got all he can use now," Selvey answered. "What he ain't got is command and control, the smarts to use what he's got. What he could use is military advisers, but ain't no one gonna go that route these days," he concluded, falling back on his Tennessee vernacular, a kind of irony which didn't endear him to Bondurant.

Ignoring him, Becker asked, "What if elements from across the river infiltrate during the night to reinforce the rebels? What if they link up with the workers party in Malunga and proclaim the peoples republic they've been talking about on this clandestine radio?"

"What clandestine radio?" Reddish said.

"We've had a report that a clandestine radio is operating from the workers party headquarters in Malunga," Lowenthal explained, dropping his voice. "The French think they've picked up the transmissions."

Bondurant gazed at Reddish curiously. "You doubt that?"

"I'd be skeptical. The party compound is demolished, the buildings burning."

"This was at five o'clock," Lowenthal added.

"The French don't have that kind of capability," Reddish said. "They couldn't pinpoint a transmitter in Malunga with that kind of accuracy. Their commo people can't even stay in their own operating frequencies."

"Then you do doubt the report," Bondurant said.

"Yes."

"But we still have to contend with the probability of foreign support for the rebels, maybe from the African radicals, from Brazza, possibly even the Cubans. Whether they have a transmitter or not, they may claim themselves a provisional government, like the old rebel government at Stanleyville. The question is, Do we move now or wait until it's too late," Becker asked, "thereby risking Dr. Kissinger's ire, as well as everyone else's?"

"Move against what?" Reddish said, annoyed. "How? The only thing you've got out there are a lot of scattered kids with Soviet weapons. The paras will be potting off singles all night."

"I don't think we need hypothesize about an imaginary scenario when the real one is ambiguous enough," Bondurant commented. "Reddish may well be right, but that remains to be seen. The fact is we seem to be blundering about in the dark without the faintest idea of where these guns came from, what the intention was, or where this bloodshed is leading us. I spoke to the *présidence* over two hours ago and told the President's aide that we'd do nothing that would imply a loss of faith in this government. If we were to begin evacuating our staff, at least five other embassies would follow suit, and that, I'm convinced, would simply play into the hands of those who are responsible for that mischief out there. At the time, I had no idea that the situation was as confused as you now describe it.

"Meanwhile, here we sit. You can't tell me whether it's a coup, a revolution, or a street brawl. You don't know where the guns came from or what they're doing with them. Someone is in the streets attempting, for all we know, to bring down a regime we've invested years in—money, military equipment, time, prestige, political capital—and you can't even give me a coherent assessment of the situation. Something like this takes people, it takes planning, it takes time! Yet you sit there squabbling among yourselves and tell me it has no paternity, that it just happened! Virgin birth, is that it!"

The room was silent. Bondurant had lifted himself from his chair and moved to the bar cart near the bookcase. He noisily filled his glass from the ice bucket and poured out a double whiskey.

"I assume that if the ministry of finance had pocketed some of the port improvement funds, I'd be told," he resumed sourly, turning back across the room. "Or if the minister of defense had been surprised en *flagrant delit* atop the privy council table, as Major What's-his-name told us at last month's country team meeting, we'd all know of that too. Yet a bloodbath is taking place, people are being shot down in the streets, guns infiltrated into the communes to be used by the hungry, the sick, and the frightened, and you know nothing about it. We've failed, each of us, myself as well as you. It's as simple as that."

He sank down slowly in the chair in front of his desk, his anger gone, one hand held across his eyes, his gaze hidden. "My mind's stuck," he muttered.

"Sorry?" Becker leaned forward, startled, as if Bondurant had suffered a seizure.

"My mind's stuck," he repeated, removing his hand. His face was calm but distant. "I couldn't remember the word for virgin birth. Dr. Merton at Lawrenceville once used it constantly to remind us of our ignorance."

"Parthenogenesis," Lowenthal volunteered quickly, like a nurse bringing smelling salts.

"That's it—yes, thank you. Ignorance was virgin-born, he used to say. 'Parthenogenetic nincompoops,' he once called us. Intimidating too. I've always had difficulty remembering the word, probably for that reason. Freudian, would you say?" He sat up, as if he'd wakened in another room, looking about calmly. "Help yourself, please. Everyone get a drink. Why don't you lead the way," he suggested to Becker. "Then the three of you can get your heads together in the next room. I'd like to talk to Reddish alone for a few minutes."

They sat alone in the study, Bondurant nursing his whiskey, Reddish not drinking at all.

"I take it that it hasn't been a very good day for you," Bondurant commenced sympathetically.

"Not very good, no."

"When is Haversham coming back?"

"Next week, probably."

"Ill-timed, wasn't it, his vacation?"

Haversham had taken a holiday in the Kenyan bush after the African Division meeting in Nairobi.

"It usually happens that way."

Bondurant nodded, putting his glass down. "If we know so little

at present and have claimed so much in the past, I can only conclude we're not telling all we know. That's reasonable, isn't it?" He
studied Reddish in disapproval, massive head cocked forward, eyes
peering over the reading glasses. "What are you concealing?"

"Nothing."

"Nothing?"

Reddish's eyes were a clear gray-green under the sandy brows,
but his cheeks were flushed. "Nothing at all, no sir."

"I find that incredible," Bondurant said in disbelief, sitting
back. "I find it impossible to believe that you of all people could be
so ignorant of what's happening out there. Where are the ministers
you're said to control still, the ones whose pockets you've been lin-
ing all these years, the ones with the Geneva bank accounts and the
Côte d'Azur real estate, the men whose loyalty you're said to own,
lock, stock, and barrel?"

"Shot. Bought off, scattered. They wiped me out."

"Who wiped you out?"

"I don't know yet."

"But they're dead. As dead as those in the streets? How much
did it cost you and the Agency? How much? How many millions?"

"I've stayed with the Soviets since you came," Reddish said.
"Those were my instructions, my OD. I bailed out of internal politics
a year ago when you took over." He didn't want a showdown with
Bondurant. If Langley and State got wind of it, he'd be finished. Not
an embassy or a station chief would touch him.

"You still had your ministers, like Yvon Kadima," Bondurant
said harshly. "You can't deny that, never!"

"Because of their jobs. Because they were helpful. Because they
cooperated in tracking the Soviets and East Germans."

"You weren't buying intelligence!" Bondurant shouted, losing
his temper. "That's a myth, your operational fig leaf! Don't sit there
and tell me that. You were buying influence, the same today as it
was three years ago, trying to control policy within the cabinet and
presidency as you once controlled the embassy! Maybe you can fool
Haversham, but you can't fool me."

"I'm not trying to fool anyone."

"Those days are over, finished! You're finished. When I came
here, that's what I insisted upon! The DCI himself assured me of
that, right there in his office at Langley—that the old ways of dealing with the President were over, that there would be no more midnight visits to the palace, either by you or anyone else. You might
have had a free hand in the old days, when everything was so con-

fused that no one knew what you were doing, when there wasn't a government here worth dignifying with the name, but times have changed. You haven't. You haven't faced up to it."

"I've stuck with the Soviets and the bloc," Reddish said woodenly. "I haven't talked to the President in over a year, since you came—"

"You went to Kindu a few months ago! For whom? For the President!"

"For Kadima. To look at an arms cache the army claimed was Chinese weapons."

"How did the President get the M-16 rifles? How did he manage that after State and Defense turned him down? Do you think I don't know? You got him those guns! You did it, Reddish—through your old friends in Euroarm! Don't sit there and deny it."

Reddish said nothing. Bondurant sat back in disgust.

Haversham was an open book for him, socially nimble but secretly sly, a Yale man who exuded fellowship with the other embassy undergraduates—his State, DOD, and AID colleagues—but a Skull and Bones man at heart. The secret society ethos and the condescension it bred had been apparent to Bondurant in an entire generation of Ivy League cold warriors at the Agency, many of them his close friends, but Reddish was an enigma to him. He fitted no niche Bondurant could recognize. He knew a little of his problems. He'd been an Arabist until the Soviets had wrecked his career in the Middle East; he'd bounced about the Asian and African backwaters ever since, never obtaining a post of his own. Bondurant supposed that he had a few old scores to settle with the Russians, inflaming the President's suspicions of Federov and his staff at every opportunity. He knew nothing about Reddish's divorce. Haversham had told him there was an errant daughter somewhere in a private school in New England, sent there after she'd twice run away from a Rome boarding school, once with two German youths on their way to the Middle East. Reddish had had to take leave to find her, retrieving her from a Volkswagen minibus on the beach in southern Turkey.

Bondurant had been uneasy from the first, but had tried to be sympathetic. In the old days it had been Reddish, not the previous ambassador, who'd been summoned nightly by a hapless President to discuss his problems—cabinet assignments, army nominations, tactics for dealing with the Soviets and the African radical states. The President's dependence had dated from the days of the rebellions when improvisation had been the style, Reddish had been the most adept at it, and the Agency had given him full rein. "He practically ran this country for over a year, just himself, no one else," Haversham had told him once, as if he were a rehabilitation counselor for Alcoholics Anonymous, "so what do you do with a man like that?" Langley's problem too, Haversham had implied, and Bondurant, not a cruel man, had understood. The mood in Washington had changed, the Agency was vulnerable everywhere, and he'd tried to be patient.

"All right," he said finally, aware that he'd already said too much, "I don't have time to pursue this now. We can discuss it later. But I want to see everything you send out, do you understand? Every word."

"I understand."

"Let's talk about the Soviets for a minute. Selvey told me they were Russian guns. How are the Russians involved in this bloody mess?"

"I don't know. I will in time."

"Let's hope so." Quite suddenly, Bondurant felt very tired. They'd talked for twenty minutes and nothing had been clarified.

✧ ✧ ✧ "What was it?" Selvey asked Reddish from the front seat. "A pissing contest?"

"No, not a pissing contest."

They drove along the river toward the embassy.

"I would have told him if it had been me," Selvey vowed irritably. "We put this goddamn country together for them, got rid of the Marxists, the Soviet stooges, then the Simbas and mercenaries, and they were on the road back. Then the President gets cold feet about not having a representative government and brings the old politicians back. National reconciliation! It's a fucking circus, that's what it is! We sold out—sold out the army that had whipped the rebels and mercs, gave it back to the politicians, and let the goddamn monkeys run the zoo!"

"The ambassador can't change the President's mind every time he feels like it," Lowenthal said from the rear.

Selvey turned angrily from the front seat. "The shit he can't! This isn't Paris, perfessor! It's Africa—the dead-end boonies! He could make policy inside the President's head anytime he fucking felt like it, just like the old days, right, Andy?"

"Those days are gone," Lowenthal replied from the darkness. "These are the days of coalition politics, consensus, nation-building."

"With ten political parties paralyzing this country? That's coalition politics? What the shit's wrong with you, Lowenthal?" Selvey demanded, his drawl cracked in exasperation. "What books do you goddamn city boys read, anyway? They didn't get the goddamned defense appropriation out of the cabinet until the army threatened to mutiny in the south! The staff up at GHQ hadn't been paid in six weeks! No wonder the old bird is dead on his feet!"

Selvey turned up the sedan radio. *"Citoyens, citoyens!"* the President pleaded. *"C'est votre président! Déposez vos armes!"*

The car turned away from the river. From the radio receiver on the floor, Reddish heard voices replace the static of the embassy communications net. A young Marine was talking carelessly to someone nearby, the circuit left open in the confusion: "Yeah, they're on the way back, keep an eye out at the gate. Squirrel Balls and Gomer too. Tell Gunny. Charlie Chan's with them. He didn't stay—"

Lowenthal turned. "What are they saying?"

"That we're on the way back," Reddish answered wearily, turning down the volume. "Becker must have called in from the residence."

chapter 13

❖ Ambassador Federov stood on the roof of the Soviet Embassy, a pair of binoculars to his eyes as he scanned the ribbons of fire dancing along the horizon to the south, beyond the commercial district. The rattle of small-arms fire had grown fainter. At his side was Klimov, his counselor but also the KGB *rezident*, who carried a portable radio tuned to the national station. The President's voice had been replaced by band music.

The two Russians had been drawn aloft by a Bulgarian report that the Belgian Embassy had been set ablaze by the rebels. If true, both men had seriously miscalculated the street disorders in the capital, and they too might be swept up in the anarchy, not a prospect they welcomed.

Below them, the embassy gates were locked and chained, the barrier reinforced from within by the three oldest embassy Volgas, driven parallel to the gate and left there. The shutters on the first two floors had been drawn closed, the ground-floor doors locked, and the small embassy staff told to stay off the balconies and away from the windows.

But the Bulgarian report was false. From the top of the building, the lights of the Belgian Embassy showed clear and distinct over the treetops, the vessel of Western interests, riding serenely intact, no flames in its vicinity, no gunfire in that part of the city at all. Klimov pointed off over the rooftops toward a building partially ablaze on the fringes of Malunga, an old ramshackle Portuguese-owned hotel where government ministers and politicians entertained their mistresses. It lay along the line of sight looking north from the windows of the Bulgarian commercial attaché, who'd telephoned in the report to Markov, the young cultural attaché.

"Probably Markov will be disappointed," Klimov said dryly from the shadows. Markov had been convinced the news was true.

"Just confused," Federov replied, lifting his binoculars again, "like the Cuban."

Before the Volgas had been driven behind the embassy gate, a frightened Cuban had scrambled over the fence to take refuge, pulling free from the local policeman who'd tried to detain him. He was now downstairs in the canteen with others from the embassy staff, listening to the national radio. When Federov had first learned of the Cuban's presence, he'd feared that the Cubans from across the river were somehow involved with the *jeunesse* rioting in the capital. Like his colleague Ambassador Priapkin in Brazzaville, Federov had little use for the Cubans. The Cuban military and guerrilla advisers to the Brazzaville Défense Civile were swaggering Marxist buccaneers from the Caribbean, opportunists from the left who were greedy for new romantic successes, like Che, and who threatened to drag the Russians into their hotheaded brothel brawls. The blackest of them were also racists, claiming that their African blood somehow gave them a superior insight into Africa's dialectical problems.

Federov's quickest contact with Priapkin across the river in Brazzaville was the sideband radio which was seldom used because the frequencies were monitored. He used it that afternoon, but Priapkin was in the interior. Klimov contacted his KGB colleague instead and was assured that Federov had nothing to fear: "Our warm-blooded friends are quiet this afternoon, even if the disinformation agents are at work with their lies. The Cuban protocol is being honored to the letter."

Federov was thus persuaded that the recent protocol of understanding initiated in Moscow and reluctantly agreed to by Havana was still intact. The top-secret protocol restricted Cuban activities in the region to cadre formation in Brazzaville, nothing more. Interrogation of the Cuban seemed to confirm it. The Cuban who'd sought refuge in the embassy was an X-ray technician from the Cuban medical clinic in Brazzaville. A confused, frightened little man, oblivious of the politics of the region, he'd foolishly accompanied a group of Brazza youths to the local stadium for the soccer game, borrowing a Brazzaville identity card for the visit. Returning to the ferry after the match, he found the port closed and the Brazzaville spectators being rounded up by the army. He'd slipped away, asked directions to the Soviet mission, and climbed over the side wall.

With Cuban involvement repudiated and the Belgian Embassy intact on the horizon, Federov and Klimov remained on the roof, spectators at events they had no part of, kept aloft by the night breeze and the bright moonlight on the river.

Despite what their Western diplomatic colleagues whispered of the two, if either of the Russians had an advantage over other diplomats, it was a simple one, stronger in its simplicity than the dogma both lived by or the conspiracies others credited to them: they knew what they believed. What they believed at this hour was that a military coup d'etat was taking place, its leadership that of colonels and majors, probably Western-endorsed, if not planned, provoked by the paralysis of an inept, corrupt civilian regime. The workers party in Malunga was resisting it, like the police, but the opposition would soon be swept away.

Federov wasn't involved in the anarchy, didn't welcome it, and had had no warning that it would occur. True, Klimov had heard some bizarre prophecies from an African official and informant supposedly under his control, but they put as little stock in his confused mutterings as they did his outrageous plea that for $500,000 he could ensure, for Moscow, "desirable results." "Results of what?" Klimov had insisted. His agent refused to be specific.

"It would be just as easy to buy the President for this half-million dollars," Federov had told Klimov, "and then, what would you have? What you have now, a nation headed for disaster."

Regardless of the ideological claims of some members of the so-called workers party, Federov had little sympathy for the *jeunesse* rabble of Malunga. If they'd now gotten guns, so much worse for them. They would be smashed, quickly and brutally, a fate some deserved, especially the hotheads and opportunists, whose disappearance would make the disciplined work of cadre formation that much easier. But the majority would remain confused and misguided for some time to come, as young Markov had been about the destruction of the Belgian Embassy.

As cultural attaché, Markov maintained discreet contact with students, so-called intellectuals, and the more progressive politicians of the capital. If Markov secretly believed those few intellectual sparks he'd nourished might take flame this dark night to deliver a unified nation intact to the future it deserved, Federov knew with the same dispassion that told him this was a military coup how deeply deceived he was. He sometimes met with Markov's students, most recently at a small reception given by the minister of education for ten university students whom the embassy had been permitted to give scholarships to the Komsomol Center School in Moscow. The ministry had delayed its consent for over a year, but had finally acceded on the President's instruction—out of pique, Federov had learned, at the reduction of the US AID educational grant. But even then, official annoyance wasn't so great that the ministry had paid for the food and drink at the reception. Federov had been billed for them.

Ten scholarships would be useful, but only a few would survive the school in Moscow. Others were also eager to go to Russian universities, just as they were equally willing to go to Brussels, Paris, or Geneva, not for ideological reasons but for subjective ones. Whatever their puffed-up professional ambitions, most were rabble, crowding the Russian cultural center as they crowded the French or American, eager for free films, free books, free lectures, and free educations, smelling of hunger, cramped quarters, foul beds, and dog pee. Federov knew what they were. They were rootless, self-deceived young men who hadn't yet understood their destinies. They wolfed down the fattest scraps of Marx and Lenin like starving street dogs, but left the hardest gristle on the bone. They had no teeth to find the marrow. Weak with hunger, self-pity, and self-indulgent sentimentality, how could they? Few would understand their fates during their lifetimes; most would carry their misery to their graves.

He searched nevertheless for those who would serve without self-delusion or self-pity, as he had served, but he'd identified only a few. Pierre Masakita might be one, but he was too singular. He was also a racist, and for that reason too a man whose time would never come.

In the *rezidentura* section was a dossier on Masakita, prepared as a result of his visits to the USSR. His most recent visit had taken place after he'd fallen out with the rebel leadership during the rebellions and gone into exile, resuming his old position in Cairo on the staff of the Afro-Asian Secretariat. He'd visited Russia this second time to examine the situation of African students granted scholarships under the aegis of the Secretariat. He'd visited Moscow and Frunze, in Kirghiz. He'd returned to Cairo after a month and submitted a report to the secretary general recommending that only engineers, scientists, and medical students be nominated for Soviet scholarships. A staff member had given a copy to the Soviet cultural attaché in Cairo, who'd found it offensive.

According to the report, the Soviet Union had depressed Masakita, who'd found most African students unhappy, a few despondent enough to attempt suicide. He'd argued that engineers and medical school candidates fared best in the Russian environment, their discipline self-imposed. The social science students struck him as hypocritical, but then hypocrisy was an asset in professing a faith in which one didn't believe. The simple-hearted and the idealistic fared worst of all, the former because of their simplicity, the latter because they found themselves despising the Russians as much as their former colonizers and thus had reached an emotional cul-de-sac confronting their own self-hatred.

The Russian attaché had had a confrontation with Masakita in the latter's office.

"You'd exploit our sciences but not our social sciences," the Russian had argued. "It's something we can't agree to. It's the one that built the other."

"It will reduce the health problems."

"You gathered statistics?"

"I talked with the students."

"You're a psychologist then, a psychiatrist?"

"No. I faced the same problems."

"How? As what? Not as a psychologist. How can you speak?"

"No," Masakita had replied, "as an African in a white man's civilization."

So Masakita was a racist, incapable of rigorous objectivity. Useful perhaps, but not dependable.

"Has the firing died down or am I imagining it?" Klimov asked, turning.

"I believe it's quieter now, yes."

Federov lifted the binoculars away from the river and toward Malunga. A pity about the bloodshed in the city, he agreed, but even victims, innocent ones at that, had their role. He believed in justice even more passionately than Markov and knew it was being denied. But injustice aroused in him neither indignation nor bitterness, only dedication and discipline. He had only contempt for those who savored the self-proclaiming virtue of their own compassion—"the smell of decadent roses," his Armenian counselor would say, playing Armenian folk tunes on his concertina; "crocodile tears," Klimov, a less sentimental fellow, put it.

Federov looked without despair at the present because he recognized the future. Justice and history were what he believed in, not poetry or pity. Patience was what he practiced. Impatience was heresy to him. The rootless rebels of Malunga, like the Cubans, were heretics who would postpone the future by mindlessly smashing the present. Order was what was needed, even a cruel one, like that now being imposed by a brutal army which served the same destiny Federov served.

An army truck rattled along the silent street below, and Federov looked down from the roof's edge. The truck hurtled on. The curb opposite the entrance was deserted, the policeman gone. Had he been frightened away or withdrawn?

"Probably we'd better go down," he suggested.

"There may be some news," Klimov agreed.

But Federov remained at the roof's edge, binoculars lifted again, this time in the direction of the old Belgian residential section along the river where most of the Western ambassadors had their residences.

Like the Cubans, they debased his beliefs. Through their hirelings in the local press, they accused him of fomenting sedition and subversion; yet if there were guns on the street this night, it was because the Western ambassadors had sanctioned them. A recent article in *Le Matin* had identified the Moscow Komsomol School as a "spy center" where KGB officers "like the current Soviet Ambassador" sent their "stooges" for training. There were such schools, but Federov sent no students there, and he wasn't a KGB officer. He was a diplomat, despite what many of his colleagues believed. He saw the suspicion in their faces and heard it in their innuendoes: they saw him as a sour, evil little man, practicing deceit. Cruelty and ignorance he could ignore, but these lies enraged him, not merely because they were false, but because they were malignly perverse, denying all that gave meaning to his career. He was a silent witness to the truths that events disclosed, not their satanic mechanic.

Following the most recent article, he'd taken his complaint to the foreign ministry, where he was received by the buffoon who headed the Soviet desk. The diplomat had listened in amusement, muttered a few banalities, and promised to look into it. Federov knew he would hear nothing more. The same week he'd complained about the article to the British Ambassador over lunch at the British residence.

"Well, don't take it personally, Georgy old boy," Cecil had chided, laughing mischievously, "but between us, it's perfectly clear what you're after. Of course it is. You'd like your chaps where the Americans and Belgians are, your military lads doing what theirs are doing. I dare say you wouldn't even mind your own chosen few on a local politburo, Moscow-style, sitting where the parliament sits, eh? But we all know that, Georgy. Good lord! Don't be naive. You wouldn't be doing your work if you didn't want that now, would you? And quite obviously, we wouldn't be doing ours if we weren't on to you. No bad faith, you see. It's what keeps the match in play, the teams on the pitch, precisely the sort of symmetry that holds our little diplomatic community intact—gives it equilibrium and a dash of élan too, I'll wager. I certainly wouldn't fret about it. More lemon?"

Federov had been too stunned to reply. Until that moment he hadn't guessed how his oldest friend in the diplomatic community viewed him. They'd served together in Tanzania, and he'd had earlier intimations of his English colleague's eccentricities, but none so conclusive as those words uttered at lunch.

The afternoon of the luncheon, Federov had arrived at the British residence thirty minutes early through his secretary's error in his appointment book. He was ushered into the rear garden to find his lanky colleague sprawled in the poolside sun, eyes closed, his collar undone, an aluminum contraption fitted to his neck, like a reflecting shade, to focus the sun's rays against his face.

It was so childish an apparatus that Federov was immediately embarrassed, but Cecil had shown no mortification in the Russian's discovery. He'd merely moved his feet from the cushions, unbuckled the sun mirror, adjusted the tie, and pulled on his coat. "Hullo there, Georgy. A reception this evening. Swedes, isn't it? I thought I'd better look fit. Didn't get my day on the river yesterday. Absolute sun addicts, those Swedes. Have you noticed?"

At Dar es Salaam, Cecil had been admired as a skilled sailor, the same reputation he'd won locally navigating his small craft on the crocodile-infested river; but until that moment, Federov had never divined its purpose. He was just a nautical sunbather, a diplomatic nincompoop, like many of the others, attributing to him hysterical, self-defeating ambitions which were as irresponsible as Khrushchev's had once been. Although Moscow had once had reckless ambitions for the nation, that was no longer true. Times had changed. His diplomatic colleagues from the West were years behind.

The country was a vast one, too vast. Like Russia a hundred years earlier, it was a ramshackle agglomeration of tongues and nationalities that had little sense of a collective identity. Only a strong, repressive government of vast resources could keep this abstraction they called a nation intact. By definition, its government would be a tyrannical one. But Moscow's resources were limited. Its meager financial aid was sent elsewhere in Africa, its political and military help to those clandestine guerrilla groups in Angola, Mozambique, and Guinea-Bissau, where revolutionary cadres were being forged on the anvil under the iron hammer of Portuguese rule. In independent Africa, where nominal independence had come, political cadres would require more time to mature; historical truths, like the repression of neo-colonialism, would be slower to reveal themselves.

Federov was aware of all this as a result of his experiences in Tanzania. Six months after his arrival in this capital, he rewrote the embassy's "secret" country plan and pouched it to Moscow with a five-page dispatch explaining his recommendations.

He made a simple point. He argued that if repression and brutality were required to keep this ramshackle nation intact, as he believed they were, then it better served Moscow's longer-term interests if that repression continued to be a Western-supported one.

It would be extremely foolish, he warned, for Moscow to encourage premature revolutionary activities, as the Cubans were now doing from Brazzaville, if as a result of their "success," Moscow would be required to assume the enormous financial burden now shouldered by the West. But even more costly, he continued, would be that burden of hatred which would inevitably be directed against any foreign patron that supported a regime that could only rule by oppression.

Federov argued that only when the political energies of the country were more mature—and a tyrannical Western-supported regime would speed the maturing process—would there be a greater role for the Soviet Union. He recommended imposing immediate restraints on Cuban mischief-making from Brazzaville.

Moscow agreed. Enormous demands were being made of Soviet economic, military and political resources in Southeast Asia and the Middle East at the time, and whether agreement was given out of expediency or because of the logic of Federov's argument, he wasn't sure. It was more likely that no one in the foreign ministry or the Politburo was giving any attention to the problem in any case; and for the Politburo to be told that a policy of indifference and neglect was, in fact, an imaginative and creative one would be the quickest way to obtain its endorsement. The Cuban protocol, imposed by Moscow on Havana, was the immediate result.

Whatever Moscow's reasons, for Federov the logic was so simple and so self-evident that he could never understand why his Western colleagues hadn't divined it themselves as a clue to Soviet policy in the region. Once the policy was imposed, he was grateful they hadn't.

Klimov had doubts: "A man has to be active," he'd said ruefully. "You'll grow restless, like me. You locked yourself away in that dusty little closet you call an office to think deep thoughts, a new country plan, and a week later you tell me a brilliant idea has come to you—to lock everyone away in the embassy too, like you, and send the key to Moscow. What kind of idea is that? In a few months you'll be pacing the floor, talking to the walls. Then you'll send another message to Moscow, just four words: 'Send me the key.'"

"Moscow has a short memory. They'll send back just two words: 'What key?'"

They crossed the roof and went down the stairwell. Markov met them in the downstairs hall, sent by the code clerk to fetch Klimov. He was tall and slim, his English that of an American, his French and German as good. The light fawn-colored suit was French, like the shirt; his cigarettes English Dunhills. In the canteen, he listened to American and English records. His father was a senior foreign ministry official, but the son was a changeling, switching paternity in the wink of an eye—now French, now German, now American. Like Markov's father, Federov was only a Russian; he'd never pretended to be anything else.

"Was it burning?" Markov asked.

"No," Federov replied, returning the binoculars to Klimov.

"What did you expect?" Klimov asked.

"*Merde!*" swore Markov.

Federov was annoyed. Perhaps it wasn't just pretense, these French affectations. Maybe involuntary, like the chemistry of the chameleons in the rear garden. What sort of world would that be?— hypocrisy become a reflex, a mutation fixed in a younger generation that had lived so long without revolution they couldn't recognize one when they saw it.

"What are our European friends doing?" Klimov asked.

Markov had been monitoring the emergency networks, not because this was his responsibility but because he was a born eavesdropper. How else could you explain his changeling's tongue?

"The American, Bondurant, is at his residence," Markov informed them. "He hasn't left."

"Sleeping, I suppose," Federov muttered disagreeably. He wasn't surprised that Markov was following the American emergency network. "I don't blame Bondurant," he called back over his shoulder on his way to his small office. "Not like us. If I knew as much as he knows, probably I'd be sleeping too."

chapter 14

❖ "It's certainly reassuring to know your chaps have their hands firmly on the tiller," Cecil observed, paddling himself about the pool in his wife's flotation jig, an ample rubber armchair with pneumatic seat, pneumatic arms, and even a small Styrofoam tray to one side, convenient for a glass, snacks, or a cigarette pack. "I must say it makes it much easier for the rest of us, but it does get damned tedious occasionally. Tiresome too. And so deadly serious about it, you see—"

A helicopter sped over the treetops, lights blinking, and Miss Browning's eyes lifted from where she sat on the edge of the pool, brown as a seal, her body shining with water, her bathing suit loose on her body.

"I shouldn't worry about that," Cecil continued drunkenly, "probably gone after Bondurant. Lifting him off to the President, I'd wager, for some midnight pow-wow."

"Things are certainly quieter."

"I would say confusion is usually in the mind. Dreadful racket it's making. I don't suppose they can see me, do you? All that noise—"

The helicopter disappeared.

"The pity of it," Cecil continued, paddling again, "is that it's just too bloody serious. I shouldn't be surprised if in ten years or so your diplomats didn't all look like the Russians, all baggy suits and bushy eyebrows, grim as old Georgy himself, gray peas in a pod. Do you know him?"

"Who?" she asked innocently.

"Georgy. Federov. It takes all the fun out of it, you see. I wouldn't want that. Good lord, no. Takes all the individuality away. Makes you much too tedious, too. No doubt about that. I knew at six it would all blow away. I have a keen eye for that sort of thing, like those buggers out there in the road. The bloody idiots are lost, you see. Sorry. Would you like a go at it?" He paddled toward her. As his voice stopped, his drunkenness came on again, releasing him dizzily in the pool. "Shall I show you how it works? Hideous color, isn't it? My wife bought it. She smokes, you see. Reads here, out in the sun. On the terrace there, she seems to attract gnats. So she reads in the pool. Quite fancies it. Shall I show you? You mount it as you would a skittish elephant in the Indian circus."

He slid out and stood waist deep in the water. He tried to climb into the seat, but failed and turned over in the pool. He gave up and dragged it after him toward the shallow end where Miss Browning sat.

"Do you want to have a go at it?"

"I'm sure I'd drown."

"I'm not very keen on it either, to tell you the truth." He climbed out, up the steps. "What's the radio saying?" The water had helped keep him erect, but now he tottered across the walk like an invalid catapulted from a wheelchair, knees bent, crablike, and had difficulty finding the steps to the terrace. "Just sailed the Atlantic in a dinghy, have I?" He tried to stand erect. "What's the gin look like?"

Miss Browning lifted the gin bottle from her side. "Half empty."

Half empty? Good lord? It was true then. Scuppered in gin! He shouldn't have looked, not from this beastly altitude. "Have to watch the next one, won't we?" he called cheerfully. What in God's name had she been filling his glass with—neat gin, no tonic, not even a twist of lemon? Her innocence was awesome. "Steer a straight course now."

With grave wooden precision, he mounted the steps. The wireless wasn't turned to the national station at all, but to Radio South Africa. Sy Baxter and his Sunday Sandmen were playing Stardust Melodies. A Miss Clapham from Bracken Farm, Kenya, had requested "Roses of Picardy."

Overhead, the helicopter clattered back over the trees, blades rapping like sticks in a fan, bearing to the north, toward the river. He didn't dare look up. For a giddy second he was sucked into its vortices, the earth whirling below. He reached for the table to steady himself. The radio was there, at his fingertips, but unable to focus his eyes on the minute calibrations of the panel, he couldn't find the national station. "Roses of Picardy" was simpler to locate, its familiar melodic line bringing the world back into focus. It was probably raining in Piccadilly, umbrellas up, bright lights swarming on the wet pavement.

"Are you all right?" Miss Browning asked, joining him.

"Quite, oh yes. Marvelous, these old melodies, aren't they? Bring back a whole forgotten world."

"It's pretty."

"Don't much fancy the orchestra, but I'm sure it pleases Miss Clapham."

"Miss Clapham?"

"Oh yes, at Bracken Farm, a regular Sunday subscriber. Sitting in her cottage in the highlands now, I'll wager, a few Rhodesian ridgebacks at her feet, still in jodhpurs, maybe her felt hat too, with the pheasant's quill. Her gin has a slice of lemon. I'm afraid Miss Clapham is in for a shocking surprise, Miss Browning. Would you care to dance?"

"Dance? Here?"

"She won't mind. I say you won't mind now, will you, Miss Clapham?" He rattled the radio with his hand, voice lifted. The music continued. "Of course not." He turned, ready for a fox trot, but Miss Browning was looking past his shoulder, frightened.

Two soldiers had entered the rear garden by the side gate and stood at poolside looking down into the bright lights. One pointed to the lights and then to the sky in the direction the helicopter had gone.

Cecil turned angrily. "Oh look here now, enough is enough. It's one thing to block my gate, but it's quite another to come crashing into my private residence like this."

The corporal pointed at the pool lights and then at the sky, insisting that Cecil extinguish the pool and garden lights.

"Don't be a bloody ass. Turn off the lights? Of course I won't turn off the lights. Why should helicopters come here anyway, you silly man! If they did, they'd certainly see what ruddy asses you've been, how absolutely disgracefully you've behaved out there! Now be off, both of you." He moved toward them, reeling, found the top step, missed the second, then the third and toppled like a stone into the flower beds.

Behind him, Miss Browning found the light switches, doused both the pool and garden lights, and fled into the kitchen. The two soldiers stood for a few minutes looking up at the sky, oblivious of a dazed Cecil, who was crawling forward miserably out of a gumbo of compost onto the poolside flagstones. Finally satisfied, they turned back around the house and went out through the gate.

A few minutes later, Miss Browning kneeled at Cecil's side in the darkness, a damp towel at his head.

"More embarrassed than stunned, I suppose. Silly thing. No blood is there? No, I think not. Haven't gone incoherent, have I?" He lay on his back, delicately holding the towel to the side of his face, looking up at the stars. His uncle had fought in Flanders.

She helped him into the house and he limped down the corridor to the study, where he stretched out gratefully on the couch. "To be quite honest with you, I'm not sure whether it was the gin, the steps, or the shrubbery. I think it may have cleared my head. 'Bloodied in battle.' Is that what they say?"

Miss Browning kneeled at his side, knees on the rug. "Are you sure you're not hurt?"

"Not in the slightest. Rather preposterous, the whole evening, but what's one to do?" He was painfully conscious of her suntan lotion, an almost edible aroma that lifted from her brown neck and shoulders. "You shouldn't squat there, my dear. Most uncomfortable for you."

"I don't think it's preposterous at all." Her breath touched his face.

"But it is, quite ridiculous." He tried to sit up, but felt giddy quite suddenly and sank back weakly. "I should get out of these wet trunks. You too. That's a lovely fragrance you're wearing, by the way, quite lovely." He heard an old man's voice.

"You're making fun of me."

"Oh, no, I assure you. Quite the contrary." He was aware of the damnable heat on his face, water running off in all directions from his brow and cheeks. "You're quite a lovely girl with a lovely figure and one doesn't mind saying so, you see."

"I do have a nice figure, I know, and I'm not ashamed of it."

"Oh, no. Certainly not."

"I don't mind if others notice, so long as I want them to notice."

"Of course not."

"I was beginning to think you hadn't noticed."

"Then that was rude of me, wasn't it? Is that the phone ringing?" He lifted his head but heard nothing. "I think we should get out of these wet suits," he suggested.

"I do too." Elbows raised, she undid the knot at the back of her neck and let the bikini halter fall forward across her knees. She stood up and stepped out of her briefs.

"I mean upstairs," Cecil murmured, gaping.

"You took a long time getting around to it. Why not here?" In full silhouette for an instant, she turned off the study lamp.

Having skated far past his intentions, Cecil was now floundering haplessly in dark, open water, struggling with a wrenched back, a gaseous head, and damp creeping shorts, which, stiffened suddenly by an improbable iron stay, like a balky umbrella, refused to come down.

"Move over," Miss Browning whispered. "Maybe I can help."

Cecil's was a military family, grandfather at Khartoum with Kitchener, father on the Somme just down from Sandhurst, gravely wounded, lying on his back under the wire while the tracers screamed overhead, not reading Greek, mind you, like MacMillan, but a casualty nevertheless, flat on his back waiting for the litter, as Cecil was now, unhorsed, supine on the couch, pressed down by a slippery but resolute Miss Browning who still rode her exhausted English mount over a course Cecil had jumped five minutes earlier. Lying on his back, fallen but not disgraced, not disengaged either, Cecil would have liked to remember a little Greek, something that found the quintessence of the moment in a barbaric world going berserk in the streets outside, since it seemed to him that his performance on the couch was as heroic as other English heroism on other battlefields—the lance lifted, the combat accepted, the aristocratic ideal of *arete* eloquently sustained in ways quite beyond the grasp of his American and Russian counterparts, who, somewhere else at that hour, were undoubtedly performing their drab custodial duties, gray peas in the same gray pod.

chapter 15

✧ In the dawn light the high windows of the old prison were a shade lighter than the stone walls. A gentle wind had begun to move, stirring the air without blowing away the heat. Still they waited in their separate cells, backs slumped against the walls, some lifting themselves from time to time to the high barred windows to watch. The gunfire had stopped now, and no trucks had passed on the road for over an hour.

"What do you see?" called De Groot, the South African killer with the anarchist's black beard.

"Not a bloody thing," Templer answered from his cell window. "Still too dark."

"It's over then," Cobby Molloy groaned, "and we'll rot, same as Mühler's lungs."

"Shut up, you limey bastard!" Mühler shot back from the cell opposite, lying tensely on his bunk with his hands cradled behind his head.

"W-w-when? W-w-what time?" called Sterner, the stuttering mixed-up Frenchman who'd gone berserk in a Goma bar and killed two Pakistani UN advisers. He began to rattle the door of his cell, afraid he'd be left behind.

"Fuck off!" Mühler shouted. "We ain't going! No one's going!"

"*Kangana monoko, mbwa!* Shut up, you dogs!" the turnkey cried through the small door into the passageway. "*Chiens! Mbwa!*" He beat his billy club rhythmically against the stout oak door.

Von Stumm laughed, a low guttural laugh, from the cot in the next cell.

"Dogs, is it!" Cobby Molloy yelled through the barred window of his own cell down the passageway. "Fetch your arse in here, you black bastard! Kick seven shades of shit out of you! You'll be wearing your fucking tail like a wog's necktie, blood and gravy, right around your neck! Come on! Come on in."

But the African turnkey only spat through the small barred window in the passageway door, slammed the panel closed, and returned to his stool.

"Chin up, lads," Templer soothed through the window of his own cell door. "It's not over yet, I tell you. He hasn't forgotten us, not Jean-Bernard. He's our man, you'll see. March us out of here like the Scottish Borderers, he will, with those monkeys out there blowing swamp wind out of one cheek and 'Bonny Prince Charley' out o' the other. You'll see. Jean-Bernard will send for us when the going gets quick and dirty."

"Stuff it!" Cobby cried.

"Stuff it yerself!" Mühler shouted. Von Stumm laughed again, moving to the door and looking out, his eyes as cold as bullets in the thin light. He was German, an ex-lieutenant from the Wehrmacht's Sixth Panzer Front on the Danube who'd escaped the Russians and found his way to Spain. He'd fought with the French in Indochina and Algiers before he'd been recruited as a mercenary in Marseilles. If he ever spoke in English or French, no one had heard.

"*Was ist, ein de Vaux?*" He laughed softly and went back to his cot and stretched out again.

"What'd he say?" Molloy called.

"He said, 'Stuff it,' same as you did."

"He doesn't bloody well care, because he's already dead! You're already dead, you bloody Kraut! Dead! You hear me?"

Von Stumm laughed. Sterner began to rattle his door again.

"Quiet lads, quiet now," Templer urged. "He'll come, I'm telling you." His voice no longer carried the conviction it had ten hours earlier as they realized a coup was under way. It was Templer, the cell-block leader and de Vaux's former adjutant, who'd promised them deliverance.

He was British, stout, heavy-shouldered, with a cinnamon mustache and a sergeant-major's booming voice, the same man who'd boasted to the American and British journalists before his trial that what he'd practiced with his own mercenary brigade was discipline as proper as in his own King's Shropshire Light Infantry in Korea. He'd been cashiered in Seoul, a detail he'd failed to mention. Now he was sentenced to hang for raping and murdering a Dutch nurse at a remote mission station and throwing her body into the rapids of the Lulua River.

Only twelve mercenaries were left in the cell block.

"Twelve is all, but it's enough," Templer was fond of bragging to the young, nervous British vice consul who visited him periodically. "Enough to keep the Bolshies out and the local scum from running amok." The young man's damp, uneasy face only encouraged Templer's rollicking imagination: "Enough to control this whole bloody country if it comes to that! Christ almighty, two-a-penny privates are all that's running this country, lad! Do you think you ruddy diplomats are safe down there in the capital? Never! The day will come when the streets will go up like straw, chappie! Hear what I'm saying! Those monkeys out there are just waiting to trade in their tails for a few Bolshie guns! Look what happened in Czechoslovakia! Look at Vietnam! It'll be AK-47s and Stalin Organs in the streets, and then where'll you be? Up here with us, that's where you'll be. Get the word out, lad! There's a whole bloody army in chains up on the hilltop, on fatigue for the duration, ready to get into khaki again. Law and order or the Queen's dominion, whatever you say—black and white together under the Union Jack. You're a son of the Commonwealth, are you, lad? Same as us, every one of us."

But it wasn't their governments, embassies, or lawyers they put their faith in. It was Jean-Bernard de Vaux. He had appeared at the prison unexpectedly earlier in the year, accompanying Colonel N'Sika during his first inspection of the para camp after assuming command. Darkness had fallen as the four men came down through the wire-enclosed dogtrot to the prison door, de Vaux leading the way, a Belgian automatic rifle over his shoulder.

Inside the mercenary cell block, he banished the prison guards, called the prisoners to attention within their cells, and unlocked each cell door in turn. He brought Colonel N'Sika and his two subalterns from the main gallery outside, and, as they watched, with typical bravado ordered each prisoner to step forward into the cell-block corridor as his name was called. The prison guards never dealt with the mercenary prisoners in such a way, even when armed; yet now they obliged de Vaux like trained dogs. He didn't miss a name; each obeyed silently, standing rigidly at attention in the dim yellow light.

N'Sika's subalterns hung back, but not the colonel. He coolly studied each prisoner in turn as he strolled through their ranks like a drill instructor inspecting new recruits—the haggard bearded faces, the matted hair, the lice-infested prison rags, and the bare horny feet in the fungus-dark prison clogs.

Only after the prisoners were returned to their cells and he stood beyond the cell-block door did he speak: "*Comme les chiens,* like wild dogs."

"Still disciplined," de Vaux said.

"Yes, but for how long?"

"*Nous n'avons rien à craindre des mercs*, nothing to fear," a perspiring Major Fumbe said, but his popeyed face belied it. So did Major Lutete's from nearby. Both were terrified.

N'Sika ignored them. "*Tu vas être le gardien de ces bêtes*," he told de Vaux. "You'll be their warden now."

Templer had had his ear to his grating and heard the familiar *tu*. So had Mühler. "*Tu*," Templer had whispered to the others as the jeep had driven away. "*Tu*—did you mark that, lads? Chums. Brothers in arms now."

"*Oui. Tu!* So what? What's it mean for us?" Mühler asked suspiciously, his whisper wiped away an instant later in a paroxysm of coughing.

A week later, clean cotton uniforms arrived.

"You can bet your bloody arse what it means now," Templer told them the same night. "As thick as thieves, those two, cooking up something! Brothers in arms, like the old days. He's our man, Jean-Bernard, still a bloody empire builder, like his colonel, you'll see."

✧ ✧ But now, despite Templer's promise of deliverance, the gunfire was dying out, and the former sergeant-major was growing uneasy.

"Chin up, lads!" he called. "It's not over yet. He'll come."

"In a pig's eye." Mühler swore.

"Two lorries coming," Molloy announced.

"They'll pass, same as the others," De Groot predicted from his cot.

"They're not passing! Look!"

Templer lifted himself high into the back window. "Great Mother of Mary! Come to us, Jean-Bernard," he murmured. "Come to us, you lovely lad." A jeep stopped behind the army trucks on the road above. A shadowy figure left the jeep and came alone down through the wire-enclosed dogtrot carrying an automatic rifle. "Back to your cots, lads! Look sharp now. Still as a wet dream, sleeping your way home. Not a sound. It's him."

A moment later the corridor lights flooded on, the cell-block door opened, and the cells were unlocked. De Vaux banished their cries. "No time, no time for that. Later. I need every good man I can muster. We'll go by truck to the armory on the other side of the hill

120

to draw weapons. They'll be watching, see. Discipline, that's what I want. Quiet as thieves but your backbones straight, hear me! It's not over yet, but in two hours it will be. It's good men and sharpshooters I need. Watch your clogs—like flint on steel here. Set this camp ablaze if we're not careful. Not a word now."

They followed him out silently, single file. Beyond the cellblock door he stopped, flashing his torch through the grill of a single isolated cell beyond the turnkey's table. Inside sat a Frenchman named Vitrac, the manager of a French forwarding agency in Brazzaville, Bernard Delbeques, Frères, huddled on his pallet, a thin blanket over his shoulders. His eyes lifted, terrified, into de Vaux's flashlight.

"Out," de Vaux commanded. From the corner, a light-skinned mulatto rose too, but de Vaux said, "Later for you. Go back to sleep." His name was Nogueira, a lieutenant in the MPLA, the Movimento Popular de Libertação de Angola.

"Sleep." Lieutenant Nogueira smiled. "Who will sleep this night?" He shrugged and sat down.

"Double quick, old man," Templer called as Vitrac crept forward. "No harm out here, just Christians and missionaries."

They moved again in single file up through the wire enclosure and into the truck, de Vaux the last, sitting on the tailgate as they rolled forward, rifle over his shoulder, clipboard on his knees.

Darkness still lay entangled in the trees, but the sky had lightened. The air was heavy and oppressive, tinged with the carbon of wood smoke.

"Smell that sweet air," Mühler said, wanting to draw in deeply but afraid of coughing.

"Lord God almighty, I never believed it," Cobby Molloy confessed.

"Queen's dominion," Templer boasted, lighting a crazy corkscrewed cigarette. It was his last, the one he'd been saving for this moment.

"The day will be hot," De Groot predicted, his eyes fastened to the sky, the last fading stars.

Von Stumm only smiled.

The trucks crossed the crown of hill and bounced down the narrow road between the palm trees to the secluded armory hidden behind a high stone wall. Built of stone and reinforced concrete, it resembled a small airplane hangar. A concrete loading dock lay along the wall nearest the gate. The trucks backed up to the dock, and they climbed out, de Vaux leading the way. On the far edge of the loading dock, unseen by the mercenaries, sat a small wooden figure two feet high. Crudely carved, it was touched with fresh kaolin. Its cruel cowrie-shell eyes stared blankly across the courtyard toward the far wall, where two jeeps were parked. A stuffed snakeskin was about its neck; an antelope horn projected from the orifice in its head.

De Vaux led the group across the cavernous bay. A high metal bulkhead divided the armory in two; on the far side of the bulkhead were the magazine and ordnance lockers. De Vaux quickly unlocked the door to the ordnance office.

"We'll draw weapons first, then ammo," he told them, stepping aside as the metal door swung open. "You tell me what you fancy, I'll tell you what we have." He moved away two steps, his voice echoing hollowly among the high trusses.

For the first time Templer noticed there were no guards. The trucks had gone too. He pinched the last breath of smoke from the damp cigarette butt and turned, puzzled, but de Vaux was quicker.

"Why don't we muster. Quicker that way. Step up, Templer first. Line up off the door. Molloy, you be the ordnance clerk. You're quick that way."

He tossed Molloy the clipboard and stepped further back, unshouldering his automatic rifle, though not dropping it against the bulkhead, butt down, as he seemed about to do, but stepped further away, the breech cradled. Molloy saw the larger magazine popped into the breech, heard the click of the release as the trigger was readied for rapid fire, and a split second later, heard the deafening roar which followed, wiping everything else away—the horrifying paralysis as he understood what de Vaux intended, the flame from the muzzle, the deafening reverberations from the steel plate, and Templer's bullying voice of deliverance now crushed in his chest.

He shot them all, Von Stumm first, because he seemed to have sensed danger before the others, Templer next with Molloy in a single burst, Mühler moving away, De Groot who fell sprawling, Sterner as he bolted crazily for the safety of the ordnance office, the others as they scattered in panic, still herded together, not understanding why he was doing this.

Vitrac, the Frenchman, knew. He had known as soon as he'd seen the wads of cotton in de Vaux's eardrums as he'd turned back from the ordnance-room door, giving up the clipboard—suspected as much when de Vaux had summoned him from the cell where he and Nogueira had been held since the Bernard Delbeques, Frères trucks had delivered the MPLA weapons north of Matadi. He had moved away, shrinking backwards, the last in line. De Vaux's final burst had caught him twenty meters away and sent him pinwheeling into the stone wall, glasses smashed, his face bleeding. But he was alive. His mind hovered, counting the single shots as de Vaux moved through the carnage. He had hopes, infallible hopes—his mother's memory, his wife's stooping figure in the garden of the seaside cottage near St. Lo . . . Five. Now six. His mind registered them, an involuntary twitch. Seven now! Just numbers.

A foot prodded him. He didn't move, his breath suspended in his terrified muscles.

De Vaux stood over him, seeing the eyelids twitch. "Don't pretend," he said. "Don't pretend now, Vitrac. You're dying." Still, Vitrac didn't stir. "A spineless back-crabbing little écrevisse in the nets with the sharks." De Vaux waited. "Don't pretend, little crayfish. You're dying. Five, six minutes, that's all. Do you want me to make it easier?"

Slowly Vitrac opened his eyes. He could see nothing. The numbers were gone. "No," he murmured, closing his eyes again.

De Vaux turned and walked back across the bay to where Von Stumm lay. "*Kommt nicht?*" he whispered, sensing a presence near.

Of all those in the bay, it was Von Stumm he most admired and pitied, the man whose biography he'd borrowed in part, the man he might have been. He left him there and continued out onto the loading dock.

The parking lights of the two jeeps parked across the courtyard had come on. Colonel N'Sika sat in one, chin sunk upon his chest, his hands across the automatic rifle across his knees. The shadows were lifting as de Vaux crossed the gravel toward the two jeeps. A light mist hovered over the city beyond. The finches were stirring in the trees and shrubbery on the other side of the wall.

Standing between the two jeeps, de Vaux emptied the magazine as Majors Lutete and Fumbe watched silently from the seat behind N'Sika. He put the weapon in the rear of his jeep behind his African father-in-law, who sat huddled under an army overcoat. A skullcap sewn with cowrie shells and leopard teeth covered his small head; a stuffed snakeskin similar to that on the neck of the wooden fetish hung across his thin wasted chest. No one spoke. Like Colonel N'Sika, Fumbe, and Lutete, the old man didn't move, still watching the open door of the bay, where the smoke still curled from beneath the overhang and out into the morning light.

"All right now?" Colonel N'Sika muttered finally, rousing himself, turning to the two majors. "Finished, eh? Nothing to fear?"

Neither Fumbe nor Lutete spoke.

"So they'll trust you now, eh, cousin," N'Sika said.

"His strength, not mine," de Vaux said, nodding toward his father-in-law.

"Like sheep," Fumbe muttered, transfixed.

"Satisfied, eh. Go see for yourself," N'Sika called back to Lutete. "Don't sit there. Your zombies are buried, like your suspicions. Go see. Go see for yourselves. Still afraid someone might give them guns? Are you small boys?"

Lutete climbed reluctantly from the jeep, followed by Major Fumbe. They moved too cautiously for N'Sika. "Go on! Are you afraid? Help them," he said to de Vaux. "Go show them my uncle's power. Yours too."

De Vaux helped his father-in-law from the jeep. He was still weak from the flu and coughed as he shed the heavy coat.

"What is it?" N'Sika called, troubled, his smile gone. "He's not sick, is he?"

"It's the night air," de Vaux lied. He led his father-in-law across the gravel, but the old man moved slowly, wasted by fever and now frightened by the recent gunfire, an old man who understood nothing of what had happened, only that his strength was failing. He wanted only to return to his village far in the north to die in peace.

When they were out of N'Sika's hearing, de Vaux said, "Walk strongly now. He'll be watching you."

"My power is dying," the old man muttered in confusion, gripping de Vaux's arm tightly. "Someone is taking it from me."

"Shhh. Don't say that now. It's the fever, that's all. It'll pass."

Gently, de Vaux led him up the steps and into the armory bay. The old man hesitated at the door, seeing the terrible carnage inside, white men's power he knew nothing about. His thin bony arm reached for the door frame, but de Vaux steadied him.

"What is it?" N'Sika called, standing up in the jeep.

"He's watching now," de Vaux said. "Be strong now, like Kindu. You remember Kindu, when we drove into the town and you were in the back seat? You didn't move, not a muscle. Do you remember how strong you were?"

"Who are these men," he asked, standing alone, sickened at the sight.

De Vaux told him that among them were those who burned his village in the north and murdered his two youngest daughters and left them for the vultures in the coffee-drying sheds.

The old man stood motionless in the bay door and for the first time in weeks de Vaux saw the dim light of recognition glow in his cloudy, troubled sight. It was N'Sika's coup, but the old man was part of its power, the power to safeguard and protect. He moved forward alone into the bay, de Vaux following, the two majors also beginning to mount the steps behind them, their fears banished.

book two

chapter 1

✧ During the East German freighter's voyage down the African coast weeks earlier, the weather was stormy. The African kept to his cabin aboard the *Potsdam*. Behind him spilled the cold green waters of the Atlantic—now violet, now indigo, now blue—as impenetrable as iron to the glaze of the weak autumn sun. His wrinkled twill uniform had been put away and he was dressed as any returning African student might dress after his years in Belgium or France: blue coat with flared woolen trousers, thin-soled black shoes with elevated heels and sharp toes, footgear suddenly made treacherous by high seas and the torrential rains that swept out from the coast.

One stormy morning the freighter took on water amidships. The gangways were slippery and the African slipped on a ship's ladder and gashed his knee. He was alone at the time but one of the crewmen saw the splashes of fresh blood. The ship's doctor found the African in his cabin lying on his bunk with a pencil in his hand, a notebook at his side, his leg wrapped in a towel and elevated on a metal suitcase. The doctor dressed the laceration and, as they talked, discovered that the notebooks contained sketches of small birds and mammals. The African described them as sketches he'd made years earlier as a young student in São Salvador in Angola. He could remember the day he'd begun each drawing—the hour, the day, and the season; all this from the angle of the sun through the trees and the small window near his bench in the village school.

As the days grew warmer and the storms passed, he would move about the deck during the late afternoon, ending his promenade on the fantail, from which he would watch the sun dissolve into the Atlantic. Petrels and terns swept in over the slick left by the *Potsdam*'s gliding passage; vaults of towering cloud, as black as anvils, traced the hidden African coast. When the stars were visible, he would bring his portable radio to the deck and sit on a winch cover, turning the dial until he found a signal from one of the coastal cities, bringing to him the African music he'd learned to live without. He would sit in the darkness until the sound of music was lost, drowned by the sound of the sea hissing past, in silence again, his isolation returned. But his isolation was less than it had been during the long years of exile, in the bidonvilles of Paris, in Rome, Cairo, and finally the Algerian guerrilla camp in the mountains. The recollection of those years was not so different to him from pain, but now it was eased by the knowledge that he'd survived to remember those moments, the recognition that in the very act of memory he would soon be released from them.

He was going home. His name was Bernardo dos Santos. He was a lieutenant in the Movimento Popular de Libertação de Angola, returning with weapons to infiltrate the savannahs of his native São Salvador in Angola to liberate it from the Portuguese.

Rain shrouded the Congolese port at Pointe-Noire the afternoon of his arrival, the steaming green hills hidden in the mist. In the harbor freighters lay like ghosts in the drizzle, their lights on. The wooden crates were swung to quayside, where they sat in the rain outside a warehouse, ignored by the Congolese customs officials as dos Santos waited nearby, his green uniform hidden beneath a dark poncho glistening with rain. A chief inspector finally arrived, examined his documents, told him that the shipment had already been cleared, and directed him across the port area to the administration building. Dos Santos spent an hour in the cramped overheated office, where a score of European and African traders competed for the attention of the few overworked clerks, waving their manifests and shipping forms, stuffed with francs or dollars, across the wooden counter.

Afterward, he was sent to immigration, where a suspicious clerk studied his passport, pored over his confidential ledgers, and finally waved him upstairs to the security office. He was interrogated for an hour before the clerk finally grunted his approval and stamped his passport. Downstairs, he telephoned the local office of the Movimento Popular de Libertação de Angola but was told by a sleepy clerk that the office was closed for the day. He telephoned the freight forwarder Bernard Delbeques. A truck would be sent immediately.

He walked back to the warehouse where the guns still lay at dockside among standing pools of water. He waited in the door of the warehouse, listening to the rain drum against the roof and watching the mist roll down from the hills, his hunger as keen as his despair. A dozen meters away, the *Potsdam* stood at dockside, its ventilators blowing the galley smells of the evening meal in his direction. Its world inside was warm, reassuring, habitable, like the Algerian commando camp in the mountains. His wasn't. He remembered both now with affection and regret. Thinking of the crowded customs office and the insolent clerks who knew nothing of guns transshipped through their independent nation to Portuguese-occupied Angola, he knew that he would grow to despise this country if he remained here too long. He smelled misery and hunger about him, as sharp as a serpent's tooth. Darkness fell. An old Mercedes truck with broken fenders loomed through the mist, its ancient headlights gleaming as feebly as kerosene lanterns. As it stopped near the East German freighter, he read the hand-lettered words on the door: BERNARD DELBEQUES, FRERES.

The old truck drove east from Pointe-Noire, following the narrow tarmac road that ran parallel to the railroad track toward Brazzaville. The landscape was cold and stunted under the driving rain. The truck crew was Congolese. The leader described himself as a *militant*, but dos Santos knew what he was; even before the crates were loaded at dockside, he'd asked for money to pay the others. He sat in the cab with dos Santos and the driver, a morose little Bantu who didn't speak. Behind the cab two Congolese laborers in dark blue coveralls squatted under the tarpaulin on the truck bed, trying to keep dry. The gun crates were uncovered and loosely lashed to the bed, bouncing and shifting dangerously with each curve and pothole.

They climbed the eroded hills and onto the plateau. The cab was filled with the fumes from the overheated engine leaking up from the rusted-out manifold. As the truck descended to the Niari River valley, the rain fell harder, obscuring the dense landscape along the roadway. The dim headlights barely penetrated the murk. Some miles beyond, the truck slowed to a crawl, and the driver began arguing with the Congolese who was giving him directions, speaking in Kikongo. Neither seemed sure of the road, and the driver thought he'd missed the turn. They found the secondary road ten kilometers beyond, a narrow muddy track that wound along a steep riverbank. Twenty minutes later the truck turned into a long tree-lined lane carpeted with palm husks. An abandoned planter's cottage stood in a palm grove, elevated on brick piers above the grassless yard. The driver backed the Mercedes against the high porch, and as they began unloading the crates, a light stirred from the interior of the cottage.

A man carrying a kerosene lantern came down the central hallway and out onto the porch. He was a tall light-skinned mulatto from Cabinda, wearing olive twill trousers with pouch pockets and a khaki shirt with most of the buttons missing. It hung open across his bare chest, where a crucifix hung suspended by a silver chain. His reddish-brown beard was closely trimmed; he smelled of stale beer. With a lazy smile that betrayed a canine missing in his lower jaw, he introduced himself as Lieutenant Nogueira, MPLA deputy chief of logistics for the southeast military district.

Hungry, wet, and tired, dos Santos nodded, but said nothing. He had never heard of Lieutenant Nogueira.

The rain poured from the roof onto the truck bed as they moved the crates to the shelter of the porch. The Congolese workers were anxious to leave once the boxes were transferred, but Nogueira called the foreman back and stood arguing with him. Dos Santos watched as the worker took something from his pocket and gave it to the mulatto. The truck drove away, and Nogueira gave back to dos Santos the franc notes he'd given to the Congolese at the port. He said the truck crew was paid by Delbeques. The laborer would have pocketed the money. He picked up the lantern, and dos Santos followed him into the house.

"There's no one here but me," Nogueira said. "What did you expect, a reception by the political bureau? They're all in Brazzaville this week—a meeting with the government. Someone tried to shoot the President last week, an ambush, and now they're nervous about guns. That's why we brought them here, out of the way. We'll move them later, after this latest business blows away. In the meantime, they're safer here.

"Did you bring any cigarettes? They're harder to find these days than guns. Now that you've come from Algeria, I suppose you're ready to start shooting Portuguese." Nogueira laughed. "It isn't easy. They're three hundred kilometers away. You have to cross through the other Congo first, across the river. Don't worry about it. We'll get you there. In the meantime you'll have plenty of time to think about it—to lead the intellectual life. Nothing but talk and solitude. I've been here for two years, and the problems haven't changed. I trained in Algeria too. So you're dos Santos. I've heard about you. Going to São Salvador, eh? You can take any room you like. They're all the same, all empty."

He took the cigarette dos Santos offered and lifted the lantern higher to illuminate the small room halfway back the long center hall. He continued talking, reminiscing in a mocking, unguarded way, like a man long accustomed to talking to himself and bored with it, as if existence itself had perished in the sound of his own voice. On the floor of the room were a raffia mat and several straw mattresses. Cigarette butts, broken glass, and dry palm hulls littered the floor. The rain blew softly through the broken window. Against one wall was a table and above it a primitive map of Cabinda. On the table were a dozen or so leaflets, and dos Santos picked one up and looked at it in the light of Nogueira's lantern. On one side was a picture of the red and green Portuguese flag and beneath it a crude message in Portuguese and Kikongo:

SALVO-CONDUTO

APRESENTA-TE 'A TROPA COM ESTE PAPEL E SERA'S BEN

TRADUTO UIZA KUSUNZULA KUA MASOLADI LE PAPELA

LAI IBOSI O MONA VO O TOMA LUNDUA

On the other side of the flyer, the Portuguese-printed safe-conduct appeal read:

ENTREGA ARMAS E MUNIÇÕES

E RECEBERÁS DINHEIRO.

"Bring guns and ammunition and receive money," dos Santos read, looking at the drawings beneath showing a revolver and bullet, four types of automatic weapons, a hand grenade, and a small land mine. He looked again at the front of the leaflet. "Present this to the soldiers and you will receive good treatment." He looked up. "Where did this come from?"

"Angola. Cabinda. The Portuguese helicopters have been dropping them," Nogueira said. "Those came from São Salvador. An old man brought them. He couldn't read them. Most of them can't. The Portuguese are wasting their time. We won't sell our guns. You can leave your suitcase and radio here if you like."

The other rooms were similar, except for Lieutenant Nogueira's, which contained a wooden cot and above it a wooden frame from which hung torn strips of mosquito netting. On the floor near the bed lay dozens of books, some piled atop one another, others lying open, face down on the unswept floor. There were books on geology and hydrology, physiological texts, a handbook on fluid mechanics, a biography of Marx, a treatise on imperialism and colonialism, guerrilla tactics, French erotic novels in paperback, a book on theosophy, and a translation of Lenin in Portuguese. Nogueira said that he'd studied in Paris on a scholarship given to him by a French petroleum consortium, but had left the university to enlist in the MPLA. He led dos Santos into the kitchen at the back of the house. The room was chilly and damp. Thunder echoed from the nearby hillside; the rain beat down on the roof. In the far corner a dozen beer crates were stacked against the wall. Nogueira took four bottles, opened each in turn, and put them on a wooden table in the center of the room.

"There's nothing else to drink. After a time, discipline goes to hell, but who notices? Maybe the termites and the cockroaches, no one else. Are you hungry? The beer isn't bad, and we've got plenty of that. It keeps your kidneys working. When they stop, you're dead." He pushed a bottle across the table.

"We had twenty recruits here last month from Cabinda, school kids, most of them, but we couldn't feed them. Hungry bastards. We sent them up to the training camp near Poto-Poto, where the Cubans have a mess. They ate well, and now everyone wants to go to Brazza and Poto-Poto. Do you think they came to fight the Portuguese? Shit no, for the free feed and then to learn Spanish. Get a scholarship to study in Havana. They'll go anyplace—Havana, Moscow, Paris, Brazil, Brussels, you name it. Just for the scholarship, that's all. After two years, so would I—back to Paris when I get the chance. The Cubans took fifteen last month, put them on a boat and sent them to Havana to study in the sugar refineries. Technicians, engineers. That's where the future is." He laughed.

"How many men do you have in São Salvador? Did they tell you? Already trained or is that up to you? Maybe I'll come join you. Angola's not easy these days. You have to get there first. The guns make it harder. The fascists in Kinshasa won't let you take the guns across. You can bribe them, but then the cocksuckers take your guns, your money, and shoot you in the back. It's easier dealing with the Portuguese."

Dos Santos had moved to the window. Lightning flashed through trees, and he saw a small muddy rear yard where the embers of a cook fire still smoldered under a lean-to thatched over with palm boughs. The thunder came again an instant later, shaking the windows and wiping out Nogueira's voice. The voice came back, as steady as the rain: "A woman from the village does the cooking, but she won't stay after the sun goes down. Afraid of her father's ghost. He worked here in the old days. A boiler split a seam in the cooking shed and scalded him to death. For a hundred francs she'll send a girl or woman from the village, but you have to be careful she doesn't send one of her sisters. The pretty ones have all gone to Brazza. Those that are left are as ugly as she is—meat for the maggots. If you're interested, the dogs will show you the way. That's another reason we moved the training camp higher on the plateau— the people around here. They're savages, worse than baboons. It's a pygmy plantation, that's what it is."

A few spoonfuls of cold rice and chicken lay in the bottom of the bowl Nogueira had put in front of dos Santos. He ate slowly, remembering the Algerian mess in the mountains, the smell of charcoal, and the chill morning air before the sun lifted over the broken peaks. He rolled the cold rice and chicken into pellets between his fingers and washed his mouth with warm beer as he chewed. The rice had been cooked many times. Lightning flashed as he ate, igniting the bare walls, the broken plaster, and the small geckos that crouched on the ceiling stalking the night-flying insects. Dos Santos finished the rice and pushed the bowl away as he drank from the beer bottle.

"... It's the boredom most of all," Nogueira continued. "After that, the local Congolese. They don't trust us, never mind what they say. The other Congo across the river is worse. Everything takes money these days—buying off customs, the police, the army. If we want to move a company of infiltrators to the Cabinda border, the ministry of interior has to be told two weeks in advance. The French advisers are everywhere. Do you think they don't know what we're telling the Congolese? If the French know, so do the Portuguese. That's the way it is with the metropoles. Don't tell me there's any difference between Paris and Lisbon. It's the same money, the same shit. You get fed up after a while—"

"I know Pierre Masakita," dos Santos said finally, resisting Nogueira's cynicism. He took a packet of French cigarettes from his pocket and pushed it across the table. Could he trust Nogueira? If not, what was left for him? "We were in Paris together," he continued. "In exile. Now he's in the Kinshasa government across the river. I'll talk to him." He emptied the bottle and Nogueira gave him another.

"Masakita? I don't know him. Isn't he the former rebel, the turncoat?"

"I sent him a letter, maybe a week ago. I told him I was returning to São Salvador and would need his help."

"Don't trust any of them. None of them. They're all the same, those bastards across the river. I told you, the Portuguese are easier to deal with. The regime over there is rotten, corrupt."

"Not Masakita," dos Santos said, smiling at Nogueira's reaction.

His cynicism was only a reflex; he'd been alone a long time. The rain drummed against the roof. The thunder rolled away to the northeast, down the valley. Dos Santos drank another bottle of beer as he listened to Nogueira's melancholy monologue. The empty house and the sound of the rain no longer seemed the symbols of his imprisonment. Listening to Nogueira and knowing the solitude that lay behind his words restored that continuity that had been lost to him as he stood alone in the rain at the port.

He could now think of the future again. The guns were on the porch, sheltered from the rain. Mers-al-Kabir was only a brief momentary memory: the rocking boat, the fierce sunlight, the splintered mirror of the sea. In this cottage a Frenchman had once lived. He had sat with his wife and perhaps his children in this same room; now they were gone. The windows were broken, the plaster fallen, the roof sagged; but there were lizards on the ceiling and finches in the trees outside. It was a beginning. To forget the past and restore the future would take time.

He remembered something Masakita had once told him in Paris when he was alienated from everything around him, like Lieutenant Nogueira, and existence no longer meant anything but the sound of his own voice. Masakita had told him of a Frenchman who'd written of that moment in history when the Roman gods had disappeared and Christ had not yet come, a unique moment in which neither past nor future existed. Men stood alone. Dos Santos had remembered it many times. Each time he thought of his own country and of Africa, of Western capitals like pagan Roman gods and of African exiles like himself, waiting in the slums and catacombs of Europe and not living as men at all.

He now told Nogueira of that moment, and they sat in the kitchen drinking beer until the cigarettes were gone.

The morning mist still lay within the grove of palm trees when dos Santos awoke. The house was silent, Nogueira asleep under the mosquito netting in the next room. Dos Santos went quietly out into the rear yard, stopping near the lean-to where the ashes were wet and cold under the palm boughs. He walked back through the palm grove. Standing among the trees at the rear, he could see the mist thinning over the valley below. On the heavy air he detected the fragrance of blossoms and ripening citrus. Turning his head, he saw a dozen lemon trees a few meters down the slope, their gnarled limbs still heavy with fruit. He moved down through the wet grass toward the trees.

He still hadn't returned as the battered gray Delbeques truck, with Vitrac behind the wheel and alone, came silently back down the lane and stopped near the elevated porch. Vitrac left the truck, slightly hump-backed, and moved with his head thrust forward. He wore gray shorts and hightop buckskin boots. In the doorway of the room where dos Santos had slept, Vitrac paused, studying the cheap tin suitcase and the portable radio. Nogueira slept noisily under the mosquito netting, mouth open, smelling of beer.

"*C'est fini? Tout va bien! Donc—* Come on. It's late. Get up."

Nogueira lifted himself sluggishly to Vitrac's voice. His head ached. He looked away from the bony face toward the window, found the morning sun under the shade, and sat forward for a minute before he moved his feet to the floor, searching for his rubber sandals. "You're early. You said ten o'clock."

"Early? What do you mean, early? We have a long trip. Where is he? Did you send him to Brazza?"

Nogueira rose and moved past him, pulling on his shirt. "Don't get excited." He went over to a small metal trunk and foraged among the dirty clothes. "*Pas de cigarettes. Rien.* We smoked his." He took a web belt and holstered revolver from the bottom of the trunk and slung it over his shoulder as Vitrac watched, baffled. From the tray he scooped up a handful of .38 cartridges, inserted them in the spare magazine, and stuck the clip in his pocket.

"What are you doing? We must be there today, tonight! What are you wasting time for?"

"Today." Nogueira laughed. "I've been here for two years. That's long enough to forget what I came for. Watch the books with your dirty shoes."

"Where is the Angolan? Did you talk to him? Is he coming with us?"

Nogueira didn't answer, moving carefully between the books piled on the floor. He crossed the hall, looked into the empty room, and went back through the kitchen and out into the yard, Vitrac at his heels. Standing in the palm grove, he shouted for dos Santos. After a minute he called again, and dos Santos answered from far down the hillside. Nogueira stood in the sunny silence looking out through the motionless palm trees and the growth of wild shrubbery.

"He's not a bad sort," he said finally, as if he were talking to himself, head lifted toward the blue sky where the haze was clearing. "But he's too much the intellectual. Doesn't talk, just listens. He wouldn't sell you or your Portuguese friends any guns. Wouldn't last in Angola either, not against the army there. No safe conduct for him. If they didn't get him, his kidneys would go, kidneys or bowels, all that shit built up, rotting your insides out. Like mine. It's the way you get after a while—too many ideas, too much thinking. That's what Europe does for you. Not like you bastards. You took it in with your mother's milk." He didn't move for a minute, head still lifted. Finally he shrugged, turning. "I'll go to Brazil. I think I'd like it there. What about you, back to France?"

Vitrac didn't reply. Nogueira looked with contempt at his haggard face and turned away, moving down through the trees with the gun belt and pistol case over his shoulder, like a *coupeur des fruits* with his climbing rope about his neck, on his way to the forest in search of wild palms.

Vitrac waited anxiously near the porch steps. As the first shot came, he shuddered in reflex, his eyes suddenly bright. Two more shots followed, muffled and without reverberation. He retreated to the kitchen and from the window watched the sunny hillside. Ten minutes later he saw Nogueira come back through the palm grove, counting out franc notes and dollar bills from a tobacco-colored wallet.

He called to him, still frightened, from the doorway.

Nogueira didn't answer. Bending near the wooden steps, he pulled a mattock and shovel from beneath the house and went back down the hillside.

That afternoon they loaded the crates in the lift van aboard the truck. Nogueira took with him his metal footlocker, a few books and dos Santos' shortwave radio. He burned the dead man's letters and papers, including the notebooks, which he threw in the fire without looking at. In the bottom of the suitcase he found a roll of parchment bound with a rubber band. Inside was a diploma from a French university. Rolled in the diploma was a polychrome print of a brightly plumed bird from the African savannahs—an expensive print, brittle with age, drawn by a nineteenth century French naturalist. Nogueira studied it in the sunlight of the yard, pleased.

"*C'est joli, eh?*" he said to Vitrac, holding it up, but Vitrac told him to burn it.

Nogueira only laughed, determined to keep it. "You've taken his guns, everything else, why not this." He rolled it up and stored it in the bottom of his trunk.

That night the truck crossed the frontier into the other Congo at a two-man border post on a track near the Cabinda frontier. The lift van passed through customs without inspection, as Vitrac had promised, documented as railroad parts destined for Matadi. Five kilometers beyond, Vitrac turned the truck into an abandoned sawmill. A light rain was falling. Nogueira could see nothing. Vitrac stopped the truck at an old saw shed and they sat in the cab waiting, lights out.

"Where are the Portuguese?" Nogueira said. "I don't see anyone."

"They're here. Just wait. Don't get out."

But Nogueira got out anyway. As he slammed the cab door the lights from a hidden army truck across from the saw shed came on. The truck rumbled forward and Nogueira retreated as it grew closer, blinded by the lights.

"Just stay there. Don't move!" He heard Vitrac's frightened voice call to him from the cab. "Don't move, for God's sake!"

Nogueira stood motionless against the cab door. The truck had stopped, the lights dimming out. He heard the clanking of rifles as the shadows spilled from the bed of the army truck. A powerful flashlight moved toward him through the rain, probing his face. He turned his head finally, blinded, protesting in Portuguese.

De Vaux stood holding the flashlight against Nogueira's face. "Who are you?" he asked coldly.

"Nogueira, Lieutenant Nogueira," Vitrac called eagerly from the cab. "Major de Vaux? It's me, Vitrac. On time, just as I said." His voice lacked conviction and de Vaux lifted the torch beam to the shrinking face.

"Get out." He pushed Nogueira away from the cab door. Two black paras immediately seized him and thrust him against the truck frame. "Put them in the truck," de Vaux told his para corporal, "both of them. With three guards."

"What truck?" Vitrac asked in confusion, climbing from the cab door. "My office in Brazza is expecting me. That wasn't our agreement. Listen, Major—"

But the para corporal rudely pulled him from the cab door and pushed him toward the army truck. *"Kangana monoko!"*

chapter 2

✧ Dawn was coming, the darkness beginning to dissolve in the streets. A crippled wind, laden with musk and charred wood, stirred across the rooftops.

Masakita awoke to a movement in the room, a shadowy figure hovering silently near the bed, holding something loose between his hands, like a garrote.

"Who is it!"

"It's me, Reddish." Fatigue had settled in his voice like rheum. He turned on the lamp on the bedside table, holding the bloody Mao jacket Masakita had been wearing when he'd been wounded. He was freshly shaven, his hair damp, wearing a wrinkled seersucker suit, but his eyes were tired. "You've been sleeping a long time."

"What time is it?"

"Five-thirty—in the morning."

Masakita struggled to sit up. The bandage on his shoulder was clean, professionally bound with surgical clamps, like a hospital dressing. He looked down at it, puzzled.

"I brought a nurse from the embassy yesterday," Reddish said.

"Yesterday?"

"Today is Tuesday. You've been here since Sunday. Don't try to move. It'll be a little raw." He pulled a chair from the dressing table and brought it to the side of the bed. "Are you hungry? You had a little broth yesterday. You weren't awake very long."

"I remember."

"We didn't have a chance to talk. Do you feel like talking now? I want to get a few things straight, the sooner the better."

"What things?"

"If you're hungry they can wait."

"What things?"

Reddish sat back. "The guns. Why don't we begin there. Where did they come from?" He grimaced, shifting position again, like a man with a backache. "They were new guns, weren't they? Still in oil. The ones I saw were still in oil."

Masakita sank back, staring at the ceiling.

Reddish waited. "Soviet-made, maybe Chinese," he continued. "You can't tell at a distance. The Czechs make an AK-47 too. So do a few others. Where did they come from? Brazzaville?" He waited again. "Who managed it?" But Masakita didn't reply and Reddish stood up. "I've got time. Maybe you need something to get the blood moving. What do you want—soup, broth, tea?"

"Spirits. Something strong, please."

"You still have pain?"

"A little."

"Broth would be better."

"Something strong."

Reddish brought a small tumbler of cognac from the kitchen and left it on the bedside table. "Where did the guns come from?" he began again patiently. Awkwardly, Masakita twisted to his side and sipped from the tumbler, grinding his teeth after he'd swallowed. "Brazza, wasn't it? Who managed it?"

Masakita eased himself back against the pillows. "You saw them?"

"I saw them."

"If you saw them, what difference does it make? Possession is all that matters, isn't it? Whether you can use them or not isn't important. Here you're shot for possession alone. If they were Russian guns you saw, so much the worse." He tried to sit up again, stiffened in pain, and sank back.

A siren sounded far in the distance. A night moth bounced against the window screen, drawn by the table lamp. "Where'd they come from?" Reddish asked.

"I don't know."

"You don't know. They were in your compound and you don't know. That's funny, isn't it?" He lifted Masakita's bloody Mao jacket from his knee and withdrew a package of crushed cigarettes, four letters, and three 9-mm cartridges. "Where did you get these?" He held the brass shells out in his open hand.

Masakita lifted his head to look at them. "Albert Matanda," he replied, sinking back, his eyes closed. "Matanda is the chief of the Mundi agricultural farm. He brought them to show me there were guns in the compound."

"Just the cartridges, no weapon?" Reddish spilled the shells onto the table under the lampshade.

"A pistol too, but I left it on my desk."

"When was that, Sunday afternoon?" He watched Masakita nod. "So you were in your office and this man Albert Matanda came in to tell you there were guns in the compound, is that it?"

"Yes."

"What about these letters?" One was postmarked from Paris, two from Cairo, and one from Algiers. Reddish had looked at them in the kitchen. The two from Cairo were from staff members from the Afro-Asian Secretariat, the one from Algiers from a man named dos Santos, asking for help, like the letter from Paris.

"I had them with me when Albert came in, trying to answer them."

"So you were writing letters in your office."

"I hadn't begun. I'd had them with me for several days."

"This letter from Paris is from an old rebel leader trying to put together a new rebel front, like the old days. He says he has local support in the Kivu."

"I get such letters all the time."

"So they weren't his guns either," Reddish said.

"No, certainly not."

"So whose guns were they?" He put the four letters in his pocket.

"I told you—I don't know."

"How did they get into the compound?"

"Trucks brought them."

"Brought them from where?"

"From customs, I thought. Now I'm not sure."

"When was that?"

"Two trucks came on Saturday night, two more on Sunday."

"As simple as that, just sent from customs. Guns sent from customs. What about customs documents, manifests?"

"Albert had them." Masakita sipped again from the tumbler. "They were the documents for crates of agricultural implements for the workers party farm at Mundi in the savannahs. That's what we thought were in the crates, hand tools for Mundi."

"Who was to give you the hand tools?"

"The DDR, the East Germans. They promised hoes, machetes, shovels, and mattocks. Albert was to take them to Mundi by truck on Sunday afternoon."

Reddish knew about Mundi. An embassy AID officer had visited the agricultural camp after the party had appealed to the foreign diplomatic missions for support, but he had seen no implements, no cultivation, and no crops, just an hour of close-order drill and a thirty-minute political recitative; Marxism-Leninism, he'd reported, but Reddish had wondered how the hell he knew. Before he'd

140

joined AID, he'd been a rural agricultural agent in Indiana.

"So what were you going to do," Reddish asked, "take the guns to Mundi until your people out there could be trained to use them?" He sat forward, elbows on his knees, shoulders hunched, his face beginning to come to life.

"We weren't expecting guns. We asked for support for Mundi—money, equipment, hand tools, anything. The Swedes and the East Germans were the only ones to promise donations. The Swedes gave us shovels and seed. The East Germans promised hand tools, fifteen to twenty crates, sent from Karl-Marx-Stadt. Those were the crates we were expecting."

"But they gave you guns instead. Your *jeunesse* in Malunga didn't know how to use them, not yet anyway, not until they'd been trained at Mundi. What happened Sunday? Did they get impatient, just grab the guns and run?"

"Mundi was an agricultural camp. No one was to be trained at Mundi with guns."

"Let me tell you what I know about the weapons," Reddish said. "First, they were still in cosmoline, which means they'd just been cracked from the shipping crates. Secondly, the rebels I saw didn't know how to use them. The AK-47 is maybe the most efficient weapon for its weight in the world, and these kids couldn't handle them. Funny, don't you think? They looked a little tanked up to me, like they'd been drinking *lukulu*. You know about *lukulu*, don't you? Something that gets your nerves together but not your head, not your reflexes either. People who drink the stuff do stupid things, like people fired up on dope or LSD. What was the *lukulu* for, someone's quick fix to get some untrained kids out on the streets with guns they couldn't use? What did you think?" Reddish asked, his voice gathering disapproval. "That the mobs in the streets were so fed up they'd help out too once the fighting started?"

"No," Masakita said. "*Lukulu*? There was no *lukulu*."

"So you don't know anything about that either."

"You're mistaken."

"All you know is that you were expecting hand tools—shovels and hoes—is that it?" He sat forward again. "That's bullshit, friend. You know it and I know it. Stop your lying."

"Is it for you to say? Who are you! Judge and jury both?"

"You're goddamned right. You used those guns. You took those guns from the crates and passed them out—"

"That's not true!"

"You *used* them."

"We tried to stop them! Nyembo was there."

But Reddish ignored him, his shoulders thrust forward aggressively, pinpricks of lamplight dancing in quick green eyes that, unaccountably to Masakita, seemed to be smiling. "I know people like you," he said softly. "Do you think I don't know people like you? You're not guilty, you're not innocent, you're not anything, are you? Just a homicidal little fuck-up who's always someplace else when the dying starts."

"You know nothing about me!"

"I know everything about you, friend, even your dreams. You're not a killer, you're not a man, you're not anything. You're just a sleepwalker, aren't you? Someone who'd crucify the bush and the rice paddies to prove your point, and when it got too hot for your kettle come crawling back for justice and a good lawyer like the frightened little shit-licker you are." He got up. "Drink your brandy, friend. You've got time. So do I. You'll need it."

In the rear hall Reddish called the embassy, but Sarah Ogilvy hadn't yet arrived. At the kitchen sink he drank a glass of water, looking out the window toward the river, where the mist was lifting. He searched through the cabinet for the coffeepot but after he'd found it, discovered the coffee was almost gone. He smoked a cigarette until his temper had cooled, still standing at the sink, doused it under the tap, and returned to the bedroom.

"We have nothing to say to each other," Masakita said as Reddish entered, "nothing at all." He had lifted himself against the headboard, shoulders cushioned by pillows.

Reddish leaned back in his chair, balancing it on the two rear legs. "You're making it awfully tough," he began again. "Let's try it from another angle. If you knew nothing about the guns, maybe someone else in the compound did."

"Impossible."

"Who else from the party leadership was there on Sunday?"

"No one."

"Why'd you say impossible? You don't think someone else might have arranged for those guns?"

"I would have learned of it."

"How?"

"My informants."

Reddish laughed. Nothing made politicians more pathetic than the memory of their lost empires; nothing made liars of them more quickly than their recollection. "Shit, you wouldn't have known any more than I did."

"No one with any sense would have brought guns into the compound."

"Not even your firebrand ideologues, Dr. Bizenga, Lule?"

"No one. They know Malunga wouldn't support them, that their revolution was still years away. After the anarchy of the past seven years, they had no illusions about that."

"Maybe they were out to nail you."

It was Masakita's turn to laugh, his face suddenly youthful, with that trace of spontaneity which told why the party faithful had been so fond of him.

"You don't think that likely?" Reddish asked, annoyed.

"That's poor Marxism, even for an American. People like Dr. Bizenga and Lule don't deal in personalities, just objective forces. I should know. They've lectured me often enough. No, we had our differences, but they weren't personal."

"So you had no enemies in the party?"

"I don't believe so."

"Who in the government wanted to get rid of you?"

"We know the answer to that. The army."

"Outside the government?"

"The Belgians for one. Your embassy for another—"

"It didn't happen, friend," Reddish interrupted dryly.

"Then that leaves us with the army."

"Tell me about the army."

"They exaggerated our strength in the communes, our popularity. They don't understand our weakness. They thought we were behind the student and transit strikes. They're also frightened."

"Frightened of what? Not of your *jeunesse*."

"Frightened by uncertainty, by the paralysis in parliament, by the President's paranoia, which made enemies of everyone."

"What about the Russians or East Germans? The hand tools came from there. Maybe they thought the party was moving too fast, that it was too ambitious—"

"The Russians know our weakness. So do the East Germans, much better than the Western embassies."

"You're a friend of Federov?"

"We talk occasionally. Not often."

Reddish had asked the question to see Masakita's reaction. Now he was disappointed. "You piss around in their garden, they'll plant you in it," he said irritably, getting up.

The light had moved into the room, the shadows from the lamp grown weaker. Trucks moved along the boulevard below.

"How many died?" Masakita asked as Reddish turned toward the window.

"A couple of hundred maybe. We don't have a body count yet."

Masakita despised the word, the symptom of everything else that was wrong with the Americans: the dissociations of technology, of men separated by their machines from everything else.

"And you knew nothing until Nyembo called?"

"Nothing."

"Nyembo told me you would have known, the way you knew everything else," Masakita said, but Reddish had turned away, gazing down into the street.

"Sure, like I know how I'm going to get out of this bloody mess." He came back from the window. "You say two trucks came on Saturday night bringing the crates from somewhere. Customs, you thought. Who was there to receive them?"

"I was there, alone in my office."

"Were you expecting them?"

"No, I was surprised."

"Could you identify the trucks?"

"Government trucks, I thought. The guard came from the gate and I saw them from the window."

"Does the government supply you trucks for shipments from customs or do you just requisition them?" He sat down again. "Or don't you make the distinction between party and government business?"

"Normally, we would have rented a truck to pick up the crates. But we'd been worried about the shipment. It was overdue. The customs office knew it was overdue, so I assume the director sent them on as soon as they cleared—a courtesy."

"Did he call you beforehand?" Reddish was puzzled. Customs didn't extend courtesies, even for diplomatic shipments.

"No, but I'd talked to him about the shipment earlier that week. So had Albert."

"So customs knew you were expecting a shipment of hand tools."

"Yes, everyone knew. Albert had been there twice with someone from the East German mission. They searched the warehouse, thinking they'd been misplaced. He'd made a nuisance of himself, as a matter of fact. Banda, the customs director's aide, called me to complain—"

"Banda?" Reddish broke in. It was Banda who'd called him the night before the shooting in Malunga, warning him that the army had Soviet guns.

"That's right, Banda."

"A small man, with glasses? From the Kasai?"

"I think so, why?"

"Go ahead."

"So Banda called and said they couldn't have Albert bringing East German diplomats in searching for merchandise. I explained that to Albert. The implements were important to him. Banda said he'd call me as soon as they came in."

"Did he?"

"No."

"When the crates arrived that Saturday night, did you look at the manifests?"

"No. It didn't occur to me."

"You weren't suspicious then."

"Suspicious? Why should I have been suspicious? The guard told me they were hand tools."

"You are a bloody pilgrim, aren't you?" Reddish said morosely. "No wonder the faithful loved you so. Did you look into the crates that Saturday night?"

"No, they were steel-banded. I told the guards to unload them in the rear sheds."

"What about Sunday? Did you open the crates when the second shipment came on Sunday?"

"No. I told the guards to store them in the rear sheds with the others."

"Who opened them?"

"I don't know. Albert came, looked at the crates, and went off to rent the truck from the Portuguese mechanic to take them to Mundi that afternoon. When he returned, someone had opened the crates. That was when he brought me the pistol and shells."

"Ordnance and ammo in the same boxes?" Reddish interrupted suspiciously.

"Yes, I think so. That's not right?"

"That's a bullshit scenario too, but go ahead."

"I don't understand."

"You don't ship live ammo with weapons. Go on."

"We ran back to the sheds and saw more crates being smashed open, more guns dragged out. It was a madhouse."

"Dragged out? What did they think, that the guns were for them?"

"I don't know what they thought. No one was doing any thinking. There was no time for that. The *jeunesse* had been badly abused by the army during the student riots. Two dozen were in the hospital. Three were killed. Eight disappeared, taken away in army trucks during the rioting—beaten up, clubbed, thrown into the trucks, driven to the military prison, and never heard from again.

We'd heard rumors after that that some of the *jeunesse* had armed themselves—revolvers or pistols, I don't know—so that they'd be ready the next time. We searched the barracks and the back sheds but found nothing. Then we searched those entering the compound. But we never found any guns and thought it was just a rumor."

"When was this?"

"Two or three weeks ago, maybe longer."

Reddish remembered the Belgian pistol he'd seen the rebel fire toward the paras that night in Malunga.

"So it's possible they thought the guns were for them?" he asked.

"I don't know what they thought. As I said, nothing made sense at the time. The more crates they opened, the more guns they found. We tried to explain that they were hand tools for Mundi, but that only made it worse."

"How many *jeunesse* were there at the time?"

"Twenty or thirty. The worst, the poorest-disciplined, assigned to the Sunday work detail. They attacked us with clubs and machetes when we tried to stop them."

"So you were beaten up, cut open. Where were the others?"

"At the soccer game, most of them. They were just returning as the army appeared at the front gate. Someone had told them. That's when the first shots were fired."

"What time was that?"

"A little after five o'clock."

"Five o'clock," Reddish repeated with a cryptic smile. "Five o'clock. At five o'clock the rebels were just returning from the stadium, the guns and ammo were there, like presents under the tree, and the paras show up too, like Santa on the roof. Everything like clockwork, is that it? Only it never snows on Christmas, friend, never—not in this goddamned town." He got to his feet. "You make it tough. You make it awfully tough."

"You don't believe it then."

"Let's just say I'm not convinced, not yet. You said something else—that eight party members had disappeared, vanished. Did you go to the President?"

"I went to the President, yes. He refused to discuss it. He said that I had been misinformed."

"Told you to lump it, did he? Take your licks with everyone else. What'd you expect? He's scared of the army too. Do you think the army knew what you didn't—that if the *jeunesse* got guns, there would be fighting between them?"

"I don't know."

"You'd better think about it then. The army's looking for you. They're looking for you right now."

"What about the President?"

"What President? Name your own. That's the whole bloody problem. It's all over. Didn't you hear it?" There was a radio in the living room, and Reddish thought Masakita might have picked up one of the broadcasts during the night or the previous day.

"I've heard nothing. What happened?"

The government had fallen, the announcement made at ten o'clock the previous night. A group of army officers calling themselves the National Revolutionary Council had assumed power, arrested the President and his cabinet, and declared martial law. Political parties had once again been banned and the parliament dissolved. The radio bulletin reported that the council had seized power to prevent a radical takeover supported by foreign-supplied arms. The old regime, paralyzed by inefficiency, corruption, and tribalism, had proven incapable of dealing with the threat. But the identity of the council hadn't yet been divulged; its leadership and numbers were unknown as it moved to consolidate power, smash the remaining pockets of resistance, and round up potential troublemakers.

But Reddish wasn't convinced that Masakita hadn't heard the broadcast, that his whole jerry-rigged scenario hadn't been calculated to conceal the fact that he had.

"Is that what the radio said," Masakita asked, "'a foreign-inspired revolt by radical elements'? By radicals? By Marxists?"

"They didn't say Marxists," Reddish replied carefully.

But Masakita didn't seem to hear. "Marxists? Is that what they were—the *jeunesse* at Mundi or Malunga? *Marxists*? They knew nothing about Marxism! Nothing! If that's what they are, then the communes are full of Marxists! Everywhere, not just Malunga—of people searching for the quickest, simplest way of expressing their hatred of their condition! Its message is simple: 'Deliver us from futility, from poverty!' Is that so hard to understand? Must you be a communist to understand that? It's as quick as those soldiers' bullets! That's all this so-called Marxism is! 'Deliver us from the past, from the present!' That's the message. It's one of weakness, not strength! Do you mean you don't understand that?"

"I understand it," Reddish said, "but it's not me they're listening to. You either. Get your thinking cap on. I'll be back this afternoon."

chapter 3

✧ A faint pall of smoke from the fires still smoldering in Malunga lay over the commercial district. The morning sun was bright on the deserted streets, the silence broken only by the occasional shriek of a siren and the rattle of army trucks deploying fresh troops or bearing away another group of political detainees.

"It's a classic case, isn't it?" Lowenthal said to Reddish at their nine-thirty meeting. "A military takeover, textbook style. They've smashed the rebels, taken the *présidence*, and dissolved the parliament."

"Too classic."

"But why no names yet?"

Reddish's mind was elsewhere. He'd run out of cigarettes and now lit a cold cigar he had no appetite for. "I don't know. Maybe they're still running scared." He chased away the smoke with his hand.

"Scared? Who's left to be scared of?"

At seven o'clock the previous evening, the commo chief from upstairs had brought Reddish the first intercepts from army GHQ to units in the interior, appealing for support for the new Revolutionary Council. By ten, when the radio announcement had come announcing the fall of the regime, only three of the five army commands in the interior had pledged their support.

"Everybody," Reddish said. "The army in the bush, us, the Belgians. You name it." His eyes roamed the desktop restlessly. He knew what Lowenthal would write of Sunday's events, and he was worried. "Masakita's still on the prowl and that probably scares them too."

"Some say his body was found in the wrecked compound."

"Like the phantom transmitter?" Reddish asked, his gaze resting coolly on Lowenthal's anxious face.

148

"I admit it's still a little confusing, isn't it? But certainly you must have some suspicion about the new council, who the leader is. You must have a few clues."

"None at all." He wasn't prepared to write the political section's cables for them.

"Selvey seems to have drawn a blank too. I find that a bit puzzling, I must say."

Maybe a solitary, Reddish had thought, someone whose genius wasn't recognized until it was there; the man who'd remained hidden all these years, lying beyond all conceivable expectations until his actions declared him no longer incognito. "It's all screwed up," he said.

Lowenthal got up, leaving behind on Reddish's desk a copy of the political section's cable reporting the regime's fall. "Military Frustrates Radicals' Coup Attempt," read the subject caption. "If you get anything new, let me know, will you?" Lowenthal asked, still disappointed. "Becker and I are working on a wrap-up cable."

"It's not over yet. You'd better wait."

But Lowenthal didn't turn as he went out.

"My, aren't we grumpy this morning," said Sarah Ogilvy as she crossed in front of his desk with a small green watering can. She was in her mid-forties, as thin as a rake, with salt-and-pepper hair and an acerbic tongue that was the despair of the younger secretaries at the embassy. They saw in her the inevitable spinsterhood of the career service; she found in them the irresponsibility of girls who hadn't yet decided whether they wanted a career, an affair, or a husband. She'd worked with Reddish in the Middle East and had rejoined him in Africa, hoping to recoup her savings with the local hardship bonus after a five-year posting in Paris.

She opened the blinds and watered the potted plants she kept on his windowsill where the morning sun reached them.

"We've got enough to do around here without that," Reddish complained.

"It must be the cigar," she replied acidly, still watering the plants. "It's really too early for cigars, especially half-smoked ones."

"Why don't you find me some cigarettes then?"

Part of Reddish's frustration lay on the desk blotter in front of him. The previous day he'd searched the files for any recent reports on clandestine arms movements which might explain the Soviet-made guns in Malunga. Sarah had searched Haversham's reading file and had discovered a cache of reports bundled together and squirreled away in Haversham's safe drawer. There were six re-

149

ports in all describing Soviet arms shipments to MPLA units in Angola and Cabinda, all in chronological sequence and obtained within the past two months from intelligence sources in Istanbul, Antwerp, Algiers, and Paris.

She'd also brought with them a routing slip from Colonel Selvey's office which she believed had been attached to the six reports but had fallen free. The routing slip was from Major Miles, the army attaché, to Colonel Selvey, but the handwriting was barely legible: "Re Major Lutete: we've been [indecipherable] this guy for ten months. Can Les help out? We need more stuff."

"This still doesn't make sense to me," Reddish complained now. "Are you sure this buck slip was attached to these reports?"

"Positive." She put down the watering can and crossed to his desk, looking at it again. "Yes, I'm sure."

"Then what the hell's it say?"

She studied the handwriting again, frowning as she brought it closer. "We've been—" She stopped and began again. "We've been . . . avoiding this guy for ten months. Can Les help out? We need more stuff."

"Avoiding?" Reddish asked dubiously, taking back the slip. "Avoiding?"

"I'm sure that's what it says."

"I don't read that as an a."

"It's a very poor a, but the whole thing is a terrible scrawl anyway. What difference does it make?"

"Can Les help out? How could Haversham help out if they were avoiding this guy Lutete?" He looked up at her, waiting.

"I don't know. Major Miles wanted Selvey to ask Haversham to help with Major Lutete, whoever he is. Who is he?"

"Major Lutete? Some jerk up at GHQ, I think."

"Didn't Haversham mention it to you?"

"No." He continued to study the routing slip. "I don't think that's what it says. I don't think 'avoiding' is the right word."

"Maybe your eyesight would be improved if you got rid of those ridiculous glasses."

"Yeah, and maybe my disposition would be better if I knew what the hell was going on around here."

"Probably Haversham didn't want to bother you with it," she suggested. "It's a military matter anyway."

"Are you sure this routing slip was attached to these six reports?"

"You're never satisfied, are you?" She left his office and returned a minute later with Haversham's reading file, which she spread on the desk in front of him. A few paper clips lay in the seam, fallen free from the documents within. "The six reports and the routing slip were right here, behind these letters."

"Maybe the slip was attached to the letters."

She turned over the letters on the other leaf of the folder. One was a typewritten note from Sylvia Haversham to the GSO asking for new drapes for the sewing room, the other a note from Sylvia to the commissary complaining about weevils in the flour. Haversham hadn't forwarded either of them.

"I guess that makes it official," Reddish conceded, giving her back the folder. " 'Weevils in the flour.' That's bad. Maybe Sylvia Haversham did it."

"Did what?"

But Reddish didn't answer, gazing thoughtfully out the window, as if something had just occurred to him.

◇ ◇ The country team meeting, twice postponed the previous day, was scheduled for eleven o'clock. Reddish was ten minutes late as he crossed the sunny silence of the interior courtyard, where a set of outside steps climbed to the ambassador's suite and conference room on the second floor. In the APO mail room he'd found a letter from his daughter awaiting him, postmarked from the New England village near her school. He stopped as he read the first sentences:

Dear Daddy:

Don't get excited, I'm OK. I'm writing this in the library which is pretty creepy this time of nite, trying to write a stupid paper on Thucydides and the war between Athens and Sparta.

"Hey, Mr. Reddish, sir," called the Marine receptionist from the doorway behind him, "they're looking for you upstairs. Miss Browning's been calling all over."

He moved on. In the center of the courtyard a jet of water splashed into a dark pool where a few plastic water lilies lay. An egret with soiled plumage stood at the edge of the pool, his black eyes fixed on the gassy silence about him. No fish or algae were in the pool, whose recirculated waters were kept clear with swimming pool compound following the ambassador's secretary's complaints about swamp odors in the courtyard. The egret had great difficulty balancing himself on one leg. His wings had been clipped by his proprietor, the general services officer, who managed the housekeeping staff, courted the senior officers, and lavished upon them the patronage he withheld from the nondiplomatic staff, like most of the third-floor communicators.

At the top of the steps, Reddish paused again over the letter:

I started looking through old National Geographics, finding the places we'd been, like Palmyra, Damascus, and everyplace else. I remembered the picnics we used to have, the way the sunlight was, our Arab cooks and drivers, and everyone else I loved when we were all together, you and mommy and me, and then I started to cry right here in the library with everyone looking at me like I was having a nervous breakdown or something—

"You're late," Miss Browning murmured without looking up from her typewriter. Taggert sat nearby, freshly groomed, each red hair in place as he guarded the door to the ambassador's conference room. Miss Browning, substituting briefly for the ambassador's secretary, had adopted the latter's imperious ways. The older woman disapproved of Reddish, but her instincts were social, not professional. He was never included on the ambassador's dinner or luncheon lists, seldom summoned to the privacy of his office, and was never the recipient of his telephone calls. In the absence of the ambassador's favor, she saw no reason to confer her own; Miss Browning was of the same disposition.

Taggert's duty at the outside door was normally that of one of the Marines; he would have been inside with the others except for the humiliation of the midnight dousing in the club pool, still fresh in his memory, even fresher in the memories of a few inside.

Reddish went in without waiting for the ceremonial door opening. He didn't care much for country team meetings and avoided them when he could, but Haversham's absence now made that impossible. For him, virtuosity in a crowded committee room meant little in the grayer world beyond, where clever answers weren't necessarily correct simply because they sounded brilliant around a board-room table.

The ambassador sat at the far end of the table, flanked by Becker and Lowenthal. The economic counselor and AID director sat farther along. Colonel Selvey slouched in the middle opposite a red-faced General Leggard, the newly arrived chief of the US military mission. The chairs along the walls were crowded with those of lesser rank, all invited guests on this solemn occasion, like freshmen at a graduate school colloquium.

Reddish took Haversham's vacant chair at the front of the table. To his right sat the administrative counselor, to his left Dick Franz, the USIS public affairs officer. He had once been a radio announcer and European stringer for a major news network. Wisdom and authority were present in the resonance of his voice, but without someone's prepared text he was an actor without a script, his sonority dribbling into clever quips and cleverer gossip.

Franz passed him a copy of the draft telegram that Becker was now explaining. Becker and Lowenthal had worked on it most of the morning, describing for Washington the events that had led to the fall of the old regime. Reddish skimmed through it quickly, searching for conclusions. They were identical to those of the national radio bulletin announcing the fall: the military had seized power when the President, paralyzed by cabinet and parliamentary discord, had failed to meet the challenge of the radical left armed with foreign-made guns.

Reddish wasn't surprised by the analysis, which was plausible, if premature; but only diplomats like them could have written it, and only fellow careerists back in Washington could have believed it. They had no time to believe anything else. Like most country team meetings, the cable was diverting theater but dismal history. Those around the table were often convinced of the guile and duplicity of foreign political motivation, but they had little insight into their own.

"... we think it reasonably accurate to say that a coup d'etat has taken place and that it was led by the military," Lowenthal was saying. "In the classical sense it should undoubtedly be called a countercoup, since there is undeniable evidence that foreign-made arms were introduced into the capital on Sunday, if not earlier, with the intent of mobilizing the communes and overthrowing the regime. The military struck only when it was convinced of the likelihood of success by the rebels. Quite obviously, they saw the possibility of a radical takeover...."

Reddish looked again at the cable as Lowenthal droned on.

"... we've known for some time about the paramilitary camp at Mundi," Lowenthal observed as an addendum to the cable was being passed out, "although we didn't deduce its specific purpose at the time. You'll recall we did a cable on the subject a few months back."

Reddish remembered that Lowenthal had gotten excited about

the AID officer's report on the Marxists-Leninists at Mundi and had cribbed the most colorful passages for his own cable to Washington, reporting a paramilitary brigade in the making at the agricultural camp. He also knew that few would recall.

"What cable?" he broke in carelessly.

Lowenthal gave him an injured stare: "The workers party camp at Mundi. You remember. We discussed it in draft."

"I don't remember anything about guns. Did you say anything about guns at Mundi?" He wanted to slow the momentum.

"Not at the time, no."

"So no one reported anything about guns at Mundi."

"No, not guns," Lowenthal replied, surprised now. "But certainly everything else."

Colonel Selvey stirred restlessly in his chair; Bondurant peered at Reddish, troubled. Becker lifted a cable from the file folder in front of him: "The cable's here if you want to look at it. Go ahead, Simon."

"Your sciatica acting up?" Selvey grumbled as he slid the cable toward Reddish. Reddish studied it without interest as Lowenthal described the party's radical ties, Masakita's background, and the ten Komsomol scholarships.

" . . . on the other hand there was nothing ambiguous about the origin of the weapons identified in Malunga. Every eyewitness tells us pretty much the same. The French and Belgian accounts are congruent with our own. So what we know certainly suggests Soviet involvement in one form or another, as the announcement over national radio hinted last night."

Reddish looked up quickly. "Was that the hint?"

"Sorry?" Lowenthal turned blankly.

"The radio said 'radical elements,' not Soviet involvement. Was that the hint?"

"Which?"

"That the Sovs were behind it."

"We've been through all that, Andy," Becker intruded. "We've discussed precisely what the radio announcement did and didn't say. Dick has the transcripts if you're interested."

Franz pushed a wad of wireless reports in front of Reddish.

"Let's let Simon finish," Bondurant ruled.

Lowenthal took an additional ten minutes."I think that just about sums it up," he concluded. "If I've left something out, we can pick it up in discussion."

Becker sat back, beginning to poll the table. The economic

counselor contributed a few comments. Deliberate, slow-witted, he was a man no one wished ill, but he was usually ignored in executive policy sessions. Becker and Lowenthal had ignored him that morning, and now he drew their attention to their omissions: rising prices, two devaluations, the student and transit strikes of the previous spring, all evidence of growing popular discontent with the regime.

Reddish listened as the voice rumbled on like a coal train past a crossing: IMF statistics, external debt financing, cost-of-living indices, commodity prices. . . . Lowenthal began to fidget, pencil dropped aside.

Throw him a sop, Reddish thought, teeth on edge. Get him on board, for God's sake.

"If we didn't go into those details, it was because we believed them implicit," Lowenthal said consolingly. "We've reported a great deal on the subject over the past several months."

Almost as if you knew, Reddish's gaze seemed to say as it traveled to Lowenthal.

The economic counselor nodded, not convinced.

"We were also concerned about brevity," Becker conceded sympathetically, "but you may be right. Why don't you give us some language, a paragraph or two. Don't you think that would do it?"

"Oh certainly, that would do it." He turned to the two economic officers sitting against the wall behind him. Their pencils began to move.

"Concluding that the workers party knew far better than most the economic malaise in Malunga," Lowenthal suggested. "After all, they helped organize the transit strike."

"Something like that," Becker murmured with a libertarian's vagueness. "General Leggard?"

Newly arrived from Germany and the First Infantry Division at Göppingen, the general had a soldier's sense of the battle zone, bright colors on bright maps with plastic overlays. He'd spent two days in battle dress during the Czech crisis, which had taught him a thing or two, Reddish remembered: the Russians were Nazis with atomic artillery and Fishbed fighters.

"You say here a low-risk opportunity for the Sovs," the general began, remembering his strategic intelligence brief at Frankfurt six months earlier—shipping lanes, strategic minerals, overflight and landing rights. "I'm not so sure about that. It seems to me the stakes are pretty high—the strategic stakes I'm talking about. This is the high ground in Africa. If this country goes, then everything south of here will go too in time. So I'm not sure I'd agree with that—a low-risk opportunity for the Russians."

"I meant opportunity, General, not the stakes," Becker replied soothingly. "A low-risk opportunity for Moscow. If these rebels succeeded, well and good. If not, then they'd lost nothing for the time being. The Soviets have been shut out locally, as you know. Since they weren't directly involved with the shoot-up in Malunga, it was a low-risk opportunity. I agree with you completely about the stakes. They were very high indeed."

Reddish found the language in the cable he was searching for and underlined it. *"Soviet and Cuban involvement seems clear."*

"Anything else?" Becker queried cheerfully.

"Yeah," Reddish said, sitting up. "Now that we've got your conclusions straight, why don't we talk about the evidence."

"I was under the impression that was what we'd been discussing."

"You just told the general that the Soviets weren't directly involved, but the cable reads 'Soviet and Cuban involvement seems clear.' So which sheet of music are we singing from? Do you know something I don't?"

"What we meant was that the Soviets weren't directly involved," Lowenthal put in. "Physically involved, I mean. Certainly it's not as if they fired the guns themselves. The rebels did. No one's accusing them of that."

Bondurant's frown deepened.

"But then they never are," Becker quickly added, smelling an impasse.

"You mean it's not Czechoslovakia," Reddish said immediately.

"Not precisely that, no." Becker smiled.

"Precisely what, then? You're saying the *jeunesse* were Soviet surrogates, Russian stooges."

"Is that a question?" Becker asked, still smiling, like a tutor coaxing an errant pupil.

"No, not a question. You're saying that the *jeunesse* were Soviet stooges."

Becker frowned theatrically, gazing at the ceiling. "No," he replied finally. "No, that's too blatant."

"For the cable or for the Soviets?" Reddish said recklessly.

"Come on, Andy," Selvey growled, suddenly uncomfortable.

Irritated, Becker said, "I think I agree with Abner. We aren't playing with words. We all know precisely what we mean."

"I don't," Reddish retorted. "I don't know what you mean at all.

You've tied the Russians to the shoot-up in Malunga. How? That's all I want to know. How? What do you know that I don't?"

"You mean you *don't* agree about Soviet involvement?" Lowenthal asked weakly, hurt.

"Exactly. I don't agree at all."

"I take it then you don't think the weapons came from Brazza," Becker resumed.

"I think I'd agree they probably came from Brazza."

"But you disagree about Soviet and Cuban involvement?"

"I think it's a mistake to lump the Soviets and the Cubans on this issue. Their interests don't automatically coincide."

"Agreed, but it's naive to assume the guns could come from Brazza without Soviet and Cuban knowledge. Would you agree with that?"

"Probably," Reddish said, "but knowledge doesn't mean complicity. Sanction either. I assume the Russians might have known, but it's only an assumption. What I know is that there's no hard evidence to support this statement in the cable about Cuban and Russian involvement."

"What we *know* is that the *jeunesse* had Soviet guns," Lowenthal insisted.

"We're going around in circles," Selvey muttered, looking toward Bondurant, who sat motionless, listening.

"I agree," Becker added, throwing down his pencil. "I agree completely."

Reddish said, "If we're going around in circles, it's because you always come back to the guns, and the guns don't prove a goddamned thing. Why can't you face up to it? Abner knows that as well as anyone else. A year ago there was an attempted coup in Brazza. Some of you remember. Afterwards they shot the plotters and put US-made M-14s on display at the stadium. They claimed we supplied them. We didn't, but it didn't matter. They had the guns. Abner got the serial numbers from the French military attaché and we tracked them to a 1954 shipment to the Greeks. They had our guns all right. They came out of DOD inventories, but they didn't get them from us and it wasn't our coup. We were clean, but they had our guns."

The faces at the table turned toward Selvey, who sat forward uncomfortably, half embarrassed, half angry. "What's your point," he asked, "that someone planted Russian guns on those bimbos in Malunga just to dish the Sovs? Jesus Christ, Andy!"

Bondurant peered coolly at Selvey over his glasses. "His point was that Brazzaville's evidence last year was as good as yours today. Do you disagree?"

"But we're suggesting possibilities, not writing a writ," Becker complained, still appealing to Reddish.

"Precisely," Bondurant continued. "Precisely why we must be careful here. Others will interpret it however they wish, whether it has a factual basis or not. I agree with Reddish that the language of the cable goes considerably beyond the facts that are known to us."

The room was silent. Bondurant peered about him, disappointed. "I fully recognize the need to identify Soviet and Cuban plots where they occur," he resumed quietly, "but I think we give Moscow far too much credit when we find its fingerprints on every smashed teacup in the pantry."

General Leggard and Colonel Selvey sat with suppressed anger, shrunken within their starched khaki uniforms. Becker's expression was fatalistic; Lowenthal's held the pain of a personal wound. Bondurant gazed at them, bemused. "I also happen to think it's quite dangerous," he added, "dangerous for them, dangerous for us."

"I wonder if you would amplify a bit for us," Becker suggested politely, the acolyte now returned to the procession.

Bondurant hesitated. The room was respectfully silent; the silence drew him on. "For what it's worth," he began, "I believe that Soviet weapons support for an obscure little party with no popular base and no hope of achieving one would have been irrational. Soviet behavior may sometimes be rash, but it's not unpredictable. Nevertheless, most of you seem convinced, even without evidence, that Moscow is capable of that kind of recklessness. I'm not, not yet, at any rate. It's possible that Soviet policy may one day go suddenly berserk, whether in Africa or elsewhere, but I don't believe that day has yet come.

"I think we bring it closer, however, when we accuse Moscow of irrational behavior on the flimsiest of evidence. Accusations of that nature get circulated elsewhere as hard fact. They also make it impossible to understand what Moscow is really up to. You can't anticipate an adversary if you continually falsify his actions. The most you can do is stir up those in Washington and elsewhere who are already frightened enough of what they refuse to understand to believe the worst."

He gazed about the room, not confident he had their understanding, even if he had their attention. "When that happens," he continued, "then our own policy voices take on the same clumsy aberrant character, with the result that neither side understands any longer what the other is talking about. To me, as I said earlier, that is truly dangerous—two frightened, confused, dangerously armed men shouting at one another in a language neither understands. To the other, his adversary is a lunatic. For me, both soon will be." He put his reading glasses back on and peered at the draft cable in front of him. "So that is what I meant. Coping with real problems in Washington is difficult enough. Coping with fictitious ones makes policy coherence impossible. So that's all I meant. What Mr. Reddish has in mind, I'm not sure. In any case, the language suggesting Soviet and Cuban involvement should be struck from the draft, as Reddish proposed."

"I sometimes have the impression Bondurant is a bit too generous," Dick Franz observed, descending the outer stairway. "He imagines *they* think as he does—a Moscow version of the Foreign Affairs Council." He slipped on his sunglasses.

"Why didn't you tell him then?" Selvey demanded, irritated at Franz's silly smile.

"Oh, it wouldn't do. A law of survival, isn't it?"

Selvey saw Reddish leave the door at the top of the steps and waited for him in the courtyard below.

"Whose ass were you covering, anyway?" he wanted to know. "What the shit were you afraid of, that some GS-18 back at the Agency would think you let the goddamn Russians come sneaking in the back door while Les was on leave."

"It was a bad cable."

"Maybe you know something we don't."

"Not yet."

"Then you're covering your ass."

"Vigilance against policy incoherence," Franz quipped.

In the privacy of his office, Reddish retrieved his debriefing of the Cuban defector from his safe and sat at his desk, still troubled, rereading the Cuban's paragraphs describing the sudden moratorium on Cuban activities, including his claim that the Russian Embassy in Brazzaville was behind it. The defection was one of Reddish's few successes in recent years, a clue as to Soviet tactics in the region, but it was a fragile one, suspiciously received by those in the Washington intelligence community unable to credit any evidence of Russian quietism—and by those at the Agency who remained skeptical of Reddish himself since Damascus. To either, the flimsiness of any evidence asserting that Soviet policy was aggressively predatory, as the Becker/Lowenthal cable suggested, wouldn't matter.

"I heard you got them to change the telegram," Sarah said as she came in with a folder of incoming cables.

Reddish nodded uncomfortably, quickly burying the Cuban debriefing memo beneath the correspondence on his desk. "Who told you?"

"I heard Selvey bellyaching to Walker. It's nice to know there's something you and the ambassador agree on."

"We won the battle, not the war."

Winning the war was why Masakita mattered to him. He was up for reassignment, possibly a post of his own.

◇◇◇ A dark green sports car waited in the embassy courtyard near the front steps, the top down. A woman sat behind the wheel, her eyes hidden by sunglasses. She wore a sleeveless white blouse, made brighter by arms tanned by the sun and she was reading a French newspaper propped on the steering wheel in front of her. She'd ignored the warning from the Marine guard that she was parked in a reserved area. She lifted her eyes occasionally to glance at the faces of the embassy staff as they left for the day.

It was a little after five when Reddish left the building, the courtyard nearly deserted by then. He saw the dark green sports car but didn't recognize the face, even after she'd honked the horn and lifted herself in the seat to call to him. Only after she'd raised the sunglasses to her forehead did he finally recognize her and cross to where she waited.

"Where are my sacks?" she asked plaintively.

"You didn't get them? They were in the back of the embassy station wagon."

"No, I didn't."

She'd been half asleep and a little disoriented as he'd put her into the embassy station wagon the morning before to be driven to the Houlets'. The curfew had just lifted.

"The driver probably brought them back. Maybe they're in the motor pool."

They walked around the side of the building and into the rear courtyard, where the dispensary and motor pool lay. Her two burlap bags were recovered in the dispatcher's office, piled on a table in the corner with a few other lost or forgotten parcels from the chauffeur-driven American community.

"I was a little worried," she admitted as Reddish carried them back to the car. "They're tribal masks. I bought them from a trader on Sunday. I was sure I'd lost them."

"You mean they're valuable."

"I've no idea. Sentimentally, I suppose. They're all I have and I won't have the opportunity to look again. I know a few of the people at the Musée de l'Homme, where they have a perfectly incredible collection. They told me what I might look for."

"You're leaving then?"

She turned, as if she thought he knew that. "Yes. Very soon probably." The color had come back into her face, which was more remote than ever, the face of a fashionable French tourist who could travel from Cairo to Nairobi, Nairobi to Capetown, and never seem more than ten minutes away from her hairdresser or her flat in the Seventh Arrondissement in Paris. Some Manhattan women had, for Reddish, the same annoying look.

"Too much for you, is it?" he said, tempted. He wondered how much she'd told Armand and Houlet about Sunday night. Probably the whole bloody story.

"It's been very difficult, very confusing."

He thought her smile a little brittle, like the mouth—old family porcelain to be looked at behind glass, too fragile for everyday use. He wondered for the first time about her personal life and who her husband was. "You give up too easily," he offered carelessly. "Things are beginning to quiet down now."

"During the day, yes, but we heard gunshots last night. They were quite near."

Like weevils in the flour, Reddish thought.

She opened the door and he put the burlap bags behind the front seat.

"I see you've got a new car."

"It's Madame Houlet's. She's been very generous, much more so than Houlet. A plane leaves on Sunday, and he'd prefer that I be on it. He believes it quite dangerous even now—unpredictable, he said. If I can't drive about, there's nothing to see. If there's nothing to see, there's no reason to stay."

"As simple as that, is it?" Recklessly, not caring any more, he let his gaze travel her ankles and legs as she got in. "What is it you want to see?"

He thought he saw her color as she settled behind the wheel. "The *cité*, some of the countryside, a few of the villages." Her attention was on the ignition switch as she probed with the key. "Houlet says it's impossible."

He closed the door after her. "Maybe not. You'll be here tomorrow?"

"Yes, still here."

"Why don't I give you a call then. We could go down to the *cité* for a drink, maybe dinner."

She looked up, startled. "I wouldn't want to put you to any trouble."

"No trouble." He wasn't sure whether she was surprised, insulted, or calling his bluff. "Getting away from the diplomats for a night might do you some good." He was smiling.

She ignored it. "Yes, that would be nice," she said vaguely. "All right then, tomorrow?"

"Tomorrow."

One of us is lying, he thought, watching her drive out the gate.

chapter 4

❖ Army trucks and armored cars still commanded the main intersections, but they were permitting traffic to pass. Some of the roadblocks along the side streets had been removed. The streets were stirring again. The iron shutters that had closed the Portuguese, Greek, and Pakistani shops had been rolled open. The small green market near the port was active again. Spoiled fruit rotted in the gutters below the garlands of fresh flowers in old coffee tins. African vendors stood or squatted in the shadows under the tin roofs. The riverboats were unloading passengers and cargo.

Groups of blacks crowded the streets near the port, barefoot women in faded washworn *waxes*, with thin black scallions of pigtail sprouting from their uncovered heads, women whose shy loping flight across the wide boulevards identified them as newly arrived migrants from the interior. Reddish eased his Fiat to a stop, letting a group of women pass. They carried on their heads cloth- or leaf-wrapped packets of goods, lard tins, or orange vessels of palm oil. The old riverboats were moored two deep adjacent to the boat sheds, and he stopped again to look, wondering if the ferry to Brazza was in operation. It wasn't. The only boats moving were those carrying domestic cargo, their debarked passengers still visible on the streets, as they would be for several hours along the boulevards before they vanished into the outlying communes, into the hives of clay, tin, and brick whose walls would conceal their faces, their cooking fires, their small pallets, their songs and dances.

No one knew their numbers. It was the anonymity that made the diplomats and the old *colons* restless and uneasy, faceless thousands infesting the tin and mud hovels in squalid candlelit rooms without water or electricity, five or six, sometimes ten to a dwelling, sometimes more. It was the postulation of that deprived, oppressed population that preyed on their minds and still nourished, as recently as Sunday, the imaginations of those who waited in the old Belgian residential section or the embassies of the European city, behind spiked walls and compounds, fearing the worst.

But after the migrants left the riverboats or the trucks—pulling to their heads the rags of their possessions, carrying the sandals and dodging the cars as they scurried to the safety of the sidewalks that belonged to the *flamands*, the Portuguese, and Pakistanis who sat in the cool shadows of their shops and sold them cheap cloth, salt, oil, cutlery, and plastic dishes—they sought only some tiny parcel of dirt yard where the smoke eddied from the ash of a hearth fire as it had once in the Kwilu or the Kasai, where the pots steamed and the wooden manioc pestles thumped the same, where in the darkness the same thin pallets would be unrolled, the songs, sounds, and laughter the same. Because inevitably they found some community of their own kin, their own blood and bone, brothers, sisters, aunts, and cousins, gathered together in mutual cohesion against the terrifying intrusions of that polyglot brothel capital, where the sanctity of family and tribe sustained them still.

How much longer? Reddish had often wondered. He didn't know. The *colons* in the shops and the diplomats at their cocktails talked of savagery still, but after all these years where were the savages? What savages? Who had cruised these rivers and coasts for centuries now like sharks among herring, devouring everything, even their past, and who now faced alone the limitless ocean of their own annihilation?

"Next time it will be bad, very bad," grumbled the old Portuguese shopkeeper as he passed the tea, coffee, sugar, and tinned milk across the counter. "You heard about the two Belgian police advisers at Bakole? Cut their throats. In Malunga, it was worse."

Cut yours, Reddish's look seemed to say as he turned back silently toward his car at the curb.

He entered the flat by the rear door and found the small bedroom behind the kitchen empty, the bed made. He left the parcel in the kitchen and went quickly into the living room. Masakita stood on the small balcony studying the river, which was at its most magnificent in the late afternoon, when the dying sun bathed the western sky and river in bronze fire. The golden light was shot through with the dark clusters it couldn't ignite: the towering thunderheads over the savannahs, the trees along the far bank at Brazzaville, and the pirogues drifting upon the silk of river like water spiders, like long-legged flies.

"So it's over," Masakita said finally without turning. "The river-boats are unloading again."

"Not quite, but almost."

Masakita opened the sliding door and left the sunlight, moving back into the shadows of the small living room. His dark face was tired, scarred by pain, his eyes listless. He hadn't shaved.

"Has Nyembo come?" he asked, slumping down on the sofa. His arm was still in a sling, but the bandage was gone from his forehead.

"He didn't report for work. I don't know where he is."

"Picked up by the army?" A few books from the bookshelf in the corner lay on the table. He picked one up, glanced at it, and pushed it away. "Whose apartment is this?"

"A transient flat. People who come in for a few days for a visit or special projects."

"Do you bring people here to offer them employment, people with secrets to sell?"

"No." Reddish stood flat-footed, coat and trousers rumpled, searching his pockets for his notebook. He was in a foul temper.

"So what is it you expect of me?"

"I want to ask you some questions. What the hell else?"

"And after that?"

"I'll cross that bridge when I come to it."

"Out of the country, is that what you have in mind?"

"That's one possibility. Whoever these people are, they're scared of you still. It's not going to be very pleasant when they find you."

"Maybe they should live with that uncertainty."

"It's not a toothache," Reddish said. "Scared people do ugly things. They're scared of you."

"Will shooting me make them braver? Will it give truth to their lies? What about you? You were in Malunga. Are they going to shoot you too? You saw it. You know what happened."

"Not all of it. Some of it. That's what I want to talk about, how it was done."

"What does it matter how it was done," Masakita said. "It's done now, finished! If these soldiers want to claim foreign guns were responsible, Russian, East German, or whatever, they can say so, and no one will have the courage to doubt them! Not the Americans, not the Belgians, no one! So why does it make a difference to you?"

"It matters. Don't think it doesn't."

"Why? Because they cheated you, these soldiers? Because they smashed your President while your back was turned, because they didn't ask your permission? Are you humiliated because of that? What do you want? Revenge? Revenge because nothing can happen here without your knowing it? What about the Africans they humiliated?"

"I want to know what happened," Reddish said.

"So it's the truth then, just the truth. Of course, certainly," Masakita continued. "The thieves are swindled, and suddenly they're interested in justice. What kind of justice? Like everyone else, you've lived here with injustice for years. So why, then? For scholarly reasons, reasons of pedagogy, intelligence pedagogy, to refine methods, techniques, to improve on performance next time so that you can't be tricked while your back is turned?"

"I told you—"

"I know what you told me, but the truth isn't celibate, is it? It has its own secrets, its own reasons. Don't misunderstand me, but you must see how strange all of this is. You say I'm not a prisoner, that I'm free to go as I choose. Go where? You don't know. Go when? You don't know that either. So I am a prisoner—to those soldiers out there, to your questions here. Questions for what? For revenge?"

"I'm not looking for revenge, so get that out of your head. I've been screwed before, by people a lot quicker than the fuck-ups that pulled this job off, so there's nothing personal in all this. If someone had told me Sunday before I drove into Malunga that I'd be bringing you out, I'd have told him he was crazy. Nyembo must have thought so too, because he took off like a jackrabbit in the other direction, and now no one can find him. O.K. I'm stuck with that."

"So now it's your problem to solve, eh, your problem to liquidate—"

"Just shut up for a minute and listen!" he said. "You're right about one thing. I'm nobody's Good Samaritan, not Nyembo's, not yours, not anyone's. You're a private pain in the ass as far as I'm concerned. I've got enough headaches just sticking to what I know. What I know is that I went into Malunga, saw some people get shot down because they had guns they didn't know how to use. And now you're here, everyone else is either dead or gone to ground, and the ones still on their feet are lying about what happened in the streets two days ago. So my ass is half in, half out. If I quit now, maybe next time it might be the embassy holding a smoking gun it didn't use."

"So you're talking about injustice."

"Let's just keep it simple and say I want to keep it honest, like Nyembo did when he called me."

"What is it you want to know?"

"Where the guns came from," Reddish mumbled, pulling his glasses on to sit in the armchair across the room, idly turning the pages of his small notebook. The glasses were repaired with adhesive tape at the bridge.

Masakita waited, weary of questions he'd already answered that would lead them nowhere.

"How do your radical friends in exile see you these days," he began quietly, "still the leader of the cause?"

Puzzled, Masakita didn't reply.

"You keep in touch with them, don't you?" The gaze lifted calmly. "You had a few letters with you the other day. One from this MPLA officer dos Santos, another from someone in Paris ready to lead an army into the Kivu. What is it they're asking—help, support, tactical advice, a few dollars?"

"They ask for advice, sometimes money. Some ask about local conditions, whether they should return or not."

"No grudges?" Reddish waited. "You left a few of your exile friends high and dry when you came back here from Cairo."

"Grudges? No. A few misunderstandings, that's all. That's what some of the letters are about."

"But some still see you as the hero of the rebellions, the leader of the opposition."

"If they do, they don't understand my position."

"Sure," Reddish offered dryly. "You set them straight on that, do you?" He got up restlessly to wander the room, jacket left behind. "Like this fellow who wrote you from Paris, ready to begin a new peasants' war in the north. Let's say he tells you he's got a warehouse of guns in Bujumbura and a thousand guerrillas back in the bush behind Goma, ready to go, what advice are you going to give him? To give up the guns and throw in with national reconciliation?"

"Under certain circumstances."

"And if he doesn't, what do you do then—tell the internal security directorate or the army that there's some lunatic with a warehouse of rifles in Bujumbura ready to shoot his way to the capital?" Reddish turned, waiting.

"Certainly not."

"So you haven't come that far yet, have you?"

"I don't stir up needless suspicions, no."

"So you're a vice minister but not a loyalist, a sympathizer but not a fanatic, a radical but not a radical. What the hell are you?" He moved away to the glass door overlooking the balcony, where the haze of fading sunlight fell like smoke, obscuring the streets below.

"I don't understand these questions."

"Just shut up for a minute. Neither do I." He stood at the glass door silently studying the river. "A few weeks ago I was over at Kindu," he began again, "looking at a cache of guns uncovered on a trader's truck south of Uvira. Chinese guns, the army command over there said. Just a clutter of old mercenary hardware, half gone to rust, most of it. But let's say they found new guns someplace close by—the same idiot officers—still in oil, still in crates, intercepted maybe on the river north of here, on their way to Angola, where most of the clandestine trails lead. But this time they don't tell the President at the morning cabinet meeting, they don't raise the hue and cry, not a freaking word. The army just keeps it to itself, hides the guns away for a few weeks, bides its time, waits for its opportunities."

He turned back to the chair, threw his coat on the floor, and leafed idly through his notebook, puzzling over the page he finally found.

"Someone called me on Saturday night, someone from customs. He said the army had guns and was going to overthrow the President. He said two trucks had gone out, two more to be sent on Sunday. I didn't know what he was talking about. He didn't either. What he was talking about were the trucks you thought came from customs. They were army trucks. Somehow he'd found out what was in the crates they were carrying, knew they were para trucks, and thought they were on their way to the para camp. But he had it backwards. The trucks were headed for your compound in Malunga, with the crates to be left there until the paras moved against your compound on Sunday afternoon. Why two more trucks on Sunday, I don't know, but it's academic. Everything had been worked out, the powder primed."

He raised his head from the notebook. "I think the guns in the compound were hijacked guns, guns the paras or the army found someplace else, sat on, and then delivered in place of those East German agricultural implements. They probably weren't meant to be used, not all of them anyway, just found there. That would have been enough. At the same time the paras were shooting up your compound they were sneaking in the back door at the presidential compound. That's what they were really after. You and your party were just the excuse, the *casus belli*, as the experts say—that's Latin for small beer."

Reddish put the notebook away indifferently, looking at his watch.

"How do you know this?"

"How the hell do you think I know it?" he said. "I just know it. You don't have to find the body to know it smells. This one smells all over town. It's the only way it makes sense." His voice faded away and he got to his feet again, relentlessly prowling the room, glancing occasionally at his watch.

"Where did they find the guns?" Masakita asked.

"I don't know."

"From outside the country?"

"Probably. What about this rebel leader, the old guy that wrote you from Paris. Did he say anything about guns?"

"No."

"Dos Santos, this MPLA officer?"

"No."

"So you know as much as I do."

"Then you have no proof, no evidence," Masakita concluded, disappointed.

"I don't have a leg to stand on—nothing." He stood at the window again, hands thrust in his hip pockets, gazing at the sheen of river. "But we're dealing with a state of mind here, like that old mercenary iron at Kindu, like you, the rebellions, and everything else. When you understand that, everything falls into place." He might have been talking to himself. He glanced at his watch again and grunted. "It's six o'clock, time for a drink."

Masakita watched him turn back across the room and disappear through the door toward the kitchen, like a businessman meeting a long-awaited mistress on a late-arriving train. He understood his restlessness. Wearily, his shoulder stiff, he rose and followed him, wiser now, his suspicions gone.

◆ ◆ Darkness had fallen beyond the windows. Reddish had gone out and brought back a roast chicken and rice from a Belgian restaurant. As Masakita finished the chicken, Reddish's questions had taken a different turn. Masakita thought the questions irrelevant; Reddish, that he was being evasive.

"You were brought up a Catholic. Do you still go to church?"

Reddish asked randomly. Masakita said he didn't. "A Catholic who doesn't go to church, a revolutionary who no longer believes in revolution. Are you still a Marxist?"

"I've been asked that question so many times I don't know how to answer. Each time, I find myself answering in a totally different way, which means that for me it's no longer a meaningful question."

"So it's not important to you now." A hint of cynicism lingered.

"If it weren't, why would you be asking?"

"Call it habit," Reddish said nonchalantly, emptying the plates.

They returned to the small living room, where Reddish took up his place in the cloth-covered American armchair opposite the couch, notebook on his knee, as detached as a credit clerk filling out a questionnaire. Most of his questions had been provoked by the Agency's Secret personality profile on Masakita which he'd looked at in his office.

"Others still think of you as a Marxist," he resumed deceptively, as if it were someone else's question, scanning myopically a scrawled page.

Masakita sat uncomfortably on the couch. "In public, you accept the fact that you'll be misunderstood. You accept that, but it's not important. The work is."

Well rehearsed, Reddish thought idly, crossing out a line. "Quite a few European journalists still look you up. What kind of questions do they ask?"

"Always the same: Why did I return? What are my political beliefs? Why do I cooperate with a regime which continues its corruption—"

"Continued," Reddish corrected, head down, drawing loops in the margin. "Past tense." He didn't look up.

"—under another name. Do I consider myself a socialist, a Marxist, correspond still with Fanon, write essays, believe in violence? Always the same."

"What do you tell them?"

"What I've told you—that I can't declare myself on these questions, that a man who can't declare himself shouldn't be in politics, but that this isn't important. Others can do these things."

"You said that before. So they misquote you, do they?"

"Accuracy can be trivial. No, they don't misquote me."

"But they get under your skin. Why do you agree to the interviews?"

Sometimes he didn't, refusing to talk with journalists, rejecting dialogue completely, as he always did when words had grown

170

stale—refusing to attend meetings, draft speeches or party position papers, going for days clothed in silence, rejecting himself like a Trappist, until something would unexpectedly arouse him—a word from his wife, a smile from an old woman in the *marché,* a witless remark by the President at a cabinet meeting, or even the sight of Dr. Bizenga, the party ideologue, standing ridiculously in the sunlit yard of the compound, chamois in hand, wiping away the finger-prints from the polished chrome door handle of his Mercedes. "Sometimes it's simply enough to have eyes," he concluded.

"What about your old Marxist friends?" Reddish asked. "How do you manage their questions?"

"I listen, as always."

"What do they say?"

"What they always say," Masakita said without enthusiasm, as if he'd repeated it many times. "They talk of state ownership of land on a continent where communal land has been traditional for centu-ries, of nationalizing industry where none exists, of trade union movements that mean nothing to rural peasants. They talk as they've always talked, of a world that doesn't exist."

"Here maybe," Reddish agreed, "but not Russia or China. They talked of those things too. Now they exist."

"The party exists."

"And what the party has done."

"They're the same," Masakita corrected. "The party is whatever it says it is." He recognized Reddish's puzzlement. "If you were blind and I weren't, I could describe this room to you in any way I liked and you would accept it. That's what happens in China or the Soviet Union when the party tells the masses that it has achieved this or that. The same thing happens in Africa when the party ideo-logues tell the party faithful that conditions now exist for the revolu-tion."

"And you don't believe they do."

"Not yet."

"No faith in the ideology?" Reddish asked, smiling.

"Possibly not."

"In what then?"

"Hope I don't understand the pathological element," he an-swered.

"What the shit's that mean?"

"The two of us sitting here the way we are, talking about who or what I am, questions which are totally without significance."

"Fancy words," Reddish muttered absent-mindedly, as if they

were of no importance. His eyes returned to the pages of the note-book. "When you were in exile in France, you were close to the Algerians. You worked for the Exterieur Division of the Algerian Liberation Front, a courier apparently." He lifted his gaze. "Are they the ones who gave you your start, taught you your bag of tricks?"

"In what way?"

"Insurgency, terrorism, how to plant *plastique*, how to run a clandestine network."

"I learned a few things, yes."

"You knew Ben Bella in Paris?"

"Slightly. He had a flat in Rue Cadet and so did I. At the time I didn't know who he was."

"Did the Algerians recruit you in Brussels and bring you to France?"

"No."

"But you worked for them in Paris?" He watched Masakita nod. "Doing what besides dropping a few satchels of explosives around Paris—in parked cars, Métro entrances, civil servants' flats?"

"I was a courier for the most part, smuggling currency up from Marseilles or from Geneva."

"Just currency?"

"I didn't always know what I was carrying, what the satchels contained," said Masakita uncomfortably.

"And you didn't look either, did you—like those crates in your compound? You are a bloody intellectual, aren't you? Dry hands, dry socks, just delivering a little mail-order homicide around town on your way to the Sorbonne or the Louvre. How long did you work for them?"

"A year."

"Another myth," Reddish said cynically, drawing a heavy line through a scrawled sentence in the notebook. "What about your French wife. Wasn't she a member of the French communist party?"

"I lived with a Frenchwoman who was a communist, yes, but we weren't married."

"Did she push you politically?"

"She was an influence, the way most women are. I'm not sure about her ideas."

"You still keep in touch with her?"

"She writes, yes."

"Still active in the party?"

"She was never very active in the party. Her father left her a little money—he manufactured plumbing appliances—and she lives as she pleases, generous with both her life and her money."

"What's she doing now?"

"I'm not sure. The last time I heard from her she was living with a blind man she met on a train."

Reddish looked up, annoyed.

"These are trivial questions," Masakita said. "Why do they matter?"

"They matter. Don't think they don't. I want to tell my people something about you. The only thing they've got is secondhand."

"Biographies are always false, always fictitious. Why create another?"

"For Christ's sake," Reddish muttered in dismay, closing the notebook. "Go ahead, tell it your own way."

◆◆◆ There was little to tell.

He hadn't been brought to France by the FLN but had gone there on his own, to Paris, to finish his education and find work in heavy industry. Later he'd met a few Algerians at a small café off Rue Cadet, where he'd taken rooms, just as he'd met a few communists at the evening study groups held periodically at a small socialist reading room nearby, including the woman he later lived with for a few months. But all these were temporary arrangements. He'd helped the FLN because he sympathized with their goals and they trusted him; but more importantly because he was free to move about, as they weren't. The associations he'd formed with the Algerian Exterieur Division of the FLN would be useful for the decolonization of his own country and all of sub-Saharan Africa. He thought the Algerians he'd met were committed to far more than their own national struggle.

He'd associated with communists and socialists, true, in the small study groups and elsewhere; but his studies in Paris went far beyond the study of Marxist texts.

One night that first winter he was sitting at the front table of the socialist reading room—where he went to escape the cold, his isolation, and the poverty which allowed him few newspapers and fewer books—when a little Frenchman paused near his chair, pulling on his beret and scarf and looking scathingly at the books and newspapers on the table—Kautsky, Lenin, Rosenberg's *History of Bolshe-*

vism, Souvarine's *Stalin,* among others. The old man was as small as a dwarf, his fingers stained with nicotine. "There is much more to our bookshelves than what you have on your table," he'd told Masakita censoriously, and with that pulled a small book from his pocket, very dog-eared, the spine torn, the title unreadable. Masakita thought he meant merely to show him the book, but he gave it to him. It was a copy of Pascal's *Pensées.* He never saw the man again, but he kept the book and read from it too, just as he read from the old editions of Montaigne and Saint-Simon he'd brought with him from Brussels.

"Why'd you leave Belgium in the first place?" Reddish interrupted.

"I was expelled from the university."

He had been sent to Belgium to study engineering, but had changed to the economics faculty the third year. The summer before he was to receive his degree, he'd joined in a student demonstration in Brussels, was arrested and released to the university officials, who ordered his expulsion. His passport was withdrawn and he was put on a ship to be returned to the Congo. He jumped ship at Dakar and two months later reached Spain, smuggled in with a group of Senegalese workers bound for France. They were led over the Pyrenees in early autumn by their Corsican *passeur* when the first snows were on the peaks but not yet in the passes. In Paris he shared a room in a bidonville with a fellow Congolese, sleeping in shifts on a single cot. He found work in a slaughterhouse, hauling away the bloody skins from the butchering rooms, while he continued to search for work in heavy industry. With a little money saved, he found a room in Rue Cadet. A few weeks later he left the slaughterhouse and took a job as a sweeper and laborer in a foundry that cast linings for industrial furnaces.

At the university in Belgium, abstract notions of property and capital had no more meaning for him than the oppression of an industrial revolution long over—the smoke of Birmingham or Düsseldorf, the cotton mills of Lancashire, workers moving home by gaslight, up frozen lanes and canals, filing into lifts on bitter winter mornings, cold and hungry, despising their condition.

As an African, he'd found it impossible to understand what his socialist or Marxist colleagues were saying when they talked of the socialist embryo in the bourgeois womb or the socialization of the productive process that would shape a new social character. Imperialism, like hatred or exploitation, was easier to understand. As an African, he could explain the misery of his own country as the product of Western wealth, artificially created by the division of labor forced upon colonized Africans by the industrial metropoles that denied them the rewards of their own resources and labor, but his knowledge was incomplete.

He'd sought work in heavy industry to bring those abstract ideas to life, to feel on his own shoulders the crushing burdens of capital, to know himself the socialization process that followed.

"Fancy words," Reddish muttered in irritation.

"Of course—just words."

"So what happened? Did you find out what Marx was talking about?"

Masakita was slow to respond. "Many things," he said finally. "I worked in the foundry for two years. After the rebellions here, I went back there for a few months—the factory, the room in Montmartre, the small socialist library. The Algerians were gone by then; their work was finished." He shrugged. "I was naive in those days, believing that change was simply doctrinaire, as finite or as manageable as the linings we cast at the foundry."

Late one February evening he happened to catch sight of himself as he passed a bakery window. He saw a wretched figure wrapped in a woolen coat, scarf hiding the African mouth, the dark face above as gray as a corpse's, mantled with the dust of the annealing rooms at the foundry, the boots on his feet shapeless lumps of leather warped by rain and snow and sucked dry again by the heat of the catwalks above the furnaces. Was that the man he'd hoped to become—miserable, deprived, oppressed? To anyone passing him in the streets at that moment, probably; but what did he feel? He felt fortunate merely to be there, a man like any other, suffering through that winter cold as generations of Europeans had before him in the same frozen streets and alleyways.

But the foundry closed. Two weeks later he abandoned France and his life there to go to Cairo to take a position on the newly created Afro-Asian Secretariat.

"This was the first time?" Reddish asked.

"Yes, the first time."

"So what had you learned for all those years?"

"Simple things," Masakita answered.

He'd gone to Europe to study engineering but had discovered Marx and trade unionism. He'd gone to escape those Jesuits who'd taught him at the mission school at Benongo, convinced, as the village elders were, that certain books of the Bible had been carefully edited or eliminated to deny to Africans those secrets to wisdom and self-respect which enabled the white man to rule, and he had discovered Montaigne and Pascal.

Before he'd left the mission school, an old chief had sent him an elaborately carved box, a receptacle for those secret books Masakita would discover in Belgium and return with to his village.

What should he have put in the box? he now asked Reddish. Marx? Montaigne? Pascal? Perhaps the latter two, since their message was simpler than that of Marx, simple enough even for the chief at Funzi to understand: this European civilization that Africans looked upon with such awe and respect was as fragile as their own.

Tired and disappointed, indifferent to riddles, Reddish lifted himself from his chair to stalk the room. "You say you knew a few communists in Paris. Did anyone ever try to recruit you?"

"Of course not."

"What about during your trips to the Soviet Union? You haven't talked about those."

"No."

"China?"

Masakita didn't answer.

Reddish turned to see the look of silent scorn. "Tell me something about China—what you saw, the facilities you visited, the dog and pony show they put on," he continued stubbornly. "They didn't take you to their nuclear testing facility, did they? I think it's in Sinkiang." He looked again at Masakita's immobile figure. "For Christ's sake, make it interesting this time!" he shouted, suddenly angry. "Something I can get my teeth into for a change."

It was late autumn when Masakita reached Peking, traveling under the auspices of the Afro-Asian Secretariat, which had sent dozens of Africans and Arabs to Chinese guerrilla camps. In Peking he was received by officials from the African Solidarity Committee and the Peking Institute of Foreign Affairs. He was given a week's familiarization course at a guerrilla training center at Da Kien, near Linchow. The techniques taught weren't original or even useful for Africans. The evening hours were spent repriming old cartridges and melting down old lead for new bullets for the firing range. He visited Nanking and was given ten days of medical training. With a group of workers from Canton, he was taken to Mao's birthplace and then flown to Manchuria, where his army hosts drove him to the Korean border near Pusan on the Yalu, where the Americans had been defeated during the Korean war.

The mountains were covered with snow, the wind savage, the landscape forbidding, as silent and empty as the thirteenth-century landscape the Mongols had crossed on their great drive toward the Danube in 1241. Listening to his Chinese guides explaining the tactics which had led to the American defeat, he'd felt nothing but the cold, a cold so numbing that the mind was annihilated, the body a burden to be escaped at any cost, even death, which came like a warm breath. Standing inside his thick quilted Chinese jacket with the fur parka, the Asian snow in his face, ice in his nostrils, gazing out across those frozen mountains and river, he found himself incapable of mental or physical response. *How had they done it?* His guides continued to congratulate themselves, like schoolboys, as if their victory had occurred that morning.

Returning to the Chinese army post in the closed jeep, their elation was gone, their faces blank again, Masakita again a stranger; and he saw in their expressions the same neuter self-absorption he'd seen in the guerrilla instructors at Da Kien as they retreated from the blackboard, the tactical lesson over: a lump of racial indifference no ideology could thaw.

At the end of his visit to China he decided that the soldiers he'd seen that day on the Yalu were no different from those of any other army, moved as much by boredom, apathy, fear, and blind obedience as anything else, their condition no more measured by the slogans of the cultural revolution that festooned the walls and rattled in the wind outside his Peking hotel room than Russian success could be judged by Soviet mathematics or the corridors of the Moscow subway.

High over China, with the sunlight flooding the nearly deserted cabin of the Pakistani jet returning him to Cairo, he'd tried to understand the Chinese, wise when his own ancestors were still puzzling over iron smelting or the phases of the moon. His hosts had been considerate, always gracious; yet even at the airport their formality and politeness seemed exaggerated—an ancient people on a vast land mass welcoming a black stranger still grappling with the first pangs of political birth.

What best summed up the Chinese were a few lines scrawled on the blackboard of a classroom in Peking, written by the Chinese instructor who taught English. Masakita knew a few words of English, but the lines didn't make sense, not even after his guide had translated them, and it wasn't until a few minutes later that he understood them. They were simple lines, almost an ideograph, but what they expressed about the Chinese was expressed in no other way. The lines, English in origin, read:

When Yenan was a market town
London was Derry Down.

"So they didn't take you to Sinkiang," Reddish summarized wearily, anxious to bring the talk to an end. "You didn't see anything very interesting except a nursery rhyme on a classroom blackboard, and the ice and snow, which just about wiped you out. I was in Korea too and got clobbered one night by a bunch of Chinese firemen blowing bugles. I'll tell you about it sometime. It wasn't snowing."

Nothing Masakita had told him would be of the slightest interest to his headquarters, not even enough to qualify him for a free plane ride to Frankfurt.

Masakita was silent.

"So you worked as a foundry laborer, read Marx and Montaigne, did a few jobs for the FLN, knew some French communists, but got fed up and hired on with the Afro-Asian club in Cairo, a Third World neutralist drafting agenda papers that wouldn't hurt anyone." He looked over his glasses at Masakita. "Right. Then you came back here to teach school in the Kwilu after independence, led a guerrilla war against the central government, but broke with the rebels and went into exile." He hesitated again, but Masakita made no comment. "Then the President offers you a sub-cabinet job at the same time the rebels-in-exile wanted you to head up their own government abroad, but you came back here—not as a Marxist, not as a revolutionary, not as anything else I can understand.

"What the hell are you? No one recruited you or even tried. Did they know you were there? You've been to Moscow, Leningrad, Frunze, Peking, Da Kien, and a few other places, all of them interesting to you, but nothing you can make very interesting to anyone else. All right. That happens too. People carry things around in their head so long they don't even know they're there, not until someone pries them loose. Others know they're there, but don't want you to find them." He lifted his eyes from his notebook. "What are you hiding?"

Masakita sat in silence.

"You're holding something back. What is it? You've got to come clean sooner or later. You can't hold out like this. Why'd you accept that cabinet post and return here after your radical friends offered you the leadership? That never made any sense to me. What was behind it? Did the Soviets recruit you? Someone else? Come on, God damn it, open up! Make it easy for me to understand. I'm trying to help."

"It was nothing like that," Masakita replied. "I've told you all I can."

No wonder the army couldn't get its hands on him during the rebellions, Reddish thought, descending alone in the elevator to the basement. Who could? A Marxist riddle in 130 pounds of pure Cartesian ectoplasm.

chapter 5

✧ The dawn light was still gray in the kitchen when Reddish took the telephone call. He had come downstairs to put the coffee-pot on, dressed only in his pajama bottoms. He'd sat up until after midnight in the study trying to patch together a cable to Langley, but the cable wouldn't write and he'd given up. A vascular flush dulled the whites of his eyes, as if he'd just awakened from a drinking weekend in the saltwater sun. The call was from his ex-wife, telephoning from her house in the Washington suburbs.

"Who'd you think it was, anyway," she demanded suspiciously, "that Vietnamese tramp who used to send you pictures of her kids?"

"I wasn't sure," he answered guiltily. Her voice scraped across his scalp like fresh pain from an old wound.

"Yeah, I'll bet. All right, Papa-San, where's her tuition check? That school you put her in has been pestering me to death, and I'm sick of it. What do you expect me to do, pay it myself?"

It was midnight in Washington and the connection was poor. He knew she'd been drinking. She only called when anger and al-cohol dulled her judgment enough to make her forget the transatlantic toll charges. In the morning she would remember and send him the bills.

"*Listen*, are you still there? If you hang up on me like you did last time, I'll jerk her out of that school so fast it'll make your head swim."

He thought sometimes that she was only what he'd made her—the anger, the drinking, even the language. She'd been a secretary at Aberdeen Proving Grounds when they'd first met, a happy, outgoing blond girl from rural Maryland with two years of college in a small denominational school in the Maryland mountains. She liked to bowl, play hearts for a penny a point with her brothers and father, and attend the local football and basketball games in the autumn and winter. Her father was the manager of a Western Auto store. The family lived on five acres outside of town, had a chicken dinner every Sunday after church, and a stocked pond where they jigged for bass and crappies on Sunday afternoons after the horseshoe and croquet games. He was working on a special weapons project at Aberdeen when he met her.

She'd adjusted to living in the Virginia suburbs but, after he'd joined the clandestine services, not to the life overseas. She'd never been abroad before. The first year had been interesting for her, but the years that followed a nightmare. She was frightened by the foreign environment, often a hostile one, by Reddish's absences, the smell of the *suqs*, the servants, cocktail-party decorum, and his colleagues' wives. Insecurity and self-consciousness made learning a foreign language impossible. She had a nervous breakdown in Syria and was evacuated to a US military hospital in Germany. While Reddish was in Vietnam, she stayed in Bangkok, where she fell in with a group of NCO wives from the US military mission. They gave each other permanents, played canasta, bowled, shopped in the commissary, and taught her to dye her hair. Reddish flew to Bangkok as often as he could, but not often enough. She met a Voice of America stringer as mixed up as she was, and the marriage fell apart after that. She'd returned to Washington alone.

Reddish said, "I mailed the check last week."

"You'd better have. Have you sold the house yet? I need the money. Living in Washington isn't cheap these days. Starting a business isn't either."

They'd bought a house on the Atlantic shore near Rehoboth, Delaware, twelve years earlier, the only permanent home their daughter had known. The VOA man she'd met in Bangkok had resigned to start his own public relations firm in Washington.

"I'll buy you out. It'll take me a little time to get the money together."

"You told me that last winter. What's wrong, aren't you making it big these days? What about that hardship post you're in? Don't they pay you big bucks for that these days? What are you spending it on—booze, women, or what?"

"I'll get the money together."

"Yeah, you said that before too." She turned away from the phone. "Hey, would you turn that goddamned TV down!"

He saw them sitting in the small ugly overheated living room of the red brick bungalow in the Washington suburbs, the dinner burned and cold on the stove, both of them drinking and worried about money, both getting uglier, drunker, and more frightened, talking about money.

". . . we can't all be on the government dole, you know. I mean, some people have to work for a living. You could save us both a lot of grief if you took Becky out of that rich man's school. She could live here, with me—"

"She's happy where she is. We've been all through that."

"She'll never be happy with you putting all those fancy ideas in her head. She'll end up the way you did. She could live out in Aberdeen with Mom and Dad."

"Look, I'll be back there in a couple of weeks. I'll talk to you then."

"You're coming back? I heard on TV that the government fell apart over there. God, you must have screwed it up royally again, just like Damascus."

"I've got to go. I'll see you in a couple of weeks. In the meantime, try to get yourself together."

He went back upstairs to shave. In the kitchen again, he made breakfast and listened to the seven o'clock bulletin over the national radio announcing the names of the new Revolutionary Military Council. Colonel N'Sika was the chairman, his deputies Majors Fumbe and Lutete.

Lutete? He paused as he scribbled the names. Which Lutete? Ten men formed the new council, all of them military officers, none above the rank of colonel.

✧ ✧ The sun was still pale in the courtyard as Reddish climbed the embassy steps. His seersucker jacket was wrinkled, his thin hair untidy. A few strands fell forward over the high tanned forehead. The Marine who opened the door thought he smelled whiskey beneath the pungence of the cigar that smoldered in his fingers. Taggert, freshly groomed in South Africa suntans, trailed Reddish across the reception hall reeking of the spice of an aftershave lotion once popular in the PX's of the Far East, as deeply embedded in Reddish's memory as the stinking rice paddies and the snow-swept mountains of the Korean war. It came in blue bottles and looked like embalming fluid. He despised it. It reminded him of a terrible drunken weekend he'd once spent in a Seoul bordello where the Korean girls wore it like perfume.

"They say you were once a weapons man," Taggert said in a bright whisper as he followed Reddish up the stairs. "Small bore, handguns, cold guns, what have you."

Reddish paused on the landing to twist the cigar butt into the urn. "Who told you that?" he asked softly.

"The commo people," Taggert told him uneasily. "The reason I'm asking is that I've got a problem with mine—a Beretta .38. I was wondering if you'd look at it."

Reddish stood searching his pockets. His daughter's letter was there, together with a half-dozen telephone call slips, some scribbled messages from Sarah, and others he'd scrawled to himself. He pulled his steel-rimmed spectacles from his pocket, scrutinizing a slip of paper he'd almost forgotten, hardly conscious of Taggert. He looked at that moment less like a diplomat or an intelligence officer than a broker on small margins, a man without expectations.

"I'll look at it," he said finally, folding the slip away. "But don't tell me what the commo people told you—me or anyone else."

Sarah hadn't arrived in the second-floor suite. The offices were empty, the coffee maker cold. He took a coffee mug from the table and went down the corridor to the defense attaché's suite. Colonel Selvey's office was deserted; so were the cubicles where the army and air attachés sat. A solitary Air Force corporal sat at a lighted desk in the outer office as he typed a cable, a dictionary open on the desk in front of him.

"How are you making it, Mr. Reddish?"

"All right, I guess." He crossed to the coffee table, dropped a dime in the saucer, and drew coffee from the urn.

The corporal bent forward at the keyboard, fingers lifted, hesitated, and then brought his fingers down, his head ducking forward immediately to look at the typed word. "God damn it. I knew I shoulda looked that little mother up. How do you spell guerrillas, Mr. Reddish? Not the ape kind, either."

"Two r's and two l's."

"I shoulda known. The colonel can't spell for shit." He pulled an eraser pencil from the drawer and scrubbed at the cable. Reddish sipped the hot coffee, studying the wall map with the plastic overlay. Marked with a grease pencil were the locations and command structures of the army units in the interior. He searched for the units that hadn't answered the National Revolutionary Council's request for support two days earlier, wondering if the release of the names of the council members meant that they'd fallen in line.

"Is this map up to date?"

"Pretty much. Major Miles keeps it up pretty good."

"Where is Major Miles? I haven't seen him." He put down the cup and brought from his pocket the forgotten routing slip he and Sarah had puzzled over.

"He's in Jo-burg. Went down on a MAC flight last week and now he's busting his ass to get back. Wants us to hold up the god-damned coup for him."

"Do you type Major Miles's reports?"

"Yeah, most of them. You think DIA reads all that shit?"

Miles was an over-age major a year away from retirement un-less he was promoted. Now he was a compulsive report writer and busybody, trying to overhaul his career in a flood of make-work, all of it useless.

"Maybe. See if you can read this for me. It's a note from Miles to Selvey. Haversham left it, but I can't read the writing. That's Miles's handwriting, isn't it?"

The corporal took the slip and held it closer. "Yes, sir, that's his scratching. He's left-handed."

"What's this word here—'avoiding'?"

"What's it say? 'Re Major Lutete: we've been [something] this guy for ten months. Can Les help out. We need more stuff.' No, not 'avoiding.' Couldn't be. 'Stroking.' That's it. 'We've been stroking this guy for ten months. Can Les help out.' That's what it says."

Reddish took back the slip. "Stroking? *Stroking* Lutete?"

"Yes, sir. That's one of the major's buzz words."

"What the hell's it mean?"

"Lutete's a major up on the GHQ G-2 staff, foreign intelligence, I think. Major Miles got him a training tour back in the States last year, Leavenworth, I think it was, and Miles has been in his britches ever since he came back. Only don't say I said so. Lutete's responsi-ble for most of the shit Miles grinds out—order of battle, new weap-ons talks with the Europeans, all of it."

"So Major Lutete's on your payroll, a controlled source?"

The corporal glanced uneasily toward the open door, and his voice dropped. "Yes, sir. Only don't say I said so. Miles has been feeding him stuff too."

Startled, Reddish said, "What kind of stuff?"

"He's been bootlegging DIA studies to him. From what I heard, G-2 and the foreign intelligence staff was in piss-poor shape when Lutete got assigned there, so Miles was helping him out. You know, giving him DIA staff studies on the Middle East, the Arabs, the Chi-coms, and Soviets. DIA gave him the go-ahead, but it was pretty low-grade shit. Most of it had been cleaned up, sanitized."

Reddish looked at the slip again. Can Les help out? We need more stuff. "How did it work, did Lutete ask for material or did Miles just bootleg what he thought would be useful?"

"Both ways, I think."

"Did he ever give him any of our material?"

"You mean Agency stuff? I don't know."

"I'll ask Selvey then."

"O.K., but don't forget."

"Don't worry. Mum's the word. Thanks for the coffee."

Sarah was standing at her desk as he went by angrily, her face fresh, her purse open on the desk in front of her as she rubbed her hands with lotion, her typewriter still covered.

"Open my safe, will you. Bring me those reports we found in Haversham's safe."

She lifted her head, following his plodding back. "Do you know how long I waited for you to come back last night?"

"I told you not to wait." He moved behind his desk.

She stood in the door.

"You most certainly did not."

"Then I told someone to tell you. It comes to the same thing. Bring me those reports. My box too."

"What's so special about these all of a sudden?" she asked as she left the six reports on his blotter. "I thought you'd forgotten about them or that they didn't matter."

"They matter. Major Miles passed them to someone up at GHQ, a major at G-2, foreign intelligence staff."

"Isn't that usual?"

"Sometimes." Intelligence liaison with G-2 required Washington's interagency approval, granted for DIA documents but not for CIA material. He scanned each report in turn, moving them aside. When he'd finished, he read them again, this time arranging them in three separate piles. Only a single report remained on his desk as he returned the others to Sarah. "This one may be it. The others are too old, too vague, or too far away."

"May be what?"

"Where the guns came from," Reddish said. "Shut the door." He picked up the packet of letters he'd found in Masakita's jacket and sorted through them until he found the pale blue envelope postmarked from Algiers three weeks earlier. Dos Santos had written in French, very good French, but the stubby, fluid script was hard to read. He'd recently finished a training school in Algeria and was bound for São Salvador in Angola. He would be arriving at Pointe-Noire, Congo, and needed help in arranging his return to São Salvador, but the nature of the assistance he was asking wasn't at all clear. At that point, the narrative thread vanished—the French illegible, the words hasty, the reminiscences too furtive for Reddish to follow.

"Maybe and maybe not," he puzzled, frowning as Sarah watched, returning again to the CIA report obtained in Algiers a few weeks earlier. The report was attributed to a lower-level Algerian official with good contacts in military and shipping circles whose reporting had been consistently substantiated. It read:

1. THE EAST GERMAN FREIGHTER *POTSDAM* TO BE OFF-LOADED AT POINTE-NOIRE, CONGO, CARRIED THE FOLLOWING ORDNANCE FOR THE POPULAR MOVEMENT FOR THE LIBERATION OF ANGOLA (MPLA):
    —650 MAKAROV PISTOLS
    —500 AK-47 ASSAULT RIFLES
    —50 DEGYAREY LIGHT MACHINE GUNS
    —20 81-MM MORTARS
    —1,500 GRENADES
    —UNSPECIFIED QUANTITIES OF AMMUNITION FOR
        THE ABOVE WEAPONS.

2. THE ABOVE LISTED ORDNANCE WAS SHIPPED IN WOODEN CRATES MARKED "AGRICULTURAL IMPLEMENTS" AND CONSIGNED TO BERNARD DELBEQUES, FRÈRES, POINTE-NOIRE. (HEADQUARTERS NOTE: BERNARD DELBEQUES, FRÈRES, IS A BRAZZAVILLE FREIGHT FORWARDER WHICH HAS COOPERATED IN THE PAST WITH FOREIGN SHIPPERS SENDING MATERIALS TO THE MPLA.)

3. THE MPLA ARMS WERE LOADED ABOARD THE *POTSDAM* ON SEPTEMBER 15 AT MERS-AL-KABIR, ALGERIA. THE ORDNANCE WAS ACCOMPANIED BY AN UNKNOWN MPLA OFFICER WHO RECENTLY COMPLETED TRAINING AT THE ALGERIAN SKIDA COMMANDO SCHOOL.

"If you'd explain to me what you're doing, maybe it would help," Sarah offered, sinking slowly into the chair at the side of the desk.

"I don't need help. I need a goddamned Ouija board."

"You said, 'where the guns came from.' What guns? The ones in Malunga?"

"Agricultural implements again," Reddish mumbled disagreeably. "Coincidences all over the place—too goddamned many. Street brawls don't happen that way." He sat hunched over the Agency report, then turned aside to the blue envelope, puzzling over the Algiers postmark dated September 12, the bright green stamp, and the watermarked envelope. Something else caught his eye. A coffee ring stained the right center of the envelope, washing away a few letters from Masakita's name and title. His own coffee cup was empty; yet he reached for it. How long had Masakita said he'd had it? A week? He put his mug on top of the envelope. The base was too large. Puzzled, he picked up the letter again and re-read it slowly. Suddenly he frowned, turned to the back of the first page, looked at the last word, glanced at the top of the second page, and then quickly at the back, sitting up startled. "For Christ's sake, you stupid pilgrim, don't you read your own bloody mail! A page is missing!"

chapter 6

❖ The local office of Bernard Delbeques, Frères, was closed and locked, a heavy chain shackling the iron shutter. The small fenced yard behind the office, opening to the alleyway behind the port, was also closed, the gate padlocked. Two empty lift vans stood on the loading dock, but Reddish saw no trucks. He returned to his car and drove on to the apartment house.

"They were reading your mail," he told Masakita in the sunny silence of the kitchen, still sweating from his jog up the stairs. He wiped his brow and neck, still standing as Masakita gazed up at him blankly from the kitchen table, where he'd been reading. "It was dos Santos."

"I don't understand."

"The letter from dos Santos, remember? Someone got his hands on it. My guess is that the help dos Santos wanted was getting guns to Angola. The missing page may have told you that, or it may have given you more details than they wanted you to know. How long was the letter on your desk?"

"A week, maybe more. What difference does that make?"

"Who had access to your office?"

"At party headquarters? Everyone. The door was never locked. What difference does it make? Dos Santos didn't say anything about guns. If he had, I would have remembered. I would have told him it was impossible—"

"Read the goddamned letter!" He pulled the envelope from his pocket and thrust it at Masakita and stood watching as he read it slowly. He read it a second time, even more carefully, puzzling as Reddish had between the first and second pages.

"It doesn't make sense," he admitted finally. "Something has been left out."

"A page is missing." Reddish lit a cigarette impatiently. "They pulled a page, the one that probably talked about the guns dos Santos wanted help with."

"But this was the letter in my office—just two pages."

"Then they intercepted it before you got it. They had you on a watch list at the post office and maybe the ministry too. This thing was probably cooking a long time. These guys may not be bright, but they're not stupid. They had the dos Santos letter asking for your help with the MPLA guns. They knew about the hand tools you were expecting from the East Germans. Someone had told them that a few *jeunesse* in the compound had guns of their own and were ready for a fight. You put all that together and you've got what they had—a scenario for wiping out this regime."

He took the letter back, disappointed at Masakita's reaction.

"So you know about things like this. You said yesterday that was how it was done."

"I told you—it's not something you know; it's something you smell. There were too many coincidences. That's not the way things work. Someone was pulling the strings."

"But not just Colonel N'Sika and his council. More men were involved. If my mail was being intercepted, then the internal security directorate was involved. Kadima."

"Probably," Reddish conceded. "People from your own party too."

"How did they get these MPLA guns?"

"I'm not sure. Bought them maybe, stole them. Who the hell knows?" He doused his cigarette under the tap. "You'd better start thinking about what you're going to do. The radio bulletin this morning announced a mass rally tomorrow. N'Sika's going to show the nation the traitors and their guns at Martyr's Square. This crowd is still running scared. Maybe they'll come running here. They're looking for you—"

"So now that you know how it was done, you no longer feel cheated, is that it?" As his strength had returned, so had Masakita's anger; Reddish felt it now.

"I told you. It's not over yet."

"But you have the advantage now—you, the Americans. You know how it was done. You could expose these lies for what they are. That gives you the advantage."

"What advantage?" Reddish said with quiet contempt. "Use your head. This wasn't a very popular regime this past year or so. Look at the headlines—strikes, student riots, the threat of an army mutiny. It was dead on its feet. So we know how they buried it?

Fine, but who gives a shit? Where's the proof? A screwy letter with a page missing? But even if we had the proof, who cares? A few journalists maybe, not because they liked the old President but because it grabs an editor's eye back in Paris or Brussels, where they're trying to sell papers. No one out there in the streets is going to worry about the old regime and how N'Sika put the gun to its head. They're going to start thinking about whether rice prices or cooking oil prices are coming down."

"But not injustice," Masakita asked, "not your government either?"

"For Christ's sake," Reddish said, searching for another cigarette. "Do I have to explain your own people to you?"

"Explain to me why your embassy can't confront N'Sika and his council with what you know."

"Because that's not the way the game is played, not yet anyway. It depends upon N'Sika, what kind of man he is. When we know that, maybe we can start thinking about a way out. But right now I wouldn't bet on it. In the meantime you'd better start thinking about where you want to go and what you want to do."

"But you know what N'Sika's going to say," Masakita said. "Of course you do. Why should that matter? I listened to Nasser in Cairo for years. Strong words every time, and next month even stronger. This nation is weak. The people are poor, every day growing poorer. N'Sika will speak tomorrow, strong words, but in a month nothing will have changed, and so his next speech will be even stronger. Do you think I haven't made such speeches myself in the interior during the rebellions? So regardless of what kind of man this N'Sika is, every speech will be stronger than the last. N'Sika will understand that too, and at last he'll realize that there is nothing he can do to change their condition or his, not in their lifetime. So regardless of what he hopes to do, he will change, only he, not the condition of the people; and he'll end up what Nasser is, a demagogue. There's no escape from it."

He looked at Reddish as if he were expecting him to deny it. Reddish said nothing.

"It doesn't change," Masakita said hotly.

"I suppose not." Reddish looked at his watch. "I've got to go."

Masakita followed him. "I remember a time during the rebellions when a delegation of churchmen came to talk to us at the headquarters of the new provisional government in Stanleyville— the rebel government. All faiths were represented—the Catholic fathers, the Baptists, even two sheikhs from the Moslem commercial community. Suddenly they'd felt the change in the air, a new beginning, the old despotism dead, and they'd all become millennialists, all leaving their pulpits to join the masses in the streets, all expecting a new era of social and economic justice.

"They were disappointed. In a week nothing had changed. In two weeks it was worse than before. In three it was intolerable. Why? Because we were weak, their leaders, because the people were still poor, justice still an abstraction, and Caesar still Caesar except more tyrannical than ever, which was why the pulpits were there in the first place. But they were churchmen, churchmen, men of the cloth! What right had they to be there! What could we say to them? Nothing! The expectation never dies, you see, buried even in those who've forsworn it, men of the cloth! It doesn't change. The rebel government lasted two months, you remember? It was over then, all over. And when the government troops took Stanleyville, you remember what happened, don't you?"

Reddish was at the rear door of the kitchen, the limits of Masakita's world, anxious to go. "I remember."

"They hanged the churchmen with the rebels," Masakita said. "Do you understand? They hanged the churchmen with the rebels, those men who had no right to ask anything of us!"

chapter 7

◆ Reddish thought the diplomatic life something of an anachronism, in style, ceremony, and much of its substance. The personification of its archaic order was the ambassador himself, who—in an age that had leveled empires, titles, and the cutaway coat—still survived at the very core of diplomacy's mystique, pursuing an elaborate code of preening manners and wooden decorum as alien to the workaday world as an aviary of tropical birds. The few aviaries Reddish had seen were in public zoos; the few ambassadors he'd known had been resident in gardens like this one where he sat now examining the bright banks of flower beds as he waited for Bondurant to conclude his conversation with Cecil, the British Ambassador.

It was late afternoon; the day was hot. They sat at poolside where the two Americans had been deep in conversation when Cecil had interrupted them, desperate for information on the new National Revolutionary Council, whose leadership had been revealed that morning. Bondurant was trying to be responsive to Cecil while at the same time attempting to conceal those ugly details he'd just learned from Reddish, who sat to one side saying nothing. Embarrassed by Bondurant's predicament—his attempting to be forthcoming enough not to be thought totally ignorant of what had happened, as Cecil was, yet circumspect enough not to yield his diplomatic advantage—Reddish had tried to excuse himself for a walk about the garden, but Bondurant had waved him back to his chair.

Cecil was disappointed that Bondurant could clarify so little. He'd arrived in the expectation that the new council was well and favorably known to Bondurant, to be told that contact had already been established, and that the full details of the events of the past two days could now be explained to him.

Bondurant had quietly disabused him of those hopes. Cecil's

face had fallen. "I'm most anxious to reassure London, you understand, but I rather suppose it will all come clear in the next few
days, don't you? I mean it usually does. The city is already peaceful
again, despite those gunshots during the night. The question of diplomatic recognition won't arise, will it? We recognize nations, not
regimes like you chaps. We may be a bit slow establishing contact,
however. God knows we don't want to go running about encourag-
ing colonels everywhere to go smashing established authority, do
we? Well, I suppose, we're all in the same boat," he offered sympathetically, "drifting in the same fog. If it's any consolation, the
French, Belgian, and Israeli embassies are as much in the dark as
everyone else."

"It isn't," Bondurant replied. "No other country has provided
military and economic assistance at the same level as we. No other
embassy was thought to know as much as we either."

"Quite, oh yes. One forgets that side of it." Cecil's look traveled
toward Reddish, as if the rebuke might have been intended for him.
Extraordinary eyes, he'd often thought—brutally cold, they seemed,
like some of the South African farmers he'd met. The way they got
after treating some of these Kaffirs in their own coin, he supposed,
all the color bleached out. He had forgotten to ask Carol Browning
about Reddish. He assumed Bondurant had been very cross with
him, as he'd been with Major Murray, his own attaché, who'd
proved to be such an ignoramus as the streets were going berserk.

"That does make it more difficult for you, I suppose," Cecil
sympathized, remembering a piece of information that might cheer
Bondurant up. "By the way, I understand our Russian friends are to
be sent packing. The French and Belgians are convinced of it. Quite
inevitable, as a matter of fact. I find the logic quite compelling.
Have you heard anything?"

"I heard something this noon from Simon Lowenthal," Bondurant said without enthusiasm.

"What's the logic?" Reddish asked.

"Straightforward enough," Cecil answered cheerfully, eager to
explain something to the Americans. God knew his opportunities
were rare enough. "If N'Sika does as the radio announcement
promised, put the rebels and their weapons on display at Martyr's
Square, he has no choice but to send our Soviet colleagues packing.
The weapons were Russian-made, after all. N'Sika can hardly accuse Federov of subversion, of attempting to overthrow the old regime while maintaining the *status quo ante*, can he? The Russian
Embassy is at minimal staff level now. The next step backwards will

be a rupture in relations." Cecil smiled eagerly, trying to win some enthusiasm. "This Colonel N'Sika will have no choice." He waited, his smile fading. Bondurant's apathy seemed unshakable.

Bondurant and Reddish watched Cecil go back up the walk to his car.

"If it were logic we were dealing with, I might feel reassured," Bondurant confessed, "but after what you've told me, I don't feel reassured in the slightest. What do you think?"

"I think they've got enough problems without taking on the Russians. I don't think they're interested in making more enemies."

"Are they sophisticated enough to understand that?"

"I don't know."

"That's the whole problem, isn't it? None of us knows what kind of men we're dealing with, except that they're killers. How much do you trust this new source of yours?"

Reddish had told Bondurant everything that he'd told Masakita, attributing it to a source in the workers party. But he hadn't told him about Masakita or the defense attaché officer supplying Agency reports to Major Lutete at G-2.

"He was there. He saw it happening."

"But do you trust him?" Bondurant watched him suspiciously.

"I trust him," Reddish said indifferently.

"It's grotesque, irrational!" Bondurant exclaimed, his disapproval vented: Reddish might have been talking about his broker. "All of this simply to justify a murderous grab for power by a few hoodlums! Several hundred terrified, untrained, undisciplined Africans given access to useless guns and then shot down in cold blood to justify bringing down the regime—"

"Some of the *jeunesse* already had guns of their own. I'm not sure they planned on the *jeunesse* using those guns in the crates."

"Then that's even more irrational. They must have known we'd discover it in time, that they couldn't conceal it from us." He turned to see Reddish's reaction. "They were too clever."

"They were worried about us," Reddish said. "They were getting ready to knock off a regime we'd helped create, we supported. So they were worried about what we might do. They cooked up a plot that sounded credible, a reason to legitimize the coup—a radical grab for power which the President couldn't cope with." The adrenaline he'd felt earlier that day had drained away; Bondurant's agitation seemed far remote to him. "If we found out about it, we'd be too late. We'd have to lump it, like everyone else. I think they're still worried about us. They're soldiers, this new council. They're in over their heads. People who are in over their heads do stupid things. Someone needs to calm them down, tell them to take it easy."

"That's preposterous."

"They're killers and they're scared," Reddish continued. The breeze lifted again from the river, and he watched it move high in the trees, not touching the motionless waters of the pool. "Someone needs to talk to them, settle them down, give them some sense of security. A word from us might do it."

"Do you mean to sit there and suggest that we hold out our hand to these people? To tell them that we've seen through this murderous little charade, but that's all right now!" He leaned forward contemptuously, trying to draw Reddish's gaze, but Reddish deliberately avoided him, looking toward the front gate, where Becker's sedan was entering.

"They're not Russians, they're Africans," he replied, "but what you said yesterday at the country team meeting still holds. They're armed and they're blundering around in the dark. There's no use sitting here babbling to ourselves about it, getting pissed off. We ought to open up a channel to them. We will anyway. It's just a matter of time." Even without turning, he felt Bondurant's choler rise.

Lowenthal and Becker left the sedan with Colonel Selvey. The houseboy pointed toward the rear garden, and the three men started down the walk toward the pool; but Bondurant, too provoked to reply to Reddish's proposal, stood up impatiently and waved them back to the house. "I'll be with you shortly! Go on inside, have a drink!" They turned and Bondurant remained standing, watching them enter the house. "You haven't mentioned this to them?" he demanded, still furious.

"No, not to anyone."

"Then I prefer that you not." He picked up his poplin jacket from the back of the chair. "I understand now why you were so obstinate yesterday in the country team meeting, refusing to suggest any Soviet complicity. You knew this then."

"No, not all of it."

"But most of it."

"It wasn't a good cable. I debriefed a Cuban defector two months ago. He told me Havana had imposed a moratorium on Cuban activity in the region and that the Russian Embassy in Brazza was enforcing it, so I didn't think the Cubans or the Soviets were involved. His documentation was better than Becker's. It was a poor cable."

"And your own, have you written yours yet?" Bondurant's voice was still chilly.

"I was waiting until I talked to you."

"Good," Bondurant said. "Have yourself another drink while I deal with them. I want to talk some more after they've gone. And I don't want you to breathe a word of this to anyone, not even Langley, until I decide how we're going to handle this bloody mess."

Bondurant went back to the residence. A few minutes later a white-coated houseboy came down the walk to the pool carrying a silver tray with a gin and tonic. He didn't know Bondurant's servants, and he didn't know this one; but the man was smiling at him as if he were an old friend and jabbering all the while in Lingala. At last, after a few questions, Reddish understood what he was saying. He was telling him that his brother had once driven Reddish from Kikwit to Idiofa in a government Landrover with the provincial governor. They had had lunch together, Reddish and his brother, in his native village, where his sister had given them palm wine. Did he remember?

Reddish remembered. The trip was two years past and three hundred miles away, but the houseboy, who hadn't even been there, described it as if it had happened yesterday. How they knew these things, he didn't know, but they knew them, enclosing foreigners like himself in a gossamer skein so finely drawn that a breath might blow it away; few saw it, fewer knew it existed; yet it was there, embracing them all.

The sedan drove away, and Bondurant returned carrying copies of two telegrams. "Becker's heard that the new council will break relations with the Soviets," he said, sitting down again. "Decidedly conservative apparently, these colonels—right-wing hoodlums—although that's not what their cable says." He handed Reddish the cables. "Does that offend you?"

"Does what offend me?"

"Characterizations such as that. Is that why you're so anxious to establish contact with them—to re-establish that special relationship you enjoyed with the former President?"

"I hadn't even thought of it."

"But if they were a little to the right of center, these army officers, that would make it all the easier for you, wouldn't it?" Bondurant waited, thinking he'd guessed the strategy. "Majors and colonels are much more malleable than social democrats, aren't they?"

Reddish didn't reply, reading the cable. Becker had written:

COLONEL N'SIKA'S PRINCIPAL ADVISER IS MAJOR JEAN-BERNARD DE VAUX, A BELGIAN OFFICER WHO FOUGHT IN INDO CHINA AND ALGERIA AND DISTINGUISHED HIMSELF AS A MERCENARY MAJOR DURING THE INFAMOUS SIMBA REBELLIONS. HE WAS HELD IN HIGH ESTEEM BY THE FORMER PRESIDENT AND THE ARMY HIGH COMMAND WHO CONSIDERED HIM PART OF THE GHQ "BRAIN TRUST."

LIKE COLONEL N'SIKA AND THE OTHER COUNCIL MEMBERS WE HAVE BEEN ABLE TO IDENTIFY, DE VAUX IS A POLITICAL MODERATE AND PRO-WESTERN IN HIS ORIENTATION.

"You know de Vaux?" Bondurant asked as Reddish returned the two cables, as disappointed as Cecil had been.

"I know him."

"Selvey believes he has access to the council," Bondurant continued. "Evidently, he's been cultivating a Major Lutete on the foreign intelligence staff at G-2 who is a brother or cousin of this other Major Lutete who's Colonel N'Sika's deputy. Do you know him?"

"No."

"If we're to open up a channel to this new council, I'd prefer it not be Colonel Selvey," Bondurant considered, wavering. "I told him to do absolutely nothing for the time being."

They sat in silence. The wind stirred again in the trees, high up, where the golden light of late afternoon lay entangled. The shadows were beginning to encroach from the garden wall; the night guard appeared to turn on the pool lights.

At last Bondurant stirred. "We both know what will happen," he admitted. "You have to be fatalistic about it, I suppose. If Colonel N'Sika proves to be someone we can work with, as Becker and Selvey believe, then no one in Washington is going to be too concerned about how he seized power. They're not going to be inclined to look behind the facts as they know them. But you may be right. Frightened men do irrational things." He paused, his silence burdened with misgivings. "As much as I despise it, it might be wise if you were to open up a back channel to this new council. I suppose you could manage it?"

"I think so."

"Tonight, if you can. Assure them that they have nothing to fear from us, but that we're concerned about internal stability. There should be no more bloodshed, no more killing. What's done is done."

He stood up wearily, putting his empty glass aside. They circled the pool toward the walk, Bondurant still thoughtful. "I find it curious that Colonel Selvey was so eager to exploit this connection of his. This Major Lutete." He lifted his head as they went back up the walk toward the residence. "I take it Colonel Selvey wasn't in any way involved in this?"

The same idea had occurred to Reddish and still troubled him. "No, I don't think so."

"Not you either, I assume." Bondurant stopped suddenly, the possibility occurring to him for the first time.

"No, we weren't involved, not in any way."

"I'm to take that on faith, am I?"

Reddish groped for reassurance. "If it had been my coup, I would have just taken the presidential compound. If I'd planted guns in the party compound, I would have told them to pop the pins, give them old Belgian ammo gone to green cheese, then cover their tracks later." He continued along the walk reflectively, head down. "But maybe someone wanted a shoot-out, which was stupid. They butchered it up, whoever planned this thing. They were lucky it didn't blow out of control. No, it wasn't me."

He stopped, looking back at Bondurant, who'd stopped in his tracks, terrified. Now he caught up with him. "A few hundred bewildered, untrained Africans are given guns and then shot down to justify someone's obscene grab for power, and you tell me the idea wasn't at fault, just the execution. You amaze me, Reddish—absolutely bewilder and amaze me."

"You asked me whether I was involved."

"I know what I asked you! Good God, man, listen to yourself sometime! Just listen! You think like they do! No wonder you found them out so quickly! But it's not just them. You've got us all at a disadvantage!"

He left Reddish standing there, like a leper, and went back to the house.

Reddish couldn't reach de Vaux that evening. The switchboard operator at the para camp refused to put through his call. He drove out through the dark streets to the hillside para camp where the new Revolutionary Council had its headquarters. The lieutenant at the gate refused to let him through. Reddish folded five hundred francs in his *carte d'identité*, passed it to him through the window, and explained that de Vaux was expecting him. The lieutenant motioned him to the side of the road beyond the gate, where Reddish waited, still stung by Bondurant's rebuke.

In the Far East once, one of Reddish's fellow case officers had been sent home by the ambassador after he'd bought a local newspaper editor and had been found out by the minister of information, a notorious anti-American voluptuary. The ambassador had known informally of the arrangement, but after the recruitment was publicized he had sent off an outraged self-righteous cable to State demanding the case officer's removal. Langley had obliged. "I'm fucking tired of doing their goddamn donkey work," the recalled officer had told Reddish the day of his departure. "I do their fucking stud work for them and then the lights come on, they get caught, and they snivel on their pillows like a convent of bloody virgins—the ambassador, the DCM, the whole crew. But turn out the lights again and see what happens! They all come back to the dildo, every last one of them."

Like Bondurant, Reddish remembered, watching the lieutenant through the Fiat window. Ten minutes later, the officer crossed the roadbed from the guard shack to tell him that the council was in night session and de Vaux unavailable. He said he would send a message to de Vaux telling him Reddish had been at the gate.

He returned to his villa, fixed a drink, and sat in the study, tired, fed up, and lonely. The telephone awoke him three hours later, the drink barely touched on the table in front of the sofa.

"I'm sorry, Mr. Reddish," the commo watch officer said, "but I thought I'd better give you a call, just in case. We just got it over the ticker. Agence France Presse, Reuters, and AP put it on the wires about five minutes ago."

"It's all right. Put what on the wires?"

"The executions. They shot the President and six cabinet ministers at zero hours thirty, local, something called the National Revolutionary Court. AFP says the executions took place at the old para camp prison. They also executed fourteen mercenaries for crimes against the people, quote unquote. Do you think I should call the duty officer or do you want to tell the ambassador and Becker yourself?"

chapter 8

❖ "Tell me about Lowenthal," Cecil asked slyly, nibbling a biscuit. "Is he really the Francophile he appears to be?"

"He's nice, actually," Carol Browning replied.

It hadn't occurred to Cecil that "Francophile" might require definition; he decided to let it pass. He sat propped up in bed, pillows at his back, his nakedness half covered by a spread. She sat on the edge of the bed, hair in disarray, wearing only his wife's dressing gown, a size too large for her. Cecil was helping himself to the biscuits and cheese they'd brought from the kitchen to the upstairs guest room an hour earlier. Two glasses and a bottle of claret sat on the bedside tray with the plate of biscuits.

"Nice? That's a rather bland word, isn't it? Something of a nit, I should say."

"Besides, he's very intelligent, despite what people say."

"Oh, I'm quite sure." He could only guess at what she meant by intelligence, since hers, he'd discovered, seemed almost nonexistent. Cognition was, for her, largely intuitive and tactile, but he had no idea what these signals meant to her as they reached the cerebrum. "What about the colonel, Colonel What's-his-name, the little chap with the buttonlike eyes?"

"Colonel Selvey? He's all right, but he isn't very smart. Diplomatic, I mean."

"He seems quite pleasant. My wife is quite fond of him, fancies that most Americans should speak that way. He's from the South, isn't he? What about Reddish? Curious man, don't you think? Actually, I've never had much of a conversation with him. Never seems to have much to say." He cut a slice of Camembert to decorate a biscuit. "Tell me, is it Reddish or Haversham. Or Becker?"

"What?"

"The CIA majordomo. The man in charge."

"We really shouldn't talk about these things."

"Really? Not talk about them? Don't be silly. Of course we should talk about them. We have no secrets now, do we? How does Walt get on with him?"

"With who?"

"Reddish. Weren't we talking about Reddish?"

"I don't know."

"Sees quite a lot of him, does he?"

"No, not at all. Almost never."

"Are you sure?"

"Of course I'm sure."

Cecil brushed the crumbs from his fingers and moved the tray aside. "Really. Then it must be Haversham or Becker."

"Do we *have* to talk about these things." She sighed impatiently and let the robe slip from her shoulders.

Cecil looked the other way. "The Camembert is a little dry, don't you think?"

She leaned forward and turned off the bed lamp. Cecil immediately reached down to switch on the radio on the lower shelf of the bedside table.

Her shadow loomed over him. "Why do you always want the radio on?" she demanded from the darkness.

"But I thought you liked it."

"You're trying to shut me out!"

"Oh, but I'm not at all. It's soothing. Don't you think it soothing?"

"It's awful. It's like a dentist's office."

"Really? A dentist's office?" His head lifted. Another scrap of Americana. "American dentists have music in their surgery? How extraordinary? You mean to lull one to sleep. Is that how they do it?"

"You want me to go." Her voice had an edge to it.

"Not at all. Besides, you couldn't possibly go. The curfew has begun. No, on the contrary, I quite enjoy having you here."

"But not physically. You just want to gossip."

"My dear, in the physical sense, as you put it, we've been sharing this bed since the nine o'clock BBC. I'm fifteen years older. You must make allowances."

Furiously, she ripped off the spread.

"I wonder what poor Federov is doing," he muttered, trying to ignore her as he groped in the darkness for the spread, sitting up. "He was always out of it, you know." His fingers touched her naked midriff, as soft as velvet. "Sorry. It must have been quite humiliating for him, posted here with absolutely nothing to do."

"Don't you ever stop talking shop?" He heard her angry breathing.

"Is that what you think? Oh, but you mustn't. I'm not at all as serious as some make me out to be." Her naiveté, deliberately cultivated, seemed to him not so much innocence as a grosser form of stupidity. He imagined that she was in love with him and he found that touching. He was moved not to dalliance so much as gallantry, treating her with a tenderness which might awaken a spoiled sensual child to finer things. "Do you hear that?" he now asked.

"What?" The phone had rung three times since they'd climbed the dark stairs for the guest bedroom. They'd let it ring without answering.

"The radio. It's Brahms, isn't it? The variation on Haydn?" He lay back. The music filled him with peace.

She leaned across him, her soft, fragrant body crushing his, and snapped off the radio.

The room was dark and silent. Still she lay across him, obliterating all else with her sheer physical presence. He didn't want to offend her, but he was physically exhausted. He didn't have the strength to begin. At last she moved and touched him where he wasn't accustomed to being touched; he waited, like a passer-by on a beach watching a drowned man being revived. Then, from deep in the ashes, that old flicker of heroism lifted once again. As she moved to position herself, the blood throbbed in his ears, the tide lifted, and he knew that one simply couldn't help loving a woman like that, stupid or not, just as some old soldiers loved war, a gross, sensual, fickle, brutal woman too for all the heroism she occasionally inspired.

❖❖ Ambassador Federov, like Reddish, had been awakened with the news of the executions. An old cardigan pulled over his pajama top, he sat at this desk on the fourth floor of the Soviet mission, his short fingers tracing out the lines of the teletyped message in front of him, just brought from the *rezidentura* teletype, his hair still tousled from sleep.

"Shot. *Shot!* Still more? How many? Six? *Fourteen?* By whose authority?"

Klimov sat fully dressed in the deskside chair. Slightly behind him stood Ryabkin, the Tass correspondent, wearing trousers and a pajama top.

"The Revolutionary Court," said Klimov. His blond hair was combed back over his skull, his blue eyes pale, the jaw muscles standing out as powerfully as biceps. Federov looked up quickly to catch the irony in his face, but it was the Tass man's tired face that drew his attention.

"All right. Yes, go back to bed—go on. Button your trousers too, or your wife will think something else of these midnight messages. We've had enough scandal here. Thank you, yes. We can manage now. Go back to bed."

Ryabkin nodded gratefully and backed out, shutting the door behind him.

"You know them, the six?" Federov asked, still astonished.

"The worst, the most corrupt—like the President."

"So they did it, just as he told you they would," Federov marveled, "just as he predicted." His eyes were still fastened to the press report as his right hand fumbled with the middle drawer of the desk. He paused, hand groping inside the drawer, then brought out a bottle of brandy, which he passed to Klimov. "*Shot* them—just like that? Something called the Revolutionary Court? Did he predict that too?"

"He simply said it would be done." Klimov rose to fetch the tumblers from the glass-fronted cabinet against the opposite wall. "He said six would be executed with the President."

"Six? Why six? Because they were the most corrupt?"

"He said there would be six. But the numbers don't matter. He told us it would be done, and so it was. 'Properly,' he said. 'In ways Moscow would understand.' "

Federov's skepticism returned. "So just like that, a revolutionary court materializes out of thin air, like this magician himself, and shoots the worst of them. In the worst of prisons. Materializes like this mysterious Revolutionary Military Council, like this phantom Colonel N'Sika, of whom nothing is known! No, no, Aleksandr, he's a charlatan, this man of yours—a circus performer. Just tricks, nothing else. So he pretends Colonel N'Sika and these others are his revolutionaries. All right. So let him pretend. But nothing will come of it—nothing at all. So six men are shot, six ministers. The President was executed too. So what does it mean? What does he want now? Money?"

"Patience, that's all he asks. To be patient, not to be concerned about the guns, they will show tomorrow. He said that it will be managed, managed in ways we will support."

"And what does that mean?"

"After the executions, there will be no turning back. N'Sika will make that clear tomorrow. Disengagement with the Belgians and the others will take time. Patience is what he is asking."

"Patience?" Federov leaned forward scornfully. "Patience? What does he know of patience? To shoot six or seven corrupt politicians is nothing at all! He's playing with words, this man of yours. And what is it that N'Sika will say tomorrow? What can he say? Nothing at all!"

"N'Sika will nationalize the economy, the extractive industries first, then the waterways and railroads."

Federov laughed. "And did he tell you who will manage this new revolutionary economy? The Bulgarians? The North Koreans? Are trained cadres going to materialize out of thin air too, like this phantom Revolutionary Court? The man is a charlatan, admit it! Disengage? Disengage from what? Who'll buy the copper, eh? He's a fool!"

"He says they'll need help, managing the economy. N'Sika will send for you."

"N'Sika will send for me and then it will all come easily, eh, this new revolution."

"He said there will be a few problems," Klimov admitted. " 'African problems,' he said. But after these problems are disposed of, the revolution will follow its own course."

"What African problems?"

"Some council members are weak. There's the Belgian, de Vaux, but N'Sika will handle them in his own way."

"So he speaks for N'Sika?"

"N'Sika knows he's been in contact with us," Klimov said.

Federov smiled. "So you're tempted, is that it? You're tempted to believe this liar and hypocrite?" He left his desk to open the shades at the rear window, where dawn had begun to show in the eastern sky. "So he tempts you, does he? You need more activity, that's all—more to do, like all of us. Shut up like this, day after day, boredom makes us stupid, tempts us with imaginary excitement. It's the tedium. Like the code clerks upstairs. Shut up all day with their machines, they're like monks cloistered inside, pretending they talk only to Moscow or to God. No wonder the prophets' imaginations were so lively. Men in prison show the same disorders. When I was in the Urals, it was that way too—cut off from everything else. So what shall we do?" He smiled ambiguously. "Shall we pave the tennis courts, put a duckpin court in the basement, or give this little charlatan a few rubles, pretending that the hour of our deliverance is at hand?"

Within the confines of the small Soviet mission—his cramped office, and the shabby living quarters where he dined alone not because he despised the comforts the Western envoys enjoyed but because he couldn't reciprocate their invitations in a style that would do credit to Moscow—Federov's tone was often one of self-mockery. Admitted to his tiny little flat, smelling of cabbage and garlic from the Armenian's rooms across the hall, how could one take seriously either his ministry or that of Moscow's imperial city.

In his self-effacement, Federov would never substitute his ambitions for Moscow's, but Moscow was far away on that gray African morning. Watching him as he plodded back and forth across the worn carpet, Klimov suspected he was also tempted.

chapter 9

❖ The African youth sat sleepily at the dirty wooden table, his dry mouth foul with sleep, his long black arms folded across its grimy surface, warm with morning sunshine. The closed courtyard was bright beyond the open window. He could smell the cooking charcoal from the morning fires, hear the chattering women in the compound yard and the sound of the faucet filling the pots and jugs from the pipe in the center of the lot. His room was small and dark, with unplastered concrete-block walls and a hinged wooden window opposite the door to the passageway. A wooden cot covered by a straw-filled pallet lay in one corner. Two folding wooden chairs stolen from an open-air bar leaned against the wall. A tin lantern stood on the wooden stool next to the bed. The concrete floor was littered with flattened cigarette butts; more filled the sardine can on the table next to the enamel bowl crusted with manioc from yesterday's meal.

He tried to forget his hunger and concentrate on the dog-eared paperback pressed open by his folded arms. On the wooden shelf above the window were a dozen more paperbacks. On the wall over the cot were a few yellowing newspaper clippings torn from the Sunday soccer supplement, one of which showed him standing with his *cité* teammates at the stadium after they'd won the President's trophy. Next to the clippings were pictures of Pelé, Che, Nkrumah, Mao, and Patrice Lumumba. Bright light filtered through the incomplete construction at the top of the wall, where the tin roof and wooden beams atop the concrete block shell were without a fascia.

In the courtyard outside the window four small boys were kicking a loose cotton wad back and forth against the wall. The sunlight touched the yellowing thumb-worn pages of the old Gallimard paperback edition of Camus, and he pushed it forward into the shadows. Two pages were missing, like the front cover, and he'd lost the narrative thread. He frowned and dropped his chin closer to the text. In the dark eyebrow above his right lid was a sickle-shaped scar which curled to the hairline, the result of a soccer match on a stone and glass-filled clay lot.

The cloth ball had flopped into a mud puddle, no longer usable, and the small boys were now flinging it against the building, shrieking from just below the window. Crispin lifted himself out of his chair, seized the sill, and pulled himself forward. "Get out of here! *Go on! Get out—out!*"

The boys fled across the clay yard and he sat down again, picking at the crust of manioc in the bottom of the bowl, but he'd again lost the thread. He pushed the book and bowl away abruptly, took his dirty towel from the foot of the bed, and went down the passageway and into the sunlit courtyard.

He shoved his way through the gaggle of women gathering at the faucet with their pails, bottles, and pans, gossiping idly as they waited in line. Two younger women with black babies hanging from their shoulders like marmosets were at the faucet. Crispin pushed through them, bent over, and rubbed his face and hair with cold water, then splashed his chest and arms.

A middle-aged woman in a dark, filthy cotton *wax* watched him cunningly, head cocked, picking her teeth with a straw, her plastic pail at her feet.

"What are you looking at, old grandmother?"

She clucked to herself, removed the straw, and told the other women he'd been hiding in his room for days, like Kimbi the basket maker, except for a different reason. The wife of his cousin Kalemba, the postal clerk, fed him each day like one of her five children. The woman leaned forward, sucking rapidly with her lips, eyes closed like a suckling child, as she told Crispin to climb onto her shoulders and hang there like one of her infant grandchildren.

"Green mamba." A young woman laughed, holding a naked child on her cocked hip.

"Listen, mama," Crispin cried, pointing to the older woman. "I saw you burning your son's green uniform. I saw you!"

She laughed. "They're coming to get you," she told him, pointing across the compound toward the wooden door opening into a back alley of Malunga. "N'Sika's soldiers. Coming through the wall. Mamba." She clucked contemptuously. "Mamba. *Ntoka.* Green serpent."

Crispin hadn't left the compound for days, hiding in his room since that evening he'd returned from the soccer game to find the party headquarters in flames.

"Mamba! *Ntoka!* Green mamba!" two small boys shrieked as

they followed him back across the yard, lifting their knees like soldiers, voices raised in those cries of derision that followed the *jeunesse* through the lanes of Malunga, but only after they were out of sight: "*Ntoka!* Green serpent!"

He turned savagely, but they bolted and fled in opposite directions like frightened pullets.

Inside his room he pulled the green twill uniform of the *jeunesse* from beneath the pallet, searched the flap pockets for cigarettes, found none, and flung it under the bed. He sank down at the table again, swept the paperback aside, and took a ten-franc copybook from the table drawer. His name was carefully printed on the cover: CRISPIN MONGOY. On each inside page he had entered chapter headings, usually in the form of questions that had occurred to him while reading Franz Fanon, Nkrumah, or Lenin: "What is the Revolution?" "How is it Won?" "What is Discipline?" "What is the Bantu Proletariat?" "What is the Bantu Bourgeoisie?"

Under the chapter headings he had entered those thoughts that had occurred to him as he was walking the lanes of Malunga, as he sat selling Kimbi's baskets in the *grand marché* and the Ivory Market, or as he sat here at this table night after night long after the lamps were extinguished. "You are the Revolution," he had written under the first entry. A dozen or so lines preceding it had been scratched out; only this sentence had satisfied him. He had added to it as the months passed: "You are the Revolution—your skin, your hopelessness, your anger, your pride, your humiliation!"

The words had excited him when he'd first discovered them. They excited him now.

The notebook had been his conscience and mentor, born of necessity. The party meetings and debates left him confused and tongue-tied, humiliated by his lack of education. His lack of education hadn't been an embarrassment when he'd been a well-known player with the local soccer team, a sure candidate for the national team if a torn Achilles tendon hadn't ended his career. He was recruited to the party *jeunesse* at a time when his life seemed over, assigned to the disciplinary brigades not for his scholarship or mental ability but for his popularity and leadership. He'd transferred to the party the hunger for recognition that once nourished his soccer ambitions. Daydreaming about his success and that of the party, his fantasies continued to define themselves in the regalia of his old soccer days—the party triumphant; Crispin and his colleagues ascending the victor's box at the stadium to be acclaimed by a wildly grateful nation; Crispin in cleated shoes, leg stockings, and shorts, holding a soccer ball.

He knew how immature were these fantasies which one day would expose him to ridicule before those far better educated than he, clever in ways he wasn't. As he succeeded in the party, he would be expected to make speeches, chair meetings with members far more agile than he, and prepare programs for younger members with secondary school degrees. The notebook had been his tutor.

His first speech had come a month earlier, after he was chosen deputy chief of the disciplinary brigade. He spoke to an incoming group on party discipline and social responsibility. He'd drawn upon his notebook for his remarks, but his delivery had been faltering, his phrase-making lacking any larger intellectual context, his embarrassment evident.

After the larger meeting, a private critique was held in the party committee room. Dr. Bizenga, the party ideologue and deputy, chaired the critique, flanked by the *jeunesse* executive secretariat, most of them university undergraduates who disdained the green twill of the disciplinary cadres.

Dr. Bizenga was critical of the speech in a lengthy discourse of his own, employing the same poisonous epithets of which he was so fond and which made his monthly address to the assembled party plenary so obscure—"oligarchic parasitism, monopolistic capitalistic combines, obscurantist revanchism."

Pierre Masakita, who had wandered in searching for the party librarian, was intrigued by Dr. Bizenga's remarks, and sat down to listen. The *jeunesse* secretary gave him a copy of Crispin's speech. Bizenga told the group that Crispin's speech was amateurish. What was its origin—*vanity*? A wounded vanity? Bitter, yes, but the social conscience was still embryonic, now punishing words in place of a leather ball. Perhaps it was what might be expected from an ex-soccer player. A wounded vanity had little to do with the struggle for political, social, and economic justice.

"I think it's a good speech," Masakita had disagreed. "Vanity is useful. Even humiliation is a revolutionary impulse, isn't it? Who said that. Marx, I think. What matters is strong roots, not the soil that nourished them. So humiliation can make strong roots too. No, I think Mongoy has made a good beginning."

Dr. Bizenga disagreed violently and launched into another tirade as Masakita listened patiently.

"Well, it's not my business," he said finally, "but you have to be careful about these speeches of yours—careful that your words don't become an end in themselves. Otherwise they'll soon be bought up by the bourgeois press, by the broadsheets where salon intellectuals purge their literary consciences." He seemed to be smiling as he spoke, but Dr. Bizenga wasn't amused. "But the end of humiliation isn't words," Masakita continued. "It's action, social action. 'Clowns, they chase after words!' Who said that?" He looked at the students who sat at the table with Bizenga. "Was it Lenin? Possibly. But that's not important either, identifying authorship. Does the fact that it was Lenin make it any more true? No, of course not. Pedantry becomes an end in itself, doesn't it?—like words? No, I think it was a useful speech, and I'm sure Mongoy has learned from it."

After Masakita had left, Dr. Bizenga had again disagreed. As an ex–soccer player, Crispin had understood.

But now Masakita had disappeared along with Dr. Bizenga. Many of his friends were dead. Had he found a gun too, he would have joined them, fought as they fought, and won his martyrdom in the streets of Malunga as they had won theirs. In the bottom of his tin suitcase under the bed was a small nickel-plated Belgian revolver he'd bought from a young boy in the Ivory Market, a purse-snatcher, to add to the cache of small arms concealed at the compound; but even if he'd had it with him, it would have been of little use. Only four rusty cartridges were in the chamber.

He felt physically ill, denied first the heroism of dying in Malunga and now denied his future as well. For a second time his life had been taken from him. This afternoon, N'Sika would speak in Martyr's Square. The captured *jeunesse* and their guns would be shown to the nation.

It was almost noon, and the heat beyond the window was hellish, the yard nearly empty. Flies drifted out of the scalding light of the dusty courtyard and into the hot shadows. In the deathless, sterile silence, his despair knew no bounds: body and mind floated free. The universe floated like dust around him; the thin, weak life-giving aromas of cooking manioc and rice that stirred from the dark doorways where the midday meals were being prepared made him giddy and nauseated.

He peeled off his shirt and went out to the courtyard again weak with vertigo, to bend to the faucet to drink, and then to slap his body alive with cold water.

As he returned, an old woman stirred indolently through the heat to gather up the clothes that had been spread to dry in the sun over a small leafless shrub near Kalemba's door. She was chewing on a piece of goat meat, isolating the fatty gristle as she chewed without touching it.

He looked at her with loathing. She spat the meat into her

hand. "Is the green mamba changing its skin to a fish?" she asked, looking at his wet shoulders and face—"to a strong wet fish, *mbisi makasi?*"

"One day you will talk the gold out of your teeth, old grandmother. Why do you eat my feet like this?"

In his room he changed into a clean shirt, slipped into a pair of rubber thongs, pulled a pair of sunglasses on, and went down the corridor to the room of Kimbi, the basket maker. Kimbi sat as he always sat in the darkened room, his back to the door, facing the gauze-covered window, the powerful stump of his body rising from the burlap mound, his strong fingers weaving the mats, baskets, and imitation tribal masks which vendors bought from him to sell in the tourist markets. Next to the burlap mound was the wooden dolly on which Kimbi sat when he left his dark room, his weaver's hands protected from the gravel, concrete, and laterite by a pair of rubber pads cut from old automobile tires.

He only left the room at night. The same lorry accident that had amputated his legs had taken away his face. The flaming gasoline had left only the skull, the bone covered by the sheerest membrane of pink flesh and scar tissue. The stubs of his teeth stuck out at odd angles, like stumps in a burned-out field.

Kimbi didn't turn as Crispin entered. His hands stopped. He waited as Crispin took a few baskets and mats from the rear wall, reached behind him to take the numbered scraps of newspaper that Crispin pulled from each item, and didn't move again until the door had closed.

The old woman laughed as she watched Crispin, the ex–soccer player and *jeunesse* militant, carrying the baskets across the yard like any girl or old woman, off to the Ivory Market near the foreign embassies to sell his wares to the tourists and *flamands*.

"*Mbisi!*" the old woman called. "Don't let the fishermen catch you!"

❖ ❖ In the gathering dusk thousands gathered in Martyr's Square under a sickle moon, some carrying placards and banners, others with wares to sell, like Crispin, but all of them eager and restless. The soldiers came first in trucks and weapons carriers. The speed and recklessness of their arrival terrified those close to the barricades near the wooden platform in the center of the square.

They surged away, pressing wildly against those who were crowding forward, many of them clapping their hands rhythmically, urged forward by the paid political hucksters who moved through the throng. The soldiers restored order with their gun butts.

The motorcycle brigade followed the trucks, gliding eerily through the dusk without sirens, lights on. Military officers emerged from the sedans and dispersed themselves along the platform, but only a single figure climbed the steps and stood in the glare of the strobe lights, his voice amplified a hundredfold by the sound trucks which surrounded the open square and sent it reverberating far into the dark streets and boulevards.

He spoke in Lingala, not French. The crowd throbbed and chattered, straining from the rear ranks to better see the distant lonely figure who confronted them. The voice brought him closer:

"... learning of the insurrection in Malunga, we went to the President, who'd locked himself away in the palace with his lackeys, terrified of the news that the *jeunesse* had guns, but even more terrified of what the poor wretches in Malunga might do, those whose daily companions weren't guns but misery and deprivation. So what did we find? A President terrified by the misery of his own people ..."

Wet black faces, kerosene lanterns here and there, the clatter of a distant helicopter. Few turned to look. The words, sentences, and paragraphs came pouring out:

"... and what strange state of affairs is this? A President so terrified by the suffering of his people that he hasn't the courage to lift one finger on their behalf! Listen! Listen to me! Did you come here to chatter like parrots, like old women! ..."

Crispin moved closer, carrying his unsold baskets, oblivious of the soldiers dispersed through the crowd.

"... so we put a simple proposal to the President! We would put down the fighting in Malunga ourselves! The soldiers would do it, imposing martial law, and after calm was restored, we would return to our barracks! We would let the people decide whether what we did was right or wrong! But the President betrayed us, just as he betrayed you! He sent word to the national police that we were to be arrested—me, N'Sika, Lutete, and Fumbe—all of us. Could we permit that? No! Never! If we were to be arrested let it be done after the rebels in Malunga were disarmed. If we soldiers were to be brought to justice, then let us be brought before the people with Pierre Masakita, Lule, and those others who gave guns to their followers in Malunga! Let us be brought to justice with those *vin rouge* intellectuals who would have made the blood run in the ditches of Malunga as the *vin rouge* had run in the veins of the colonizers, the same *vin rouge* these killers had drunk to get their courage up! *Vin rouge* imported from abroad, red wine, the white man's drink, not ours, not *masinga ya mbila*, the palm wine of our own forests!

"If we soldiers were to be brought to justice, then let us be brought before the people with the President and his cabinet, with those politicians who talked the money out of the people's pockets and into their own, who talked of economic progress and social progress, of education for the masses, maize for the hungry, and unity for the nation, who talked of this and that, night and day, day and night, who talked of everything but their villas in Belgium and Switzerland, the Mercedeses in their garages, their fleets of taxis and trucks, their coffee and palm oil plantations, their lackeys and whores. Progress here, progress there, but what progress? *Quel progrès?* What progress? *Progrès à wapi!*"

Crispin stopped, distraught, as the roar swept the front ranks first and then engulfed the rear, drowning N'Sika's voice:

"*Progrès à wapi! Progrès à wapi! Progrès à wapi!*"

"Listen to me! Shut up and listen! There are other things too! Other things we discovered! After the minister of finance and the governor of the national bank heard about the fighting in Malunga, they tried to flee the country! Why would they do that? Why would they run away like criminals? Were they criminals? Of course they were criminals! Listen, the old President once talked of how vast our cash reserves were, as vast as the great river over there behind you! Was that true? Did you believe him? Of course it wasn't true! So these two thieves were discovered hiding away in the airport baggage room, where we found them, their suitcases filled with dollars. Diamonds too! Of course.

"And what about these reserves, all this money that the country had accumulated, all these reserves! Do you know what these reserves were, what they are! Just three pieces—underwear, pants, and shirt! That's all! Just what you're wearing—underwear, pants, and shirt! Three pieces, that's all. Where has the money gone! To Belgium, of course—to Belgium, France, and Switzerland! And what did these Belgians and Frenchmen give back in return? Peacocks for the presidential garden! So we shot them! The Revolutionary Court sentenced them and we shot them! So we shot these thieves, this scum that these years of confusion and anarchy had given us—shot them as we'll shoot others who'll be tried and sentenced by the Revolutionary Court . . ."

The crowd was deathly silent.

Canvas-covered trucks had moved slowly down the closed street and stopped near the wooden platform.

". . . so we cast out the politicians, just as we smashed the rebels in Malunga. What choice did we have? We had no choice! Because their leaders, the provocateurs Masakita and Lule, had given them something more dangerous than the drunkenness of foreign ideology! What was it? You know what it was—something that kills like the mamba, something that kills ten, twenty, thirty men with a single flick of his red tongue—*moko, moko, moko*, one by one, all of us, each of you. . . ."

He held up the automatic rifle, holding it high over his head as the crowd roared its anger: "*Te, te, te!*"

The soldiers dragged the ragged, frightened youths from the truck beds and herded them, fifty or sixty strong, along the cockpit of green grass in front of the platform. Their uniforms were torn, black with grime and blood, their hands shackled behind their backs. Many were in their early twenties, but they looked younger now, as helpless as Ivory Market thieves trussed up by the police after their capture. Some were in their teens, the orphans of the Kwilu or Orientale, their families dead in the rebellions, harvested from the dense green forests and savannahs by an inept government to rot in the urban slums.

Crispin was too far away to recognize any of the faces.

". . . and there you see the green mambas of Malunga, the hoodlums and thieves who were misled, betrayed, corrupted, first by the old politicians, and then by the *vin rouge* ideologues! But look at them now! Their jaws are empty, their fangs drawn, their poison gone!"

They brought the guns. The paras carried them from a pair of flatbed trucks, slung heavily in tarpaulins or pine crates and dumped in the roadbed with that heavy ironlike resonance unmistakable anyplace on earth. The flashbulbs flared in the darkness. Photographers and cameramen leaned over the restraining ropes.

". . . revolution is a man's work, not a child's. It's our work—forget about the green mambas! Listen to me! Listen! The revolution is won together or not at all. But it takes work, hard work! *Eeer wa!* Do you hear me! *Eeer wa!* We must push and pull together, all of us! . . ."

Crispin listened as the crowd began to take up the work chant of the riverboats and barges, fields and forests, heard wherever two or more Africans had labored together, driven under the lash of that primitive chant.

N'Sika was holding something aloft, a paper taken from his pocket, lifted in the glare of the klieg lights, but Crispin had missed his words.

"... and it won't be easy! Never! Many will be against us. They will talk against us, lie against us, plan against us! They will say we've cheated them! All right! Let them talk! But it's our copper we're taking back, our mines, our minerals! The order is here—in my hand! We won't change that—never! We can't change our pride, our manhood, our revolution! Can we be children again, crawling back through our own filth? No! Never! So let our enemies know that—that we can no more change our revolution than we can change our race or the color of our skin! No! Never! And if others seek to humiliate us because of that, we must either submit to our own degradation or we must fight! Only weak men and women, prostitutes and lackeys, are accomplices in their own degradation! We are what God has made us—Africans! We will fight! But it is the revolution that will carry our battle, not plots or counterplots! Only hard work will win it, not words or foreign guns! So together we will change the condition of this nation! But peacefully, with hard work and sacrifice! I have talked too much tonight. I'll talk to you again. For tonight, it is enough. There is much work to do."

Crispin stood hollow and frightened in the surging crowd, baskets at his feet, watching N'Sika leave. N'Sika had nationalized the economy. His party's revolution had been stolen by the new regime, his life denied him for a third time.

❖ ❖ ❖ Reddish stood on the fringes of the crowd near the wooden barricade.

"*Flamand*," a nearby voice whispered to him. "*Flamand! Ecoutez, flamand! Monoko non ngui! Français te. Français na yo te!* Listen, European, white man, or whoever you are! Listen! He speaks our language, not yours! Lingala, not French! What are you doing here? Go home, eh. Home is where you belong, *flamand!*"

Reddish turned to see an old man stick his tongue into his fist and then hurl its imaginary demon to the ground.

The crowd was slow to disperse. The faces Reddish passed as

he moved away still wore the exhilaration of victory, like spectators leaving a victorious soccer match. On the boulevard a limousine from the Belgian Embassy led a cortege of diplomatic cars through the thinning crowd. The driver stupidly tried to force his way through the foot traffic and honked his horn furiously. A crowd surrounded the limousine almost immediately, a few beginning to rock it back and forth as they took up Colonel N'Sika's work chant, "*EEER wa! Eeer wa!*" The mood wasn't ugly, just jubilant. A squad of soldiers put an end to the demonstration.

He walked back to the embassy through the dark streets. Lowenthal was in shirtsleeves at his desk, the outer suite in confusion as old files were being rifled for copies of the Belgian minerals accords and the treaties and agreements protecting Western investment. The embassy didn't yet have a copy of N'Sika's speech, but Dick Franz at USIS had taped it, and one of the USIS locals was translating it.

"They say he didn't mention the Soviets," Lowenthal greeted him in agitation. "He didn't talk about Russian guns?"

Reddish sank down on the sofa next to the door. "He talked a little about foreign ideology—*vin rouge*—but it was ambiguous."

"But certainly the Soviet guns were there. He couldn't hide them."

"The guns he showed were a grab bag—Belgian NATO rifles, some old Enfields, some Soviet carbines, even a few M-14s."

"So he's not going to throw the Russians out? Everyone thought the mob would march on the Soviet and East German missions. That's where most of the press corps was, on the street outside the two embassies, waiting."

Reddish said, "N'Sika tricked them off the scent. No one was thinking nationalization. They were thinking about the guns. He couldn't very well nationalize the economy and shut down the Russians. He needs to keep his options open." He searched his pockets for a cigarette, but the package was empty. "But it was a good speech. It worked. I didn't think he could do it, but he did."

"It doesn't worry you?"

"A lot of things worry me. I just haven't had a chance to think about them. Hello, Abner."

Colonel Selvey stood angrily in the doorway. "What the shit's going on? I almost got my goddamned window busted out again."

"Andy and I were just talking about it," Lowenthal said.

"What'd N'Sika tell those baboons, anyway?"

"What they've been waiting to hear," Reddish replied.

"So what kind of regime are we talking about?" Lowenthal asked.

"N'Sika's," Reddish answered laconically. " 'Moderate and pro-Western in its political orientation.' Isn't that what you guys wrote in your cable two days ago?"

"Hindsight is twenty-twenty," Lowenthal said.

"So it's all fucked up again," Selvey put in.

"Pretty much," Reddish conceded.

"How do you write that State Department-style?" Selvey asked Lowenthal. "What do you tell the White House? 'Dear Doc Kissinger. If you birds think you got troubles in Vietnam, we just wanted to let you know. It's worse over here, and these bimbos ain't just wearing black pajamas. It's all black.' "

"That raises an interesting point." Lowenthal remembered. "What about the Soviets?"

"Raises shit," Selvey snorted. "You birds couldn't raise a bamboo dildo in a Bangkok nooky house, and that's the best there is. C'mon Andy. I wanna show you a gadget DIA just farmed out."

"What about the Sovs?" Lowenthal called out.

"We'll talk about it," Reddish said.

Selvey found two cans of beer in the closet refrigerator, popped the lids, and gave one to Reddish. He led him into his office, brought a jar of peanuts from his desk drawer, poured them into a clay pot, and closed the door.

"Maybe I'm not smart in the same way you birds are," he began, sinking down behind his desk, "but I'm not the redneck or the Tennessee plowboy everyone thinks I am. I don't talk their talk and they don't talk mine." He drank from the can, sighed and sat back again, his feet lifted across the corner of his desk. "But I just don't understand what the hell's going on. None of it makes any goddamn sense to me. I had a contact up at G-2, a major we sent to the US last year for training who's been giving us a little stuff. His name's Lutete. Maybe Les told you."

"I heard about it."

"For the past month, this bird's been after us to give him everything we could on Sov or Chicom arms shipments and military supplies—to Brazza, Burundi, Tanzania, the liberation groups, you name it. So we went along. The whole fucking time GHQ knew Masakita and his crowd were expecting guns from someone, but the little fucker doesn't say a word about that." Selvey sat forward suddenly. "You know who his cousin is?"

"N'Sika's deputy."

Selvey was disappointed. "Who told you that? Miles?"

"Bondurant. He said you wanted to open up a channel to him."

"Channel, shit." Selvey sank back. "Miles saw him at the airport last night when he came in. They're shipping him out to the command in Bukavu. Miles couldn't get squat out of him, just that he was being reassigned. They diddled us, diddled us good."

Reddish said, "That's the way it goes."

Selvey studied him morosely, still angry. "Just the same old shit for you, is that it? All the time this shoot-up was coming, this asshole we trained in the States knew something was up and didn't say a goddamned word."

That's not the way it happened, Reddish was tempted to say. He said nothing.

"So answer me this, doctor," Selvey grumbled, fixing Reddish in his stubborn gaze as he leaned forward. "How the shit do you birds put up with it year after year?" Reddish smiled, not in amusement but in sorrow. "Africa too. How the hell do you get the handle on it, on baboons like this Lutete?"

"Europe never interested me much." He stood up. It wasn't an answer but it was as much as Selvey would understand. What could he tell him? As a younger man, he had found the life more interesting out in the hinterlands where there was still a sense of the frontier, of a border not yet crossed, a future still to be made. That was where he'd always gone. The capitals of Europe had never tempted him. The problems there weren't the problems of order but of arrangement. Along the frontier and among societies still in transition, the risks were what mattered; nothing was ever certain. The man you talked with one day might be in prison the next, hanged the day after. Men risked everything for the sake of a future not yet defined, and when losses occurred they were absolute.

Yet it was a lonely life, whatever its consolations, and the strong paid the price along with the weak. Arrogant or ambitious men were protected by their self-esteem, their triviality, or their pride, but not the others. Semi-exiles, like Reddish, had nothing to insulate themselves against self-discovery. They had only themselves, their memory: it was essential that you never forget who you are. His wife and daughter had been equipped with much less.

"So don't tell me," Selvey said, putting down the beer can. "I wouldn't understand anyway."

An hour later Reddish drove to the flat. Masakita had gone. He'd left behind no message, only the houseboy's borrowed trousers and shirt, neatly folded in the center of the bed. On the kitchen counter was the radio and alongside it a pad with a few scribbled notes, probably written by Masakita as he'd listened to N'Sika's speech. The scribbling grew more fragmentary down the page and finally trailed off altogether, as if he'd realized that, like most demagogues, N'Sika had reduced his own elusive lien upon the truth to inconsequentiality.

The apartment smelled of stale air, medicine, tobacco, and the dusty vacuity of safe houses everywhere. The futility of his detective work was also there, smelling very much like the rubbish of old scholarship in dusty old libraries, of gray, desiccated men prowling the past, where their minds fed and their bodies lived because more audacious and cunning men had denied them presence among the living.

Reddish wasn't sorry to see him go. He'd become a burden and a nuisance. He was tired of himself, the embassy, and his solitude. He wanted to buy a woman a drink, listen to her voice, and take her home afterward, to think about other things during these last few weeks left to him.

chapter 10

❖ "I'm divorced," Gabrielle Bonnard said after her second drink. "Madame Houlet is my aunt. Does that surprise you."

"Which?"

"Either."

"I'm always surprised," Reddish said. "I'm a professional at it."

"I came here for a vacation of sorts. I intended to do some traveling in the interior. We were going to a lodge near Goma, the Houlets and I, but then the fighting broke out."

"So now Houlet wants to put you on a plane."

Her fingers were long, the nails unpainted. She wore a sleeveless white dress, sandals, and a small scarf about her neck. For the first time he'd noticed the gray streaks in her hair where it was cut short above her neck.

"He worries a great deal. She has a car, but he won't let her drive alone."

"The interior is quiet these days, not like this."

"No gunfire at night?"

"No. You could probably still take that trip." Their talk had been random, desultory, an escape from performance. Their initial self-consciousness overcome, they were two strangers in a mirrorless room.

"Do you come here often?" she asked.

"Not too often."

The bar in the *cité* where he'd intended to take her was closed.

"Because it's a European bar?"

"Probably—now that you mention it."

It was still early evening. A fat Portuguese money changer in a shiny silk suit sat hunched at his usual table near the door, a Robusta coffee and brandy glass on the table in front of him. A tall Senegalese sat with a West African in a tailored suit too warm for the

220

season. He was sweating and mopping his face as he argued with a dark-skinned Greek. At the bar, two Belgian planters in khaki shirts sat on stools staring at their faces in the tinted glass behind the bar as they talked in moody exchanges punctuated by silences as deep as the snows of the Ardennes. In the nearby dining room, a Congolese marimba band was playing "Lady of Spain" to a dozen empty tables.

"Armand is often at the Houlets'," Gabrielle said, lighting a cigarette. "It's impossible to avoid him. Do you know him well?" She held the cigarette inexpertly, like the minister's wife at the local bridge club.

"Not too well. Just professionally."

"I think he's probably typical of a certain kind of Frenchman who'd been a diplomat too long. I don't mean to be unkind, but I doubt that the work interests him any longer."

"He's worn out, I suppose," Reddish said. "When did you tell him about being in Malunga?"

"The other night at dinner. They were quite surprised, Armand as well as the others. They'd assumed it was total chaos."

"It was. How did you happen to be talking about it?"

"I shouldn't have?"

"It doesn't matter."

"You're not angry? I should feel terrible if you were."

"No, there's nothing to it."

"Was it indiscreet?" Her eyebrows lifted.

Reddish smiled, aware of a spontaneity long suppressed. "No, not at all."

"One never knows with diplomats," she admitted. "Perhaps it was indiscreet. Houlet was very cross about my being in Malunga, very upset about everything, as if my being there was somehow a reproach to the embassy for not having someone there too. I think diplomats prefer not to have problems—don't they?—not to be reminded that they may sometimes be remiss or mistaken. Have you found that? You think of diplomats as someone prepared to take risks, but I find that isn't true at all. They're as conservative as doctors or lawyers. I'm sure Houlet is counting the days until I return to Paris. My ticket is for next week, but I've seen nothing of this country, nothing at all. Armand told me you've traveled widely in the interior, more than anyone else."

"I once did. Not much any more."

"You've tired of it then?"

"I haven't had the time." His eyes wandered the room. Cailloux, the middle-aged Belgian hotel manager, sat drinking and smoking at his table near the cash register.

"Are you expecting someone?"

"No." He turned back to her. "I'm sorry. I was wondering what brought you to Africa. There are better places for vacations."

"I suppose I've been to most of them."

"Something new this time?"

"Not really. I took a trip last summer to the Greek islands—Paros, Naxos, Santorini. I've forgotten some of the names now. I was alone, the first time I'd taken a vacation alone for almost fifteen years. I enjoyed it. I made no bookings beforehand, just discovered the pensions and hotels as I needed them. I could always catch a boat in the morning or evening when I was bored. There was always a boat going someplace and when I was tired of one place, I could always imagine something extraordinary waiting elsewhere. I found sometimes that just getting on a boat was enough. Travel has a momentum of its own, don't you think?" She looked at him for a response, but he wanted to listen, not talk.

"I think so. I discovered the new excavations on Santorini—the Minoan ruins. I took a few books with me, not many, just a few, books I'd put away years ago and hadn't looked at since." Her eyes were turned away. "I reread Stendhal. Do you know Stendhal?"

"I've heard of him."

"I reread a fragment of his autobiography in the Pléiade edition. It was rediscovering Stendhal that started me off. It's rather odd, the way it happened." She was looking down at her glass, twisting the stem slowly, her voice fading.

"Odd how?"

"Finding the book. It was just after the divorce and I was sorting books on the shelves, trying to decide which to keep for myself, which Robert might want, which to give away, when I found the Stendhal. I was kneeling on the floor, all dusty, the teakettle was whistling, and the apartment was empty. It was a depressing day, nothing was going right, the packers were coming, and I only wanted it all to be over. Then I found the Stendhal. I couldn't remember ever looking at it. On the first page I found why he was writing it—not an autobiography but a fragment. It gave me the most curious feeling. One October day in 1832 he found himself standing on the Janiculum Hill in Rome and remembered he'd soon be fifty." Her dark eyes were still lowered to the glass, still puzzled, her lips touched by the faintest of smiles, as if hardly conscious of Reddish at all.

"So what happened?"

"Nothing, really. Just that. He couldn't believe the years had gone by so quickly. His best works were behind him, but he decided it was time he got to know himself—just then, at that moment. Then that night, alone in his rooms, he did a very curious thing. He wrote a note to himself in the waistband of his trousers—just to himself, no one else—contracting the words, like a code, so no one else could read them. 'I'm going to be fifty,' he wrote, just as simply as that, but I understood. It was exactly what I might have done—what I felt like doing—that moment, all dusty, strangers coming, the teakettle whistling. A month later I went to the Greek islands. Now I'm in Africa. Perhaps it was childish of me. In *Henri Brulard*, Stendhal tells us he was still a child during most of his life."

"Most of us are, but you're not going to be fifty."

"At the time, I felt like it. Fifty, sixty, it doesn't matter. I'm sure most women feel that way after a divorce. Women much more than men. Suddenly discovering how quickly time has passed is a very personal thing. Was it too impulsive?"

"I don't know about the Greek islands. Africa isn't the same. There's no boat every night. No, I understand what you felt."

"But I didn't come simply as a tourist. Last winter I attended the lectures at the Sorbonne's African studies center. I didn't expect the Greek islands again."

"But so far you're disappointed?"

"Yes," she said slowly, "yes, but only because what's happened here this past week has shut me away from things I'd like to discover for myself. I went to Chad first with a group of friends. Then to Uganda. It was impossible there. My English is very poor. My friends went on to Nairobi and Capetown. That didn't interest me so I came here to see the Houlets and to travel in the interior. A mistake, you see."

"Not a mistake, just poor timing."

They finished their drinks. The Portuguese money changer had gone. The Congolese band was playing "Ticket to Ride." As they crossed toward the door, Cailloux lifted his sleepy eyes from the Belgian newspaper and asked Reddish if he'd heard the N'Sika speech in Martyr's Square.

"I heard it."

"Another thief," Cailloux muttered disagreeably, looking briefly at Gabrielle and then back at Reddish. "A big-time thief, like Leopold. Now it's the copper mines."

They went out through the great Moorish lobby to the street, where a warm rain-laden wind blew from the west. The streets were quiet. Two African prostitutes in mini-skirts and white doeskin boots leaned against a nearby car watching them sullenly.

"How did you happen to go to Chad?" Reddish asked as he drove away. "There's a civil war in Chad. It doesn't make the headlines, but it's still there." She was leaning forward, looking up through the windshield at the few stars that showed just beyond the scalloped edge of a thunderhead moving in from the sea.

"I wanted to see the Tibesti Mountains." She sank back against the seat, already a voyager, no longer earthbound, her face bathed in the amber glow of the dashboard, a traveler again, high above the equatorial forests and the canyons of cloud, far above the wrinkled waters of Lake Chad, and the stony wind-swept silence of the Tibesti. How many times had Reddish made that same flight?

"They were always something I wanted to see," he recalled.

She sat alongside him, head back against the cushion, looking out the windshield. "If I've told you something about myself, it's by way of apology," she said after a minute. "I had no right to violate your privacy in that way. Your being in Malunga that night to help your friend was entirely your own affair."

"It doesn't matter."

"But it's still a terrible thing—to take away someone's privacy, to have your private life violated by others, by those who care nothing." She sat up. "That night at dinner, I was suddenly very tired of everything that was being said. They talked as if no one knew what had happened in Malunga except themselves. For someone to have been shopping, a tourist too, and to have gotten where she didn't belong was a scandal, especially since she was probably hysterical at the time."

Reddish laughed.

"But I am very angry about that," she continued. "Very angry. Must one be a diplomat to understand what has happened? I told them the three men I saw had been shot down in cold blood, unable to use the heavy guns they carried. They said I was imagining it, that if a woman sees someone being shot, which she has no right to see, she will naturally sympathize with the victim. How can they be so narrow-minded? It seemed to me that their premises are quite false. If they are so wrong about what happened that night in Malunga, then they are wrong about other things too. But it was cowardly of me to speak out like that—very foolish, very selfish."

They had dinner at a hilltop restaurant overlooking the city, sitting outside on the deserted terrace, watching the rain clouds move in. She told him about the lectures she'd attended the previous winter in Paris. He described a few of the more remote regions of the interior that interested her. As they left the restaurant, the rain began to fall, huge sporadic drops at first, but then in sheets as they reached the old Belgian residential section, flooding the tarmac and flailing green leaves and purple blossoms from the trees. The Houlets hadn't returned.

"Please, come have a brandy," she suggested. "It's raining so terribly."

He had no interest in seeing the Houlets. "It will pass in a minute. Thanks for the evening. I enjoyed it."

"But I must ask you something. Please. It's quite important."

He let her out at the front door, drove forward to park his car at the edge of the drive, and ran back through the rain to join her in the hall. She led him to the front salon. The green marble fireplace held a small grate piled with kindling and ceremonial logs. A felt-covered card table had been readied nearby, decks of cards, coasters, and ashtrays in place. An Empire sofa faced the fireplace across a small Chinese carpet.

"Not bridge you were talking about, was it?"

"Bridge? No. I don't play. Do you?" She brought glasses and a crystal decanter from the antique cabinet. The rain rushed through the trees outside and flooded the spouts beyond the windows, pouring from the gutters. She stopped, listening. "Have you ever been to Entebbe in the rain, hours and hours of it, just like this? Just gray skies and rain." She shivered in recollection, the chill touching her. "Like prison, destroying the will that way. It had that effect on me. *Africa*, I thought. I don't want to remember it that way. Did it affect you the same way at first?"

"Asia did, during the monsoon. Not here so much. It goes pretty fast."

"The wind on Santorini affected me that way too. My hotel was high on the mountain and the wind blew all night long. I had to fight against it. It was dreadful, terrible at first. It took away my courage." She removed a folded map from the cabinet drawer.

"So it wasn't all vacation, the Greek islands."

"No," she admitted. "There were many nights like that, mornings too." She turned toward the front windows.

He guessed that she wasn't planning to catch Houlet's plane after all, but was thinking about a trip to the bush and wanted his advice.

"It's a car," he said.

She put the map away. The Houlets entered a few minutes later, voices unnaturally loud, still amplified by the din of the crowded reception they'd just left. They were accompanied by Armand and a young brunette from the French cultural center. Houlet was short, plump, and bald with a cherub's wet mouth; Madame Houlet was more stately but also plump, her brown eyes warmer, with a curiosity her husband's lacked. Her perfume filled the room, which suddenly seemed very alien to Reddish, very French, very uxorial.

"Back so soon, Gabrielle? No more adventures? Ah, Reddish. A very great pleasure. You know my wife, I believe, and Mr. Armand. And Miss Foucart, to be sure." His voice was still very loud, even aggressive. A late supper was waiting, but Houlet decided to have drinks first. He energetically searched for glasses and whiskey. Gabrielle had withdrawn silently to the sofa near the fireplace.

"I didn't see you there," Armand recalled, speaking of the reception. "You were right not to go. The usual crowd. Wretched food. And no one from the new Revolutionary Council was there, not a soul."

"Does that surprise you?" Houlet asked.

"No, not much," Reddish said. "Still feeling their way, I suppose."

"Of course. Precisely. But of course, Gabrielle wasn't there to enlighten us." Houlet called across the room to Gabrielle. "I was just saying to Reddish that we had no one at the reception to enlighten us."

"*Shhh,*" Madame Houlet said, hand lifted to her silver-gray coiffure. Fixing her eyes suddenly on Reddish, she smiled.

"But of course you and Gabrielle had much to talk about, I'm sure," Houlet continued loudly.

"Extraordinary, isn't it," Armand murmured with a vague smile, "that you could have been in Malunga while the assault was under way and then drive out quite calmly, past the bodies in the road, guns going off in all directions. Gabrielle has told us."

Houlet winked at Reddish. "And to see everything so clearly," he added. "Was she really so composed as all that, even to describe the number of bullets fired—"

"*Shhh,*" Madame Houlet urged, setting out coasters. "Do you play bridge, Mr. Reddish?"

"Not very well, I'm afraid."

"I'm sure Gabrielle was very heroic," Armand said.

"But of course," Houlet announced, clumsily pouring out

drinks. "But of course she was heroic. *Le livre du moi est toujours héroïque.*"

Thunder roared in the distance and pealed across the rooftops. Houlet flinched in mock fright. The rain came harder. "What was that?" he asked as he restoppered the decanter. "Gabrielle's guns again?"

"*Shhh,*" Madame Houlet insisted from the sofa, where she'd gone to join Gabrielle. "Shall we light the fire."

"But why all this *shhh?*" Houlet continued. "Why all this silence." Madame Houlet studiously ignored him. "My wife is a romantic," Houlet volunteered to Reddish, lowering his voice. "Like Gabrielle. But Africa's no place for romantics. God, no. Writers either." His voice dropped even further. "God save us from those who've come to Africa to discover themselves, eh? From writers who've come to discover Africa for us. Do they think Africa exists just for their own salvation? But what is that you're drinking?"

Identifying the brandy in Reddish's glass, he was apologetic. "The thieves' brandy, of course. The houseboys'," he whispered. "The best is kept hidden away." He unlocked the bottom of the cabinet and brought forth an old bottle. "Try this. This is much better."

"No, thanks. This is fine. I'll be on my way in a minute."

"Gabrielle?" Houlet lifted the bottle in her direction.

But she had overheard his whispered remark and was looking silently at Reddish, her eyes lost to him again, as they'd been that night in the elevator, and she didn't answer Houlet at all.

chapter 11

◆ As de Vaux left the rear porch of his cottage early that morning, the old sentinel was stooping near a palm tree where something lay hidden in the grass. De Vaux's two small children played during the day in the swing and sandbox nearby, but at this hour they were still in the house with their nurse, who was scolding them through breakfast. The old sentinel moved to a squat, knees against his chest as he cautiously reached for something hidden to de Vaux, fingers extended, as if stalking a lizard or toad.

De Vaux joined him and saw it wasn't a lizard at all, just a wooden figure as mute as the one they had discovered a day earlier, no more than two meters in length, a wooden creature with a coat of beaten bark daubed with dried mud, a blunt snout and four stubby reptilian legs, evilly carved to resemble those of a pig or crocodile. A child might pick it up impulsively; a European would be curious but cautious; a wary African wouldn't touch it at all.

De Vaux believed it was meant for the children. He crouched down beside the old guard and with the barrel of his revolver prodded it to its side. Hidden beneath the bark fiber were the poisonous metal barbs, tiny fishhooks whose shanks were embedded in the wooden core, their snelled tips exposed but bent downward in the bark, unfelt by the grasping hand but immediately alive as the creature was lifted, the snelled teeth biting deeply into fingers and palm. He wrapped his handkerchief about the snout and lifted it into the sunlight, belly up. The hooks were smeared with a viscous substance. It was an old fetish, as old as the iron fishhooks, but the toxin was as fresh as that found on a similar fetish a day earlier.

"Green mamba?" the old sentinel ventured aloud as he identified the venom-barbed hooks, parroting what he'd heard on the national radio: the *jeunesse* were everyone's enemies.

De Vaux told him to search the grounds again, and he carried the fetish back to the cottage and down the hallway to the far wing and his father-in-law's room. Behind the closed door, the darkness stank of his sickness. He lay on the thin pallet, ill and feverish, head back, his eyes closed and his mouth open, like the cleft beak of an old tortoise. His black skin hung in loose seams from his ancient face, arms, and thighs. About his waist was a dusty crimson sash; a stuffed snakeskin wrapped his right ankle, a bracelet of yellow leopard teeth the other. The long thin reed pipe with the fire-blackened clay bowl no larger than a thimble lay on the bedside table among the medicine bottles. A week had passed since he had last smoked it. For three nights that same week he'd been driven through the dark streets searching for Pierre Masakita's whereabouts. The last night, he had spat blood.

It was all de Vaux could do to look at him in this condition. Once the strength and power of his people to the north, he was now dying.

The old cousin who attended him sat on the stool at the foot of the cot, his head against the wall, his ash-caked hands hanging loosely over his bony knees. Once a minor fetisheer, whose power had failed, he was trying to recover it on the old man's behalf. Gathered about him on the dark floor were clay pots, vessels, and fetishes, some with antelope horns projecting from their wooden heads, others with dried viscera, fingernails, scraps of body hair, teeth, shriveled cauls, or embryonic bones in their concealed body cavities.

"He must go home to his village," the old cousin told de Vaux listlessly, opening his eyes. "He must go, all of us—"

"In time," de Vaux answered, bending over his father-in-law, his ear at the old man's lips. The breathing was weak and irregular.

The old cousin sat forward, identifying the object de Vaux carried, straining his neck but not leaving his stool. "What is it?"

"We found it in the garden. Do you know it?"

De Vaux took it to him, but he shrank away, lifting his forearm. "No! No! Is it theirs?"

Like de Vaux, the old cousin knew that the fetish found in the garden was a sign and a portent, proof that someone knew the old man was dying, and his power with him, the power that had once protected this household, this daughter and her children, de Vaux himself, and his nephew Colonel N'Sika. Power being challenged was power no longer feared; illness or death in this family was proof that the power was broken and the magic of someone stronger had prevailed. A challenge must be answered by even stronger magic, but de Vaux's father-in-law had no strength left.

Colonel N'Sika had begun to suspect the truth. He'd visited the cottage twice in three days, both times late at night and both times alone, seeking his uncle's counsel. The colonel hadn't slept well; he'd lost his appetite; Pierre Masakita had eluded his uncle and his troops; and his tongue had been paralyzed for a few minutes during an all-night session of the council, humiliating him in front of majors Fumbe and Lutete and others he mistrusted. "Which among them are my enemies?" he'd asked his uncle.

De Vaux knew better than his dying father-in-law what N'Sika's problems were—twenty-two-hour days, all-night working sessions, no sure sense of where their revolution was taking them, and an inept, divided council afraid for their lives and frightened by N'Sika's uncompromising leadership. But the old man had had little counsel to offer. He'd taken back the small ivory amulet N'Sika wore about his neck, studied it silently for a few minutes, and retired alone to his room. When he returned, the ivory amulet had a deeper, richer luster to it, and the old man wore an identical one around his wrinkled neck.

Yesterday, de Vaux had seen the amulet discarded on N'Sika's desk in a container of paper clips and pens.

N'Sika had arrived unannounced for his second visit, and de Vaux hadn't been present. N'Sika had discovered the old man lying in the darkness behind the door, attended by the old cousin and his primitive fetishes. He'd left troubled and uneasy, complaining bitterly to de Vaux on the following morning that the old cousin and his filth were corrupting his uncle's strength and that the cousin should be sent home to his village in the north.

But de Vaux hadn't sent the old cousin away. There was no place for him to go, just as there was no place for his father-in-law to go. If the relics the old cousin had assembled on his father-in-law's behalf seemed primitive and obscene to N'Sika, they were still the articles of the old cousin's faith, and de Vaux had been taught by his years in Africa to take nothing for granted in such matters.

Years ago he'd been victimized by relics as barbarous as these.

✧ ✧ He was driving a truck up near Bunia at the time and had broken an axle on the track a hundred kilometers to the west, returning from Stanleyville. Darkness had already fallen and he was too exhausted to pull the bearing and replace the axle with the spare; so he lit his lantern and he and his African helper returned to the isolated village whose cooking fires they'd passed eight kilometers back.

The village was dark when they entered, the Africans vanished into their huts. The few who finally came forward into de Vaux's lantern light were sullen and suspicious. They offered them nothing to eat, but all de Vaux wanted was charcoal for his kettle and a spot to lay out his bedroll. He was willing to pay for it. They wouldn't accept his money, and an old man pointed through the darkness to a hut at the end of the village and said they could sleep there. But they had no charcoal.

When they reached the hut, the African helper refused to enter, claiming that the villagers didn't want them in the settlement and had sent them to the deserted hut to get rid of them, since it was still possessed by the dead man who once lived there.

De Vaux was too tired to argue and suspected his helper was lying to him. How did he know who had lived there? He gave the helper his torch and told him to go back to the truck if he was frightened. After the helper left, de Vaux spread his bedroll inside, ate a cold sandwich, drank his cold tea in the light of the lantern, and went to sleep.

He didn't talk about it afterward, not to anyone, not even his Congolese wife, years later, whom he told everything. It was the most terrifying night he'd ever spent in his life, but it was nothing anyone could ever describe, nothing you could either believe in or not believe, as the Europeans were always asking: "What about this witch doctor or fetisheer business? What do you think? Is there anything to it?"

That was the wrong way to put it. It wasn't anything you could think about at all, no more than you could a raging fever. What was that—mental, something your mind was seized with? He could define it no better. It was just an experience, a condition that drove your terrified little mammalian mind from whatever crypt or fissure where civilization had hidden it away all those centuries and stalked it, right out there on the jungle floor. That was why the Europeans would never understand.

He'd been awakened in the middle of the night to find something in the hut with him. *A rat? A reptile? Maybe a snake?* Probably. It had happened to him before. He reached for his lantern. It was as cold as ice. And just as suddenly the cold clutched at him too, blowing across his face like Antwerp fog from the winter streets, a sinister breath that filled the thatched hut and condensed like hoarfrost on the cold metal of the lantern, which from that moment on would be useless to him no matter how many times he replaced the wick or the candle.

So he was sleeping, he convinced himself, just sleeping, just an exhausted victim of one of the uglier tricks of sleep after a brutal day on the track. In an act of will he woke himself, but consciousness was much worse; the icy lantern was there, just as this paralyzing coldness was there, trapped outside himself—an evil stalking presence that rose wrathfully from the darkness and struck at him, something foul, cold, and unspeakable.

He scrambled away against the thatched wall of the hut, where he braced himself, eyes straining in the darkness to know his captor. He didn't know what it was. It was without shape—no face, no body, nothing tangible except its coldness—yet it was there, its icy presence licking at his bare ankles, then his arms, and neck, but retreating each time he struck out at it. He flung his cigarettes at it, his wallet, his wristwatch, kicking at it finally with his feet, trying to push himself through the wall thatching to escape into the warm darkness outside the hut, still holding the lantern up to shield his face. But the vines and raffia rope held the thatched wall in place and he was its prisoner.

Caught momentarily in the tangle of fiber rope, he felt its coldness reach his neck and jaw. He cried out, freed himself, and rolled to his side, kicking as it retreated, cold, gray, as palpable as sea fog; and in that moment, in the terror of his condition, in an instant of clairvoyant insanity de Vaux understood the terror of its own. It was a dead thing—his helper had been right—but no longer in the physical shape, the blood and bones his Creator had given him, but in this other, set loose in this unspeakable condition and now trying to hide its formlessness away in de Vaux's warm flesh and bone, to escape that very nullity de Vaux was recoiling from in terror.

"You bugger! You won't do it! Not me, you bastard!"

His discovery seemed to him so clear, so remarkable, and so terrifying in its simplicity that in that instant it seemed to him that through raw fear he'd divined what philosophers and theologians searched a lifetime for through their dusty texts without discovering. There would be a ton of gold in that philosopher's stone—death was even more unspeakable, more terrified of its nullity than life—and if later he was to feel cheated of that discovery, at the time it gave him the courage to continue battle. He had no idea how long he fought off his assailant. Only when the first dawn light showed through the trees and he could see the outline of the door did the oppression lift, the cold withdraw. As he crawled through the door exhausted, the mist had begun to stir from the black river that thrashed through the sunless jungle behind the village.

He gathered together his kitbag, his bedroll, and lantern, and retrieved his pocket articles from the earth floor of the hut. In the dawn light he saw, hanging from the roofpoles outside, the gnawed gray sticks tied and knotted with viscera. Some were old, weathered by the sun and rain, but at the side of the hut he found a pendulous goat horn sealed with a wad of fresh entrails.

The villagers stirred from their huts to watch as he struggled down the path to the road, more exhausted now than he'd been the night before. He made a good show of it, trying to walk a straight line, shoulders back. He didn't look over his shoulder at those mute savages who watched him go, didn't care who had lived and died in the abandoned hut; and if the poor buggers he'd left behind continued to be oppressed by something dead trying to crawl its way back to life, more terrified of its condition than they were of theirs, maybe they deserved that too.

By the time he reached the truck eight kilometers away, his discovery no longer seemed so remarkable. His pounding feet and aching head had driven everything else from his mind. Maybe it was only his own exhaustion after all; maybe bad pork or contaminated tea. In the hellish heat of the day, his philosopher's stone of the previous night dissolved, fled like quicksilver in a memory of acute delirium.

But his fatigue was real; so was the lantern. The helper was waiting when he reached the truck. "Start the engine up and let's have some warm water," de Vaux told him. "What's the long face for, lad? Didn't sleep well or didn't expect to see me? Should have stayed put, like me. Slept like a stone, I did."

The lantern was still cold to the touch; he put it on the engine hood before he set to work. He took the spare axle from the work chest, pulled the wheel and wheel bearing, and replaced the broken axle. Afterward, he ate some cold biscuit as he shaved, and finally retrieved the lantern from the hood. It was now neutral to the touch, but on the warm engine cowling was a pool of milky water, larger than any condensation which might have been explained by the damp African night and too curious in color to be the result of any leakage from the lantern well.

"Manioc dust," de Vaux explained to the curious driver. "Must have been a manioc mill in the next hut, eh? Buggers thought we were going to steal their manioc sacks."

But when the truck reached Bunia that night, the milky track was still there, although the fluid had evaporated, leaving a foul corrosive scar down the blue cowling.

So de Vaux—mechanic, planter, and petty empiricist—had concluded that something had been with him in the hut that night: a dead man's spirit, his memory, or some grisly avatar set loose by those tied sticks the village fetisheer had hung from the roof pole. He didn't know what it was, but it was his business, not to be shared with anyone else. Whenever he passed those bush savages on the track with their grotesquely tied sticks or primitive talismans carried to escape the destinies that stalked them through the thick green African twilight, he was reminded of the lantern.

He thought about it also as he grew to despise those others, the Europeans, for their contempt for what these black men knew, just as he despised them for the superiority of their belief that reality was identical with their own European understanding.

They called it belief. He called it madness, as mad as the fevers of avarice, dogma, art, and redemption that they called civilization.

◇ ◇ ◇ The Revolutionary Military Council's security committee met daily at seven o'clock in the evening. The working hours of the first days of the crisis had now become routine. N'Sika worked through the night, slept from noon until five, and returned to work. The other members of the council had adjusted their hours to his.

At six that afternoon, de Vaux left his jeep in the gravel drive in front of N'Sika's headquarters, climbed the steps past the armed guards, and went down the tiled corridor to his small office directly across the hall from N'Sika's suite. Inside, he telephoned for the afternoon intelligence summaries and the daily reports from military and police units in the interior. De Vaux prepared from them the daily intelligence brief which would be presented to the seven o'clock meeting of the security committee. N'Sika chaired the committee; de Vaux was the *rapporteur*.

Dusk was falling outside as he crossed the hall to the committee room adjacent to N'Sika's office, carrying a map board. In the garden outside, council members were already gathering on the chairs and divans of the small terrace that had become N'Sika's waiting room. Many sat there through the night waiting for an audience. N'Sika rarely appeared on the terrace, but his presence was there nonetheless, as it was everywhere else in the capital, even as his person had become more elusive than ever.

De Vaux knew N'Sika had always had the ambition for power, but he hadn't realized until after the coup how completely he commanded its instincts. He'd always kept himself remote from others, not only because of the stammer which had been such a humiliation in his younger days, but because of those warnings of ambition which come to many unique men who believe far more in their own destiny than they'll ever be able to admit to others, suffering that burden in solitude, as N'Sika once suffered his stammer. Solitude had made him stronger than the other members of the council, who were only now discovering how totally he was their master.

It was N'Sika who'd decided to nationalize the economy, N'Sika who'd ordered the recent executions, N'Sika who'd led them forward by making it impossible to retreat, and N'Sika who now had made them all his hostages. In his own strength, intolerance for their weakness would grow. The old President, hysterical in his last days and final hours, had been the first to feel N'Sika's malice. N'Sika despised him not only because of his weakness and corruption but because for years his ambition had made him the accomplice of the President's venality and paranoia. As N'Sika's strength gave way to grandeur, his colleagues on the council would feel that malice too. In not recognizing N'Sika's own genius during those long years of suffering and obscurity, they too, like the old President, would be judged guilty by N'Sika, accomplices in his own degradation.

De Vaux wondered who would be next. In the dimming light of the garden, he watched Majors Fumbe and Kimbu, N'Sika's closest confederates, talking quietly with the three Belgians sent from Brussels to open compensation negotiations resulting from the nationalization of the copper mines. Both were still useful to N'Sika—Kimbu for his brutality, Fumbe for his blind obedience.

Major Lutete sat near the arbor smoking as he edited a news release. Lutete was a question mark, like Dr. Bizenga, who waited in the shadows far to the rear, listening to a tall Senegalese in a white *boubou*—probably the envoy sent secretly from the Organization of African Unity in Addis Ababa to pledge support but to insist that the executions cease. Dr. Bizenga wasn't a member of the council but an economic adviser and gadfly. His bony repellent face, steel-rimmed spectacles, and obsequious manners set him apart from the soldiers. He might be useful in the copper negotiations. Already he'd suggested through Lutete that N'Sika give him a diplomatic post abroad, either at the UN in New York or in Paris.

At the front of the garden two council members were talking heatedly to N'Sika's personal secretary. Both were members of the security committee, both clumsy and thick-witted, their only advantage to N'Sika the troops they commanded. But N'Sika's popularity in the army made them less important now. As de Vaux watched, they turned, walked to their separate jeeps, and were driven away.

Did that mean N'Sika had canceled the seven o'clock security meeting?

He went back to his office, where his aide was waiting with the folder containing the reports from the interior.

"Anything more from Funzi?" de Vaux asked. Funzi was on the fringes of the old rebel areas; a police post at Funzi had been raided for weapons the night before. Near Funzi were the forests where Pierre Masakita's rebels had launched the old rebellions.

But the aide said nothing, looking at de Vaux in confusion.

"What is it? More attacks near Funzi?"

He shook his head and gave de Vaux the folder. It was empty. On the outside cover leaf where the names of the security committee members were listed, de Vaux's name had been struck off by a single stroke of N'Sika's felt-tipped pen.

chapter 12

✧ "I don't wonder they're behind barbed wire," Bondurant declared nervously as they drove through the steel gates of the para compound. He'd been summoned by N'Sika following Washington's request that he urge the council to cease the executions. Three days had passed before N'Sika had answered the ambassador's request for a meeting. It was almost midnight. Soldiers with automatic weapons were strung out along the road under the palm trees. Muzzles were three times lowered against the hood at internal checkpoints. Despite the calm in the city, the para hilltop resembled a night bivouac for an army doing battle somewhere out in the darkness.

"You'd think they would have sent someone to meet us," Lowenthal complained.

"It's over there," Reddish told the uneasy Congolese driver, pointing off through the trees, "where the floodlights are."

Paramilitary troops cordoned the side terrace to which the major who'd met the car led them. A row of old armchairs was lined up on a strip of red carpeting under the trees, feebly lit by double strands of electric lights strung from the trees and a few iron poles.

They waited in the armchairs while the major went back through the arbor and disappeared up the steps to N'Sika's office. Guns surrounded them in the shadows. Soldiers patrolled the villa perimeter; others stood just beyond the wash of electric light, silently facing the terrace. Overhead the dry palm trees rattled in the throat of the night wind.

Bondurant sat back woodenly, hands folded. Lowenthal's head was set, chin propped against his closed fists, staring at the red carpet. Reddish looked up through the palm trees, searching for stars.

"A little like Baghdad after the revolution," he recalled.

Someone coughed in the darkness behind him and he turned.

Beyond a small wall screened with potted plants was a second terrace where members of the new government were waiting to be received.

"Like a dentist's waiting room," Reddish suggested, sitting forward and searching for a cigarette. "I hope to hell this is the head of the queue."

"A little macabre, isn't it?" Bondurant asked in distaste.

"Think about Kissinger," Reddish proposed.

Bondurant was intrigued. "In what sense?"

"The statesman as hero," Reddish said.

Bondurant laughed. Lowenthal smiled.

"He gets a good press, doesn't he?" Bondurant mused. "Much better than the Secretary."

"Why not? His answers are better-educated than the reporters' questions," Reddish said. "He's trickier with words."

The major reappeared. They followed him back through the arbor and up the steps between two red-bereted bodyguards with M-16 rifles. The high-ceilinged room they entered was empty except for a small group of plush armchairs surrounding a low coffee table in the far corner. The room was lit by fluorescent tubes along the wall and ceiling. An old carpet with its nap worn to fiber led to the group of chairs. At the head of the low table was a larger red plush chair with a yellowing antimacassar over its back.

Colonel N'Sika took the chair after he entered a moment later, motioning to them to sit down. Bondurant sat to N'Sika's right, Lowenthal and Reddish next to him. N'Sika was accompanied by Major Fumbe and Major Lutete. He wore a Colt .38 in an open holster on his right hip and was dressed in wrinkled khakis, dark with sweat at his neck and under his arms. The two majors also wore side arms. The three men looked tired and smelled of their fatigue, of sweat, gunpowder, lack of sleep, and missed meals. N'Sika and Fumbe both carried portable radio receivers opened to a security channel. Both put them at their feet as they sat down.

N'Sika sat for a few minutes without speaking at all, head thrust forward, reading without enthusiasm a few handwritten notes prepared for him. He was in his late thirties, his skin jet black and unmarked, heavy in the jowls and neck. His face was wooden. No animation showed in the thickly lidded eyes, only a weariness that bordered on sullenness, but he dominated the room. His two majors were smaller, their eyes livelier, but it was fear that moved their muscles, and it was N'Sika they feared. He rarely looked at them; their eyes seldom left his face.

The palm trees outside clattered in the wind as they waited. The static from the radio stirred from beneath the table. Finally he folded the notes away in his shirt pocket, took out a crushed package of cigarettes, and put them on the table.

Then he began to speak, slowly and laboriously, telling Bondurant why he'd decided to abolish the old regime and nationalize the economy. He spoke French, not Lingala, and he spoke it clumsily, his monologue broken only by an occasional pause for a forgotten word, which Major Fumbe supplied in a whispered voice. As he spoke, he didn't once look at Bondurant, Lowenthal, or Reddish. His eyes brooded instead across the table in front of him, traveling across the watermarks, the peeling varnish, and the cigarette burns, which he occasionally covered with his long fingers, the nails as strong and smooth as soapstones. He smoked continually.

He might have been talking to himself. Nothing in his voice or face conceded any recognition to his three visitors. The battered old table was more real to him, its scars familiar, its history known. It was as if he'd decided that these three white men could never understand what he had done or experienced, his world as closed to them as theirs to him. To Reddish, it was obvious that this long, tiresome monologue he was dutifully performing as chief of state was as dead to him as the three men to his right were dead to him.

A bodyguard brought Coca-Cola and Fanta, the bottles uniced, like the glasses. A second bodyguard fetched N'Sika a fresh package of cigarettes and emptied his ashtray.

He waited until the two men left the room before he resumed. He didn't like the Belgians, he began again, but the interruption had broken his train of thought. "The dwarf of Europe," he summarized. "A white pygmy in our forests. They are nothing—ticks on an elephant. Leeches. Like that. *Rien plus.*"

He asked for continued American support; he expected more from the Americans than the others. The United States had never been a colonizer. Its hands weren't stained by the blood of the past. He hoped the United States wouldn't join with the Belgians in forcing harsh terms as compensation for the nationalizations. The Belgians weren't to be trusted. Belgian guns had been identified among those seized in Malunga. Now the Belgian Embassy was spreading lies about that too, saying that only Soviet guns had been found. The dossier was there, with Major Lutete, who would discuss it with them. The fact was that the provocateurs in the workers party had been in touch with many imperialist agents, not only African—like the Angolan turncoat in the MPLA—but European as well.

It was then that N'Sika's disability betrayed itself. He'd been talking for forty minutes without interruption, and he faltered over a word—a momentary block that crippled his palate and jaw for an instant before it released them. He had a stutter.

"The dossier is there," he concluded finally, waving toward Lutete and sitting back in his chair, as if the subject didn't interest him.

Major Lutete sat forward, lifting a thick dossier to the coffee table, his hot eyes on Bondurant. "It is all here, Mr. Ambassador, as the President says. The complete file, which will be turned over to the Revolutionary Court. It includes the serial numbers of the guns, a letter from the Angolan turncoat the chairman mentioned, dos Santos, to Masakita, promising to supply the party with weapons, as well as the import licenses from the European firm, Societé Générale d'Afrique—"

"I'm sure it's complete," Bondurant interrupted, "and I appreciate your willingness to discuss it, but it's a matter for your courts, not for me."

Reddish had stirred forward at the mention of dos Santos, only to sit back in disappointment.

Major Lutete was confused: "Excuse me?"

"This is an internal matter. It's not one that concerns my government."

No one spoke. Bondurant waited patiently, turned again toward N'Sika, who muttered something in Lingala to Lutete. The major sat back in relief, returning the dossier to his briefcase. N'Sika sat in silence, head forward, studying the table. Finally he lifted his eyes, examining Lowenthal and Reddish.

"Why did you bring these two men?" he asked Bondurant.

"They're my counselors," Bondurant replied, surprised.

"Which one is Reddish?"

"There, at the end."

N'Sika looked closely at Lowenthal: "*Olobaka monoko nini ndako na yo?*"

Lowenthal flushed. "Sorry—"

"I regret he doesn't speak Lingala," Bondurant explained.

N'Sika studied Reddish coldly. Abruptly he launched into a long tirade in Lingala, his anger sometimes carrying him to the edge of his chair and back again as he complained bitterly of the crime and corruption of the old regime, crimes which the Americans had allowed to go unnoticed, unpunished. He sometimes jabbed his finger in Reddish's direction, as if he held Reddish personally responsible. He held one hand out, fingers apart, and with the other counted off the names of those who'd cheated, embezzled, and thieved from their ministries. Was the embassy blind? Was Washington blind? How could it be blind? Its agents were everywhere. Of course it knew what was going on, just as Reddish had known that Sunday morning when he'd come to talk to de Vaux about the workers party guns. Yet all Reddish was protecting was his own people, his embassy, his ambassador. Didn't the embassy or Washington care about the people who were suffering? All the people, everywhere! In his village in the north, all one saw was sickness, hunger, death! Why? Was the United States a pygmy, like the Belgians? Why hadn't the Americans done something? . . .

N'Sika's two majors sat sweating in terror. Bondurant, watching N'Sika's angry face, was frightened himself.

At last N'Sika sat back. Bondurant asked Reddish to give him the gist of N'Sika's words, but N'Sika interrupted him. He could talk to Reddish later. Weary of the meeting, he asked Bondurant if he had anything to say. Bondurant raised the points supplied by his instructions as N'Sika listened sullenly, without comment. Only when Bondurant asked that the executions cease did N'Sika's face come alive again. He hunched forward eagerly, interrupting Bondurant.

Did the ambassador want to talk about the executions? Very well, he would talk about that. He waved to Major Lutete and told him to translate from Lingala into French. He was tired of French. For three minutes he harangued Bondurant in Lingala and then sat back.

Major Lutete took a deep breath and moved forward in his chair. "Monsieur l'Ambassadeur," he began in a faint, dry voice, "notre président a dit que . . . il a dit que nous, nous—we understand, yes. It is logical and natural, Mr. Ambassador, that you should be concerned about these men—these thieves, rapists, killers, and so on who were sentenced by the Revolutionary Court. Certainly, Mr. Ambassador, we well understand, since this is your responsibility, to preserve order and to improve understanding among nations. That is a diplomat's responsibility. But here on this hilltop, Mr. Ambassador, the President has his own responsibilities, but there is a great difference—"

N'Sika interrupted him angrily, motioning him back in his chair, and pointed to Reddish. "Tell him," he commanded. "Tell him in English." He seized the front of his damp shirt with one hand, and with the other lifted the ambassador's helpless, shrinking arm from the chair rest, dangling it aloft by the sleeve.

241

Reddish translated as N'Sika spoke:

"In this uniform—this shirt, there is a man. Just one man. Now, if you lie or make a false report to your foreign ministry, and someone discovers it is a false report . . . a lie . . . they won't take you out and shoot you because you failed, will they? . . . They won't hang you, will they? . . . No, of course not! . . . But if I fail, they will shoot me . . . They will shoot me or hang me or whatever! . . . So I must be careful not to fail—and I must be careful to teach my enemies what justice is . . . not abstract justice or diplomatic justice, the kind you deal with in telling me you are troubled by these executions, but not so troubled that your tears or your grief will kill you tomorrow if someone else dies! But if I can't teach my enemies what abstract or diplomatic justice is, send them to Brussels or Paris or America to the universities to learn as you've learned, I can show them what my justice is."

N'Sika released his shirt and dropped the ambassador's sleeve, standing now in front of his chair. He took from his pocket the handwritten note he'd studied at the beginning of the meeting, the remarks prepared for him by his advisers.

"And do you know where my justice is? Not in the universities or the foreign ministries! Do you know? Not here in this room with us, in your words or in my words, no! Who sent you these words? The same men who gave me these words?"

He ripped up the paper contemptuously and threw it across the table, then flung his arm out behind him, pointing down the hillside:

"My justice is down there, against the stone wall of that prison on the hillside. Would you like to see it? To visit it for yourself? I'll take you, yes, because I have nothing to hide. I mustn't hide it—never! My justice is against the stone wall of that prison and I want everyone to know what it smells and feels like! It smells and feels like death, because that is what it is—for me, for my council, for all of us! Not paper or parchment. It smells and feels like death, and if you don't know its smell, then it will never find you, but if you do, it will—wherever you're hiding, in whatever commune or village! Because as surely as I'm talking to you this way, if there are those out there in the darkness who have no reason to fear me, to smell and know my justice, then as surely as we sit here this minute, those men will be the ones who one day will put me against the wall and shoot me!

"But you don't understand that, do you? No. How can you. When they shoot you, they'll only shoot the name your father gave you, the idea of your name, whether it is good or bad. When they hang you, they'll only hang the uniform away someplace in a dusty closet that doesn't smell of death, but of ink, parchment, papers, and everything else diplomats worry about. But you will keep your pension, your villa, your children, and your wife. But when they shoot me, it will all be butchered together, everything—collar, sash, medals, bones, and meat, like *mwamba,* and afterward it will all be thrown in a ditch like the carcasses of the dogs the street sweepers find each morning in the capital, and in that ditch I'll smell of death too, not pensions, or ink, or dusty closets where foreign ministries hang the sashes and medals of diplomats who fail. So that is the difference and that is why I shot those men, and if you still don't understand, we will go down to the prison and see for ourselves, just the two of us, you and I, no one else."

It was N'Sika speaking, not the man fabricated by his policy and protocol advisers, but the man Reddish had heard speak at Martyr's Square, the man behind the coup d'etat and everything that had followed. Bondurant and Lowenthal sat stricken, like Majors Fumbe and Lutete, eyes never leaving N'Sika's face. The darkness pressed in on all sides from beyond the windows; the sounds of cartridge belts and rifles, metal on metal; the low, sibilant voices in the garden; the clatter of the dry raffia palms.

Reddish knew that he had dared all, this man. Whatever psychological taboos had been inflicted by decades of foreign rule, he had violated. Whatever quietism was implicit in his own tribal tradition, he had violated too. He had devastated the social fabric, smashed the polity that held each in place, and torn himself from the peaceful anonymity of a corrupt social order to declare himself its master. Now he had described the consequences. He had triumphed, but the agony of will remained. The nation was still an abstraction; there was no historical, legal, or social authority to which he or his majors might appeal if they failed, just the same barbarism that had awaited the old President. Even as village boys they'd known that one day they would die, but their triumph had made the extinction more absolute, the knowledge more dreadful, and the moment itself more terrifying.

He wondered, as they filed out silently, how well Bondurant had understood that.

❖ ❖ Becker was waiting in the ambassador's study with Carol Browning as they entered somberly. Becker looked from the ambassador's ashen face to Lowenthal, who was even paler, and finally to

Reddish. Bondurant hadn't uttered a word during the long drive down from the para camp.

"Apart from that, Mrs. Lincoln," he inquired of Lowenthal, "how was the play?"

"Appalling," Lowenthal whispered, sinking down in an armchair.

Bondurant ignored them both and moved heavily to the bar cart. Becker followed him with his eyes, puzzled, and looked back at Lowenthal.

"Brutal and primitive. I trust I shall never again have to witness an episode like that. Fear so thick you could cut it with a knife."

"What did he say, this Colonel N'Sika?"

Encouraged by Bondurant's silence, Lowenthal sat up, like a stand-in thrust center stage. Carol Browning still waited with her stenographer's pad in front of the couch. The ambassador noisily filled his glass from the ice bucket. Watching this drawing-room tableau, Reddish, for the first time that night, was suddenly depressed.

"About the executions?" Lowenthal continued. "He told us in a wholly bizarre, improvisatory way that because of circumstances over which he had little control, moot in any case, I must say, that these draconian measures must continue—"

"Fix yourself a drink, Simon," Bondurant interrupted, his back to them.

"Sorry?"

"Fix yourself a drink and sit down. That's not what he said at all."

Bondurant crossed the room deliberately, drink held to his chest carefully, like a vicar moving to the congregation, chalice in hand, and sank down in his favorite armchair. The whiskey was very strong, the glass filled to the very brim. "Do you have your pad, Miss Browning?"

"Yes, sir."

"Good. What did N'Sika say? What did he say indeed." He sipped from the glass and put his head back, gazing off into the middle distance. "He said what Napoleon said when he explained to Metternich at Dresden in 1813 why he couldn't surrender." He took another swallow, his eyes brightening. "He said quite simply that others' fear was his strength, that he was an orphan of history, which is quite correct, that kings might surrender a dozen times, yet go back to their thrones as royalty still, like diplomats with their pensions or their retirement cottages at Bar Harbor, but not men like him, which is also correct. He could surrender only once, he said,

244

and when he did, he would be killed for it, dead in that absolute way neither bureaucrats nor diplomatic royalty can ever understand." He turned his gaze to Lowenthal. "How primitive is that?"

"That puts a fine point to it," Lowenthal said.

"The point was perfectly made."

"He quoted Napoleon?" Becker asked, astonished.

"I quoted Napoleon, just this minute, but it's not the Schönbrunn Palace atmosphere I'm trying to evoke, Dresden either," Bondurant replied, his irritation muted. He looked back at Lowenthal. "You frighten me sometimes, Simon, more than N'Sika." He looked at Reddish. "What do you think?"

"The point was clear."

"Good. I don't believe he would have managed it in French, do you?"

"Probably not."

"I thought not. A very impressive man, this N'Sika. Keen, tough, and very intelligent. And a way of projecting himself too—a bit sly, perhaps, like an actor, but that's a quality such men always have. Molotov had it, so did Spaak and Adenauer. So now we know who the revolution belongs to, don't we?"

The telegram to Washington reporting the talk went through two drafts. There may have been an incipient paranoia in the efforts of Becker and Lowenthal to paint the most flattering portrait, that of a beleaguered African nationalist beseeching American support, detectable even in their bureaucratic jargon, which didn't deal with the subconscious. Tired of their tinkering, Bondurant rejected their rewrite and adopted his original draft.

chapter 13

❖ The midday sun splintered on the azure lozenge of the Houlet swimming pool and the leaves of the lime and avocado trees nearby. Reddish followed the white-jacketed Bakongo houseboy out the french doors and across the shaded courtyard to the pool. Gabrielle lay on a zebra-striped lounge chair, her eyes hidden by sunglasses. Yellow and green finches scolded and thrashed in the shrubbery.

She sat up slowly, surprised. "I was in the neighborhood," he began, almost apologetically. "I thought I'd see if you were still here."

She quickly pulled a terrycloth beach robe over her bikini.

"That was very kind of you. Please, do sit down."

"I can't stay very long." She'd been swimming and her hair was still damp. "It's my lunch hour."

"But you'll have something to drink, won't you?" Masked by the sunglasses, her face seemed different to him. She may have been conscious of it. She removed the glasses as she called the houseboy back. Her face was the same as he remembered from the other night, and he sat down. On the metal table were a book and a few travel brochures.

"Planning your next trip?"

"Not really. Houlet suspects I'm not anxious to return to Paris. He brought me those. He thinks a trip to Capetown or Durban might be interesting. I'm told the Capetown beaches are lovely. Have you been to South Africa on holiday? I'm told many diplomats go."

"No, I've never had time for it."

"It's not the Africa I wanted to see."

"I guess not." They sat in silence for a minute. She didn't seem to know what to say. "I'm sorry about what happened the other night," he offered.

"Yes." She nodded, still looking at the travel brochures. "I'm sorry too."

The houseboy brought Reddish a gin and tonic.

"It is very depressing sometimes," she began after he'd gone. "I was very upset. I made up my mind to leave as soon as possible. It's only a matter of deciding where to go." She stood up. "Do you mind if I change into something comfortable. I'll only be a minute."

She left him alone on the terrace holding the drink on his knee. The pool surface was unbroken, reflecting the drifting cumulus overhead. In the silence his gesture seemed wasted, inconsequential, less important than a wet bathing suit or the prospect of the white sand beaches of the Atlantic. He pulled Masakita's letter from his pocket, received that morning by Nyembo at the embassy, delivered by an anonymous messenger. Now, in light of the events of the past week, it seemed a letter from a stranger. He found the sentences that most troubled him:

The interior is peaceful. I've decided not to seek exile, whatever happens, but to search for a permanent solution to this problem between the government and me. But I will need the help of those powerful enough to convince the N'Sika government to agree. The Americans would benefit from such an accommodation, as would the entire country. Should you wish to contact me, you have simply to come to Benongo.

"I'm glad you came," Gabrielle said as she returned wearing a denim skirt and cotton blouse. "After the other night, I wouldn't have expected it."

"We didn't get the chance to talk," he answered, folding away the letter. He watched her sit down again. "I was wondering which you were, the romantic or the writer."

She gave a small laugh. "The writer, I suppose, the journalist," she added in despair, "but a failed one. A failed romantic as well."

"Is that why you're here?"

"It is difficult to explain."

"Like Stendhal?"

"Yes, like that story. I would have explained the other night, but then the Houlets returned and everything was impossibly mixed up."

"I thought maybe you wanted some help on planning a trip someplace."

"Yes, that too." She turned her head away for a minute, looking across the garden, as if trying to find a way to begin. He waited

247

silently. "I haven't been completely truthful with you, either about why I came here or why Houlet wants me to leave. I went to Chad to do a story on the French military offensive against the rebels in the Tibesti, France's African war." She turned to him.

Her voice was different, even her eyes. He didn't know how to answer her so he said nothing.

"I've learned since I came here," she continued, "not to be too direct, at least among diplomats, like Houlet, who concede to you only what they concede to their wives, their secretaries, or their mistresses. If they give you only that advantage, that of being a woman, it's best to use it, and not to be too ambitious with your own ideas."

"Fair enough," Reddish said. "I think I know the problem. What happened in Chad?"

She'd gone to Chad with a photographer and an anthropologist she'd met at the African studies center in Paris; the latter had worked among the nomads of southern Algeria and Libya and spoke Arabic. The French Ambassador at Fort Lamy was suspicious, and the French military commander denied them permission to travel to the north in the Tibesti region, where the unpublicized French military action was under way. They were restricted to Fort Lamy.

"There was no water at the hotel, no electricity some nights. It was beastly hot. My two companions began to lose their appetites for the trip. The advance we'd gotten hadn't fully covered our expenses, and I made up the difference. I had a furious argument with the French Ambassador one night, and then with them. They were both worried about keeping on the best of terms with the French authorities. The anthropologist had been doing some work among the remote villagers of Tunisia, funded in part by the French government. The photographer was simply a coward. They proposed doing an article on the fishermen of Lake Chad instead, the African fisherman, and I refused. At the French Embassy the next day, the two made their amends with the authorities and prepared for the Lake Chad excursion. I refused and my visa was revoked by the Chadians, who put me on the next plane. To Entebbe, as it turned out. For three days, nothing but rain. It was a complete disaster, all of it."

"So you came here."

"I thought Houlet could help me with the Quai and have my visa reissued, but he wouldn't even try. I'd researched the Chad background for five months and was totally unprepared for anything else. So I was bitter about that. The political situation here bored me—I'm sorry to say that, knowing how you feel about this country—but it did. It was so predictable, so corrupt, so unoriginal. But then the coup came. The more I saw and heard, the less I understood. The situation in Malunga seemed to me quite different from what Houlet and others were claiming, but I didn't fully understand why. I tried to do a little investigation of my own, but without success. I knew so little, no one was prepared to help, the foreign ministry is in chaos, like the university—"

"How did Houlet react to that?"

"I didn't tell him, but he probably suspected. Why should I take Houlet or Armand seriously? Then that night at dinner I quite lost my temper. I told them what I'd seen, how brutal it was, how totally absurd the idea that a radio station was operating out of the party compound, or that the blacks in Malunga were preparing to smash the government—"

She stopped, her bitterness gone suddenly. "I'm sorry. I didn't mean to say all of this."

"No, I think I understand."

"Do you?" She turned toward the sunlit garden again, leaning back in the deck chair. "You're quite lucky," she continued after a minute. "You have a profession you can claim, something that claims you. That's important not to forget. You don't have to justify yourself every minute, every hour, every day."

"Why should you feel that?"

"But how else can I feel? Ten years doing nothing. What resources do I have except my own? You see?" she said after he didn't answer. "Why should you understand? You've never had to recover your life from someone or something, to take it back from nothing, to begin again."

"So that makes you ambitious."

"No, not ambitious. Just to know yourself again, is that ambition?" She gave a dry, bitter laugh. "You don't understand at all, do you?"

"Maybe not. What does your former husband do?"

"He's a lawyer. Yes, a very successful lawyer. Too successful, I suppose. In his success he didn't understand why his brilliance shouldn't suffice for everyone else. He had no interest in family talent not his own. He didn't understand what was happening to him. After so much success, his career had become a substitute for life, his cleverness a substitute for thought. He was bored with what he had become, and he met a young woman who made him feel he could live again. But it wasn't his fault, not completely. I helped too. It's a very simple formula and that's why it happens. But you're divorced too. Was that the price of your success or did others pay it?"

"I wasn't successful and others paid it," Reddish said. "All of us."

"Your mistake or hers?"

"Mine."

"Then there's still a chance, isn't there?"

"No, no chance."

Madame Houlet came into the garden with her rose shears, a limp straw hat on her head, a basket over her arm. Reddish stood up. She paused to talk for a few minutes and then continued on, disappearing behind the screen of flame trees in the rear.

"The places we went were pretty far off the beaten track," he continued, looking at the sky, "not what she was used to. She would have been happier in Europe. She couldn't have been happy here, never."

"I know how she feels," Gabrielle said. "I think I'm beginning to despise it too."

"No, you aren't," Reddish said, putting down his glass. "Give yourself a chance. It's a big country. Put the pieces back together."

"In what way? Write about it, you mean?"

"Why not? No one else has."

"Are you talking about the coup or the country?"

"Both," he continued. "They're one and the same. I may be going away for a few days, maybe a week. You ought to get away too. It would do you some good. Here everyone is saying the same thing, journalists and diplomats both. It's different in the bush. If you don't know the interior, you don't know this country. If you don't know the country, what happens here in the capital won't make any sense either."

"Where are you going?"

"The interior."

"For what reason?"

"To see what's happening, how they're reacting to the new regime." At the country team meeting the day before, the AID mission director had presented a report from the public safety adviser that a police post at Funzi had been raided for weapons by a group of rebels. The report raised questions in Bondurant's mind as to whether the dormant rebel regions might again become active in opposition to the new military regime. He'd suggested that someone visit those regions, someone from the political section; Lowenthal, not anxious to leave center stage, had proposed that Reddish go.

"Where would you suggest?" Gabrielle asked.

"The Kwilu maybe," Reddish said. "Let me think about it. I'll give you a call tomorrow. You'll still be here?"

"I'll still be here. Are you serious?"

"Why not?" he said.

❖❖ "I thought you weren't going to take any more trips," Sarah reminded him after he'd returned from the ambassador's office.

"Just this last one," Reddish said. "Is anything in from Langley yet on our cables?" The day following their meeting with N'Sika, Bondurant had instructed Reddish to report to CIA headquarters the coup details as he knew them—the hijacked MPLA guns, the assault on the party compound, and the seizure of the *présidence*.

"Nothing, not a word. I still don't understand about this trip."

"Some of the old guerrilla trails may be coming to life again—at least that's what some people think."

In the niche between the glass-topped desk and the typewriter table was a cork mat to which were thumbtacked the sun-faded ethnological maps of the interior, the various tribal atolls, islands, and archipelagos marked in different colors. He stood scratching his temple with the steel letter opener, following the thin blue vein of river to the north and the great lake at the edge of the rain forest, the equatorial wilderness which had once been Masakita's foraging ground. Funzi, where the police post had been raided, was just north of Benongo, where Masakita had attended the Jesuit mission school. Near Funzi was an AID-funded fishing cooperative. Reddish wondered if anyone had visited it recently.

"What the hell's wrong with Langley?" he asked suddenly. "It's been almost a week now."

"I'm sure I don't know. Why does it have to be you going on this trip? Haversham is coming back on Thursday. He'll want you here."

"Because I'm tired of this place. There's nothing going on here, nothing the others couldn't handle."

"Why doesn't Selvey go?"

"Because he doesn't know the area. What's wrong with you anyway? What difference does it make."

"Wednesday is my birthday," she said coolly, turning back to the door, lips drawn thin. "I was planning something. I'm sorry I ever asked."

He telephoned the AID project officer and asked him about the fishing cooperative near Funzi. The young officer was uncertain, a little vague, and finally apologetic. No, no one had visited the project in over a year. It wasn't a very high-priority project anyway. The economic rationale was somewhat dubious, the venture pushed by the ex-minister of finance, who'd been shot. For that very reason, it would probably die on the vine now. In the meantime, the AID country plan had shifted emphasis—new target goals, a new emphasis. But the project was still on the books. If Reddish was planning a trip in the area, he might look in. But don't encourage any additional funding, no, quite impossible now.

"Do you people over there ever finish anything you started?" Reddish demanded.

"Oh yes. As a matter of fact, we recently completed—"

He hung up.

❖❖❖ "And who did he say is the ideologue these days? Who is pulling these rabbits out of the hat?" Federov asked, turning to Klimov as his car sped toward the para camp through the midnight streets. "Whose ideas are these we read about every day in the newspapers?"

"N'Sika's," Klimov admitted.

"So your charlatan is no longer the maestro, eh, no longer pulling these strings that are all tangled in confusion." He was in an expansive mood after a small party at the embassy celebrating Navakian's fifty-fifth birthday. The wine Federov had drunk—and he'd drunk too much—had even persuaded him to extemporize on Navakian's concertina.

"So what socialist text has he borrowed, this colonel, for his first five-year plan?" he continued, determined not to let this night be ruined by another bullying lecture at the para camp. He'd been abruptly summoned three hours before. Klimov, contacting his informant on the Revolutionary Council, had learned that Federov would be told that Russian support for the MPLA guerrilla forces must be reduced, if not eliminated; the same guns were finding their way into the hands of those in the interior opposed to the new regime. Another imbecilic protest at another imbecilic hour.

"N'Sika has no text. He admits that."

"And so where has N'Sika studied? If N'Sika is the ideologue, not this hired charlatan of yours, where does his mind hide—in the jungle where he learned his brutal ways? Is that where he studied? Who taught him the French he uses to terrify us or have Fumbe terrify us—ten verbs and twenty nouns, always the same. What kind of book can you write with ten verbs and twenty nouns? A very primitive book. No, don't look for bones in this nasty egg they call a revolution—never."

"He's willing to learn," Klimov suggested. "He must learn. It's a vacuum. He has no time to think, not with all these decisions to be made."

"A vacuum?" Federov turned. "Whose words are those?"

"My words."

"So you'd hatch this egg, would you? A vacuum. But it's not a vacuum. There is something there—a bullying impulse to humiliate the Belgians and Westerners. More than just an impulse. To turn on his tormentors, to electrify his audience every time he opens his mouth. What happens when he runs out of words, when he grows tired of shouting? I'll tell you what will happen. He'll go creeping off to Brussels and ask for mercy, ask for the technicians and monopolists to run his copper mines. Of course. And he's a racist too. So being Belgian-trained, he'll know the proper kind of servility when he stands on his hind legs in Brussels and begs for their understanding. A racist, that's what this man is, and if you don't see that in his eyes, you don't see anything."

"I see a man willing to listen," Klimov answered.

Federov studied the armed guards at the para camp gate through the sedan window. Their bullying disgusted him; so did their brutal self-conceit. They insisted the driver leave the car over Klimov's protests. Oh, there are no bones in this egg at all, Federov's mind sang, suddenly detached from this macabre comedy, this circus of zombies which frightened even the moon peeping through the fringe of ragged palm trees, guns everywhere, black blood still warm against stone walls less than a mile away.

In the salon with its vulgar chairs and weak, gelid light—like that of a bath house, Federov thought—Colonel N'Sika's purple-black face seemed wearier, the eyes lackluster. Federov was cheerful, almost lighthearted, his gray eyes shining behind the iron-rimmed spectacles. N'Sika had just completed a six-hour session with the Belgians, whose wooden stubbornness had blocked any movement on the copper mine negotiations. He had intended to cancel his meeting with the Russian, but Major Fumbe had been unable to reach Federov prior to his departure for the para camp.

Major Lutete began by describing several recent raids on police posts in the interior by rebels carrying Russian weapons. One occurred within a hundred kilometers of the capital, another at Funzi, to the north. The council had reason to believe that the rebels had been armed from Brazzaville and supplied with Soviet-made weapons intended for the MPLA.

Federov dismissed the reports with a wave of his hand. "I will make it perfectly clear to you now, as I have before, that neither Moscow nor Brazzaville, whose authorities our ambassador across the river has consulted, has any intention of arming these confused, frightened rabble in the bush, whoever they are. We fully respect your government's policy of positive neutralism announced last week. We are motivated solely by the wish for coexistence, so we don't regard ideological differences or differences in social systems as in any way a barrier to this new era of cordiality. We arm no rebels. We regard this country as one which plays a most important role in Africa."

"So you do not agree that these are guns supplied from across the river?" Fumbe asked.

"There are those who pretend to see Moscow's puppeteering strings everywhere," Federov replied, turning to N'Sika. "Of course. Do they also give us credit for the moon hanging in the trees outside? Perhaps. But I can assure you, Mr. Chairman, that we don't hang cardboard moons in a cardboard sky for these rabble at Funzi or wherever to bay at. Of course not." Amused at his own metaphor, he smiled. "We didn't create your revolution, either, did we? No. You created it, you and your men here. Did we create those objective internal conditions that brought about the downfall of the old regime? Not at all, no more than the moon I spoke of. The moon is out there in the trees because its time has come. So it is with your revolution."

Encouraged by N'Sika's childlike attention, he continued: "So it is too with progress and social justice, to which you say you are committed. Revolutions succeed not because they are announced over national radio but because their time has come, because internal conditions have ripened and created them, created the will for men to understand their condition and change it." At his side, Klimov stirred restlessly. Federov ignored him. "Are two hundred million Africans waiting for Moscow to tell them to waken, to rouse themselves, and stand up? Of course not. Only people who are ignorant of history can say such things. So examine the situation objectively, as you have your own revolution, and you will see that we have no reason to give arms to these rabble."

N'Sika studied the Russian's lively face, the quick gray eyes, and the hairy eyebrows. His tie was askew, a white collar button showing. A claret-colored spot, like berry juice, stained his shirt-front. His shoes were dusty.

"People accuse you," he said.

"Of course they accuse us, as they will continue to accuse us. They accuse us out of weakness, not out of strength. But we know what these imperialists want. It is very clear. They want the best of all worlds, past, present, and future, yours as well as mine. When a repressive, corrupt regime is maintained, social and economic justice denied, the masses deprived, hungry, and sick, that's a triumph for peace and stability. When anti-popular criminal regimes are overturned, that's a threat to peace and stability, and Moscow is accused of sowing sedition and revolution abroad.

"So what is stability? It's doing nothing—nothing, you see! So we know what these imperialists want—they want the same world tomorrow as they have today or they had last year, but what does that deny? It denies progress, it denies history. So of course they won't have what they want. Why? Because you can't deny progress. You can't artificially trifle with the objective processes of historical development, not in the name of stability or anything else. History will turn these charlatans out."

N'Sika listened silently, puzzled by the twists to this strange little man's imagination. "Objective processes of historical development"? What was he talking about? Did he mean that the forces which overthrew the old President were the same as those which hung the moon in the sky? If progress was inevitable, why was it that the dead President had ruled as oppressively as the Belgians, that the people in his own village in the north were worse off now than fifteen years earlier? The Western envoys feared this man, as the old President had feared him, but why? Not the man, certainly. He had no strength in his arms or neck. Did they fear his secrets? Did they fear what was hidden away in his books, the way the old fetisheers feared the missionaries' Bible?

"Objective processes?" he asked. "A leader must be objective. What we did was done for the nation, not for ourselves. So that is objective. I understand 'objective' in that way." He hesitated, reluctant to bare his clumsiness in front of Fumbe and Lutete, who talked easily and quickly of such things. "But what else did you mean?"

"Objective in the sense of understanding those laws by which societies revolutionize themselves," Federov replied. "But first you must understand why these things happen . . ."

N'Sika listened as Federov explained. His words were difficult. He had little time. Tomorrow the Belgians would come again, followed by the French, the Americans, the Germans, and the Israelis, then the Arabs, each with their own interests, their own problems of investment or trade, their own veiled warnings. In the meantime the ministries were in chaos, like their balance sheets and deposits. The council was more frightened and divided than ever, as terrified of de Vaux as they were of Masakita and the old rebels in the bush, whom they claimed Masakita was now organizing, perhaps to be joined by a few mutinous army commands. De Vaux was no longer of use to him. He'd betrayed him by concealing his uncle's illness and could no longer be trusted. So he trusted no one on this hilltop, no one at all. He needed to be ten men to do what needed to be done, but he was alone; what strength he had was being leeched from him each day in a hundred trivial decisions. The powers of his ancestors were forsaking him as his old uncle wasted away; his education had been that of a soldier, not a politician.

So something was missing. He searched for quick and simple solutions to these problems which a month earlier he hadn't dreamed existed. Bullets had been quick, but the burden they brought was crushing. What could he invoke in his search for simplicity? Bullets? No. God? Which god? Mammon had been the old President's god, the key that unlocked all doors, bought allegiance and loyalty, silenced dissension, and fueled the engines of government. What else was left? The Belgian colonialists had thrown the other on the rubbish heap of history during their long period of plunder and exploitation, like the old fetishes burned by the Catholic priests in his village. After he'd executed the old President and his cabinet ministers, he'd felt no remorse and seen none in the faces of the civil servants and the people in the streets. He knew it was true—that the body of the Belgian Christ could be as easily forgotten on the rubbish heap as the old fetishes.

But what Federov was telling him was something else, something new entirely, as simple in its design as those laws which kept the planets in motion overhead. Exploitation was something he could understand even better, and now Federov was describing Western exploitation of Africa in Marxist terms.

N'Sika listened, not understanding everything he was being told, but impatient to be told more.

"What did you do before you became a diplomat?" N'Sika interrupted suddenly, as interested in Federov as the lessons he was teaching.

The Russian said he'd been a schoolteacher in the Urals.

"What did your schoolhouse look like? Was the roof tile or was it thatched?"

Federov described the schoolhouse.

"And the children, did they have enough to eat? Did they wear shoes? Did they sit out in the sun and rain or did the government put a roof over their head, give them food to eat?"

N'Sika's aide interrupted to say the Pakistani Ambassador was waiting to discuss the cancellation of a contract for textile machinery, but N'Sika sent Lutete to meet him and continued to talk to Federov.

Lutete didn't mind the interruption. It seemed to him that they weren't talking politics at all; more importantly, he knew that the Pakistani would pay to have the contract restored and the foreign exchange released. He intended to get his share of it.

◇◇◇◇ Crispin was at his table in the afternoon sun, bent over his copybook, when he heard the knock at his door. He turned quickly, crammed the book back into the drawer, and heard the voice of his cousin's wife: "Crispin! Crispin! Are you asleep?"

He opened the door and saw a stranger standing next to her, a black oilskin bag over his shoulder. He wore a wrinkled white shirt, a black tie, and a black serge suit that smelled of diesel fumes. He was a traveler, maybe an evangelist. Pinned to his lapel was a fiber cross, still green from the interior.

"Crispin Mongoy?"

"*Ehhh.*" The African took a letter from his oilskin bag and gave it to him.

"Give him some money," Crispin told Kalemba's wife, who gathered her skirts about her and shuffled barefooted back along the corridor.

The pastor continued to eye Crispin disapprovingly. "Are you a Protestant?"

"No," Crispin said.

"The man who gave me this letter said he was a Protestant."

"Where did he give you the letter?"

"On the lake at Benongo."

Kalemba's wife returned and gave the pastor a few coins, which he silently counted as he pinched them into his leather purse.

"God be with you," he said, nodding to Mrs. Kalemba.

The letter was from Pierre Masakita:

Dear Crispin:

I passed Kimpiobi on the track today, and he told me you were safe under Kalemba's roof. I have no news of any of the others.

If you're able, I would appreciate it if you would begin to make discreet inquiries as to the whereabouts of the old members of the political bureau of the party.

Decisions need to be made within the next few weeks. All of us must recognize the new reality which faces us and come to terms with it. An accommodation must be made which enables you, and others like you, to take up their work and their lives again.

I will be in touch with you again.

Pierre M.

Thirty minutes later, Crispin was crossing the *grand marché* on his way to a small bar on the edges of the commercial section, Masakita's letter in his pocket. The owner of the bar was a cousin of the politburo's recording secretary. The burden lifted from his shoulders, he strode through the clutter of stalls and babbling old women as he had once marched through the back lanes of Malunga; but at the rear of the market he was brought up short by a small poster tacked to a telephone pole. He identified the face even before he read the name and inscription:

PIERRE MASAKITA
1,000,000   Francs
Ya Matabisi
Sambu Na Mtu Na

Pierre Masakita had a price on his head. The poster was new, so new that it still attracted some curiosity, including that of two policemen who stood in the shadows of a nearby stall, unseen to Crispin. A few urchins gathered to look too, standing with Crispin. Perhaps it was their presence which provoked his response. Angrily, he ripped the poster from the post and stuffed it in his pocket.

The two policemen saw him and immediately blew their whistles. Crispin bolted away into the *marché*, the urchins after him. Hearing the policemen's whistles and seeing the fleeing figure, others took up the chase, believing him a thief. A dozen African workers unloading a truck jumped to the ground to block his path. He leaped sideways into a stall, fell over the counter, and sprawled among cassava and beans. Before he could regain his feet, a dozen

258

youths had tackled him while the old woman who owned the stall beat him savagely with her staff.

He was bleeding, his nose and mouth dripping blood, his shirt torn, as the two policemen and the largest of the pursuing youths led him off to the police station.

In his pockets they found a nickel-plated Belgian revolver, the poster he'd torn from the post, and a letter. The revolver had been stolen from a Belgian shopowner almost a year earlier; the poster was government property. The letter interested no one until it was discovered by the lieutenant at the central prison.

book three

chapter 1

✧ Reddish spent the third night of his trip at a palm oil plantation on the banks of the Kwilu River, hundreds of miles to the east
of the capital, the guest of his old friend Faustin Kaponji. He arrived
at dusk, driven in the old Landrover Kaponji had sent to Kikwit to
fetch him.

Kaponji was waiting for him on the porch of the guest cottage,
eager for news from the capital. He was a Maluba. "A Jew of the
Congo," he'd called himself when they'd first met three years earlier. A small man in his early fifties, with a dark puckish face and a
lively imagination, Kaponji was a man of parts. He was a businessman who professed no interest in politics, but he had an insatiable
curiosity, as well as a great deal of money. As a youth he'd been a
diamond smuggler in his native Kasai and had accumulated enough
capital to launch his career as trader, planter, and businessman. He
owned the palm oil plantation, which included a half-dozen Belgians on the staff, had a small office in the capital where he traded
in German steel, Thai sugar, Japanese appliances, and Czech hand
implements, as well as an office in Brussels, where his Belgian wife
lived. His Maluba wife lived with their children on a second plantation in the Kasai. His plump métisse concubine kept another home
for him in the capital. He was also a Rosicrucian.

Kaponji had assembled the Belgian and African staff in the
plantation recreation center for a small cocktail party. In the muggy
African twilight, Reddish shook their hands and answered their
questions, Kaponji at his elbow. The Belgians had brought their
wives, tired middle-aged women who sat silently to one side, anxious to return to their own cottages, where their dinners were waiting. Their husbands gave to Kaponji the same extravagant servility
they'd once given their Belgian overseers.

As the two men returned to the main house, Kaponji tried to

cheer Reddish up, convinced he was depressed by the overthrow of the old President.

"Well, everything has its dark side, but that's not what you should look for. I suppose the old man got what he deserved, the others too, but it's bad enough just remembering your own youth, isn't it?—the tricks, the deceit, the sharp practices. Crimes too, of course. We've all committed them, no doubt about that. But we're lucky, each of us. The mind's recuperative powers are enormous, André. Thank God for that. You see the new boiling vat over there, still in the crate. Just arrived—from Germany. So just be thankful for the power you have in your own head! It's enormous! Positively immoral, the strength there! Guilt is only in books, *mon ami*. Only in books, thank God for that. Otherwise we'd all be dead—dead of grief or remorse. Any one who says differently is a fraud—intellectual trash. I'd rather be a Rosicrucian these days than these grief-stricken Catholics or socialists. Better social doctrine than what these communists or capitalists have to offer, too. No one's putting Rosicrucians in jail these days, are they? Of course not. There's no reason to—no intellectual pretense to it at all. It's all just mumbo-jumbo, simple humbug, that's all. So it frees your head for other things."

In the salon of the main house, Kaponji rummaged through a drawer and brought out an old bottle of Indian elixir to add to their gin glasses. "This will bring your spirits up. In five minutes you'll be a new man, freshly minted."

During dinner alone in the dining room, Kaponji talked about the new Revolutionary Council. He knew a few of the names. Major Fumbe was too stupid to be a rascal, like the old President. He didn't know Lutete. Colonel N'Sika was a strange man. Perhaps a little primitive, but not stupid. No, he certainly wasn't stupid. When you find a politician who isn't merely stupid or venal, that makes you uneasy. So he was uneasy about N'Sika.

Kaponji explained that N'Sika credited his uncle, an elderly *chef coutumier* or traditional chief from the north, with lifting his career out of obscurity. But de Vaux was probably behind it, the *éminence grise* of this new regime.

"In what way?" Reddish asked.

"The plane crash," Kaponji said. "You remember the plane crash in the north, the one in the storm at Mbandaka where the old general was killed?"

Reddish remembered.

"The old general was N'Sika's enemy, the man who'd been blocking N'Sika's career. So there you are—the plane carrying your worst enemy blows up in a rain squall. Was it lightning or a bomb? Who knows? Not N'Sika. But if you can manage both, dynamite and a detonator, a fetisheer and his power, you have the best of both worlds, don't you? And this fellow de Vaux can, believe me. But not N'Sika. You see the power that gives him? Of course, quite simple."

The following morning, Kaponji took Reddish on a tour of the plantation and pressing factory. At ten o'clock, the launch was ready at the boat landing to take him upriver to the missionary landing strip. A pilot would fly him from there to Lutu at the end of the lake, where he'd catch the evening packetboat for Benongo.

Kaponji was still reassuring him as they walked down to the river: ". . . put all this business out of your head, André. It happens and then it's all over. There's only one law—decay and regeneration. We're all freshly created creatures. You can't change the rest, never. Wars, crimes, obscenities, executions—they all happen. We recreate ourselves every day, in the wink of an eye. The past is no more. Otherwise how could you walk back through that village along the river, looking at its poverty, its disease, its superstition and filth. All those wretched creatures. Can we die every day? No. Be grateful for it. Commerce recreates you every day in the same way. A new man is what you are. Politics will kill you before your time in this country, mark my words. Don't think about the old President— that shyster! Politics was what he wanted, politics was what he got —a bullet in the head. Yesterday's cruelties and abominations are forgotten, of course. Let your recuperative faculties work, your brain cells regenerate. *Commerce!* Commerce is the answer, André!"

Reddish made the overnight trip to Benongo in a creaking fetid cabin, the wooden bunk airless, the mattress under him as thin and stiff as a copra rug. The warped door to the cabin wouldn't close and was slammed to and fro constantly by the movement of the dogwatch hands from the fo'c'sle as they shuffled barefooted back and forth. The matchwood walls shuddered and pounded from the vibrations of the pistons below.

On the other side of the cabin wall the Belgian first mate blew and spat, thrashing in his bunk and grunting hoarsely from time to time, as if a woman were with him, one of those cool, dusky, long-legged girls who had silently moved aboard at Lutu, an isolated village where the women were unspoiled by bars, beer, or the single white man who lived there, an elderly Swiss pharmacist who lived in eccentric celibacy with his malarial dreams and his collection of old masks. Reddish had caught sight of the first mate at Lutu—a sixty-year-old *flamand* with jaundiced eyes and tobacco-stained whiskers who'd watched hungrily as the girls came aboard and squatted down in the evening shadows of the deckhouse, unburdening their shoulders of the freshly fermented palm wine they'd brought aboard in wicker-wrapped bottles cooled with damp palm leaves.

Reddish slept for only an hour or so, defeated by the hellish heat of the cabin, and spent the remainder of the night in a canvas chair behind the wheelhouse watching the white billows churned up by the paddlewheel. On the deck below dark figures lay sprawled on mats. He fell asleep finally, but awoke to watch the dawn leach the horizon, draining it blood-red at first, then pink; soon the night was gone and the silver bowl of sky was the color of mackerel from the gulf.

The packetboat docked at Benongo, south of Funzi, in the early-morning sunshine. A crowd of fifty or sixty Africans waited on the collapsing wooden pier as Reddish crossed the timbers, climbed the path up through the palm trees, and carried his bag down the dusty lakeside road to the old mission house, where the Catholic brothers were expecting him.

Two hours later he was at the grassy airstrip south of town. The small twin-engine plane circled the field twice and drifted in from the lake, kicking up dust and chaff as it scuttled across the field. He watched from the shadow of a tulip tree as the plane unloaded, his rented Italian jeep behind him with the other vehicles from town. Near the metal utility shack lay the weed-grown hulk of a T-26 trainer used during the rebellions, the victim of a foul-weather landing and a permanent reminder of the lake country's unpredictable weather.

Two Belgian priests came alert as the door opened. Two provincial officials alighted first, followed by Gabrielle, who paused uncertainly, her eyes searching the faces waiting near the wing. The two Belgian priests saw her too and dropped their thumb-crushed cigarettes into the dust. "*Tiens,*" the shorter one exhaled sharply.

"*Mais non, non—pas possible,*" said his companion.

He was right. As Reddish reached Gabrielle, a stout Belgian sister left the cabin door, sharp-chinned and sharp-eyed, her face as yellow as a brick of cheese. She carried a small medical bag and wore white stockings over her bulging calves.

It was dark and the equatorial heat lay like a blanket over the second-story gallery where they sat—Reddish, Gabrielle, and a

264

Catholic brother—looking out over the black lake. The trees hung still, their leaves motionless. Not a breath stirred. The chairs were wooden, with stiff cane seats, dressed from the logs cut and planed in the sawmill at the rear of the station. The floor was wooden, like the gallery, which traveled the length of the brick mission house two degrees south of the Equator.

Frère Albert described the recent raid on the police post at Funzi—a local dispute, nothing more. The policemen at the post had confiscated smoked fish and beer from a passing truck, and the villagers had retaliated, making off with the police rifles.

He was Flemish and spoke French with careful precision, like an old servant handling ancestral china not his own. He was lean and gnarled, with gray teeth, a gray beard, and bright brown eyes, as bright as those of the hawks they'd watched with Gabrielle's binoculars on the marshes that afternoon. He smoked a pipe, a thumb-worn briar held loosely between his calloused fingers, oil-stained by the repairs he'd been making in the mission generator room. The current pulsed feebly through the naked bulbs overhead.

Beyond the mission gate the native women plodded by on the dusty road, black shadows swaying against the moonlit lake. Heavy wicker baskets bent their faces into the road. Their backs were laden with firewood gathered along the shore and in the stump-filled fields nearby.

"You've been here a long time?" Gabrielle asked cautiously.

"Since nineteen thirty-two." He'd made only two trips to Belgian since then. One to visit his dying mother. The other? He'd forgotten—a lung infection perhaps. But he was content here. Where else could a man his age go these days? As a young man, he'd visited North America. He nodded toward Reddish and said he'd forgotten that during their last talk. When was that, two years ago?

"North America?" Gabrielle asked.

North America, but not the United States—his English was much too poor for that. Quebec City and Montreal were the two cities he'd visited. The recollection of that frozen, sepulchral countryside had haunted his imagination ever since. He would like to see the snow again before he died, but he supposed that was impossible. The purity perhaps—that was what had haunted him, seeing that virgin frontier as the first French missionaries and trappers had seen it. As a young man, he'd read of the martyrdom of the first Jesuits by the Hurons and Iroquois. That was what he'd wanted to ask Reddish. Were there Hurons and Iroquois near his home? "Where was it—Wisconsin?"

"Wisconsin." Reddish was surprised he'd remembered.

Frère Albert turned toward the women moving along the road. The country had changed since he'd left the boat at Matadi so many years ago. Perhaps he had changed too. He'd seen many strange things—lightning bolting from a blue sky to strike an isolated hut at the edge of a village where an old sorcerer lay ill. Did madame believe the impossible? The impossible sometimes happened. There were many things not written, many things witnessed by the priests themselves, who refused to write about them. That merely meant they hadn't been understood. One found in books only answers for which an age, epoch, or civilization had questions. But the minds of those Africans out there in the road carried another civilization, richer in many ways than their own. Much remained to be explained—ways of perception, for example. Two days before Reddish's message had arrived, the wash boy in the scullery had told him that he would be coming.

His chair creaked. His gray pipe smoke lifted into the flickering yellow light. The husbands of the lake tribe killed their wives with labor and fished only sporadically now. The lake was poor in fish. There was no way to evacuate their meager catches. The Portuguese trader in town had a dozen flatbottom scows that arrived three times a week with wares, all the scows equipped with new outboard motors. A virtual monopoly. Remarkable entrepreneurs, these Portuguese.

Reddish remembered that AID had supplied outboard motors for the fishing cooperative they would visit tomorrow.

The bell from the refectory rang for dinner. Gabrielle and Reddish followed Frère Albert across the porch and watched him go down the outside stairs. He invited them to join him if they returned early from the commissioner's dinner. He had a bottle of brandy. They would see his light.

"He's lonely," Gabrielle said. "Could we walk along the lake? Do we have time?"

They left the compound and crossed to the beached dugouts and canoes where a few fires still smoldered and the fishermen were folding their nets. She walked to the end of the small jetty, looking up at the stars. The moon was a full, brimming silver disc high over the lake. The far shore was hidden from them.

"It isn't what I imagined. It's different—strange—but so lovely, so peaceful."

"Stagnant."

"I would hate it if it were like the capital. There's life here, but it's gentler. Would you change everything?"

"No, not everything."

Their adjoining rooms off the second-floor gallery of the mission house were identical: whitewashed walls, high narrow beds covered with mosquito netting, wash tables, and tin shower stalls. Lodged adjacent to Reddish was the Belgian sister.

Gabrielle was ready before Reddish and stood in his doorway waiting, her hair combed, wearing a white dress, conscious too of the sister who sat next door in the lamplight reading from a small book.

"What are you doing?" she called in a whisper.

He was studying a typewritten list in the light of the table lamp. "It's a list of provincial officials," he explained. "They're going to ask me for everything from nylon nets to Landrovers."

The sister next door noisily cleared her throat.

"*Shhh—*" Gabrielle whispered.

"So I want to know who I'm dealing with. What's the matter?"

A black sedan waited in the sand road at the foot of the gallery steps, sent by the district commissioner. His *chef du protocol* was extravagantly servile, holding the rear door open for them. "*M'sieur l'ambassadeur,*" he breathed, bowing into the dust.

Reddish felt obliged to correct him. Correcting him now would reduce the size of everyone's expectations.

Smoking flambeaux flared in the shadows beyond the verandah of the district commissioner's lakeside villa where the guests gathered on overstuffed chairs brought from the salon. Gabrielle sat with the women, across the verandah, Reddish to the right of the commissioner. His black tribal cane leaned against the table in front of him, where the drinks were being poured—great whacks of whiskey, uniced, dumped into tall glasses by native hands accustomed to serving up Fanta, lemonade, or beer. Both the commissioner and his wife were from a region far to the east, five hundred miles away, as much strangers to the local people as Gabrielle or Reddish.

The talk was about N'Sika, the new council, and the perfidy of the dead President and his regime. None mourned him, despite their appointments under his administration. Reddish was regaled with tales of malfeasance and murder. Why had the Americans waited so long, when a gentle push would have done in the old hypocrite years ago? A black cleric showed Reddish his scarred black wrists, lacerated by iron manacles from a month in the jail at Lutu.

The commissioner's plump face was needled with tribal scars. He wore a dark Nehru jacket and trousers. Had Reddish been at

Martyr's Square when *le président* had made his speech? *Incroyable!* There was a great chief for you! What dignity! What courage! He'd given the Belgians a hiding, hadn't he! Lashed the skin from their backs, broken the whip across their shoulders, and then thrown it at their feet! He'd taken back the country from the foreigners—no more *vin rouge!*

Slyly he touched Reddish's hand with his fingers. "But he hadn't done this alone, eh? The Americans had said, *ça va*, right?" He winked at Reddish. " '*Ça va?*' Isn't that what the Americans had said?" The Americans were omnipresent, omnipotent. Weren't they sending an astronaut to the moon?

During the dinner toast, the commissioner catalogued his needs—trucks, Landrovers, tractors, nylon nets, a freezing plant for the fish. The police needed jeeps. How could they patrol the old guerrilla trails bringing guns from the Cuban training camps in Brazzaville without vehicles? The new minister of interior must come to Benongo to see for himself how the district had been forgotten by the old regime. Reddish must persuade him. Then Reddish must persuade the new President to come. They must both come together.

As the commissioner bade Reddish and Gabrielle farewell at the foot of the front steps, he apologized for being unable to accompany them to the fishing cooperative at Funzi. He had been summoned to the provincial capital, as had all district commissioners. Regrettably too, since he'd not visited Funzi for almost six months. He shrugged. No vehicles.

It was after eleven when the commissioner's car returned them to the mission guesthouse. Frère Albert's light was out, and they silently carried their chairs to the far end of the gallery, facing the lake, away from the visiting sister's window.

They had a nightcap, Gabrielle silent as she gazed off into the darkness. "Do they truly think you can do all that?" she asked finally. "That you can supply all those things he mentioned?"

"No, not really. But they feel they have to ask. It's a ritual now. It also helps them explain why nothing gets done."

"But they're all strangers here. None of the wives I talked to was from this region. All of the officials are from elsewhere."

He explained that the old President had managed the interior that way in attempting to break up the tribalism of internal politics.

The wind had risen on the lake; they could hear the sounds of the surf stirring against the beach. "In a way, they feel abandoned out here," he continued, "like Roman consuls at the outposts of the empire. Antioch, Palmyra, Tyre. They don't even feel that these lake people are part of their nation, unless it's an inferior part—not Romans at all, just Syrians, Jews, barbarians."

She sat in silence as he brought the two lanterns from their rooms. He filled their wells with the kerosene Frère Albert had left for him and set the wicks.

"That would never have occurred to me," she murmured finally, lifting her head, "what you just said."

He didn't see the African at all, didn't hear his footsteps down the gallery until he heard Gabrielle's small cry. He turned and saw a man standing halfway between their chairs and the staircase. His face was hidden, blocked out by the wash of light from behind him.

"*Mbote*," Reddish called.

"*Mbote, patron.*" He didn't move. "*Ozali Reddish?*"

"*Ehh. Nazali.*"

The man nodded. "*Buku na you.*" He said he had Reddish's book and came forward, his hands extended, head lifted, not bowing as he gave Reddish the book, the way most villagers would, but standing stiff and straight, his small shoulders thrust back. He was short and wiry, also barefooted. His tattered shorts and shirt smelled of smoked fish and gasoline.

Reddish looked at the book Pierre Masakita had borrowed from the flat in the capital. "Where's the man who gave you this?" he asked. "*Azali wapi?*"

"*Lobi*—tomorrow we go."

"Tomorrow I go to Funzi."

"*Namsima.* After Funzi."

"How?"

"Pirogue."

"The man who gave you this book is your friend. *Azali moninga na yo?*"

"*Ehhh. Ndeko*—my brother." He nodded to Gabrielle, then Reddish; he moved backwards as lightly as a shadow and went down the steps. They both went to the gallery rail and looked down into the darkness, but he was gone.

"What did he say? What did he want?" Gabrielle asked, still frightened.

"He wants to take me someplace."

"Not tonight?"

"Tomorrow."

The lights flickered for a moment, dimmed, and then expired. Gabrielle moved to the front of the gallery with Reddish, looking out over the lake. The generator had been turned off. As the seconds passed, the curtain of obscurity lifted and they saw the deep bowl of sky, the scattered stars, the broad silver lake lying under the moon, the milky strip of road, and the frosted trees.

On the lakeshore, they saw the small pirogue move away, sculled by the same little man who'd returned the book.

In the heat of the morning Reddish walked down the dusty lake road and found a Portuguese trader's shop where he bought cigarettes, Chiclets for the children at Funzi, and bottles of mineral water. A few Africans stood mutely in front of the scarred wooden counter clutching coins in knotted scarves. The Portuguese owner sat on a stool behind the cash box, a cigarette in his mouth, a cup of coffee on the tray in front of him. His wife was a fat raven-haired woman with a tired face and deep shadows under her dark eyes. She fetched merchandise to the counter for her customers' curiosity with silent impatience.

"You're the American," she said to Reddish as she waited on him. "It's worse than ever. You were here before, eh? I remember. Now the army thinks it can steal everything from us, like they took the copper from the Belgians. They steal from our boats, our trucks—worse than thieves. Thieves you can punish."

"Goods are scarce," Reddish said, "especially here."

She laughed. "What do you expect when they steal from our trucks. If we close down, where these people go, eh? You think I live in this hell-hole lake country for my health, my looks? I been here thirty years. Each year it gets worse."

Her husband encouraged Reddish to pay in dollars, but he paid in francs instead. After he put the cash box away, he said, "You like the dinner last night? Whiskey, beer, wine—everything O.K., huh? Very nice." He reached under the counter and pulled a thick wad of invoices from a cigar box, holding them up. "All right here—beer, wine, whiskey, coca. All for the *commissaire*. Last night, two hunnert dollar maybe. You wanna pay?" He threw the invoices back into the cigar box. "Who gonna pay this, huh? Six months maybe to get my money. Maybe I never get it. When you come to my house, you drink palm wine, coca maybe. Next time you come, bring plenty people, O.K.? Plenty dollars."

Gabrielle was waiting on the gallery steps, a leather camera bag over one shoulder, wearing a denim skirt and a sleeveless white blouse.

"I was worried," she said. "I heard a plane take off."

270

He told her it was the commissioner on his way to the provincial capital.

After lunch they drove through the village and out through the mangrove trees that fringed the lake along the track toward Funzi. The narrow dikelike road twisted through the marshes, left the swamps behind, and traversed the rain forest, impenetrable ten meters beyond the verges. In the shadowy green twilight, blue and yellow butterflies flocked by the hundreds in the wet ruts where the ditches had overflowed, fluttering before the rented mission jeep like a sheen of crystals. The jungle retreated and they emerged onto burned-over meadows where farmers were hacking at roots and burning stumps as their wives moved with hand hoes along the rows of silver-green manioc or the rot of decaying banana trees. They passed through a few isolated villages, none containing more than a handful of reed huts. The men sat smoking and talking under the reed sun shelters; the women glanced up from fire-blackened caldrons and manioc mills; naked children flocked out onto the track after they passed, waving their arms and shouting.

It was midafternoon when they left the main track and turned back toward the lake. The forest thinned and the trail grew steeper. After an hour they saw figures ahead of them hiding behind shrubs and trees along the track. As the grinding jeep approached, they would turn elusively and sprint up through the wild palms toward the fishing village. Most were young children. The jeep gained the final grassy knoll on the crest overlooking the lake, and they saw the green palm fronds, freshly cut, stuck in the sandy soil to give welcome. At the edge of the village they drove under a green archway of palm boughs tied with vines and garnished with red flowers.

A hundred Africans were waiting in the center of the village, moving rhythmically in front of a wizened old chief and his wife who stood with wooden dignity in red robes awaiting the jeep. The territorial administrator in a European suit bustled here and there, like the director of a mummers' pageant.

"*Notre proconsul*," Gabrielle murmured, watching him rudely shove aside a few old women to make way for a pair of younger village girls bearing flowers.

The women looped a wreath of yellow blossoms about Gabrielle's head, the children pressed bouquets of wild anemone into her arms. Seeing her bowed head, her smile, and her affectionate embrace of the young children, the crowd spontaneously swept away the administrator's hand signals and he was swallowed up.

Behind the chief's hut the lake sparkled and bickered like an

271

enormous iced mackerel. The breeze fluttered the pennons of red cloth atop the thatched huts. Gabrielle's face and blouse were wet as they moved into the cool shadows of the chief's hut, but she seemed exhilarated, still holding the anemone. The yellow wreath had been lifted; a few yellow petals still clung to her hair.

The chief took the seat of honor at the table, flanked by his wife and brother. About his neck was a leather thong on which hung four leopard teeth, polished like old ivory. On his head was a red cap beaded with cowrie shells. After he was seated, he folded his dark arms against the table and didn't move, following the administrator's stage management with his ancient red-veined eyes with the same mute primal indifference with which a caged lion follows the antics of a peanut or popcorn vendor beyond the bars. In the shadows of the room his dark face was as blue as gunmetal; the four leopard teeth shone like pearls against his wet black chest.

Clay pots of peanuts and watermelon seed were set out. Beer, soft drinks, and palm wine were brought from the scullery hut. The chief drank palm wine from a wooden goblet, staring silently through the sun-filled doorway and into the yard, where his tribesmen still plunged back and forth, goaded on by the administrator's factotum. Their thudding feet sent warm dust as fine as talcum back through the seams of white sunlight to settle on the damp faces of those inside the hut.

The chief didn't speak; the administrator spoke for him, requesting more financial help for the US AID-sponsored fishing cooperative—more boats, more motors, more nylon nets. After he finished, he took a petition from his attaché case and presented it to Reddish on the chief's behalf. It was typewritten and in French.

After the feast, Reddish wiped the mwamba paste from his fingers, washed his dry throat with beer, and made a brief speech in Lingala thanking the chief for his hospitality. The chief and his retinue retired to the cool shadows of their family huts.

The administrator took them for a tour of the fish-smoking kilns, the docks, boats, and pirogues. As they climbed back up the hill toward the jeep, Reddish stopped, identifying the small figure squatting alone down the shore near a beached pirogue.

"Where are the outboard motors?" he asked the administrator.

He told Reddish they were out on the lake.

"In this heat?" The solitary figure near the pirogue got to his feet, dusted his trousers, and climbed toward them. Following Reddish's eyes, Gabrielle saw him too, puzzled, her hand to her eyes, shading the sun. "They don't fish in this heat," Reddish continued. "Where are the motors?"

"*En panne*, broken down, most of them. There may be a few on the lake."

Reddish pulled his kitbag from the jeep, but left Gabrielle's flight bag on the front seat. "It's the man from last night," he told her.

"You're going with him?" she asked, startled.

Reddish asked the administrator if he had a driver. If he did, he'd pay him to drive Madame Bonnard back to Benongo.

"But you're not going back now?" the administrator asked.

"Later. The fisherman over there has a sick child. I said I'd look at him."

"I see—yes. But in a pirogue?"

"No," Gabrielle pleaded suddenly, guessing Reddish's purpose.

"I have my car," the administrator explained. "I could drive her—"

"Impossible," Gabrielle insisted. "I'm going too."

The administrator, still puzzled, said, "But I can take you. I'm returning now. You are welcome."

But Gabrielle had already snatched up her bag and was running down the long sloping hillside to where the pirogue was beached.

❖ ❖ They followed the edge of the lake, skating across the silver shallows, the blunt nose pointed north. Gabrielle sat forward on a small wooden stool, her hands gripping the ax-hewn gunwales, Reddish amidships. The boatman crouched in the stern, hand on the tiller of the ancient paintless outboard motor lashed to the stern by a pair of planks. The sun sheeted the lake with silver, blinding them as they looked west. In the reeds and rushes, they sometimes passed small thatched lean-tos built atop pilings only a few feet above the lake where solitary fishermen slept, their pirogues drawn alongside and lashed to the pilings, waiting for the sun to go down.

No sound came except the throb of the old motor drifting blue-gray smoke out behind them. The sky was a metallic blue, with a soft batting of clouds to the east. They passed other dugouts, black slivers of matchwood far out on the lake, sculled by single oarsmen, heron-slim in the stern.

The dugout at last began to veer toward a hidden river channel overgrown with weeds and hyacinths. In the early morning and at dusk, hippopotami would cruise for water plants among the reeds;

but they saw only a few egrets, as motionless as cattails. The river narrowed a mile beyond its mouth, and the thickening canopy of cypress, umbrella trees, oaks, and wild nutmeg blotted out the sky. The air was heavy and foul; the river blackened in the shadows; yellow snarls uncurled where the current moved against rotting trunks.

As the channel narrowed, Gabrielle turned and looked at him anxiously, her face small and frail against the towering backdrop of purple tree trunks, massive ferns, and trailing vines. The channel narrowed further. The fluted tree trunks glistened with dampness and were scrawled with yellow and gray lichens. The water ahead of them was motionless in the dense green light, then abruptly wrinkled here and there by some devouring jaw hidden far beneath the surface. Flies, gnats, and mosquitoes swarmed in gray shrouds. From his trouser pocket the boatman took a thin fly whisk with a polished bone handle and began to twitch it back and forth unconsciously, with that sure muscular knowledge of a nervous system trained to precision by years of discomfort. Not once did he move his yellow malarial eyes from the channel ahead of them.

The dugout slackened, sending a yellow tongue of water ahead of them into the small slough where white film lay over its surface like scales on a dead skin. A few meters beyond, the helmsman guided the dugout between two water-filled pirogues beached on a mud bank. Two small Africans were waiting, crouched silently on the bank, each holding a thin switch with its bark peeled, moving it constantly across shoulders, neck, back, and ankles. Their legs, arms, and bellies were thinly covered with wood ash. At a nod from the boatman they scrambled into the water and helped pull the dugout onto the beach. Neither looked at Reddish or Gabrielle. Reddish helped Gabrielle onto the bank, shouldered the packs, and followed the boatman through the screen of bamboo thicket and up the narrow path. He had guessed by then who the boatman was: the polished bone handle of the fly whisk hinted at it; the silent obedience of the two men on the bank and their refusal to look at the two strangers confirmed it—he was the village chief.

The village lay a quarter of a mile above on a promontory overlooking the swamp and river, surrounded by dense trees whose foliage forty to fifty feet overhead sheltered the dozen thatched roofs like an umbrella, shutting out the sky and admitting only a chiaroscuro of brilliant light here and there on the black earth. The village itself was bathed in a green submarine dimness. The women were naked except for bolts of dirty raffia cloth about their hips; the men wore raffia skirts or cotton shorts; their children sat with swollen bellies and ruptured navels, looking up with fly-blown faces as the procession passed.

The chief led them to a single hut at the far end of the village behind a thicket of decaying banana trees. Beyond the hut a twisting path climbed higher, and farther up the slope they could see the blowing grasses of a small meadow open to the sky. The chief held aside the raffia curtain, but didn't enter. He said his brother would come later. Then he spoke a few quick words in his own tribal dialect, not Lingala, his eyes searching Reddish's, and when he saw no recognition there, shook his head and went back to the village. The hut was already touched with evening shadow, the clay floor recently swept, as dry as a bone. In the corner was a single raffia mat, on the crude table a new candle in a carved wooden holder and a box of matches.

"I don't understand," Gabrielle said, wiping her damp face with her handkerchief, when they were alone. "Are you staying here—in this hut?"

"It looks like it."

"But this isn't what I expected."

"It never is," Reddish said, unpacking the battery lantern from his kit, "but I hadn't planned on you coming."

"Please don't be angry."

"I'm not angry, but it won't make things any easier."

A dark hand brushed away the raffia curtain and a young boy entered carrying a wooden tray with two bottles of warm beer, their labels stained with rust. He put them on the table without looking at Gabrielle and Reddish, trying not to smile, like the walk-on in a grade school play, and went out. A minute later they heard the sound of shattering wood and saw two other youths building a fire in a circle of ash-covered stones in the yard. Gabrielle watched them silently, lifting the raffia curtain aside, and finally raised her eyes toward the golden meadow.

"Do you think we could walk up there—now, before the light is gone?"

They left the village and ascended through a patch of yams and manioc. She moved ahead of him carrying her camera. As he followed her up the path toward the crown of hill, leaving the shadows of the village far below, he saw a few brickbats and seams of crystallized mortar almost hidden in the grass at the edge of the path. He kicked at the brickbats curiously and heard Gabrielle call to him from the top of the hill: "Come! It's splendid!"

He climbed slowly after her into the dying sunlight through deep, bending grass as thick as buckwheat. They climbed higher toward a farther knoll crowned by a few flame and citrus trees whose waving leaves still held the fading sunlight from the west, the sun gone now, far out to sea, beyond the coast, and the old Portuguese forts. The western sky was crimson.

She waited for him on the path, looking out toward the vast silver dish of lake. "It's magnificent," she cried, the color showing in her cheeks again, the sullen heat of the village and river below blown away by the evening breeze. Reddish gazed out over the basin of lake, the circling forests and swamps, the fading crimson of evening sky.

At their feet nearby, moving slightly with the breeze, a single yellow rose lifted its head from the tangle of thorn and weed. Gabrielle saw it immediately, calling to him as she dropped to her knees, "But look, look what it is—a rose."

He turned, saw it, and was climbing higher as she reached forward to take it, still kneeling in the grass as she brought it to her face. He was standing in the weed-grown courtyard when she joined him, looking into the gnarled, fire-stunted lime trees, into the vine-grown shell of brick and mortar of what had once been a small cottage dominating the surrounding countryside. Only the outline remained—a low brick foundation overgrown with vines, weeds, and wild creepers. A few ancient fire-blackened joists still lay like charred bones within the obliterated rooms. At the front of the cottage had once been a flagstone terrace enclosed by a low stone wall. A few stone pilasters remained, like broken teeth in a bleached jawbone.

"Oh, André," she murmured, gazing about her at the devastation as she sank down on the step, the rose still in her hand, "so petite, so tiny, so cruel—" Reddish circled to the rear, looking down the slope toward an abandoned track that disappeared into the green forest beyond where the trees grew in parallel rows as far as the eye could see, like the sentinels of some abandoned empire. He knew the bark would be scored and mutilated, hacked like the breastplates of those other old warriors of empire; these windrows would be empty of life too, as empty as the vaults of Petra or the broken columns of Palmyra under the Syrian sun, looking out over a frontier the wilderness had reclaimed. He walked back to where she sat slumped on the step looking up at him sorrowfully.

"Rubber," he said, "miles and miles of it."

"Rubber?" From the village below, the smoke from the evening cooking fires threaded slowly through the trees. "And the people?" she asked. "The woman who made this garden, who planted this rose?" She gazed about her at the desolation of the courtyard, where crimson and blue anemone grew in the cracks. Leaning down, he picked one and gave it to her, and they sat together on the broken step, listening to the wind. A few kites and fish hawks sailed high on the warm currents of evening air.

"I despise this country," she said finally, without bitterness, breaking the silence. "I do. At moments like this, I do, and I'm sorry, but I do."

"The house was built for the rubber, probably during the war. Now it doesn't pay."

"This house was deliberately, cruelly burned."

"It could have been lightning. That's why the village is down there, not up here. This is storm country."

"Just rubber? That's the only reason? Sometimes what I hear from you is so terribly matter-of-fact it's cruel. It is."

"So was this house."

Impulsively she held the rose toward him. "And this?"

He looked at the rose and then at her lifted eyes. "And the village down there? Roses on the lawn—and hookworm, yaws, and malaria in the work camp? What did the people who owned this cottage leave here? What'd they leave—Roman law for the bedouins, a few French irregular verbs for the overseers, the twenty-lash law for everyone else? They tapped the rubber trees and left."

"She left this—this rose."

"What's that mean?"

"A woman lived here, André. I know. A woman who sat here in her garden, who loved this hilltop. I can feel her, the way she sat here—"

"But not an African woman, is that it? This afternoon the girls at Funzi gave you flowers. They were as black as Erebus—"

"You're not fair."

"Maybe she was a métisse. Half black."

"I don't understand you," she cried. "I don't. I've tried, but I don't! I don't understand why you would come to a place like this, or to that ugly village down there. I don't even understand why you are in Africa—with men like Armand and Houlet. I don't understand anything, anything at all; but when I try to understand—when I see a devastated house like this, so small, so fragile, in a country so dark, so ominous, so murderous—when I try to understand and try to feel what someone who once lived here must have felt, like the woman who planted this garden, you deny it! You do! You deny it! It's in your face, your words! Why do you punish me? Why do you punish yourself? When I see a house like this, burned and ruined, I'm moved by that, but you say, 'No, no, you mustn't be moved, you mustn't feel anything. Just commerce, just greed, just ugliness again, and it's your civilization that has done all of these cruel things.' But I can't help it! That's not the answer, not the full answer. I feel what is here."

He saw the brightness come suddenly to her eyes, but just as quickly she turned her head away. Looking at her averted shoulders, he remembered again that night in the Houlets' salon when she had looked at him silently from the sofa following Houlet's thoughtless remark. In that European salon among complacent white faces whose arrogance he'd come to despise, her solitary gaze had made him aware more painfully than ever before of how deeply he'd shut himself away.

"I'm sorry. That's not what I meant," he said.

"But it's what you said."

"It's what I said." The twilight was thicker now. "Maybe it's because I sometimes think we're a little extinct too, like those rubber trees," he began again. "That's what hurts, knowing there's so little you can do. We've helped destroy their past. Now we're destroying our own too, maybe the future as well. Neither seems to exist as an idea any more. Stupidly too, that's all. Just doing stupid things."

They sat in silence for a long time watching the western sky grow dark. She stirred suddenly, her head back, breathing in slowly. "Do you smell that?" Eyes closed, she breathed the fragrance of the stunted old lime trees within the courtyard, still in partial blossom after all these years.

chapter 2

✧ Reddish had expected to be taken to Masakita someplace nearby, but he arrived at the hut the same evening. Gabrielle was kneeling over a tin basin sponging away the dust from her neck and face when the raffia curtain was jerked aside and a man came into the hut, glanced about, looked at Gabrielle and Reddish, and called to someone outside. He wore a webbed cartridge belt with an empty holster. He turned abruptly and went out.

Masakita entered alone a few minutes later, wearing a dirty white soutane, his right arm in a sling. He pulled the soutane off immediately and folded it over the chair. He was dressed in a tattered gray shirt and shorts. His thin legs were gray with wood ash.

"Welcome," he said with an apologetic smile. "Welcome, both of you."

Reddish told him in Lingala that Gabrielle didn't know who he was, but he merely shrugged. "It doesn't matter. She was in the car that night, wasn't she?"

The man with the webbed belt brought in a tray with three bottles of beer and three plastic glasses.

"My cousins told me it would be a trick, your coming to Benongo and then Funzi, that you were conspiring with the commissioner for the million-franc reward. My colleagues in the bush were also suspicious. They said, 'He'll come but he'll bring the army.' So I told them to watch for themselves. So they watched the pirogue come and were still watching until ten minutes ago. But if the army doesn't come by sundown, they can't come at all. This is my uncle's village. My father's too, but he was dead. When I went to the mission school at Benongo, I claimed my mother's village, near Funzi. No one from this village had ever gone to the Jesuit school. It was a hunting tribe, smaller people too, you noticed. *Bena singe*, say the tribes up the lake—the monkey people. So my papers, my records say I'm Bolia from up the lake, but it isn't true. This is my village, my people."

"But you're not living here now?" Reddish asked.

"No, deeper in bush to the east, an old rebel camp abandoned for years now. You enter by pirogue, like here, only much more difficult. The missionaries avoided it, like this village."

"So they're searching for you among the Bolia."

"Yes, but not searching very well."

"I thought you'd left," Reddish said, "to Brazza or someplace else."

"I've been in exile. There is no place to go now. For others, yes, but not for me. I've been in exile, in Cairo, Prague, Brussels; in Peking and Moscow; in Algiers. In Paris four years. But now there is no place to go. To go outside, to go into exile once is necessary, I think. To go twice is more difficult. But to go a third time and a fourth is death, alive in the body, yes, but death in everything else. No, there is no place for me to go now. My place is here, with my own people."

The tree frogs thumped in the distance. The candle smoked in a sudden draft and Masakita leaned forward to extinguish it, then trimmed the wick. After he relit it, he moved the raffia curtain aside to let in the night air. "I won't go again."

"What's the alternative?" Reddish asked.

"There's only one—to reach an accommodation with this new government. We've had our insurrections, our guerrilla wars. They've failed."

"You think they'd fail now?"

"You know that as well as I do. Of course they'd fail. This country is exhausted, worn out. Who would lead a rebellion? Those few tribesmen of mine out there in the dust? Who would follow them? A few of their tribal cousins, no more. And what would guide them—nationhood? What nation? Where is our nation today? An abstract idea, nothing more. But there are always a few tribal malcontents ready to fight. They're ready to take to the bush again—to burn, pillage, and terrorize. But who will they fight? The government? But where is the government? A few pitiful soldiers, policemen, administrators, and commissioners, like those you dined with last night, who are as frightened, confused, and miserable as they are?

"No, the government doesn't exist out here. You know that as well as I! It exists only in the capital, where Colonel N'Sika and his council sit on the para hilltop. How can a government exist in a country this size when you can walk ten kilometers into the bush and no one will ever bother you or know you exist, like these people here. But of course they don't believe you when you tell them that, these rebellious malcontents.

"So they begin their rebellion right here, fighting a government three hundred kilometers away, and end by destroying this village and those suffering people out there. That's all they would accomplish. Yes, they could recruit a few tribal outcasts from other villages, thieves and braggarts from this one, murderers from another; and if together they declared themselves revolutionaries, maybe Moscow or Peking would give them guns, but it would be a fictitious war, a war to declare their revolutionary spirit at any cost, to punish those who lack it, and to force their will on those who simply want to be left alone. But the rebellion would spread no further than the banks of that river there"—his lifted arm pointed off into the darkness—"and the road behind us, because the Bolia are in that direction, the Tumba below that, and they all despise this tribe, just as the hungry worker in Malunga grew to despise the *jeunesse*. So that's the sort of exhaustion I'm talking about, an army and three hundred tribes, not a nation at all. So insurgency isn't the answer, not now."

"Then you're talking about exile," Reddish said.

"This is my country," Masakita began again, "the only country I want. The government is my own, a black government. This isn't Angola or Namibia. The Portuguese and the South Africans aren't my colonizers. This is my country and these are my people. I can understand why an Angolan is in exile, a Namibian, a South African black, certainly. To go home there is to agree to your own degradation, to acquiesce in it. I know why dos Santos fights his battles, why he claims Marx as his father—what other father do the Portuguese permit him?—but I am not dos Santos and the Portuguese are not here."

"You could go back to Cairo and take up your work there—Africa and the Third World."

Masakita sat back contemptuously. "Yes, Cairo. Cairo or Algiers, take your choice. To do what?" he asked, his voice rising. "To ask them for sanctuary? For asylum—to tell them I'm not a free man in my country and ask for permission to be free in theirs? But what sort of freedom is that? The Egyptians and Algerians are my brothers, but do you know what it is to be a black man in the slums of Cairo or Algiers, in Jidda or Oman? Do you?"

"I know it's not easy."

"You've been to Cairo. You know the expression 'If you want a brother in arms, buy a Nubian; if you want to be rich, an Abyssinian; and if you require as ass, a Swahili'—a Bantu, like myself. Yes, go to Cairo. Go to Cairo and help liberate the continent. What continent—the Sinai? Where are the troops Ben Bella promised black men like me in 1963—ten thousand Maghreb soldiers to liberate southern Africa. Where are they? Where have they gone? I helped the Algerians. Have they come here to help me? No. And what's the purpose of Nasser's Afro-Asian Secretariat? To fight Africa's liberation wars? No, to make us blood brothers against Zionist imperialism! So go there, you say—go back to Cairo. And how long am I to stay? Five years, ten years, a lifetime, like others before me? To stay as they've stayed, in the suqs of Jidda and Aden, the black men you find in the filth of the alleys selling peanuts in cones of Arabic newsprint, the Arabized Swahili or Bantu whose tongue is split with the speech of the Hijaz, his eyes still dusted over with the sand of the slave caravans—the captive of Islam and the brothels of the Middle East who now believes Mecca is his spiritual home. Is that what I'm to do—become an Arab or European's eunuch again? No. Never. And in exile, that's what I would be!"

He leaned back in his chair, wiping his face on the front of the lifted soutane. Gabrielle watched him in bewilderment.

"No, I've been in exile. For years, for decades. I won't go again."

"They'll find you," Reddish said uneasily. In front of him he saw a different man. "Sooner or later they'll find you and shoot you."

"And you can do nothing?"

"Not here. I've got a Haitian passport and a UN laissez-passer with me. It'll get you out of the country."

"So you've brought me no news."

"This is the best I can do."

"So what does this mean—that your embassy is now willing to fully acquiesce in this plot?"

"It means there's nothing I can do."

"I'm grateful for what you've done already. You know what happened in Malunga; and if you know, so does your government."

"N'Sika would never trust you, never. You know that."

"But your government has influence. You have power. N'Sika isn't a stupid man like those around him. He's clever and he's intelligent. He knows where his interests lie. The other men on the council are weak. But you can reason with N'Sika—"

"To tell him what? That you somehow matter to us, that this

282

charade has gone far enough? We asked him to stop the killings. He said they were necessary. You're the one that matters most. They're frightened of you, all of them."

"The others are weak! N'Sika isn't!"

"I'm telling you to save your own skin."

"You came here to tell me that! All this way, just for that! Just to tell me *that!* That you accept no more responsibility?"

"What the hell do you expect of me? Am I your goddamn keeper? Hell, no—not any more than I was the old President's."

"*My* keeper?" Masakita stood up. "*My* keeper! I'm not asking for charity. I'm asking for justice."

"You won't get it, not from N'Sika, not from us, not from anyone else. It's up to you. Get out while you can."

Masakita hesitated, but he turned, picked up his soutane, and went out without a word. A moment later the man with the pistol entered, glared about angrily, and hurried after Masakita.

Gabrielle sat motionless on the stool watching Reddish, who still crouched over the table, beer glass in front of him, a cigarette between his fingers.

"You came all this way to tell him that?" she asked in disbelief. "To *shame* him into exile?"

"I want to save his neck."

"But such a terrible way—so cruelly."

Reddish got up impatiently. "You don't belong here. You shouldn't even be here. The whole thing is a goddamned mess. I was crazy to even come. I don't know what the hell I thought I was doing, who I thought I was. Another fuck-up, like going to see de Vaux that Sunday afternoon—"

He was speaking in English now, ignoring Gabrielle. He shoved brusquely through the raffia curtain and went out into the warm night.

"When in Christ's name is someone going to get something right for a change!" he shouted into the darkness—"when, for God's sake!"

But no one was there.

He awoke in the thin morning light and sat up, sore from the hard clay floor. The raffia mat in the far corner was empty, Gabrielle gone. The hut had been brutally hot during the night, sleep intermittent, touching his consciousness only lightly, never fully releasing it. He found her outside kneeling near the ashes of last night's fire, trying to roast plantains in their skins. They'd hardly exchanged a word since Masakita's angry departure. Her face was as tired as his, her limbs as stiff. The sun was on the meadow above them, but the village was suspended in aquamarine light under the canopy of trees, the smoke from the morning fires hanging in unbroken parallel planes.

She burned her fingers on the hot plantains, jerked her arm back, and they slid into the fire. He gave her raisins and dried fruit, and she heated the mineral water in a tin cup for the Nescafé. As they sat silently on the log near the coals, faces gritty, limbs sore, a young village girl brought them limes and mangoes in a fiber basket, dropping the basket ten feet away and running off frightened. A few old women moved out of the forests, bundles of faggots on their backs.

"A real tropical paradise," Reddish said. "Maybe the Club Mediterranée could open a Tahiti tourist village here. You could write the brochure."

She didn't answer.

"You shouldn't have come," he continued. "It was my mistake."

"You said that last night."

"Maybe I'd better say it again. If word gets out about my coming here, there's going to be trouble. For him and me both."

"I know that."

"Just so we understand each other."

"You are beginning to sound like Houlet," she said coolly.

They repacked the bags in silence. Masakita appeared an hour later, alone. The sun had penetrated the screen of banana trees. Masakita took a dirty white envelope from his pocket and handed it to Reddish. It was addressed to N'Sika. They went inside the hut.

"I've been thinking about our talk last night," he began quietly, his anger gone. "You came here, you told me what you believed you had to say, and it was freely done. I understand that—"

"He was trying to help you," Gabrielle interrupted.

"Yes, I understand that too. He was saying that whatever his own preference, he can do very little. He has no faith in his own government, no hope in mine. So I understand that too. So it's not what he wants or what I want, what the people of this village want, but others. All right. But that mustn't prevent us from trying. I've written a letter to N'Sika, explaining that I want to live here, live here in peace. He can confine me here if he wishes—to this village, to Funzi, to Benongo—but someplace where I can work in my own country, with my own people. He would recognize that I'm less of a problem here than elsewhere.

"I've told him that I've no intention of going abroad, none whatsoever. That time has passed. Others can go, younger men, men who haven't lived as I have with the revolutionaries in exile, with their empty talk and their parasitic life, their appetite for publicity, food and drink, cars, women, and God knows what else. Because unless you have some special sainthood or genius, like Lenin or St. Paul, what happens to revolutionaries in exile is what happens to monkeys in a zoo, their lives more and more dominated by boredom, paranoia, and exhibitionism, by inner emptiness and public masturbation; but I'm not a saint and I have no genius. So either I work here or I'll die."

"Doing what?" Reddish asked.

"Whatever is needed. Whatever is required to bring about those things N'Sika talked about in his speech at Martyr's Square. What has happened has happened. N'Sika has made a new beginning. The past is finished. But if he is serious about justice, now is the time to begin. My goal has always been the same—social action—"

"And you'd work with N'Sika to achieve that?"

"Yes. I would live here, in this village. In Benongo, in the capital, wherever. Education, administration, I don't care. But the anarchy must end. The first thing anarchy strikes is education. If killing a neo-colonial politician closes a classroom for a year, then spare him. It's the child in the classroom who matters, and when the classroom is destroyed, it's the demagogue who stands in the rubble, everyone else blinded by his dust. It's the future I'm talking about—"

"And how in God's name do you think you can convince others that you're serious," Reddish asked, "that you'll work here in peace? Do you think N'Sika is going to believe that? He's as primitive as those bastards that put those guns in the compound."

"Primitive, yes, but he's learning. He's not like the others. Whatever else he is, he's also a serious man. By now he must be beginning to realize how vast his problems are and how few the people he can rely on. But you're right. It is difficult. It's very difficult to convince frightened men that your way is better than their way. But we must try. What else is there? It's never easy, not here, not anyplace else. But what do you expect? As a Christian, what else can you expect? Nothing is less Christian than to promise suffering people an end to their pain and a lasting reign tomorrow for their own decency and goodness today. We can make no promises, just as you could make no promises last night.

"So it is difficult. It is difficult to convince hungry, angry men that patience is wise. Your country knows that very well. Yours is a conservative country now, which only means that your workers aren't starving. Because of this, your government regards this as proof of its own virtue, and your politicians demand that starving or oppressed men be patient. But patience takes time. A starving man who follows this advice will soon be dead. Time and suffering sometimes make a man wise, but in a hungry, angry world, the world I live in, there is no time for wisdom, just ignorance and desperation. I know that. You asked me that night in the flat what I was hiding from. I was years in exile, a desperate, violent man. And out of those years of exile perhaps my own anger died. Perhaps I died with it, in ways people do die before they're even aware of it.

"Can I now deny that with nothing left to me, in those most terrible years of homesickness, confusion, and loss, a Catholic-trained African living in Paris those years, sitting in my library chair those frozen winter nights when I had no place to go, sitting there like a tongue-tied Pascal, can I deny that I wasn't tempted, that I didn't feel in the darkness around me the agony of Christ for all men, black and white alike? And can I tell you how terrifying this is for a black man like me, how terrifying that knowledge that puts an end to action and buries him in the silence of mortification, with a white man's words on his gravestone? So you understand now why I won't go into exile, no further into exile—that for me there could be no return."

Gabrielle turned to look at Reddish silently, her face so full of pain that he knew there was nothing he could say to her, to Masakita either; and he turned and left the hut and went out into the hot sunshine, looking blindly at a village so bleak, so naked, so brutal in its poverty, that he knew he'd never seen it before.

He was still standing there when Gabrielle touched his arm and shoulder: "Please," she asked softly, still stricken, "come talk to him."

chapter 3

✧ It was midafternoon as Reddish drove the Italian jeep into the mission yard at Benongo. The sun scalded the white dust of the road and flashed in lonely semaphore across the glinting surface of the lake. Nothing moved in the metallic heat—no gulls, no kites, no pirogues, no women in the road.

Gabrielle showered and fell exhausted into bed. Reddish showered, tried to sleep, but couldn't, and instead prowled restlessly back and forth on the gallery, smoking. At five, Gabrielle still hadn't wakened, and he left the mission house for the police station.

Despite the heat, the police captain was sitting in his dusty office reading a month-old edition of *Le Matin* from the capital. His gray khaki shirt was damp, his pop-eyed face beaded with water. In the sunny compound outside, three Landrovers sat in rusty dismemberment, axles, wheels, or engines gone. A fourth vehicle sat in the driveway under the trees, its metallic gray paint and yellow wheels still bright and new, its hood wrinkled with the pleats of compression following an accident, full tilt against some immovable roadside barrier. The new windshield still held the twin stars of compression where the two unlucky policemen had vaulted the dashboard.

The police captain had been a guest at the commissioner's dinner. He apologized for his lack of refreshment, but brought a sack of groundnuts from his drawer, spread them across the corner of his desk, and invited Reddish to help himself. He couldn't answer Reddish's question—whether the arrival of the internal airline's small Cessna could be confirmed for the following morning—but sent his radio operator to contact Lutu at the head of the lake and report back.

While they waited, Reddish asked him about the reported attack on the Funzi police post. He shrugged it off, repeating what

Frère Albert had reported two days earlier. The assailants were first thought to be rebels, but the captain had gone to Funzi to investigate firsthand. They were local villagers, angered by the police post's confiscation of a truck of smoked fish. The villagers had been placated, the guns returned, the incident closed, except for the final report, which would be forwarded within two weeks to the provincial capital. The captain hadn't yet corrected the original teletyped message claiming that rebels were responsible. Landrovers were in short supply; patrolling the old guerrilla trails still required Landrovers; and he had only one in operating condition. The urgency of the original message might convince the ministry that his own vehicle needs were more compelling than those of other districts in the region.

The radio operator returned with the news that the plane's scheduled arrival couldn't be confirmed. A storm was moving from the west toward the far shore of the lake. But the packetboat would come as scheduled the following morning, returning to Lutu at nine o'clock.

Gabrielle was still sleeping when Reddish crossed the gallery in the gathering dusk and knocked at her door. Frère Albert invited him to join him for dinner in the refectory, where they sat together at the plain wooden table long after the other priests and fathers had departed. The overhead lights had been extinguished; the shadows of the table candles were long on the brick walls, the high arched roof lost in shadow as they finally left and went out into the warm night air.

Frère Albert had been describing the history of the mission and the mission school. He'd told of the African students, where they'd gone and how they'd distinguished themselves. One was studying at the Vatican; another was a bishop in Luluabourg.

But one name was missing; and as they went out into the dark courtyard, Reddish asked him about Pierre Masakita. "I understand he was a student here once. Do you remember him?"

Frère Albert stopped to light his pipe. "Oh yes, I remember him. Everyone remembers him." The gray face flared in the light of the match and was hidden again. He waved the dying match, still standing on the path, looking up at the night sky.

"You didn't mention him."

"No. He was different, very different. In some ways, he was the most extraordinary student who was ever here. The fathers will tell you that, those of us who remember. Then he went off to Belgium, got into trouble—anarchists, communists, I don't know what. They don't talk about him. He came back once, I remember, and they don't talk about that either. He came back once, that was all. He brought a small wooden box for Father Joseph, who was the prefect then—a wooden box carved by the Bolia up the lake. It seemed that the chief there had asked Pierre to bring back certain texts from the Holy Scriptures, those they thought had been deliberately withheld from them. You probably know the superstition. So after his return from Europe that first time, he gave the box to Father Joseph. In it was a copy of Montaigne. Yes, Montaigne. Two other books too, but I've forgotten their titles—books on science, on skepticism, I believe. Yes, he was remarkable, the most remarkable of all."

"But they don't talk about him."

"No, hardly at all."

"What do you remember best about him?"

They stood at the foot of the gallery steps. Frère Albert considered the question silently before he removed his pipe. "I remember the boy in him, not the scholar. The boy in the machine shop and the sawmill, curious about everything. Just the boy, but that was unique too. You knew that when he left these lakes and forests they would take that away from him too, the way they take everything else, and so they did."

Standing in the African darkness, Reddish saw Masakita's face, half hidden by a scarf, gray with annealing dust, looking out into the winter night from a bakery shopwindow in Paris near the Rue Cadet.

He didn't sleep well. He finally drifted off to awake again long after midnight, hearing the crash of surf against the beach, and he saw the ghostly white curtains standing away from the window. Rain swept across the wooden gallery and against the screen. He sat up. Across the wet planks of the gallery floor he saw the oblong of yellow light from Gabrielle's room next door and knew she'd finally awakened. He got up, pulled on his trousers, and slipped out the door. Outside the window he heard the intermittent click of her portable typewriter. She was wearing a cotton shift, sitting in a chair with the typewriter on a second chair pulled near, the kerosene lamp on the table to her right.

He called to her, and she sat up startled. "It's me," he said, opening the door. "How long have you been up?"

"Just a few minutes. I couldn't sleep."

"I tried to wake you three times yesterday evening. Are you hungry?"

"No. Please."

As he came closer, she quickly rolled the page from the carriage and got up; but she knocked her leather writing portfolio from the chair, spilling the typewritten pages across the rug.

"What's the trouble?"

"Nothing. Please—it's all right." She kneeled to snatch up the typewritten pages from the floor near his feet.

"You type fast. Did you type all of that—"

"Yes. Yes, I did. Please, I'm very tired." She lifted her face, still frightened; her cheeks and forehead, saddled with fresh sunburn, exaggerated the hollows of her eyes.

"You've been up a long time, haven't you?" She couldn't answer, and Reddish understood why. "You were writing about the trip, weren't you? About our talk with Masakita."

"Yes—no! Don't ask, please. It's personal, just personal."

"You said you wouldn't write it. You told me that."

"I knew you would think that!" she cried. "But it's only for me—no one else!"

He turned and went out.

By morning the storm had moved to the east, but the clouds were low over the trees and a fine drizzle was falling. As she left the room, she saw that the wicker table on the gallery contained only a single cup, napkin, and plate. Looking in through Reddish's doorway, she saw that the bed was made, the mosquito netting neatly folded over the canopy, his bags gone.

The serving boy who brought hot water, Nescafé, and a croissant from the refectory told her that Reddish had eaten breakfast very early in the dining hall and had gone off in the Italian jeep.

She sat alone at the wicker table, looking out over the desolation of the road and lake, able to eat but barely able to swallow, unable to separate herself from the gray overcast and the sodden trees and road. Benongo was ugly in the rain, now another of the desolate, futile places she'd sought out and then fled from, alone again. The memory of the past two days had become a nightmare for her, the small wretched village under the trees even more wretched on a morning such as this, the ruined cottage just a meaningless rubble of mortar and weeds.

She heard the sound of a vehicle on the beach road. Turning mechanically, she saw the Italian jeep splash through the puddles at the gate as it turned into the mission compound and stopped at the gallery steps, only the roof visible. She sat paralyzed as Reddish climbed the stairs, a wet slicker over his shoulders, his head bare. She thought he'd forgotten something. He would pass the wicker table on his way to his room, and she knew she hadn't the courage to speak to him. She sat forward and emptied her cup quickly, then rose from her chair to return to her room.

"It's all right," he called out as she turned away. "Take your time. We've got a few minutes yet. Are you packed?"

"Packed? Not really." Her voice faltered.

"We'll be going by boat. The plane's not coming."

He'd gone to check on the plane's arrival. The flight had been canceled, and he'd booked passage on the boat to Lutu at the head of the lake. She ran to her room to pack her luggage.

"Have you ever been on a paddlewheel before?" he asked as they went down the gallery steps for the last time. "It's an all-day trip, not too bad. Worse at night."

She didn't know what to say.

The gangway was greasy, like the decks. A fine rain was still falling as the old paddlewheeler churned away from the dock. They stood at the rail outside the cabin watching Benongo until all they could see were the palm trees that hid the Catholic mission house and the commissioner's lakeside villa.

"I thought you'd gone," she managed to tell him finally, when there was nothing left to say. "This morning I saw your empty room and I thought you'd gone."

"Gone? Gone where?"

"After last night."

"Last night you said it was personal. I hadn't slept well. I shouldn't have come in like that."

"No, I understand why you did. It was rude of me."

The shore retreated in the distance, pressed down by the overcast, a single sedimentary stratum.

"What did you learn last night," he asked, "writing it all down?"

She was slow in responding. "I'm afraid I simply confused myself. With some things it takes me a long time to understand. I think I'm very slow that way, my mind late in catching up."

"Which way?" They were alone at the rail below the wheelhouse, shrouded in mist.

"Understanding why I feel certain things the way I do, understanding what my emotions mean. Sometimes I'm not very clever that way."

"Maybe you'll catch up at fifty, like your friend Stendhal."

They stood at the railing looking out through the mist, thicker now, fully obscuring the coastline. Patches of fog hid the lake ahead of them. "What was it he said—that at fifty it was high time he got to know himself?"

"You remembered. Yes, I suppose he was trying to catch up too."

"What did he say when he finally did?"

She considered the question silently, looking out toward the shore, but there was nothing there. "The last page was sad"—she remembered at last—"as if he were finishing a long overdue letter to an old friend and suddenly realized that it was too late, that he had nothing to say, that his friend was dead." Reddish turned to look at her. "'I'm very old today,' he wrote, 'the sky is gray, I'm not very well.'"

He waited for her to continue, still watching her face, but she said no more. The fog had enveloped them now, obscuring the wheelhouse, the bow and stern, the paddlewheel, which had stopped suddenly as the boat glided forward. The mist hung suspended in a fine feathery vapor, chilling their faces and bringing each surface nearer: the beaded railing, the curve of her upper lip, the drops in her dark hair.

"That was all?"

She hesitated as he waited, as if he might misunderstand. "No, one thing more. He said, 'Nothing can prevent madness.' Those were his final words." She seemed to smile. "But I don't think that's what he meant at all, not madness." She lifted her eyes to his calmly, her self-consciousness gone. "What he meant was that you can't live your life over. That was what he had discovered."

◇ ◇ The day ended as strangely as it had begun. The night was dark as they disembarked, the steamer late, the fog far away, but the rain that had prevented the plane's arrival still drifted down across the muddy lanes and eroded banks of the village at the head of the lake, puddling the compound at the water's edge where the shipping line maintained a few primitive guest accommodations for lakebound travelers. The double cottage to which Gabrielle and Reddish were led was bare, the beds hard, the linen musty. There was no restaurant nearby, no hotel, no meals to be found except at the Italian atelier and depot which served as a kind of caravansary at the terminus of the overland and water routes.

They found their way through the dark lanes along the hillside to the atelier and its enclosing compound, but no lights showed and Reddish guessed that, like everything else, it was closed for the night. They entered nevertheless, like refugees, through a muddy passageway where goats and cats foraged, and found themselves suddenly surrounded by live shadows, shoulders and heads turned away, watching through the mizzle a wide window of light against the far wall which opened miraculously to Saharan dunes, soldiers in kepis, and isolated Moroccan forts, scarred by the cracks and imperfections of the ancient film and the stuttering lens frame of the battered projector itself, which stood near the center of the compound, draped over by an improvised tarpaulin suspended from a truck bed. Several dozen spectators crouched, stood, or sat there—truck drivers, mechanics, warehousemen, Italian fathers, stranded visitors, and rural officials, all immobilized, despite the rain, by the thirty-year-old film.

To the side, off a narrow verandah, was a plain common mess with wooden tables and benches. The meal was over; yet the plump African cook, still in the kitchen, recognized what had brought Gabrielle and Reddish there and silently fetched soup bowls filled from the simmering pot-au-feu which served all guests, drivers, mechanics, and laborers alike. At the far end of the plank table where they sat, a dark-skinned Indian or Pakistani sat hunched over his bowl, an ancient copy of *Time* magazine lifted in front of his devouring eyes. The soup was hot and filling; the bread, left from the earlier servings in the small woven baskets on the table, was dry and hard. They ate in silence; a pair of tabby cats prowled the table legs, brushing their ankles. Outside, the mist drifted, the rectangle flashed with shifting images, the laughter lifted and fell.

As they finished and stood up, Gabrielle searched the room silently for some evidence of their host. The African woman was in the kitchen rattling her kettles, humming to herself. The dark-haired Asian read his magazine. She looked at him silently: *I have no idea where I am or what I'm doing here,* her look seemed to say. *Do any of us?* He left franc notes on the table.

As they recrossed the courtyard, she paused in the lee of a truck cab, sheltered from the drizzle, to look at the film, her curiosity aroused by the laughter. It was an old French comedy, one she'd seen in her youth. She turned away at last, still scanning the silent silhouettes over her shoulder as they entered the narrow passageway, Reddish's flashlight probing the path ahead of them. It was as if no one had seen them enter, no one seen them leave.

The generators at the guest compound had been shut down by the time they returned. He left her there and went down the hill in the darkness to the police post to check on the plane.

Her room was strange at first, as those others had been, growing no more familiar as the candles burned down. She waited uneasily for his return, standing near the window, holding the last of the brandy from the flask. She saw his flashlight on the path and ran to unlock the door.

"The plane will be here," he told her, shaking out his slicker, "the weather's clearing to the east." She held out the paper cup. "That's for you," he said. "Mine's finished."

"No, please. You look chilly."

His bag was on the floor near the door, his room waiting across the porch, but he took the cup. "It's a little silly," he said, looking back at her, "putting you to bed again like a maiden aunt."

"Was it deliberate?"

"Maybe at first."

"Then your style is like mine, a little old-fashioned." She was smiling. "We never seemed to have much time for ourselves, did we."

"Not before, no."

They stood in silence and then he put aside the cup and brought her to him. Her mouth tasted of brandy. His face was cold with the rain, and he felt her shiver as she withdrew, her face still lifted.

"You're cold too," he said. "Finish the brandy."

"Not now."

There was nothing more to say. The candles burned down. They were lovers that night in the chilly cottage at the head of the lake. In the darkness the mist at the windows brought the sounds of the water nearer, brought the fragrance of smoke from the village fires, as at Benongo or the village above the swamp, but by then they both knew where they were.

294

chapter 4

◇ The old man was dead now, and except for de Vaux the cottage was empty. He'd sent them away, first his wife and two children, then the old cousin and his wife, and finally the old man himself, whom he'd smuggled out the front gate, the dead body wrapped in a wad of laundry. His wife and children had flown to Kisangani and would go north from there, into the bush to wait for him in the village near the Sudan frontier where they'd waited out the mercenary rebellions.

The old cousin had left the previous day to go to Kisangani by boat to await the old man's body, but it was only a device to get the old cousin safely away. De Vaux had no intention of having the body embalmed and shipped by plane or boat to the north. If another fetisheer had won N'Sika's confidence by claiming responsibility for the old man's death, he'd want the bones and vital organs too. De Vaux meant to deny them to him.

After he'd got the old cousin away, de Vaux had smuggled the corpse out the gate in a laundry bag. In the *cité*, he'd rented an old *deux-chevaux* from a Belgian mechanic, changed into blue overalls, and driven east into the savannahs, where he'd buried the body after dark along the Black River.

De Vaux hadn't talked to N'Sika for over a week, but that evening he'd received a note from N'Sika's headquarters summoning him to an eleven o'clock meeting.

He sat under the reading light on the sun porch, the appointment an hour away, reading a book about upland sheep raising. Sheep were impractical in Africa, but except for *Robinson Crusoe*, the book was the only one he had. Like the Defoe novel, it had been left from the UN peacekeeping contingent's reading room, borrowed, like the other, from an English lending library and never returned. A circulation slip was glued to the endleaf. Whoever had borrowed it owed a king's ransom, maybe five hundred pounds sterling. N'Sika was King Croesus by then, but he was no better off than the poor sod who'd borrowed this book.

He sat quietly in the chair, the automatic rifle at his feet, a pistol on his hip, a quart of beer on the nearby table, his mind engaged by the mysteries of upland sheep raising. Perhaps he could begin again in New Zealand or Australia, but then he remembered the immigration laws that excluded Africans—his wife, and two children—hesitated, ripped off the cover, and threw the book aside.

At ten-thirty he left the cottage, crossed to the headquarters compound, and for the first time in two weeks joined those who sat on the chairs under the palm trees awaiting N'Sika's summons. The electric lights were as dim as ever, the mood still sinister, despite the general amnesty which had been announced the same week.

The number of foreign visitors had grown—European businessmen, board members from the great banking houses of the Continent, envoys from the smoke-encrusted foreign ministries of the metropoles or the communist East, international civil servants from the World Bank, the IMF, and the UN.

On this night, de Vaux was surprised to see two Chinese in dark blue uniforms sitting with Dr. Bizenga in armchairs along the strip of red carpet. They weren't from Taiwan, but from Peking's embassy across the river in Brazzaville, come to discuss purchasing the regime's copper. Dr. Bizenga led the two Chinese into the salon and returned alone to join Major Lutete and Major Fumbe, who were talking about the deadlocked negotiations with the Belgians. Of all the civil servants and advisers summoned by N'Sika to the para hilltop, de Vaux considered Dr. Bizenga the most obsequious—laughing at the council members' jokes, flattering their dull grunts into philosophic profundities, and embellishing their banalities like an alchemist filling decayed cavities with carious gold.

De Vaux turned away from Bizenga's voice and listened instead to two captains talking about the recent amnesty. They claimed that two hundred insurgents and outlaws had registered at police and military posts in the interior seeking amnesty. Four hundred *jeunesse* had registered with the police in the capital itself. All day long, mothers, grandmothers, sisters, wives, and fathers had queued up along the road outside the para hilltop waving palm fronds and chanting rhythmically each time a military vehicle sped through, hoping to catch a glimpse of Colonel N'Sika to show their appreciation. In the late afternoon, N'Sika had agreed to receive a delegation of old women brought from the front gate. Moved by their words of appreciation, their tears and flowers, he'd accompanied them back to the front gate to speak to the crowd gathered there.

But he was furious when he returned to his office, and he immediately sent for Majors Fumbe and Lutete and the new minister of interior. He'd supposed that the outpouring of emotion had been spontaneous; but as he stood in the rear of his jeep addressing the throng, he'd seen the municipal buses that had brought them there from the communes.

De Vaux thought he knew what N'Sika wanted. You steal what you've got, and after a few weeks you believe it was brought to you on a golden calf, carried on a golden throne. But it wasn't gold at all, and when they took it away from you, you'd be hauled away by the heels, like a dead cat by the collector of dead cats.

The two captains rose and went back to the refreshment room; de Vaux sat alone, unable to escape Dr. Bizenga's voice as he described the Belgian negotiating team. Everyone on the national side had been willing to give into the Belgian demands—everyone except N'Sika. In the end, Bizenga predicted, he would be forced to give in too:

"You can't change these men," he explained. "They are just burghers, narrow-minded, rigid, dogmatic. They have a certain density, an opacity you can't avoid. When you meet them on the street in Brussels, it's like walking into a lamppost. And everything they say is said with the sort of hollow iron ring a lamppost makes when you walk into it."

Major Lutete laughed in amusement, as he would at a dog in a circus who walked on his hind legs.

". . . 'It is cold,' he might say, the European way, looking at you very seriously. Are there icicles in your beard too? Frost in your nose? You feel to see. They expect it, these Europeans. The world exists only to verify their own existence—meat, drink, and hard fact. Or, 'I lost ten thousand francs at backgammon at my cousin's last week,' or, 'My mistress locked me out.' Whatever. Things happen to them, you see, these burghers I'm talking about—absolute things. And as a result over the years they've finally succeeded in creating themselves as a series of palpable iron objects. It's true, Major. He finds something admirable in his corporeality, his bulk. His thoughts may be timid and hare-brained, but they belong to him, no other. When he gets wet, he reminds you of something in the rain—a tree or a fireplug. Most men of intelligence would far prefer to see themselves in this way—as an object, a palpable object. Not a subject at all, no. But that's the intellectual's weakness and why it's so easy to deceive him.

"What did Marx say? . . . Well, I can quote Marx in this company, can't I, since we must borrow from both worlds, East and West? Well, Marx said that the only antidote to mental suffering is physical pain. So the truth is that Marx didn't want to be an intellectual either. Secretly, he hungered to be a burgher—an iron-ringing object, a collection of iron-ringing molecules that can't be altered one iota by dreams, by sight, by touch. He wanted to get all of these phantoms out of his head.

"What can you do to dreamers? You can smash them but you smash nothing. Dreams, vapors! But with this other man, this European burgher, the physical object remains—like the fireplug in the rain. If you walk into it, too bad! The physical object is what you feel, simple corporeality. Compare this to the man of feeling, the man of intelligence, of noble thoughts. He can't breathe, but he dissolves a little of his substance in your face, the tiny atoms of which he's composed. So deadly serious, yet, but a stench really. The breath of Marx or Lenin, fifty years dead now. But the European intellectual is no different, is he? He dissolves himself and his world in your face, this literary gentleman, like a ripe carcass sending up clouds of blowflies. I'd rather walk into a Belgian lamppost, like the delegation that was just there. He tells me that I exist, just as the intellectual and his blowflies tell me it's completely his world."

He laughed again. A few laughed with him.

"Who leads the Belgian delegation?" Major Fumbe asked.

Dr. Bizenga mentioned a name. "A terrible invention, this man. He's walking proof of everything I've said. His grandfather was a count. His mother ran off with a French perfume salesman. An iron-ringing lamppost right there."

De Vaux finished his glass of beer, seeing the Chinese leave silently. He believed he would be the next summoned. Twenty minutes later, N'Sika's secretary slipped from the rear steps and de Vaux went to meet him. The secretary said that de Vaux was mistaken: the meeting wasn't for this night, but for eight o'clock the following morning.

De Vaux returned to his cottage at the edge of the hill. The porch light and the lamp on the sun porch were still lit; his sentinel crouched on his stool under the palm tree. He unlocked the front door, still annoyed at whoever had deceived him.

Inside, he immediately detected a strange scent in the air and stopped, unslinging his rifle. Then on the bare floor at his feet he saw a few light smudges of wood ash mixed with something more mealy, perhaps kaolin. The track led across the salon, through the dining room, and down the hall toward the small dark room where the old man had died. De Vaux followed it, gun raised, seeing where it daubed each door in passing, touched each window and sill, and lay in a thick white crust, already beginning to dry, across the threshold of the old man's bedroom. The room was in darkness. He felt for the light switch and turned it on, but the light was out. Already he could detect a figure lying on the bed—small, dark, shriveled, as his father-in-law had been those last days; and in the horror of the recollection, he knew this body was his father-in-law; something had brought him back, the same power that had plagued his house and children this past month, that had broken his bond with N'Sika, and that lay as sinister and oppressive over the sand roads and palm trees of the para camp as it had once lain within that small hostile hut on the track to Bunia and which, condensed to its essence, had stood in a small evil pool on the hood of the old truck.

He stood there remembering it all again; and when the tall white-robed figure rose from the far end of the room where he'd been sitting silently, his breath was withdrawn and his muscles were as weak as water, his strength denied him; and he couldn't raise the weapon as he stared at the tall white-robed figure whose face was blacker than any he'd ever seen. A moment later he seemed to remember the face, but at that instant the two Africans behind him smashed the recollection from his head, and he fell forward across the cot, gun clattering to the floor, his unconscious body lying across the lifeless, lacerated body of the poor cousin that de Vaux had sent to Kisangani on the pretext of awaiting his father-in-law's corpse.

chapter 5

❖ Les Haversham was still youthful despite his forty-nine years, his brown hair untouched by gray. He was slender, loose-boned, quick with a smile or a handshake, unfailingly courteous with outsiders, always careful at a cocktail party or a reception to remember a first name, a preference in wines or beverages, details of a previous assignment, hopes for the future, where your children were. Embassy wives thought him charming, military spouses debonair, junior diplomats what they would like to become. Somewhat liberal, gray-eyed, dressed in gray tropicals, a button-down oxford-cloth shirt, and a rep tie, he seemed the embodiment of the American ethic abroad, committed to the principle that politics was a manageable dividend-paying enterprise, like any other kind of business. Imbued with that ethic, he would never deliberately overthrow a foreign government, arrange a massacre in the streets, or assassinate a president—no more than Ford would blow up General Motors, since such bad faith exceeded his operational franchise and outran his moral base. What he would search for were more practical, promotional schemes that would give him a competitive advantage over those who sought what he sought—dominance in the political marketplace.

He was annoyed with Reddish's reporting to Langley on the Malunga episode, because it put the N'Sika regime in a poor light in Washington. There were those in the State Department or in Congress eager to find excuses for reducing their cooperation with military regimes, especially those who'd seized power as brutally as N'Sika. These same policymakers were searching for ways to reduce US arms sales, and the N'Sika regime would continue to seek US military assistance. Reddish's cables, circulated in Washington and undoubtedly leaked to the Hill, would have the net effect of complicating relations with the new National Revolutionary Council.

Reddish and Haversham had had an argument in the latter's office the week following Reddish's return from the interior. Reddish was touchy and out of sorts. He had received no word as to his future assignment, although his replacement was already on the way. His own departure was less than ten days away. He'd told Haversham nothing about the Masakita episode and was skeptical about the general amnesty announced while he was on the boat from Benongo. The council had claimed that police and army posts in the interior had been alerted a week earlier and were busy preparing the inscription of old renegades and new rebels on the amnesty rolls. He'd seen nothing to support this. He thought the council was lying.

Masakita's letter was still in his pocket, undelivered. He'd twice attempted to see de Vaux, but had been unsuccessful. He'd learned that de Vaux's security responsibilities had been taken over by Major Fumbe.

The station suite was deserted that evening. Everyone else had gone home.

"I think you showed poor judgment sending those cables out," Haversham said distastefully, feet lifted to the corner of his desk as he reclined lazily in his swivel chair, toying with a letter opener. "By then, the damage had been done. It was all ancient history. No one needs to know how N'Sika pulled this job off. All a postmortem could do would be to stir up a few creeping Jesuses back in Washington who piss down their legs every time you talk about military regimes." Despite the vernacular Haversham practiced behind closed doors, his voice had the same cultivated drawl to it, like those heard around the Cosmos Club bar. "I don't want to make too much of this, Andy, but I think you've put us on the spot." He brought his feet down, avoiding Reddish's eyes. "After what you've told Washington about N'Sika's planting those MPLA guns in the workers party compound, a few people are going to worry about getting into bed with him. It doesn't do us much good out here telling them where the bodies are buried."

"What's Langley said?"

"What could they say? Nothing, not a word. I'll bet someone is spreading your paper all over town by now."

"What was I supposed to do, sit on it until you came back?"

"It might have helped."

"Helped who, you and Selvey?"

"What's that got to do with it?"

"You know how N'Sika and his crew tracked down those guns, don't you? Because you and Selvey told them where to look. You gave them our reports on MPLA arms shipments and Miles bootlegged them to G-2."

"It was routine liaison," Haversham said, coloring. "DIA had already approved it."

Reddish sat forward aggressively. "Liaison for what? What liaison? It was make-work, all of it! Major Miles's little paper mill that was going to get him promoted to light colonel! That's all it was—a piece of factory garbage, like everything else DIA turns out! You know that as well as I do!"

"Selvey asked for my cooperation," Haversham persisted. "I owed him one for all the times he let us use the attaché plane. I was trying to give him a hand."

"It was stupid, all of it! What are you really afraid of? That someone's going to tie you to that shoot-up in Malunga? You can relax then. I left that part out of it."

"Yeah, that's just peachy, isn't it?" Haversham retorted, stung. "Left us out of it? How? Do you think those guys back there are stupid? It doesn't take any little Jew-genius with some Senate committee staff to figure out that maybe it was us that fingered those MPLA guns. It's not me I'm worried about, it's the Agency. Did you ever think of that? Christ, no! You lost a few people, lost control, and tore up half this town trying to find out who shafted you. Then when you found out you sent in those cables to get yourself off the hook. By the time those cables spring a leak somewhere on the Hill or the New York *Times*, you know what it's going to look like, don't you? That the Agency was behind it, that we rigged the whole frigging mess from the very beginning. Did you ever think about that? Christ, no! You were too busy covering your own ass. So what if the Sovs weren't behind it? Maybe for policy reasons it might have been a good idea to let everyone think they were for a while. You didn't think about that either, did you?"

Reddish stood up. For Haversham, Africa was just a skirmishing ground, high-grass tactical terrain for ambushing the Soviets, nothing more. "Screw it," he said.

Haversham got up too. "What the hell's wrong with you anyway? Why are you so goddamned touchy? I come back after three weeks and you're not even here. You're off in the bush, dicking some French babe. Do you know why I stayed away—the whole three weeks? To give you a chance to show your stuff, to let you run the station for—"

"Just screw it," Reddish said, going through the door.

He had a drink that night, not at the French reception for a visiting deputy from the Quai, where he'd promised Gabrielle he'd meet her, but alone, sitting in the rear garden, wearing a shirt but no tie, coat and tie both discarded on the kitchen chair. He had no enthusiasm for the reception and no will to tell Gabrielle he'd been unable to see N'Sika. He was in the kitchen replenishing his glass when the phone rang. It was Gabrielle, worried, telephoning from the back hall of the French Ambassador's residence. She'd thought something might have happened.

"No, nothing's happened."

"But why aren't you here?"

He didn't answer, studying the clock on the kitchen wall, but it was her face he was watching, brought back by the intonation of her voice. It was as if she was there, next to him. He saw the doubt touch her dark brows when she was troubled, the way her lips still held the sound after the word was released, still in sorrow.

"Don't give me any lectures," he said.

"But I'm not giving you a lecture." He knew she would be smiling and he didn't know what he could tell her. "Is something wrong?" Her voice came back, softer than before.

"No, nothing's wrong. How's the reception?"

"Noisy. Very noisy."

"Why don't I come get you then?"

"Now?" She was surprised.

"In ten minutes. Meet me at the front gate." He didn't give her a chance to answer.

The French Ambassador's residence was near the river. The verges of the road were lit with flares and lined with sedans and limousines. A dozen policemen on foot kept the arriving vehicles moving and the gate free of congestion. Reddish ignored them and pulled into the drive. A policeman waving a red-lensed flashlight came toward him angrily, but Gabrielle appeared just as he reached the car, running lightly in front of the headlights, wearing a long skirt and shawl.

"Houlet stopped me as I crossed the garden," she told him breathlessly, her cheeks flushed, her scent suddenly filling the car. "Where are we going?"

He sensed her excitement. "To my place," he said, his eyes on the road. He thought she was disappointed and without knowing why he remembered suddenly the heart-break of his first formal dance thirty years earlier—a car like this one, a dark night, a girl with a gardenia in her hair, and a father waiting behind a porch light for the daughter a young man had promised to bring home by midnight.

At his villa, the night guard was waiting, holding the gate open. They reached the privacy of the study where the lamps were lit, still in silence. She took off her shawl, looking around at the room. "So you still have his letter." He didn't answer and she turned to see his face. "He said you had no hope in his government, no faith in your own. It's true then, isn't it?"

"Probably." He jerked the drapes closed, shutting away the flickering fire and the shadow of the night guard under the avocado tree. "You shouldn't have gotten mixed up in this."

"You've said that before. Is that why I haven't seen you?"

"No."

"Because you had nothing to tell me?"

"I can handle the letter. It'll take a little time, but I can manage it. That's not the problem."

"What is it then? Why have you been acting so strangely?"

"You—you're the problem. You'll be leaving in a few days." He was searching the desk drawer, looking for the liquor cabinet key. "You expect too much. I can't change things. What do you want to drink?"

She watched him cross the room to the small cabinet. "You believe the letter matters more to me than anything else, don't you?" she said sadly. "Just the letter."

"The letter won't change things. It won't make any difference. Nothing will." He didn't know how he could make her understand that.

"But you went all that way, all the way to Funzi, and now we're here and you'll give N'Sika the letter."

"When I find out how to work it."

"Then what more could anyone ask?"

"A hell of a lot more than I can deliver." He didn't know what he was doing. The liquor cabinet was already open, the bottle on the kitchen table, where he'd left it.

"You don't have any hope, do you?" she repeated, coming toward him.

"Only in what I can deliver."

"And you think I do. But so little that it will all be changed if you fail in this?"

She had crossed to where he stood, her face as calm in the lamplight as it had been that morning on the boat and the misty evening afterward, its mystery the same, holding him then as it held him now.

"I don't want you to expect too much, to make it too hard on yourself," he said.

The answer was already in her eyes. "But how could I expect too much when so much has already happened? Nothing will change that, don't you see? It's you who expects too much, as if you'd never failed before."

"I'm not thinking of me."

"How can I make you understand?" She hadn't moved.

"We've only got a few days left," he said uncomfortably. "The Houlets won't be waiting up for you, will they?"

"It doesn't matter."

"What is it?" He thought he saw her smile.

"Nothing." She shook her head.

"What is it? It's something."

"Nothing. I was just thinking."

"About what?"

"I'm not sure. It's all rather strange. For you it probably doesn't matter so much, you've done so many interesting things, but for me it's all been very special. It's nice to know that interesting things can still happen to you after all this time, that everything isn't locked away. It's something I shall never forget. The trip, the people we saw, everything. It's hard to believe it's over."

"Nothing is ever over," he said, relieved. He took her arm. "Let's go sit in the garden. It's better out there."

Dawn was coming when he finally drove her back to the Houlets'.

"What day is it?" she asked sleepily, her lips dry, her hair awry, her head back against the seat.

"Don't ask. Maybe Tuesday."

"Tuesday," she murmured, her head still back. "Next Tuesday I'll be in Paris."

The sky had lightened, a gray chill he didn't welcome as he took her to the door. As her face turned toward him, pale and anxious, it seemed to him now that there was nothing about this woman he didn't know.

"What time?" he asked.

"Tonight? Seven? Seven-thirty?"

"Seven," he said.

◇ ◇ Ambassador Federov also failed to appear at the French reception, his absence much more conspicuous than Reddish's. No longer the silent, watchful presence, he'd become the eager, ingratiating diplomat, discovering in N'Sika a political foundling, history's innocent left on his doorstep, eager to learn what Moscow could teach.

Federov had sent N'Sika ideological texts and books, newspapers, daily press bulletins, all in French, even a desk set with a cast-iron miniature of the Palace of Congresses in the Kremlin and an onyx inkwell. He'd also persuaded N'Sika to agree to the visit of a delegation from Moscow led by a group of African scholars from the Academy of Sciences, several officials from the Soviet-African Friendship Society, and a few middle-level civil servants from the ministry of foreign affairs.

But he'd received some disturbing news that afternoon, reported by the Russian Ambassador across the river at Brazzaville. Priapkin claimed that two Chinese diplomats from Peking's mission in Brazza had met secretly with N'Sika to arrange the normalization of relations with Peking. The same rumors had circulated in the capital for several days. Klimov had dismissed them, convinced that his own source would have immediately reported any such meeting and moved to prevent any opening of diplomatic relations with Peking. After Priapkin's report had been received that afternoon, Klimov had hastily left the embassy compound for a clandestine meeting with his source on the council.

Federov was waiting under the overhang at the Soviet chancelry for his car to be driven around when Klimov's sedan appeared at the front gate, returning him from his rendezvous. The younger man slid quickly from the front seat, not aware of Federov until he called out to him.

"What did he say?" Federov asked, smartly attired in dark suit, white shirt, and bright figured tie, his attention already drawn away to the pleasures of the evening awaiting him.

"What else could he say?" Klimov laughed hopelessly. "It's done, finished. The announcement will be made at eleven tonight."

The limousine drew to the curb ten feet away but Federov

didn't stir, frozen in place. "They recognized Peking?"

"Tonight, yes. The idiot sat through two council sessions and made no objections—none at all. N'Sika decided two days ago."

"But why? Why now?"

"Because they are idiots, like Lutete himself! Because nothing here has any logic to it, nothing at all! Just a drunken dream, like those sheep on the council."

"But N'Sika said nothing to me—"

"Like Lutete, that idiot! I must go send word."

Klimov disappeared into the foyer, leaving Federov standing in the half-light of the overhang. His chauffeur waited, holding the door open, but Federov stood shrunken and cuckolded in a vapor of eau de cologne, studying his driver's face as if he were a total stranger, a thug, or hooligan holding open the door of a Black Maria.

He turned woodenly and went back into the foyer. Waiting for the lift, he seemed to forget where he was.

The most dangerous among us are those who refuse to understand that the struggle against imperialism is a sham unless it is inseparably linked to the struggle against opportunism. You will report to the Ministry of Education in Uzbekistan where, as vice deputy for administration, you will have the opportunity for that quiet reflection which will again enable you to know the face of the enemy.

The letter was from the chief of cadres, drafted by Federov himself in Moscow and sent to an inept Soviet ambassador in Zambia. As he entered the cage, he searched for the button for the eighth floor, his old floor at the Foreign Ministry on Smolenskaya Square, but couldn't find it. The present lost to him, he stood in bewilderment, oblivious to the musky African night. Before he could collect his thoughts, the doors closed with a pneumatic hiss, the cage lifted, and he was carried aloft, a confused prisoner in a metal room, certain of nothing but the sweat that prickled his armpits and the mist that gathered like sea fog on his steel-rimmed glasses.

◇ ◇ ◇ Cecil had sent a cable to his wife imploring her return but had heard nothing. His mother-in-law was now ill and his wife had stayed over with her. He remained at his residence after lunch that day, complaining to his secretary of a mild fever, despite the thermometer reading. Examining his face further in the medicine cabinet mirror he tried to convince himself that the thermometer was unreliable and that some nameless African bacillus was polluting his bloodstream, swimming freely on afternoons like this when he felt most enervated, that in fact his body had become a virtual tropical pond of such bacilli, sapping his energy, stiffening his joints, robbing his sleep, and utterly destroying his will as well. But peering at his eyes, tongue, and tonsils, he could find no more than the Baptist missionary doctor had been able to find two days earlier in his surgery. He'd given Cecil a brown bottle of tablets for dehydration.

With a few hours of solitude ahead of him, he changed to his shorts and crept down the stairs to the library, moving like a man about to be accosted. But the house was silent, the servants retired to their quarters in the afternoon heat. In the library he found a book on the Crimean campaign which he'd been trying to finish for over a month and continued outside to the cushioned lounge chair at poolside. The afternoon was brilliant, the deep, Prussian blue sky windless, and no sound stirred—not a distant radio or army siren, no nearby cassette music, nothing at all. The surface of the pool was unbroken; in the far corner the pneumatic armchair lay motionless, like an abandoned bathtub toy. He sat down gratefully and had just settled himself back when he felt a sharp metal tooth prod his spine. Sitting forward he retrieved one of Carol Browning's barrettes, lost there during their midnight romp among the cushions. He discarded it on the metal table, eyes averted from her other possessions the yard boy had assembled there—suntan lotions and creams, two pairs of sunglasses, a bikini halter, and a tortoiseshell comb.

The book he'd brought from the library was a stern master, tortuously detailed, densely footnoted. Rereading it again, Cecil felt like a laggard schoolboy after a long holiday, his mind dissolved by August heat and summer sherbets, indolent mornings and long afternoons on the river, adrift in a punt under the willows. His attention wandered as he turned the pages, escaping Latin declensions and the smell of chalk and dusty classrooms to turn to the pool, to the shrubbery beyond, and finally to the clutter of objects on the metal table. Looking at them silently, head reclined, eyelids heavy, he knew by the relief he felt that their owner wasn't here what his secret affliction was—not fever, not bacillus either—was the indefatigable Miss Browning. He continued to gaze at them, hypnotized, consciousness diminished as he drifted toward sleep, the book slipped aside. A thought formed itself: he couldn't continue like this. Last night it had been three o'clock, the night before, two. The time had come for an honorable retreat from the field of battle. Those were the last, inertial thoughts that came to him before sleep, the first he recalled as he awoke, refreshed, the garden deep in shadow, the lights of the terrace lit.

At seven o'clock, he was standing fully dressed near the front window awaiting the arrival of Carol Browning's moped. On the desk in the study was her beach bag in which he had gathered all of the lost articles of her semi-occupancy—barrettes, suntan-lotion and shampoo bottles, sunglasses, a pair of nylon briefs, a bikini halter, three tape cassettes, and a sticky, half-empty brown bottle of exotic design containing something called cocoanut-café liqueur. In his jacket pocket was something she hadn't lost at all but had given to him secretly one evening at a reception when her moped was being repaired—the key to her flat.

By seven-thirty he'd finally chosen the words to explain his decision, regretful but exculpatory, of course. By eight, she still hadn't arrived and he'd grown uneasy, his glass empty for the second time. By eight-thirty, he'd finished his third drink and his earlier intentions seemed crudely gratuitous. He'd also begun to forget what he was going to say. She telephoned from her flat ten minutes later, very tired, kept late at the embassy by Bondurant. She'd decided on a quiet evening, playing bridge with friends.

"Oh yes, that's sensible," Cecil said, relieved at the postponement, "quite sensible. It was rather late last night, wasn't it? Probably the rest will do you good. A quiet evening at home, eh?" He guessed she would be entertaining the other American secretaries in her apartment building.

"Something to take my mind off things."

"Certainly, I understand. But I didn't know you played bridge." If he'd known she could play cards, that might have given a different texture to his fatigue.

"The Italian military attaché has been teaching me at the Belgian Club during lunch. We're going to play tonight."

"The Italian military attaché? Faggioni?"

"Carlo. Do you know him?"

Carlo! Carlo Faggioni! Of course he knew him. A muscular nincompoop, a ballet soldier in tights. "Not too well, but I understand his wife is very good. At bridge, I mean," he recovered quickly. What else could he have possibly meant? But she'd called him Carlo. "Where are you playing?"

"His wife's in Naples."

"Not at his flat, I trust." He laughed falsely, but quickly recovered, wiping his face. "I meant the bridge game." His mind squirmed beyond him, a serpent's nest of double entendres.

"I don't know," she said laconically. Her indifference gave him encouragement, but a moment later he discovered she wasn't being laconic at all. She was chewing gum. "He's going to let me know. Maybe at the Spanish Ambassador's."

Good Lord! "Look here, Carol," Cecil said sternly. "I don't want to appear too paternal about all this, but I should be very careful if I were you."

"About what?" He heard the resentment in her voice.

"About these people. I should watch my step if I—"

"You've been listening to too much gossip. I think they're neat."

"It's not a matter of gossip, but a matter of reputation. There's a distinct difference, you know. In the case of the Span—"

"Oh for God's sake, don't be such a prude. I'll talk to you later. I've gotta go."

Blood flushed to his skin and scalp, senses quivering, as alert as a hare, Cecil stood for a long time at the phone table after she'd hung up. In this cuckold's delirium he explored every word she'd uttered, every phrase, intonation, and intake of breath for its hidden text, like a code clerk decrypting a cable. What had she truly meant? What was her real relationship with Faggioni? If she was so grossly insensitive as not to recognize her own foolishness or Faggioni's designs, he would explain both to her. Was she merely stupid or was she maliciously cunning? But she hadn't attempted to conceal anything from him. On the contrary, she'd told him precisely of her plans for the evening. After all, bridge required four persons, not just two. Besides, neither Faggioni nor the Spaniard had a pool. And he had the key to her flat. No, Cecil decided, drawing a reassuring breath, there was no more to her evening of diversion than she had described. Perhaps she was intellectually curious after all.

Perhaps he could teach her chess.

chapter 6

✧ Masakita had already left the abandoned rebel camp in the swamps near Funzi.

It was dusk and the scattered villages along the sand road were in shadow. The battered Mercedes truck rocked back and forth along the ruts and through the sand shoals, and then with a lurch shifted gears and began the long descent toward the swift green river below. The air was stagnant at the lower elevation. As the truck slowed to approach the ferry, Masakita could see through the whipping canvas two trucks and a pair of Landrovers already in front of them waiting to cross the river.

The truck shuddered to a stop and the dozen cramped passengers crawled from the bed and onto the riverbank. Beyond the lip of broken asphalt where the ferry moored, the swift green current plunged northward in a dozen racing pools. The old ferry was chugging back toward them. Bats chittered in eccentric circles; frogs thumped from the lush dark weeds. The truck drivers and passengers squatted silently in the warm dust, waiting for the ferry. An old mama in a filthy cotton smock charred a few ears of corn over a charcoal fire. A mother with two children crawling over her shoulders sat fanning the flies from her roadside wares—fruit, peanuts, and a few spines of smoked fish, as black as wood bark.

Masakita bought a plantain and ate it as he stood on the ferry landing. His wife had bought "new" clothes for him for his journey, pulled from one of those bundles of secondhand apparel imported from America or Europe in compressed bales, like raw cotton, and sold throughout the interior. The khaki trousers were patched over in a dozen places with a quilt of heavy thread; the faded khaki shirt was clean but washworn. Over the breast pocket was a blue cotton medallion: FRED'S FORD MART.

Before she'd bought the clothes in Benongo, his wife had had a premonition. She'd twice dreamed that he'd been pardoned, both times before the news of the general amnesty reached them. The first time she'd dreamed that he'd received a letter from the President and had gone by packetboat to the capital, where a military band was waiting at the port together with the cabinet officers in their morning coats, their blue and gold silk sashes, and in the rear the sedan chair, the *tipoy*, of the new President.

The dream was drawn from her memory of the old regime and Pierre's return from Cairo to accept the post in the government of national reconciliation. She'd had a second dream three nights later and awoke in the darkness to tell him that she'd held in her hands the heavy vellum of the presidential envelope with its red wax seal.

Masakita remembered the envelope he'd received in Cairo.

That day they'd gone to the village below Funzi in the pirogue for cooking oil. As they were returning, they saw the police boat from Benongo flashing southward on the lake in a spume of white spray. She told him that the boat had brought the letter to the village.

But when they reached the slough below the village, the same inert water lay under the trees as they traveled the final meters, and in the gloom she'd known that no boat had stirred the dark waters since their own pirogue earlier that day. That night she wept. She cared nothing for the ceremony of public life. She had known him as a schoolboy—the boy who had gone to the mission school at Benongo, and she had known then, as the village knew, that there was something unique in him, something in the spirit of the boy and now the man so rare that he would never be permitted to keep it. There was far more in him than the Catholic fathers, Europe afterwards, and now the new government would allow him to keep. Her father had told her that and she didn't understand. Death she knew, but not murder.

When the word came two days later from Benongo that the amnesty had been announced, she'd turned immediately to him, listening as the old chief described what he had heard. He took from his damp waistband the printed circular from the police post at Funzi. Her dreams were now in her eyes, as they were there on the damp paper in the chief's hands.

Kerosene lanterns lit the deck of the ferry as it plowed the dark current toward the opposite bank. The passengers gathered along the rail searching for the breath of wind that came in mid-channel. They disembarked hastily at the landing and climbed the bank to the *sûreté* shack, anxious to pass through before the checkpoint closed down for the night. Inside a single clerk examined their documents and registered their names in an old ledger by the light of a moth-covered lantern. The passengers crowded the small room. When one of the moths settled on the clerk's lower lip and stuck there, an old woman snickered and two children laughed. The clerk stood up angrily and threatened to close down the checkpoint. A truck driver told the passengers to line up outside the door and enter as their names were called. He took their documents and the clerk sat back down again, mollified.

After thirty minutes they climbed back into the truck and continued their journey toward the capital a few hours away. At a small village they were joined by a petty administrator carrying a suitcase and a flashlight. He chased two women from their seats next to the tailgate to sit there himself, his luggage alongside, his European felt hat on his knee. After he'd settled himself, he probed the faces of his traveling companions with his flashlight, ignoring their pained, shrinking faces. "You must be careful who you travel with these days," he said. He was a government official, and government officials had to be vigilant. Were there other government officials present? No one answered. The light flashed against Masakita's face and remained there. "I know you," the official said. "You work for the national bank."

Masakita didn't reply.

"Either there or the insurance office near the railroad station." He moved the light to the patch over the pocket. "What is that?"

Masakita told him it was the emblem of a foreign company.

"So you're wearing the rags of the foreigners. You ought to be ashamed of yourself. Don't you know we have our own revolution now? No more *vin rouge.*"

The diesel fumes were heavy under the creaking canvas as they bounced along through the darkness. Masakita sat with his head against the sideboards, looking back through the arc of canvas, searching for stars. They were on the high savannahs, no villages on either side.

An old woman suddenly became ill from the diesel fumes and the truck's rocking motion. The administrator flashed his light angrily into the darkness as the nauseating smell reached him. "She'll make us all sick! Tell the driver to stop! Put her off!" A young woman told him to shut up; and after he demanded that she too be removed, someone hurled an overripe mango skin at him. It struck him across the collar and neck. His dignity gone, he flung it back, but a plantain skin struck his face, blinding him, and another knocked the hat from his knee. "Stop it! Stop this! Behave yourselves!"

"Shut up then!"

"Who are you, a *flamand!*"

"We'll put you off, like the old President!"

Outnumbered, he huddled closer to the tailgate, drawing his bag nearer.

The mutterings died away. The sounds of sleep lifted and fell, like the sound of the sea. The stars grew brighter over the tableland of the savannahs, the moon hidden. Masakita shut his eyes, remembering the old rebel camp and his own village, the faint red glow of the fire through the door of the hut where his wife slept, waiting. Lulled by the motion of the truck as the wheels left the sandy track and found the asphalt that led to the capital, he finally slept.

It was midnight when he was awakened, a cold gun barrel against his ribs. The other passengers had already left the truck and were standing in the weak electric light of the corrugated metal shack where police, army, and *sûreté* officials were examining documents at the final checkpoint before the capital. The two soldiers prodded him from the truck and motioned for him to get in line with the others. Another squad of soldiers circulated beyond the shack, herding those who'd already passed through to the debarkation point down the tarmac where they would rejoin the trucks. The soldiers' voices were strong, their movements quick, their guns and uniforms well kept, not at all like the indolent, disheveled police and soldiers of Funzi and Benongo. With a vague, uneasy premonition, Masakita felt again the raw cold will of N'Sika's revolution here on its periphery, the lights of the capital a bright glow in the distance six kilometers away.

"Your face is familiar," the *sûreté* captain said, holding the tattered identity document as he studied Masakita's face. "Where are you coming from?"

"Benongo."

"Benongo itself or nearby?"

"Funzi." The identity card gave his village as Funzi. It belonged to his wife's cousin. He'd intended to use it only as far as the capital, where he would talk first with Reddish before giving himself up at the para camp.

The *sûreté* captain looked at the card, nodded, and again lifted his eyes. "I know your face, but I've never been to Funzi or Benongo."

The dark eyes waited. It was for Masakita to explain. How

could the officer know him if he'd never been those places? He was the government, Masakita the supplicant. If what the government knew wasn't consistent with what this indigent dressed in someone else's rags could explain, then he was lying. That was the power of his office, a power that made the weak ignorant and the helpless guilty.

"I once worked in the capital," Masakita said.

"Where?"

"In the ministry of interior."

"In the ministry?" The eyes seemed skeptical, then triumphant. "Albert! Oh, Albert." He called through the door behind him, and a bespectacled clerk joined them from the adjacent office. "You worked in the ministry for ten years. This man says he worked there too. Do you know him?"

Masakita looked silently at Albert N'Kuba, whom he hadn't seen since his transfer to provincial travel control. N'Kuba didn't move for a moment, brown eyes fixed on Masakita's face, lips parted, the light of recognition still suspended. It would mean so much to be right—a promotion, a cash bonus, as the secret sûreté bulletin promised; yet it would be humiliating to be wrong, the butt of every cruel joke for years to come.

"You worked in customs control," Masakita said.

N'Kuba's fingers touched his chin in reflex. "The beard . . . the beard . . . is new."

The eyes fixed then, pupils dilated, and he took a step backward. "Yes," he murmured. "I know him. Could I speak to you . . . in my office," he told the captain, still backing away.

An hour before dawn an automobile came from the capital traveling at high speed, followed by a second automobile and an army jeep. Masakita was blindfolded before he was led from the clerk's office, where three soldiers had guarded him, and shoved into the second sedan, a black Mercedes. He was pushed forward in the seat and his hands were tied under his knees, a rope around his ankles.

Sitting in the front seat, he recognized something familiar in the scent of the upholstery—in the talcum, the bay rum perhaps, or the spice of a European air sweetener. He knew it was a Mercedes and that it was black.

"Oh, no, it's not disloyalty," the car's owner once explained to him, "not at all. It's just a car—a matter of utility, that's all. But let's not argue about it."

"But I'm not arguing," Masakita had said.

315

"Criticizing then. But you own a Mercedes as well."

"The government owns it. It belongs to the ministry—"

"*Ah ha!* So you see. A matter of utility again."

So there it was—the heart of their differences. To Masakita, his alliance with the old President in the government of national reconciliation had been contrary to his conscience but necessary for the country. To the Mercedes owner, these were personal matters, unmortgaged by moral claims.

"If you're going to pose theological arguments in terms of owning a Mercedes and advancing the revolution, between moral chastity and utility, Christ and the devil, then I'm not going to argue with you, Pierre—never. No, no. My wife's brother sold me this car. He needed the money for his cottonseed plant."

So Masakita, even blindfolded, knew the car, knew it before someone sat forward from the seat behind him and wiped away the odor of the upholstery with a crude burlap bag pulled roughly over his head and tied around his neck with a sisal cord. The dust filled his nostrils and punished his mouth and throat with the dry, acrid powder of old palm husks.

The Mercedes belonged to Dr. Bizenga.

Dawn had come as the Mercedes raced through the front gate of the para camp and sped back under the palm trees, the hooded figure on the front seat. The jeep and one sedan turned aside at Colonel N'Sika's headquarters, but the Mercedes continued down the sand road toward the maximum security prison, which had been emptied this past week, the felons transferred to the old jail at the edge of the *cité.*

Masakita was led from the car and down through the wire dog-trot, through the heavy door, and to the right along a stone corridor to a heavy iron grating covered over with steel mesh where the public cell block lay, its ceiling two stories high, like the prison itself, a square smoke hole in the center of the roof—a vestige of colonial days, when the prisoners prepared their own meals.

Only two prisoners lay in the enormous cell, backs against the stone wall, knees lifted, legs chained by ankle irons to an iron ring sunk in the center of the floor.

De Vaux watched as the burlap bag was lifted from Masakita's face, leaving the wet cheeks and forehead powdered with palm grit, the short woolly hair sprigged with husks. The two turnkeys shackled irons to his ankles and led him forward to padlock the last link to the iron ring in the floor. They replaced the cord on his wrists with handcuffs and went out, locking the iron door behind them.

Masakita stood looking about him, eyes moving along the stone walls, the wall of steel bars faced with mesh, and high into the shadows of the trussed roof where a patch of blue sky showed through the smoke hole.

"Masakita," de Vaux muttered finally through his broken teeth, his head cocked upward, one eye closed. "Am I right?"

"That's right," Masakita said, studying de Vaux's cruelly punished face. One eye was swollen closed, the face bruised and cut; dried blood crusted his nostrils and stiffened the front of his khaki shirt.

"Who?" Nogueira asked.

"The bloke they're looking for," de Vaux said, still squinting up. "De Vaux here. This is Lieutenant Nogueira, late chief of the MPLA cadres for the southwest sector, Cabinda front, now retired."

"Who did that to you?"

"Someone who wanted to find out something, where I'd hidden it. Didn't see his face, though."

"Hidden what?"

De Vaux shrugged. "The past, where I'd buried it. 'Rest in peace,' I told them. Who wants to dig up the past. Hyenas, that's all. That's what they were."

"What about this man Nogueira?"

"Scared of him, that's all I know. Found him here and didn't know why. That scared them. Do you have a cigarette?"

"No." Masakita slumped down against the wall.

"Books maybe. Newspapers. *L'Express? Paris Match?*"

"Nothing."

"Shit. Same as us." His eye fell for a moment on the burlap that Masakita's captors had dropped to the floor and which now lay on the stone floor near the door. A hood or just a blindfold? He stared at it silently, sighed, and sank back again, looking at Masakita, examining the small nose, the beard, the brown eyes, and finally the patch over his pocket. "You ever hear of Robinson Crusoe?" he asked.

"The book? Yes."

"The book, that's it. A bloke shipwrecked on a desert island. You heard of it?"

"I've heard of it."

"I told you," de Vaux said to Nogueira. "You think my head's full of shit. So is his then. I was telling him about it," he said to Masakita. "I just got to the part about the goats."

It was late afternoon when they heard a car on the road above and stopped talking, eyes lifted silently toward the high window. Car doors slammed and footsteps came down the clay path into the wire cage, the iron hinges creaked open, and two figures emerged into the shadows of the corridor. The light was dimming and Masakita got to his feet, followed by de Vaux and Nogueira. They moved as far across the stone floor as their leg chains permitted, standing some six meters short of the bars. Masakita saw a tall figure in a white robe, but couldn't identify his black face or the face of the second man, which was only a broken mosaic through the heavy mesh. But then he saw the glint of the steel-rimmed spectacles and the small white pebbles of the familiar bifocals.

"Bizenga. I knew it was your car."

De Vaux knew too, suddenly coming alive: "Bizenga! You bloody, filthy bastard!" He tried to pull free of his leg chains, tried to tear his wrists from the steel manacles, but his feet twisted and he fell against the floor, but still crawled forward, pulling himself on his elbows. "I'll kill you, both of you!"

Dr. Bizenga gazed down sympathetically. "But I'm sorry, Major. I have no idea what you're talking about."

"You liar! You goddamn liar! Where'd he come from—that zombie with you! Where'd you dig him up!"

Dr. Bizenga glanced at the tall Senegalese at his side. "I don't know who you're talking about, but this is Dr. Ba. Dr. Ba is a surgeon and pathologist, brought by Major Fumbe from Dakar to be his adviser. As you know, Major Fumbe now has all security responsibilities and he's a firm believer in fighting fire with fire, as they say. From Dakar, yes, where they maintain the best traditions of pathology—and of African folklore too, I should say. But what did you think he was? What's come over you, Jean-Bernard? What sort of seizure have you suffered here, eh? Jumping at shadows again?"

De Vaux lunged hopelessly toward the bars.

"Try to show a little hospitality for Major Fumbe's surgeon, Major. All Dr. Ba desires is your cooperation. He simply wants to know what happened to Colonel N'Sika's poor uncle. Is he dead or have you hidden him away somewhere? And if he is dead, as some of us suspect, what was the nature of his influence? Or his illness? Was it something Fumbe can cope with? A very superstitious fellow, this Fumbe. A simple exercise in pathology would tell Dr. Ba immediately whether Major Fumbe had anything to fear or not. So why not cooperate with him?"

"Never! *Surgery?* Never! That hyena wants his bones, that's what he wants—bones and everything else. He'll never get them, not from me. The old man's in peace, wherever he is. You'll never get your filthy, butchering hands on him."

"What's this about?" Masakita broke in. "Why is de Vaux being held here?"

"He hasn't told you? That surprises me," Bizenga said. "But I'm sure he will in time. Such men always do. Ask him about his past. He'll tell you—his vulgar little triumphs, his sadistic little conquests. Like a lamppost in the rain, eh Jean-Bernard? All scratched and nicked. Did someone walk into you? All iron-ringing, those molecules of yours, but hollow. Who can change you? What can change you? Nothing, fortunately."

"The amnesty was announced days ago," Masakita said, "but we're kept here. Why?"

"Oh but there's no amnesty for you," Bizenga said, surprised. "Oh, no. Not for you. You haven't discovered that?"

"A general amnesty was announced. I saw the circular myself."

"Oh yes, you saw the circular yourself. There is a general amnesty and quite a successful one. Very successful. You see how it came about, don't you? The council was quite worried about you, Pierre, on the loose again, on the prowl—Moscow this week, Peking the next. What were you planning back there in the bush, another guerrilla war against the central government like the one you led in sixty-four and sixty-five. So you see why an amnesty was inevitable, don't you, why it was necessary to liberate that rag-tag army back there in the interior from your ranks, to let them live in the peace you would deny them—"

"You don't know what you're talking about."

"Oh no, perhaps not. But the council was worried, very worried. Crispin Mongoy received a letter. You remember Crispin, don't you, the ex-soccer player. You sent him a letter asking him to contact the other members of the political bureau. That sounded suspiciously like sedition to the council. What your intentions were—well, that doesn't matter. The council doesn't trust you, Pierre, that's the sum of it. They'll never trust you, you see. Never. You're far too clever for them. Too clever for all of us. So we have our amnesty now, but it's not for you. No, no. Here in prison the law of *lex loci* rules. Hasn't Major de Vaux explained all this to you— *lex loci? lex talionis?* Come, come, Major, I'm surprised at you. What have you been prattling about these past few hours—your picaresque redemptive adventures in darkest Africa, ten thousand black savages starved, lashed, and crucified to stir again that liberal heroic soul that bourgeois Europe starved to extinction? Come, Major—"

"What does the council fear?" Masakita interrupted.

"What do they fear? They fear you, quite obviously. Why? Well, because of what I've already told you. Apart from that, I wouldn't presume to know what Major Fumbe's beliefs are, or even Colonel N'Sika's. No, no, once a belief has taken root, who am I to deny it? Would I cut down every tree in the forest because it's not mimosa, which my wife prefers? No, let's be reasonable, Pierre. Once a man believes what he believes, who am I to take it from him? Isn't that what you once told me—that I judged in you what wasn't mine to judge? It's the same case here. You and I were educated in Europe, so it's different for us. Some of these esteemed members of the council had no such advantage. Take Colonel N'Sika, for example. What Colonel N'Sika believes is his own business. As it happens, that's a mystery to the council too. Ask Major de Vaux what the colonel believes—Major de Vaux who helped nourish the root once he planted the seed. Didn't he once convince N'Sika that his power could do anything—blow up a *petit porteur* in a rainstorm in Mbandaka, whether by dynamite or demonology no one ever knew. Perhaps de Vaux can tell you. Certainly it's something N'Sika never talks about—not with any of us. That worries the council too. Tell us, Major, tell us *le secret de l'Afrique noire*, which you may have so cunningly planted in Colonel N'Sika's skull. Or did you? Tell us now. All of us would rest easier if we knew what you know—"

"You're a bloody liar!" de Vaux shouted.

"So there you are," Dr. Bizenga said with a sigh. "You grope for these things as best you can. I'm sorry, Pierre. A man believes what he wants to believe these days. God knows things are bad enough out here with what modernity has brought us—evangelists, proselytizers, Baptist pagans who have no place in their countries but rural kingdoms in ours, mullahs, Peace Corps anarchists, socialist savants, and UN macroeconomists, thousands of them, all running amok through the bush waving a new set of scriptures at every starving black man they meet. Add to that the neo-colonialists, the neo-imperialists, east and west, the neo-fascists, the Cassandras, futurologists, poets, and seers, all nightmares inherited from the Western mind, concentrations of spiritual capital that can't be rooted out, and what have you got? No, Pierre, if each of us were to try to discipline the rubbish in another's skull with the sanctimonious nonsense in our own, where would it end? Turmoil, you see. Absolute chaos. And you were always against that, weren't you? So you see how the law of *lex loci* has come to apply."

Dr. Bizenga took off his glasses and wiped them carefully with his handkerchief.

"You haven't changed," Masakita said.

"You either," Bizenga replied regretfully. "It's a pity. At a time when weak men are becoming stronger because of their presumption, their arrogance—like Major de Vaux there—stronger men such as yourself are becoming weaker because of their silence, their virtue, their righteous scrupulosity. In times like these, that's self-indulgence, Pierre, not social action at all. Autoeroticism. Onanism, pure and simple. But what can one do? Paris would have been better for you, Brussels even. There that raw talent might have been civilized for social use. You could have opened a bookshop, written epistles to Pascal—"

"You chase after words. You always have."

But Dr. Bizenga only shrugged, already beginning to show his boredom. "What else is there these days? What have they taught us, East or West? To use their words while they steal our country."

He turned to his Senegalese companion, nodded, and they went out.

The three prisoners returned in silence to the stone wall, dragging their chains behind them, de Vaux carrying the burlap that had wrapped Masakita's face. He sat looking at it silently, knowing then what Bizenga had been talking about, what it was in this man Masakita the council feared—not N'Sika, perhaps, but the others, who feared N'Sika too but Masakita more. How would men like Fumbe or Kimbu explain Masakita's elusiveness all those years—gliding through the green shadows of the Kwilu, claimed dead at Kindu, but alive again the following morning in Idiofa, in Peking one week, in Moscow the next, and now disappearing without a trace from the gutted workers party compound in Malunga.

The answer lay in his hands, in the burlap hood he'd picked up from the floor. During the days of the rebellions, a few of the rebels had presented de Vaux's mercenaries with special problems. Their power was real enough to send a village into frenzy, so he'd covered their heads with rice sacking or old burlap bags, as he had his father-in-law's once, the sight denied those fierce manic eyes, recognition denied their crazy tattered heads, sprigged out with all sorts of weird magical filth. He'd cloaked the heads of those witch doctors the same way Pierre Masakita's head had been hooded as he was brought into the old prison that morning.

chapter 7

❖ Bondurant listened silently as Reddish finished his story, the entire story, no details suppressed this time, the letter Masakita had given him lying on the desk blotter in front of him. His eyes were sometimes drawn away from the worried, stubborn face to the scarred hand holding the cigarettes and stubbing them away, one by one, in the deskside ashtray, two fingers broken and twisted in a way Bondurant had never noticed before.

Reddish had made a few mistakes, a few errors of judgment or perception, but now he was under no illusions. N'Sika would get the letter only if the ambassador delivered it himself.

He'd thought he could scare off the coup plotters, but that hadn't worked: he was wrong, just as he'd been wrong in his suspicions that the defense attaché's office or even the station might have been involved, perhaps even his headquarters itself. After he'd sent in his cables reporting the details, he'd gotten no reply for almost ten days. Washington's silence had made him uneasy, as if he'd dug up the bodies, bodies that were supposed to stay buried. But that wasn't it either. He'd been wrong again.

"You think you're at the center of their universe back there," he concluded, moisture glistening on his high forehead, his gaze moving to the side window of Bondurant's office and the lilac-colored clouds blooming high over the river in the setting sun, "every cable on the director's desk or in the evening brief for the White House before the circuits are even cold, but that's not the way it happens. It's the way you get after a while, being so far away. You know so much one day, and the next you're bankrupted, wiped out. You think it's deliberate, calculated, another conspiracy, that you've been conned, used, forgotten, tossed away. But that's not it either. You forget how much there is back there every day—how many cables, how many crises, how many people, how much confusion,

322

how short the Washington memory is. Washington didn't know any more than I did. There was too much going on—the Khartoum kidnapping, the SALT openings, the Chinese business, everything else that no one could get a handle on. It was a bloody vacuum all that time, just a couple of us sitting here. They just didn't bloody well care."

He'd been alone all that time. He shook his head hopelessly, still in despair.

"It's often that way," Bondurant said quietly, "but sometimes for the better too. The bureaucracy wouldn't understand all these things any more than they would understand a letter like this one."

He lifted the letter from the blotter, looking again at the fine dark handwriting. He had read enough to feel depressed—the letter of an intellectual, too gnomic, too convoluted for N'Sika's direct, brutal mind; but he would deliver it nevertheless, perhaps his endorsement making it simpler. It was Reddish's plight he was drawn to.

"I think it was Macaulay who once said that historians are seduced not by their imaginations but by reason," he offered reflectively, rising at last from behind the desk. "Diplomats are very much the same way—diplomats, civil servants, bureaucrats, whatever name they go by. The ablest bureaucrat, the cleverest, would never knowingly fight a battle he couldn't win, and that's why he's successful. But truth by consensus isn't a real world at all. It's an artificial one, a shadow world that reflects nothing of ourselves." He looked at Reddish for some flicker of response but saw nothing. "The life outside is much more substantial. So you were right, I suppose, not to trust the bureaucracy. Their strength is collective, not individual, which means simply that they're weaker than you. They'll betray you. Call it Bondurant's law. I learned it years ago."

He peered at Reddish sympathetically, his despondency releasing certain axioms long contemplated but rarely confessed. Still he waited, a huge hulking wintry man, thawing suddenly, like an old glacier giving up its bones.

"A bureaucrat's logic is something like a bookkeeper's," he resumed, "or an accountant's. A matter of keeping the ledgers and totaling up the balance sheet. It doesn't require brilliance, just that one not be abysmally stupid. No imagination at all. They never need lift their heads. What is it, Miss Browning?"

He looked impatiently toward his substitute secretary, who stood just inside the door with that innocent calf-eyed look he'd come to recognize.

"I thought you buzzed me," she whispered soulfully.

"I did. Call Colonel N'Sika's protocol chief and tell him I want to see the colonel immediately. Better still, have Becker do it. His French is more reliable.

"It's a pity," Bondurant continued ruefully. "Imagination is what we most need, imagination is what we don't get. We don't think of international politics that way at all. We leave foreign policy to drab little bureaucrats, geopolitical lunatics, or professional theorists, most of them behaviorists, none of whom are imaginative in the least. They have no idea of how vast the theater is in which they're working, how imaginative its demands are, or how infinitely cunning the historical process they're all trying to outwit, East and West alike. Did you ever think of international politics that way—as one giant theater?"

"I don't think I have."

"You should. My daughter is in Off Broadway theater. I tried to tell her once. Nothing touches more lives—not subscription concerts, chamber music societies, or anything else. There's nothing else that compares with it. Half the world is strutting around its stage, declaiming from a primitive nineteenth-century text, utterly discredited, utterly bowdlerized, while the other half—our half—simply doesn't know whether they're part of the audience or part of the company. The truth is that neither seems to know what it's doing. Those that do are selling programs in the aisles."

He lifted himself again from his chair. "The only consolation I can find in all this is that the Russians are in far worse shape, their own bureaucracy even more incoherent, continuing to rationalize their insolvency year after year in ways we seem to be imitating. Whatever our moral claims—and I believe they're legitimate ones— I suspect that in the political realm at least we're institutionally incapable of acting in any way other than the way we do—as a vast conservative third-rate mediocrity. We should let the Israelis or the Cubans manage our foreign policy for us. Neither can risk failure, which means they must be imaginative. What is it, Miss Browning?"

"Is Mr. Becker to go with you."

"No, I'll go alone, and I would hope that Colonel N'Sika will see me alone."

Looking at the closing door, Bondurant was suddenly aware of a more familiar ghost prowling these chilly pedagogic fogs he'd conjured up: an old man sitting at hearthside in the house on Library Place, cruelly editing his old journals, once vivid and fresh, in the morosity of old age.

"I should tell you," he said finally to Reddish, coming directly to the point, "that I haven't the slightest hope that we'll be successful in all this."

Sarah Ogilvy was waiting for Reddish as he returned to his office. The suite was deserted. He'd been with Bondurant for two hours.

"What are you trying to do, set some kind of longevity record?" she asked, slamming her safe drawer closed. "Haversham went home. He wants you to call him, maybe stop by for a drink so he can find out what the h is going on."

Reddish searched his jacket pockets, making sure he'd left the envelope with Bondurant.

"What are you looking for?"

"I thought I forgot something. Did you pick up my airline ticket?"

"It's on your desk. I'll tell you something you did forget—Taggert. He waited here for an hour, something about a special lock. What was that about?"

"For Carol Browning—a combination lock. There have been a few break-ins at her apartment house and she's worried."

"I'll bet she's worried." She followed Reddish to his office.

It was late and Gabrielle was waiting for him at the Houlets'. He grabbed his briefcase and headed for the door. "Lock me up, will you? Thanks for the ticket."

"I'll bet she's worried," she persisted, trailing him to the door. "The only trouble with her lock is she forgot who she gave the key to. Do you know who was banging on her door at two o'clock last night? The British Ambassador! Cecil!"

Reddish glanced at her as he went out the door. He'd barely heard a word. "The poor bastard," he said.

chapter 8

✦ "What does this man Masakita mean to you?" N'Sika demanded harshly. "Why do you come here to speak for him? You didn't speak for the others."

"Because I want to see justice done," Bondurant replied uneasily, the protocol dispensed with.

"He will have a trial by the Revolutionary Court. You saw the dossier. Lutete offered to show it to you, but you said it didn't interest you." N'Sika pointed at the empty chair where Lutete had sat that night, shoulders thrust forward.

"The letter is written to you, not the court," Bondurant persisted. "It is a personal letter to you." He hadn't worn a coat and tie, as Reddish had suggested, and now he felt silly for it.

N'Sika studied Bondurant's face sullenly, his gaze finally returning to the letter on the table in front of him. "I receive hundreds of letters every day, but not like this." The letter was three pages long, written in longhand. He lifted the first page contemptuously. "He tells me that he will live in peace, that he will work and live in peace. What are the rest of these words he writes? If I am to explain to the people and the council why I am to trust him now, what words can I use? My words? My words about Masakita are finished, eaten up. Nothing is left. His words? Are his words stronger? What words—French words? How can I feed the people his words when in three pages he tells me he isn't even sure himself? Is that his conscience? If that is his conscience, let him keep it. Only he will understand it, not the people. If you have something to tell the people, make it easy for them to hear you, not in letters like this one, foreigners' letters, which begin at *a* and go on to *b* and every other letter of the alphabet but always end not at *zed* but back at *a* again. The Belgians send me such letters every day, only about copper and diamonds and foreign exchange, technical matters. Is his conscience a technical matter? Let him hire a board of Belgian directors to administer it then, not me."

He got up rudely, turning his back on Bondurant, and walked to the door, calling out into the darkness in Lingala. Two bodyguards entered quickly, carrying rifles. He gave them an order and returned to the chair, his face even more bellicose than before.

"The council fears Masakita," he resumed bluntly, "not only because of this rebellion in Malunga but for other reasons which are none of your business."

His French is like a schoolboy's, Bondurant thought, his impotence rising like an echo now, a bullying schoolboy who never yields the advantage.

"They believe Masakita has nine lives," N'Sika continued, "they only one, so that is their fear." He leaned forward over the table, his voice dropping conspiratorially; and Bondurant sat forward too. "They are nine men, Masakita only one. What can I do? The council is more important to the country than Masakita, more important than me, because if the Revolutionary Council is weak, then the country will be weaker. This is important to your country too. You have not given us guns and money to see us grow weaker."

The eyes drilling Bondurant's pale Saxon face seemed so dark as to have no irises at all. He searched in vain for some focus of understanding or compassion, his neck and armpits prickly with heat. He saw nothing.

"Yes, I understand that."

"And your government, do they understand that?"

"I wanted you to see the letter. I came on my own, not because my government asked me to come. It is, as I said, a personal matter." This was a concession he would have preferred not to make and now he regretted it.

N'Sika sat back. "So that is why you wanted no one else here. You came to whisper in my ear."

"As a friend," Bondurant conceded uncomfortably.

"So we could speak plainly with no one listening. All right. I understand."

The two bodyguards returned with two quart bottles of beer and a pair of glasses, attempting ineptly to pour out the beer themselves, one with bottles, the other with the glasses, hands trembling, glasses and bottles rattling; and N'Sika brutally sent them away, pouring the glasses himself. "You see how they are," he declared, "these men who are so eager to say yes, who can say nothing but yes. Your breath blows them away." With calm hands, he set the glass in front of Bondurant and returned to his chair.

"About this letter then. What is it? Is he afraid to die, this man Masakita? It is nothing to die now. It is harder to live, harder every day. Everyone is afraid. If my mother saw these men on the council, she would be ashamed. Masakita's mother would be ashamed too, a man writing a letter like that. Bullets are easy, but they don't bring change. The hunter shoots the elephant, but the women dress the meat. Their work is harder, like our work. We must do everything ourselves here, stalk, hunt, dress, feed—everything.

"Now about the Revolutionary Council and this letter. How many are we, nine or ten? No, less than that. This one wants to go to Paris as ambassador, this one to Brussels, another to Italy—all want to go somewhere, to go outside, like soldiers after their fighting is done. Why? Because it is hard for them, too hard, and they are only soldiers. Being here is different from being in a barracks. As a soldier, you may be afraid before a fight, a battle, but after the fighting is finished, it is done, over with. A soldier may be frightened once or twice in his life. Here you can be frightened every day. So it is easier to be outside, to let other people do these things, the politicians or the civil servants who did these things in the past. So I tell the council, 'If we don't do these things, who will?' We must be objective, we must examine the situation objectively, as Africans. As a revolutionary council, we must not only make decisions but raise the political consciousness of the masses . . ."

Bondurant heard the undigested fragments of a familiar political theology in N'Sika's demotic French.

". . . but we must also raise our own, our own consciousness, here on this hilltop. The council's responsibilities are not only to the people but to itself. Do you know Federov, the Russian? I used to talk to him the way I'm talking to you, just the two of us. He sent me books, many books—books to speak for him when he wasn't here— too many books. How could I read them? He talked to me about objective conditions, about history, about the class struggle—all these things that never interested me. Who has time for it now? But because Peking's diplomats are coming here, now we don't talk at all. A Russian delegation was to come here to see our conditions, but the visit was canceled. Moscow canceled the visit. I didn't understand. I told Major Lutete to call Federov and tell him, 'You must be objective about this,' but he couldn't be objective . . ."

The ambassador allowed himself the briefest of smiles, but N'Sika lumbered on:

". . . because Peking is his enemy. So Moscow is his master, this

Russian, and it would be better if he were to go back again and send someone who can talk the way we're talking. So in the same way the Revolutionary Council would never be objective about this letter, because Masakita is their enemy, fear their master. Am I to tell them that Masakita matters more to the country than they do? He is only one man."

"It is difficult," Bondurant answered hesitantly, "but at the same time . . ."

N'Sika ignored him, his face more animated but the eyes moving away, lifted to the window, to those sounds outside where the palm trees continued to whisper in the night wind. Bondurant paused, hearing nothing except the trees. N'Sika spoke first again.

"Your government is strong," he said, eyes searching again the tabletop as they had during that first visit. "You don't understand governments that are weak. I know why the old President was corrupt, why he ruled with francs and dollars—of course I know. It is easier that way. Nothing is simpler. I know why he created this imaginary government of national reconciliation with a parliament and all those tribal political parties—of course I know. So he could hide under it like a cat under the fisherman's table. All these things I know in the same way I know why soldiers who leave the barracks to rule a country are confused and afraid, whispering together, asking each other, Where is the enemy they can see? Where are the soldiers they would fight? It is nothing to overthrow a government, nothing at all. An imbecile could do it, yes, and we were imbeciles too—we made many mistakes, but we are here now, the Revolutionary Council is out there waiting for me, and there is no one else to govern except us. No one. So you understand my situation.

"I would send myself away if I could—as military attaché to London or America, where I could learn English and read the books that Masakita, Dr. Bizenga, and Federov talk about—wise men's books, scholars and historians—but who would stay? Fumbe, who's afraid of his own shadow? Lutete, who's an old woman, now growing older? Who would watch the ministries? The same thieves who did these things before? Never! Do I know what is happening in Finance today, how much foreign exchange was issued, how many import licences approved? No. I asked the World Bank to send me two financial advisers to help me, but who do they send? Two Belgians who once worked for the copper syndicate whose mines I nationalized—the same thieves! The UN sends a new representative, a Pakistani, and he immediately comes to see me. So what does he want to talk about during his first visit. More food and medicine for the peoples in the drought area to the south? No. He wants to talk about nationality for the Pakistani shopkeepers in the north whose English passports have been taken away, the same people who have been cheating the village women for years! And now you come bringing this letter, a letter from one man! Just one man, not a village, a district or province . . ."

N'Sika looked up morosely, glancing toward the side door, where his secretary had been hovering, a slim, frightened young man holding a thick folder. N'Sika beckoned and the secretary quickly brought him the file folder, holding it open on the table as N'Sika signed a folio of documents. Seeing the secretary's success, Major Lutete followed on his heels clutching a pale green binder holding a few telegrams. N'Sika glanced at them with perfunctory interest, took the pen Lutete offered, and scrawled his initials on the cables. Major Fumbe, plump and frog-faced, waited anxiously in the doorway, a carbine over his shoulder.

"I have a visitor," N'Sika told him coldly. "Leave your gun outside." Fumbe obeyed eagerly, returning an instant later to confer with N'Sika in a fawning whisper, his departure as servile as the others'.

Alone again with Bondurant, N'Sika sat hunched forward over the table, gold watch dangling from one wrist like a bracelet as he reached for the ever-present package of cigarettes. He lit a cigarette mechanically. "They are not all like this," he resumed, troubled, as if conscious of Bondurant's unspoken judgment, "not all the council. Probably you think you know this nation, this country, these peoples—from the books you have read, from the gossip of the Belgians or Europeans, from listening to the civil servants in the foreign ministry or the *vin rouge* intellectuals the Belgians left behind, like the old President and his cabinet, those crippled old men wearing the *patron*'s coat and trousers.

"I will tell you a story about someone who could read no books or even write her own name, a woman from my village in the north who never learned what these people in the capital learned or would have taught her. She was given away by her father to an old Belgian who had a coffee farm. This Belgian gave her a cottage to live in near his own house, but she never accepted him, not in her heart, even though she was forced to obey her father. She never accepted him, even though she could do nothing when he would come to her at night, the way such men do. She lived there for eight years, denying the Belgian in her heart, never speaking to him, not one word, even after eight years when his sickness for her had become a fever, ruining his life and the life of his family, who left him and went back to Belgium. A fever, you see, rotting his life. She never spoke to him, this woman—never, not a word in all those years. When he was dying he ordered his two servants to carry his bed to her cottage, so they did—two frightened servants carrying the *patron's* bed like a chief's *tipoy* to her cottage where he lived those last months, wasting away. She fed him, washed him, and clothed him. After he died, she washed the corpse and dressed it in coat and trousers and then, because he was a fat man and she was small, she dragged the dead man by the heels up the path to the house, where the two servants were waiting to say yes to her, whatever she wanted—the house was hers then, the house, the coffee trees, the farm—but she left the corpse there on the porch, at the feet of the two servants waiting to say yes, and went away without a word, down the road and across the river to the village she hadn't visited in eight years."

N'Sika paused, the cigarette smoking in his strong fingers, brooding along the tabletop.

"But in the village they rejected her too. They thought she was mad, living in silence all those years; dragging a white man's body through the dust was an insult, something only a madwoman would do. The Belgians and their priests had been to the village, you see. So the elders sent her away. She became a midwife, a healer, and a seller of herbs; but in time she found a husband, an African from the same tribe who worked on the river and gave her children of her own. She was a woman these people here would say was ignorant and primitive, even mad, but she was stronger than all of them, a woman who could say no. There are many like her, but not in the books you read. It is only when this council finds its strength in the same way that they will know who they are. Then the country will become strong. But as strong as she was, this woman I told you about wasted her strength because no one came after her, no one joined with her, the people weren't ready for her, and she died alone at the edge of the river near a trading village where the Arabs owned the shops."

N'Sika got to his feet abruptly, as if the conversation no longer interested him. "I can say nothing more to you," he concluded. "I can make no promises. I will present the letter to the council, to Fumbe, who is responsible for security, to the National Revolutionary Court."

"I understand that," Bondurant said, relieved that the conversation had come to an end. He stood up gratefully.

N'Sika led Bondurant to the door, but he turned aside as they reached it. "I must say one more thing—between us, no one else."

"Certainly."

"This man Reddish must go. We are speaking plainly now. He must go. He was too long with the old President."

Bondurant nodded, surprised. "He's leaving in two days."

"You sent him?"

"His tour is finished," he replied quickly—too quickly, he realized immediately. He should have lied and said he had requested his recall. He knew, too late, the advantage N'Sika had over him.

N'Sika laughed, a crude bellowing laugh—the first time Bondurant had seen the slightest evidence of any humor in the man— but the note was false; it climbed his spine like a chill.

"Oh yes—finished. I understand."

N'Sika left him at the door and Bondurant found his way alone out across the garden, flushed and bewildered, like an old man who had lost his spectacles, blundering by mischance into the wrong patio, where the council members awaited their summons.

"This way, Mr. Ambassador." The protocol officer overtook him and led him toward his car.

Once struck, the false note traveled with him along the sand road and down the hill as he stared silently out the sedan window from the back seat.

What council? he asked himself, ashamed. Fumbe and Lutete had been there, both his deputies. He'd seen their outrageous servility, just as he'd glimpsed the others waiting silently in the shadows of the patio, like the indigents who'd once waited for the old President outside the royal gate.

chapter 9

✧ So de Vaux knew how Major Fumbe and Dr. Bizenga had tricked him, gotten into his skull that night at the cottage as he'd found the old cousin lying there in his father-in-law's place, tricked his nerves and muscles slack when one quick burst with the automatic rifle could have cut the Senegalese fetisheer in half, wiped him out, and that would have ended it right there. So they'd tricked him, all because of that bloody lantern gone dumb in the thatched hut on the track to Bunia that night, the lantern and the pool of white water on the engine hood. *Manioc dust, wasn't it?* Manioc or papaya dust blown there by some damp breath of swamp wind lying along the hollow below the village. . . .

The cell was warm in the afternoon heat, a square of blue sky visible through the smoke hole in the roof. The three of them sat slumped against the stone wall, legs and hands still shackled.

"So it was your idea, yours and N'Sika's," Masakita continued quietly.

"Just the two of us at first, that's right. In the beginning. We had more information than we could ever use up at G-2, all those intelligence reports we worked with on the foreign intelligence staff—Belgian, American, British, a few French, even some Portuguese. All going to waste. Who could make sense of it, eh? All that information just going to feed the President's paranoia.

"So there we were, N'Sika and me, with a network of brokers and agents bigger than any the Rothschilds ever had—the Rothschilds, Lloyd's of London, the Banque-Indochine, Barclays, or King Leopold himself. We were sitting on top of an empire, and what were we doing with it? Nothing at all. N'Sika was fed up with the old President and wanted to go blasting into the palace one night and just take it over, just like that. We were all fed up with it—the corruption, the thievery, the country coming apart the way it was.

We told him he had to be clever about it, as clever as the Belgians, the Americans, the Russians, and everyone else. So Lutete and I found out about the MPLA guns coming into Brazza that day about the time the East Germans were sending those hand implements—"

"What about the nationalizations?" Masakita asked.

"That was N'Sika—his idea. No one could talk him out of it. He wanted to make something decent out of it, like me. 'Create a world out there,' like the bankers in Brussels used to tell me when I was trying to sell shares in a tin mine up in the Kivu. 'Create a world out there and we'll manage it for you.' That's what they used to say. Not directly, you understand, but that's what they meant. N'Sika didn't want that. So he just took it over. He was ahead of us, ahead of all of us."

De Vaux grunted to his feet and rattled clumsily across the stone floor to stand in the center of the oblong of sunshine, looking up at the patch of sky. Two guards crouched on the roof, their voices sometimes heard but their black faces seldom seen.

"Hey up there!" he called.

A wet black face appeared in the opening, looking down silently, brow dripping sweat that fell through the column of sunlight and splashed on the bone-white stones.

"Hot up there, is it, laddie?" de Vaux called. "*Coo,*" he purred in a perfect imitation of the late Sergeant Major Rudy Templer, recently of the King's Shropshire Light Infantry. "Drop down here where it's nice and cool. Nice and easy like. Fetch your rifle with you. We'll show you a little close-order drill."

The man at the opening spat at de Vaux, who moved aside as the spittle floated down. "Dry as cotton, is it? Try a little beer. I could catch that."

The face went away, and de Vaux went back to the wall. "You should have packed it in and gone across the river," he told Masakita.

"You too. You could have left."

"Me?" De Vaux laughed. "Where to? Back to Antwerp? No. What's in Antwerp these days? Nothing, that's what. Shipwrecks, I'd say, like I told you before, everything else smashed. Put it in better words if you can, but that's what it comes down to with us—shipwrecks."

"That appeals to you?"

De Vaux shrugged. "It's what comes to me. I don't know too many books the way you do. That's not the school I learned in. But what I've read I remember. Shipwrecks. Wreckage from the storm, eh. Whatever comes to you, you use—like that shirt you're wearing. Fred's Ford Mart. Who'd it belong to. Who's Fred? Who the shit cares. It just came to you worn out, secondhand like it is. Like this fucking prison here."

Masakita's sympathy was stirred, guessing a secret romantic in the man next to him, a schoolboy's vanity, proud of his hand-me-down scholarship.

"It's the same—Africa, Asia, the jungle, the beach, or anyplace else," he continued. "It doesn't matter how you got there, what storm sent you off course, who smashed your keel, who the shit Fred is—you're there, wearing his shirt, all by yourself, living off your wits, dragging up whatever's left, whatever you can find, knocking a place together however you can. The bulkhead's a door, the decking a roof, everything topsy-turvy, but it keeps the rain out." He spat blood from his loose teeth and stretched out his legs.

"No more than that?" Masakita asked.

"Not much. Then one day it all comes crashing down around your ears," he said, studying the litter of the cell, the trusses overhead, and the square of sky. "Like this rathole." He spat again and wiped his mouth. "You wake up again, knowing what you should have known all the time, what that crazy Robinson Crusoe forgot. You don't build houses like this. So you sit here like this, the way we are, knowing they've beaten you again the way they did Crusoe, a poor bugger with a stinking goatskin cap on his filthy head, a freak, beard hanging down to his knees, worms in his belly, scabs on his hands, and so that's what he remembers—that he's still a civilized man, a white man too, and he hasn't measured up. What if he had to walk down the street in Brussels like that, eh? They'd lock him up in the asylum before he got ten meters. So he's rescued himself, made a new world for himself out of an island no one else wants, made a house out of a smashed ship. So what? What is it except something that no one except a goddamn bloody fool would ever live in—"

"You keep talking about a shipwreck," Masakita said.

De Vaux said, "That's the whole point, isn't it? A shipwreck means a ship, doesn't it? But think about that for a while. So you come staggering out of the sea the way he did, half drowned with salt water, half crazy the way he was. You've got to think of the ship, don't you? 'Great God, where was the ship?' He keeps talking to himself. 'Jesus, that was some bloody ship!' He even tells Friday about it. So he's still on that desert island twenty years later, still talking about the ship. 'Great God, where is the ship?' he wants to know. That's the worst joke of all. We're told of it all our lives, aren't we?—told about it in our deepest dreams, the way Crusoe was, but I can tell you something different, something we all know bloody well, which is why we keep dreaming about it. There wasn't any fucking ship, never."

chapter 10

❖ Gabrielle was gone, driven by Reddish to the airport two nights before his own departure to catch her midnight flight for Paris. They planned a week's holiday together in France on his way back to Washington, where he'd been reassigned. As they said goodbye in the nearly deserted terminal, she gave him a bound envelope, carefully wrapped—a going-away present, she'd said—her copy of Stendhal's autobiographical fragment, *Henri Brulard*.

"Something to cheer you up," she'd told him, smiling. "I don't want to worry about you. This way I'll know you're in the best of company."

The villa was empty those two nights after she'd gone. He was at loose ends, no longer part of the embassy at all. The night following, he'd brought the envelope from his bedroom, intending to look at it, but had put it aside finally, unopened.

On the day of his departure, Bondurant had still had no word from N'Sika. In the middle of the afternoon, Reddish had a brief talk with Bondurant and afterward went down to his old office to pick up a few personal items Sarah had collected for him. Another man's presence was already there in his old office, his banished. His replacement was named McPherson, a man ten years younger. The office was filled with the sweet scent of honeyed undergraduate pipe tobacco. On the clean desk were a new blotter unstained by coffee rings, a pad scrawled in a neat unfamiliar script, dinner and cocktail invitations for the embassy novice, and a leather photograph folio holding the smiling faces of a pretty wife and two children.

"He's certainly eager, no doubt about that," Sarah told him, as she entered to fill the desk drawer with newly sharpened pencils, legal pads, paper clips, and memo pads. New pictures and maps were on the walls, fresh plants on the windowsill, and the old leather chair with its cracked cushion had been replaced.

"He's younger too," she added, "which means that his disposition isn't quite so threadbare."

"Wait until he gets a load of your shorthand and parsley sandwiches," Reddish said, picking up the two framed pictures left for him on top of the file cabinet. The two pictures had been taken at a devastated tea plantation in the Kivu during the mercenary rebellions. Reddish and the old President stood together in front of a squad of paras.

"You'll notice he doesn't smoke burned-out cigars left from old dinner parties either. Did you notice? He's a pipe smoker."

He didn't answer, looking at the two pictures for a minute. Then he tore off the backing, and ripped them in pieces.

"What are you doing!" she cried, seizing his arm, but it was too late. The President had signed them. "That's a souvenir. If you didn't want them, I'd keep them."

"Souvenirs of what?" He threw them into the wastebasket.

The Havershams gave a small farewell buffet the night of his departure. The ambassador made a brief dignified speech and proposed the toast. Reddish's response was even more brief, but also awkward. Listening to him in the candlelit rear garden, Bondurant heard again the stubborn, cryptic man he'd only begun to understand those last weeks.

As Reddish sat down again, Sarah said, "You never give away anything for free, do you?"

"Just his heart, sugar, and you got it," Selvey said. He winked at Reddish. "Ain't no free diplomas in the school of hard knocks, ain't that right, perfessor?" He nudged Lowenthal, who turned quickly.

"Sorry."

Selvey, a little tipsy, whispered, "The Cubans are coming."

Ambassador Bondurant and Reddish walked alone to the car. Haversham drove him to the airport.

◆ ◆ They talked throughout the afternoon that final day as the thick finger of sunshine from the smoke hole toiled infinitesimally across the stone floor and climbed the far wall, like the secret stroke of a pendulum. No voices came from the roof or the road outside. They heard the occasional cooing of the pigeons and the chitter of swallows that nested high under the roof overhang. Then the afternoon dimmed, deepening the shadows and blackening the sky overhead. The first stars came out.

At ten o'clock a truck stopped in the road above and they heard the soldiers disembark, heard the clatter of their rifles as they reassembled in the road, and then listened to the commands of their lieutenant as they practiced, the click of firing pins echoing in empty chambers.

"What time?" Nogueira asked, head lifted toward the high window.

De Vaux shook his head. "No regrets now?" he asked Masakita. "Not the exile you said you couldn't live with?"

"No."

"Not Paris, not Cairo?"

"No, that's finished now. How about you? You could have gone too."

"No, not really. A few things, maybe. Not much." His head rolled back against the stones and his eyes lifted to the window. He seemed to grow more thoughtful now as Masakita waited, his voice softer as he began again.

No, he had no regrets. He'd started with nothing but a few ideas in his head, come out of the slums of Antwerp, his mother a seamstress, patching clothes for a secondhand shop on the street below that bought and sold garments to the merchant seamen. He remembered how she sat in the alcove with the winter light over her shoulder, her sewing basket and her cards of thread and wool on the table nearby. In the pockets of an old seaman's jacket she'd found a few postcards brought back from Leopoldville. There was a picture of a gorilla from the Kivu, an oryx, Congolese fishermen with their basket nets along the falls at Stanleyville. De Vaux had carried those cards with him for months, and when they were about to fall apart he tacked them over his cot. The gorilla's eyes had burned their way into his soul. But his first memories were those of his mother sitting in the small alcove, the light over her shoulder.

What was he to do? Go back to that again?

No, Antwerp wasn't for him, no more than exile was for Masakita. Antwerp would be the same, except death would come slower, the way it came to his mother. Always the same there. He'd seen it last time he was there, his mother still sitting in the alcove with her secondhand clothes piled at her feet—older, grayer, still sewing.

She had her toast and tea at seven each morning after mass, then turned off the gas, letting the weak winter sun warm the alcove where she sat. Always the same there. Nothing would change her.

He'd bought her a sewing machine, but she'd sold it. Nothing would change her except death. The same on the streets. The clerk or accountant read the stock closings on the bus or tram in the morning, folded his paper to glance at the headlines, and then searched the thighs of the woman across the aisle as he continued the front-page ax murder among the lingerie ads.

The sky was always gray through the windows, smoke threading over the rooftops. At ten the dentist down the street put on his smock and rinsed out his mouth. Could any of them find their way in the dark, go where he'd gone, in hellish heat or a sorcerer's darkness along the track to Bunia that night where the dead man had been waiting for him, terrified. *Cold out here*—that's what death had to say, wanting to put his shapeless hands in his pockets, his fingers in warm fingers again, to hide his terror in de Vaux's. What was Antwerp these days?

Could any of them go where any gull could go, out beyond the antipodes, Tierra del Fuego lost behind him? No. Some called the jungle a dungeon, but it wasn't that. How could he tell them what he'd found if he were to go back? No words, no words at all, and the words were what was missing. Masakita had words. But not him. But there were no words for what his father-in-law had taught him. How could you tell Antwerp that? Was there any sense left there? The secretary at the typewriter, the clerk folding his newspaper, the dentist rooting for decay among the ten-year-old molars? Sense gone dumb in them, as dumb as the stones where they sat, as dumb as the brass ferrule that taps the blind man's cane through the winter darkness to open the newspaper hutch near the train station . . .

The guard at the front door summoned his colleagues from the two stools in front of the cell door, and they crept out silently, taking their newspapers and tin pails with them. Outside, rifle bolts were being locked in place.

So the past was wiped out, forgotten, empty, like Europe these days. "It has to be," de Vaux explained. "How else could we get on, men like me. Or anyone else either."

"So yesterday is forgotten," Masakita said.

How else could he explain it, de Vaux continued. How else? The tricks the mind plays just to keep you on your feet day after day—the wars, the crimes, the humiliations, the murders? How could you face it otherwise? The daily slanders and insults, the man who robbed you last week, the one you robbed two weeks ago, the woman you made love to last year now carrying the postman's child? No, your mind was always on the dodge, keeping you going year after year. Take last year, when he'd gone to Brussels in January for a month. It had been twenty years since he'd seen him, but there he was. He'd hardly recognized him at first. He'd come around the corner near the old smoke-encrusted Banque National du Nord in the morning cold, and almost knocked him down. It was him all right—in his gray gloves and his trilby hat, down at the heels a bit since de Vaux had seen him, but it was him all right, the devil himself, on his way to an appointment somewhere. De Vaux was late for his appointment too. It was windy. Very cold. They didn't speak.

"So you knew him, even then," Masakita said.

"Swindled me three times, he did," de Vaux admitted with a cunning smile. "The last time, the worst of all."

A few soldiers were coming in the door. They got slowly to their feet, Masakita leading the way.

The old prison was silent.

"Fumbe! Fumbe, you cowardly bastard! Show us your face!" De Vaux's hectoring voice rattled under the high roof and along the stone walls.

But the shadow didn't move, standing just behind the iron mesh, the face hidden in the darkness behind the three kneeling marksmen who waited at their firing holes, heads turned.

It was N'Sika, standing alone.

His mother's memory had brought him here, invoking her strength to understand theirs. As a soldier, he'd rejected those memories because he loved them too much, the memories of her and their life along the river near the Arab settlement where she'd settled, an itinerant midwife and seller of herbs, abandoned first by her father, then her villagers, and finally the indolent, weak husband who worked on the foreigners' boats. They lived in a mud hut at the river's edge, her will unbroken, her strength wasted in poverty, where she died like a derelict, her conscience her own.

Her beliefs were his too by then. He didn't understand them. Some were drawn from the stories her father had told her, others from the gossip of the street, or the admonitions of the soothsayers in the marketplace. Still others were the images or premonitions inspired by the Western or Arab picture magazines that came to her second- and thirdhand from the coffee shop, the brightest of which she cut out to decorate the walls of the mud hut, pasted up with a mucilage of flour and honey. There were photographs of a chief in a *tipoy,* a European coronation, a woman in ermine leaving a horse-drawn coach, the mute stone sentinels of Luxor, the black hull of a freighter capsizing, bow-lifted, in the stormy North Atlantic. She had never seen the ocean, never seen the storms that battered the winter coasts, but she knew it was a vessel, a derelict, and it was something terrible to her, summoning from memory the recollection of some dream or nightmare she understood even without knowing its language.

She'd had nothing to share with him those last days, her voice taken away by sickness. The last night he sat with her alone. The tea and barley broth he'd brought from the charcoal fire cooled on the box near her pallet. The bowl of oil glimmered on the mud floor. In the light of the candle stub on the box were her two-franc mirror with the red plastic handle, the bottle of rosewater, and the tortoise-shell comb with a few strands of wiry hair still caught in its teeth from her last toilet. A red shawl lay over her shoulders. Outside, the evening idlers drifted by. The old gramophone lifted its tinny music from the coffeehouse. Two drunken boat workers argued as they urinated in the passageway. Slowly the lanes grew quiet. It was after midnight when he heard the struggle in her throat and saw some brutal force lift the small head and shrunken shoulders from the pillow. Her face was calm, her head thrown back proudly, but it was outside her then, shaking her body the way a dog shakes a bundle of limp rags. Crueler still, it flailed the small wasted body convulsively, and he flung himself over the pallet, a thirteen-year-old boy shielding her with his arms and shoulders as he struck out at the shadows that grappled for her. Her mouth stiffened and yawned open; he heard the sound of dry leaves rattling in the wind rush by his ear as she lay still. He crouched at her side until the candle dimmed out and he slept on the mud floor alongside the pallet. He awoke to the morning sun and the whistle of a boat on the river waiting to unload its cargo.

He had invoked his mother's memory and now it released him, the cloak of compassion banished as he looked through the mesh from the shadows at the men in the cell block. They were derelicts too, too strong for this weak nation, their strength and consciences their own, wasted like hers in a mud hut at the water's edge. Who could follow them?

He nodded to the three marksmen and turned away, back to the corridor, head lowered, as if his own burden had grown heavier, not lighter, as his council members had assumed.

chapter 11

❖ It was one o'clock as the tired travelers were led from the departure lounge, down the outside staircase, and across the tarmac to the waiting jet. Behind them on the esplanade a group of boisterous beery Brits were singing "For He's a Jolly Good Fellow," serenading a departing Yorkshireman from the British Embassy bag room. Reddish saw their waving hands and dim white faces as he turned back at the top of the boarding steps. The sound was still ringing in his ears as he sat in the rear of the cabin and the jet began its screaming sprint down the runway, his mind numbed mute by the stinging blizzard of speed and sound. He heard it again as the silver cylinder lifted its freight of gravity-heavy bodies into lightness once again, rediscovering speech, limbs, and appetites.

He sat alone at the rear of the jet, staring down the wing at the scattered lights of the capital, watching it fragment in detonations of black smoke as they climbed into the clouds and the city was lost in darkness. They climbed higher still, beyond the great river, the jungles and villages with their campfires and the smoke of the savannahs. Lights were consumed in darkness, but still he looked down, oblivious to the neon-lit cocktail lounge the cabin had become— passengers moving, rubber-wheeled carts whispering by, cigarettes, whiskey, and shared intimacies suddenly bountiful.

He was a stranger again, even to himself, but he was accustomed to it. He'd lived a dozen lives in twenty years, like Masakita; and now, at this moment, none of them mattered. The darkness had taken them away—friends, rooms, offices, villages, and faces. They served their tours, burned their private files, received their orders, made their departures, and then vanished themselves—anonymous deracinated men in the vacuum of transit, clutching briefcases on a night flight to yet another continent, frightened by the swiftness of their inconsequentiality, their stomachs churning with the loathing of a new beginning. Countries they had known better than their own slipped behind them silently, like barren headlands passed in the night.

He'd left a lifetime behind him. How many did he have left? None, like Masakita? Maybe he was slyer than that—loth to become, like diplomacy and everything else these days, just another fatuous, foolish profession until there was nothing left of that either.

Tired, he ordered a drink and picked up a newspaper from the seat pouch in front of him, but it was a Capetown paper and he cast it aside. He pulled his briefcase from beneath the seat and removed Gabrielle's envelope.

"Excuse me, but I noticed that you'd boarded in Kinshasa," an English voice called from across the aisle. "Do you speak English by any chance?" A South African businessman holding a drink leaned toward him from across the aisle, blue eyes eager, curious about murder and mayhem in the streets Reddish had just left.

Reddish resisted his first impulse and nodded. "Yes, I speak English."

"Were you there long or just passing through?"

"A few weeks."

"Bloody awful, I gather—the riots. You were there? You don't mind my asking, do you?"

"No, I don't mind."

He fell asleep high over the Tibesti and awoke at dawn, stiff and cramped, Africa behind him, the Mediterranean a wrinkled silver mirror far below as they veered toward the French coast. His companions were sleeping. The morning sun was bright through those few cabin windows where the shades weren't drawn.

He had had an ugly dream and was looking forward to a whiskey, but it was early morning, the other passengers weren't awake, and he doubted that the sleepy young German stewardess brought by his seat light would understand that.

Gabrielle would.

He ordered coffee instead, recovering Gabrielle's envelope from the seat beside him as he looked down at the fertile fields of France swimming into view, crosshatched in the ancient husbandry of a long-settled economy, totally alien, totally strange, not at all the corrugated green vastness his eyes had so long been accustomed to. He tried to accustom himself to the change, trying to forget those he'd left behind, to think of himself as an American again, a Midwesterner whose corridors of destruction were carved by flood,

344

drought, or winter storms, nature's carnage, nothing more; an American again, here among strangers, encouraged by the day's possibilities, beyond the reach of the past.

He opened the envelope and looked at the bound book. It was bulky—too bulky. He looked at the front pages and the engraving of a man a century dead, Gabrielle's old friend and correspondent, the Frenchman who'd discovered himself too late in a letter to a dead friend:

I am very old today, the sky is gray, I am not very well.

Nothing can prevent madness.

The book on his knee opened easily to those last pages, and as it did the fold of waxed paper Gabrielle had pressed there slipped down the spine, the petals within faded, the stem dry, but the fragrance still there, as fresh as it had been that afternoon when she'd first lifted the rose toward him on the ruined hillside above the lake, as if she'd known then what he now was just beginning to understand.